IN THE DETAILS

JULIA WOLF

PLAYLIST

"Often" The Weeknd

"Your Love" The Outfield, Diplo

"Me and Your Mama" Childish Gambino

"Sex on Fire" Kings of Leon

"I Remember Everything" Zach Bryan, Kasey Musgrove

"Casual" Chappel Roan

"Light On" Maggie Rogers

"Dog Days Are Over" Florence + The Machine

"Don't Dream It's Over" Lauren Daigle

"The Kill" Maggie Rogers

"Stargazing" Myles Smith

"REPRISE" The Lumineers

"Flowers in Your Hair" The Lumineers

"Your Love" The Outfield

"WALLS" Kings of Leon

"Stubborn Love" The Lumineers

"Motion Sickness" Phoebe Bridgers

"You Say" Lauren Daigle

"Colorado" Renee Rapp

"Rivers and Roads" The Head and The Heart

"Someone To Stay" Vancouver Sleep Clinic

https://open.spotify.com/playlist/6VzwGV3ypNPRQEp9Eaqb Vx?si=8e69ae3f88ad4532

MORE BOOKS BY JULIA

The Harder They Fall (Billionaire office romance)

Dear Grumpy Boss

Sincerely, Your Inconvenient Wife

P.S. You're Intolerable

Not So Truly Yours

The Seasons Change (Rock star romance)

Falling In Reverse

Stone Cold Notes

Faded in Bloom

Where Waves Break

Savage U (college romance)

Soft Like Thunder

Bright Like Midnight

Sweet Like Poison

Real Like Daydreams

Savage Academy (academy romance)
Save One Thing
These Two Wrongs
Jump On Three

Blue is the Color (Rock star romance)
Times Like These
Watch Me Unravel
Such Great Heights
Under the Bridge

Unrequited (Rock star romance)
Unrequited
Misconception
Dissonance

Never Blue Duet (Angsty rock star romance)
Never Lasting

Never Again

Never Again

CHAPTER ONE
Clara

Leather and wind.

A man took the empty stool beside me at the bar without asking if it was free. As soon as he sat down, his scent told me something important about him: this man was a biker. Not unusual in this establishment—simply named The Tavern—which I estimated to be half bikers and half wannabe cowboys.

Closing my eyes, I inhaled, catching the same scent on myself. I loved when I smelled like this. It meant I'd been riding for hours, nothing between me and the road except my Rossi Triumph Classic.

"Your glass is empty."

His voice rumbled across my skin, leaving goose bumps in its wake. Low and gritty, he sounded like he ate gravel for breakfast every morning. In his case, it wasn't a bad thing.

Not a bad thing at all.

I tilted my head to the side, letting my eyes skim his profile. His jaw was covered in golden-brown stubble, and the proud line of his nose was interrupted by a bump that spoke of a break or two somewhere along the way. His focus was on my glass and my hand around it.

"That's true," I murmured.

"Shame," he replied.

"Why's that?"

He hummed a clash of thunder. "Woman like you should never have an empty glass."

A startled laugh fell out of me. "Oh? You can tell the kind of woman I am just by sitting beside me at this bar?"

"Yep."

The hairs on the back of my neck rose at his single-word answer. He'd loaded a lot of meaning into that sole syllable, like he'd wanted me to hear it—wanted me to ask.

If he truly knew the kind of woman I was, he would have predicted I'd never be one to ask a man's opinion of me.

I waved at the bartender. "I'll take another, please." Then I gestured toward the man beside me. "And whatever he's having."

Motorcycle Man went still as the bartender filled two tall, icy glasses with frothy beer. She slid one in front of each of us, and I passed her cash, telling her to keep the change. She smirked at us and stuffed the bill in the pocket of her tight jeans as she walked away.

I chanced another glance at the man next to me, surprised to find him focused on me and not how well the bartender's jeans cupped her high and tight ass.

His eyes narrowed into icy blue slits, intense in their scrutiny. I lifted my beer and took a sip, acting like none of this affected me while my insides quivered. I wasn't a cool woman who flirted with growly men in bars. Pretending I was was both terrifying and exciting.

I wasn't certain I was doing a great job of it, but if me buying him a drink had turned him off, his fragile masculinity wasn't worth my time. I danced around men's delicate egos daily at work, and that was more than enough for me.

Before I could take another sip, a hand landed on my knee, and my body was spun sideways on my stool, putting me face to face with Motorcycle Man.

His legs were spread, trapping mine between them, pinning me like butterfly wings with his hard stare and the words spilling from his soft lips.

"I'd been watching you before I came over."

A shudder tried to work its way through me at the sound of his low, gritty voice. It was only by sheer will I suppressed it. He drawled each word with a lazy cadence while dropping the ends off some. Like a southerner without the twang. And it wasn't so much an accent as an economical disbursement of effort like he'd decided the ends weren't necessary, so he hadn't bothered using energy to finish them.

I raised a questioning brow, my throat too thick to speak.

"Two other men approached before me, and you turned them away." He dipped down, coming so close I felt the warmth of his breath. "Why didn't you turn me away, sweetness?"

I licked my dry lips. I couldn't remember the last time my heart had fluttered in this distinctly unfamiliar way.

"Simple," I pushed out, almost feeling silly for the precise way I spoke in comparison. "You didn't ask. You took the seat you wanted."

"Hmmm...you like when a man takes what he wants?" he asked, though I wasn't sure he actually wanted an answer—not with the way his gaze skimmed over the shape of my body, following every curve and valley like he was riding it. This he did not skimp on. His perusal was as thorough as could be.

Awareness washed over me. My nipples scraping against the lace of my bra, the seam of my jeans aligning with my center, the feel of my clothing on my skin, my hair resting on my shoulders, the way my thighs and ass spread on my stool—it all pushed to the forefront of my mind, and I forgot how to sit, breathe, drink my beer naturally.

I made an attempt to lick my lips again. "I like when certain men take certain things."

He almost smiled, one corner of his mouth kicking up. "Are you trying to be mysterious, sweetness? It's cute, but you don't need to waste time playing around. The second I spotted you, I thought you were the sexiest thing I'd seen in a long time."

My stomach pitched, and I gripped the edge of the bar so I didn't go with it. Suddenly light-headed, I sucked in a breath to steady myself. How was this man able to send me topsy-turvy with sweet words?

Probably because I was starved for attention like this.

Well, not strictly like this. I couldn't hunger for something I'd never had or known possible for a woman like me. Even though I felt like a badass when I climbed off my bike, wearing my leathers and skintight jeans, certainly no one had ever claimed I was the sexiest thing they'd seen in a long time.

That corner kicked up farther. "Did I fluster you?" he practically crooned.

"You did," I admitted.

He trailed the rough pad of his index finger along my cheek and down the column of my throat. "You're pink, CeeCee. Love that color on you."

I bit down on my bottom lip, eyeing him from beneath my lashes. Not playing coy, giving myself a moment to gather what little cool I had.

"You seem to bring it out in me quite easily, Jake."

A full grin now, he dragged his fingers through my hair, cupping the back of my skull, and pulled me into him. His mouth hovered over mine, and for a beat or two, we traded breaths.

"I wonder..." he drawled.

Before I could ask what exactly he'd been wondering, his mouth covered mine, and I lost my train of thought, just like I had the first time this man kissed me a year ago.

He pulled back, eyes on my parted lips. "Yep."

I sucked in a sharp breath. "What?"

His lips grazed mine. "It wasn't some fairy tale I made up. You are just as sweet as I remembered." His thumb took over for his mouth, pressing against my bottom lip. "You have a hotel room?"

I nodded, an earthquake shifting my insides into an unrecognizable landscape. "Yeah. Are you going to wreck it with me?"

He chuffed and dragged his thumb down to my chin. "Finish your drink, CeeCee, and we'll see where the night takes us."

We both knew why we'd shown up here tonight and while it was in me to argue that we shouldn't waste time, I didn't.

I had no idea if we'd have another night like this. Maybe I'd wise up and not return. Maybe he would.

Picking up my glass, I raised it in front of me. "To not rushing things."

He tapped his glass to mine. "To patient good girls getting their rewards."

I was nowhere near a girl. Tonight, though, I'd be this man's good girl. If his rewards were anything like they'd been the past three times, I'd be anything he wanted me to be.

CHAPTER TWO
Clara

I t was so much.

Too much.

Hands pinned above me, the rest of me trapped beneath an unrelenting man, I snapped my eyes shut, giving myself over to the feel of him driving into me. My sweat-misted body sliding against his. The sound of his huffing breath. The warmth of each exhale brushing my lips and chin. The bite of pain and pleasure as he rolled my nipple and kneaded my breast roughly. Jake over me, inside me, surrounding me...

I was helpless.

We barely knew each other, but in these twisted sheets, he reached into my inner depths and demanded everything. I'd never been one to succumb to demands. With Jake, I found myself handing it all over until he all but consumed me.

"Eyes on me, sweetness."

My lids shot open at his command. His eyes bore into mine as his intensity vibrated through him into me, rattling me all the way to my bones.

"That's a good girl," he cooed, velvet over sandpaper. "You're so good at listening to me, aren't you?"

I nodded, out of words.

He slowed his thrusts but kept them just as deep, working himself so far into me it was nearly impossible not to let my eyes flutter closed as they rolled back in my head.

"Are you going to give me what I want?"

I shook my head. "I can't. Not anymore."

His hand slid from my breast to my abdomen then between my thighs. He brushed over my tender clit, and I nearly jumped out of my skin. When he pressed down on it, I screamed. Not a cute, breathy scream. It came from my belly and wound its way up my throat with primal force.

Jake laughed, the faint crinkles around his eyes deepening. "Oh yeah, CeeCee. You've got another orgasm for me, and you're going to give it to me."

He wasn't wrong.

This man, this motorcycle-riding stranger, played my body like he knew it well. Like he had me in his bed every night, not once every blue moon. He must've done this a lot. Every weekend, taking another lonely woman to bed and fucking her until her bones melted. I didn't know how old he was, but I was certain he was younger than me. There was no way he wasn't making good use of his youth and undeniable skills whenever he got the chance.

A kernel of jealousy took root in my gut. Before it could sprout into something bigger, Jake covered my mouth with his and rolled my clit until I couldn't bear the pleasure-pain. He licked away my cries. Chuckled when I bit down on his lip. His answer was to spear me with his cock. To drive into me so hard, I was sure he'd come out the other side. I let go of his lip to soundlessly gasp at the ceiling and claw at his shoulders.

When he finally came and slipped out of me, his hot, sweaty body landing right next to mine on the mattress, I knew for sure what I'd worried about since the first time he'd ended up in my hotel room a year ago: he'd effectively ruined me for every man who'd come after him. There was no way on this green earth anyone else could do what he did to me.

It was why I'd come back three times since.

I didn't know Jake's last name, or where he lived, or who his people were. He could have been a serial killer or runaway priest. He could have been the type to post thirst traps on social media.

None of that mattered. There was no possible future here. If I were smart, I'd leave and not come back before he had a chance to figure out who I was and find a way to use my family's name against me.

Reaching over, he splayed his fingers on my stomach. "I feel you tensing already. Did I not fuck you well enough to turn that busy mind off?"

I turned to him, finding him already watching me. God, he made scruff look good. His hair, wild and mussed from my fingers, made him look even better. I'd left my mark all over him. Lips puffy from kissing and red from my teeth. Faint claw marks down his biceps and over his shoulders. There was even a little purple hickey at the base of his throat.

Seeing him like that, what *I'd* done to him, made me feel powerful in a way foreign to me. I had power in my day-to-day life, but this was wholly different. It bestowed a sexy kind of confidence that allowed my lids to lower and my tongue to peek out to wet my swollen lips.

I laid my hand over his, slotting our fingers together. My voice dropped, husky and flirtatious. "I don't know, stranger. I thought we were going to wreck this room, but all I'm seeing are messed-up sheets. Everything else is in its place."

He raised a brow. "Are you challenging me after I just had your teeth clacking from you shaking so hard?"

I shrugged as well as I could, considering I could barely feel my limbs. "It's more of an observation." But he wasn't wrong.

He rolled to his side, propping up on an elbow and squeezing my breast like he owned it. My thighs pressed together of their own accord, and the smug tilt of his lips told me he saw it.

"Don't know the next time I'll see you, so you better believe I have every intention of making good use of our time together." He plucked my nipple, eliciting a gasp from me. "Sit on my face, baby. Let me lick you until I'm ready to fuck you again."

"Jake…"

He dragged a finger along my cheek. "After all we've done, I can still make you blush. If I were twenty, I'd fuck you right now to keep it there."

And I would have let him.

Because this was a fantasy. A time and space completely removed from my real life where I could be someone different. Wanton and sensual, a little dangerous, taking a strange man to bed and fucking all night. That wasn't me. I was mature and responsible. Danger had never attracted me *until Jake*. And since this was barely more than a fever dream, he could do *anything* to me in this hotel room.

I also knew myself well enough to know this would not be the last time I took a ride from Denver to Skyridge with the intention of running into this man.

Pushing up on my knees, I crawled over him. "Make me blush, Jake."

He gripped my hips and devoured me with his eyes. "I'm going to do more than that, baby. I'm going to light you on fire."

He made good on his word.

All. Night. Long.

As my eyes rolled back from another body-shaking orgasm, I heaved a breath, smiling to myself.

Best fever dream I've ever had...

CHAPTER THREE
Clara

A warm, sticky hand gently slapped my cheek.

"Wake-up time."

My eyes fluttered, and my legs shuffled in the sheets. Was it really time to wake up? It felt like I'd just reached over and turned off the light beside my bed.

And I'd been having the best dream. I was on the back of someone's bike, wind whipping my hair, laughing at the stars twinkling in the night sky. I wasn't ready to wake up and face the sun yet.

"Mommy, open your eyes."

Nellie's sweet breath grazed my cheek, and I grabbed her, pulling her wiggly body onto my chest. She squealed with surprise, giggling as she fell against me.

"I'm not ready to wake up," I whined, keeping my eyes clamped shut.

"But you gotta work, Mommy."

She said this with no conviction, quickly settling on my chest, her small fingers tangling in my hair. I relaxed, soaking in her weight and gentle touches. If she wasn't careful, she'd put us both back to sleep.

"I'm so comfy, though." I squeezed her tight. "I think we should stay here all day. You can be my teddy bear."

That got her going again, laughing like I was the best comedian she'd ever heard, giving me a proper ego boost. Granted, she was three and it didn't take much to crack her up, but I counted it as a win.

"I'm not a teddy bear," she declared.

"You're not?" I pet the top of her head. "But you're so fuzzy."

"Mooommy, come on!"

She pushed away, scooting to sit beside me. I cracked open my eyes to look at my daughter. Her chestnut waves were a mess, and she had a milk mustache. As always, she was utter perfection.

"Did Marina feed you a yummy breakfast?" I asked.

She nodded vigorously. It was how she did most things. "Cereal and lotsa fruit."

I scrunched my nose. "I wonder if she'll make me breakfast too."

Her head tilted in thought. "I think so. You gotta get out of bed if you want to eat it."

I sighed. "Oh, all right."

I used to feel terrible, gut-churning guilt at having a nanny help me in the mornings with feeding Nellie breakfast and getting her dressed while I caught extra sleep, but my mother had put a stop to it. She'd told me women with partners didn't feel guilty for letting their partner pick up the slack or tapping out when they needed to. She had reasoned since I was doing motherhood on my own—unintentionally and rather traumatically—I should consider my nanny my parenting partner.

Now, I only had a gnawing edge of guilt over not being able to do absolutely everything for my daughter. Marina was a godsend and kept me sane. In her sixties, she was like a second grandma to Nellie. She lived in the in-law suite on my first floor and helped out when I needed her but kept to herself when she was off the clock. It was the perfect setup.

Convinced I wasn't going back to sleep, Nellie went out to play with her nanny, and I hopped in the shower to get ready for work.

As the just-short-of-scalding water slid over my skin, I let my head fall back. Flashes of my dream played out behind my eyelids.

Funny I'd dreamed of being on the back of someone's bike when I had never ridden with anyone but my father—and that had ended the moment I'd become old enough to drive myself. But since Jake had been the driver, the dream had probably had little to do with motorcycles.

I pressed against my collarbone. It was no longer tender. The bruise he'd left there a week ago had healed and faded. The ones on my thighs and rug burns on my elbows and knees had too, as if my interlude had never happened. Except...when I crossed my legs a certain way, I could still feel the ghost of him driving into me.

I didn't date or have casual encounters with men. Jake was the one indulgence I'd allowed myself since my marriage fell apart three years ago. He was exactly what I needed right now. No strings, no complications, nothing personal, just crazy, intense sex. I couldn't say if it would happen again or when, but I had plenty of memories to get me through lonely nights.

Chuffing, I shook my head. *Enough of this.*

It was too early in the morning to be thinking about the sex I *wasn't* having. Jumping out of the shower, I dried myself, then wrapped a towel around my chest. My routine was almost muscle memory now, so it took me no time to blow-dry my shoulder-length bob and flat iron the wave out.

Over my years of working in an office, I'd honed my style. Dresses were easier since they were one piece and I rarely had to fuss with them. I slipped on one of my favorites, a burgundy, high-necked, short-sleeved sheath with a built-in belt.

My reflection didn't quite match what was in my head. Since having Nellie, I had bountiful curves where I'd once been relatively straight. Then again, pre-motherhood, I'd spent hours in the gym with my ex, doing everything in my power to retain his physical ideal: small and tight. Given my Italian heritage and love of carbs, I'd been working against nature. But I'd *loved* him, so I'd considered all the work I'd put in to whittle myself down to the slightest version part of being a good wife.

Pffft.

If he'd been making the same effort to keep me happy, I'd have had more to show than ten years of lies and a very public divorce.

I smoothed my hands over my rounded hips and the slope of my stomach that seemed to be here to stay. I was trying really hard to love myself in this shape.

The added pounds certainly hadn't deterred Jake.

I met my eyes in the mirror and whispered sternly, "Not that it matters what a man thinks."

I knew better than to base my self-esteem on a man's good opinion, which could be rescinded at any moment. What I thought was paramount—and that was...a work in progress.

Today, I felt good, though. Whether it was a leftover boost from my wild night with Jake or the dress that fit me like a glove, I wasn't sure, but I'd take it. It meant my appearance would fade to the back of my mind where it belonged. My days were far too full to be distracted by the size of my thighs.

The bathroom door cracked open, and Nellie's head peeked through.

"Oooh." She pushed the door open wide. "Mommy, I like this."

"You do?" I took her hands before she could paw at me. While she was dressed and appeared shiny and clean, one never knew what could be lurking on a three-year-old's hands. "What do you like about it?"

Her brown eyes flared. "The color, and…" she guided our joined hands to my thigh where her index finger poked the fabric, "the bumps. The bumps are nice."

"That's called slub weave. I love how it feels too." I let go of her hand to tug her braid. "I love your hair, Nell-Belle. Marina is so talented."

And thank god for it. If Nellie's hair were left up to me, she'd have a lopsided ponytail every day.

She patted her head. "It's beautiful, right, Mommy?"

I bent down to kiss her forehead. "Yes, my love. Everything about you is."

My workdays were scheduled to the second. This was by design. When I was in the office and away from Nellie, I did not want to waste any precious time. Every day, I dropped her at the company day care ten floors down and hit the ground running.

This was why my brother's random visits annoyed me. Luca often wandered in, checking out the books on my shelves and view from my windows, taking his sweet time getting to the point of his appearance.

As CEO of our family's motorcycle company, Rossi Motors, he could do what he wanted. As my younger brother, he most often wanted to bug me.

When he folded his long limbs into the chair opposite my desk, I paused reading a manufacturing report to give him my attention.

"Good morning." He rested his ankle on the opposite knee, the picture of relaxation.

"Good morning. Did you need something?"

He huffed, his dark eyes twinkling. "Straight to business, huh? I remember when you weren't so serious. There was that time you danced on a bar—"

"I've never danced on a bar. Why would I do that?" The idea horrified me. First, getting on top of the bar had to be completely awkward, and once you were up there—

Luca chuckled. "You're thinking about it, aren't you? Listing all the reasons you'd never do it?"

I sighed, my hands spreading on the smooth surface of my desk. "What's the purpose of dancing on a bar?"

He shrugged. "I don't know. For fun? Attention? Does there have to be a reason to do everything?"

"Perhaps not, but I think my bar-dancing days have sailed."

For a moment, I allowed myself to imagine what Jake would do if I climbed onto the deeply gouged mahogany at The Tavern. I was fairly certain if I made it up there, I would end up hauled over his shoulder with a bright-red backside.

I blinked away those thoughts and cleared my throat. "You never did say why you're in my office."

"Besides the obvious in wanting to see my sister?"

I nodded. "Of course."

He shot me a mischievous grin. "I wanted to see how my darling niece is. Does she want to come spend the night with Uncle Luca and Aunt Saoirse soon?"

I lowered my chin, giving him a pointed look. "You know damn well if you dangle Clementine in front of her, she'll be at your doorstep with her blankie and dolly before you can blink."

My daughter *loved* their cat, maybe more than she loved me or anyone else.

She also loved her Uncle Luca. He'd been there with me when she was born and had stayed in the hospital for those first couple days. He did skin to skin with her when I was too out of it to function following my emergency C-section and hadn't failed to be there for both of us since.

His wife, Saoirse, had become my sister in all but blood, and she and Nellie adored each other.

If there were a contest, though, Clementine would win, hands down.

"If I have to bribe her with my cat, I will," Luca answered.

"I don't know." I tucked my hair behind my ear. "She spent the night with Mom and Dad last weekend. I wouldn't feel right sending her away again so soon."

Dropping his foot to the ground, he leaned forward in his chair. "Sending her away? It isn't like having a sleepover with her family is tantamount to dropping her off at the orphanage. Jesus, Clara, we love her like she's ours. You don't have to do it all alone."

"But she isn't yours." My stomach twisted with the guilt that never went away, and it made me defensive. "If you and Saoirse want a little kid around so much, why don't you have one of your own?"

He slowly blinked at me. "Being a dick won't push me away." He drummed his fingers on his knee. "Saoirse and I aren't ready for our own kids. Let us spoil yours."

I tilted my head, considering my brother. He was thirty-three and had been happily married for three years now. We weren't alike in a lot of ways, but family was everything to us. This was the first time he'd explicitly told me he wasn't ready for kids. I'd assumed their pregnancy announcement would be coming any day now. Then again, I'd been waiting for it since their wedding day.

"Why aren't you ready, Luca? Is it the job?"

He stared back at me, still doing that slow-blinking thing. More guilt rolled through me. By most standards, as the older, more serious Rossi sibling, I should have become CEO when our father stepped down for health reasons three years ago, but I had never wanted to take the helm. My role as COO was where I thrived. Being the public face of Rossi held no appeal to me.

I'd let that role fall to Luca despite him never showing any interest in the business.

Before he'd taken over, he'd been a freewheeling artist, the wild child of the family.

All that ended in one day.

As expected, Luca stepped in as CEO, and while it hadn't been the smoothest transition, he'd grown into it beautifully. Our shareholders loved the direction he was taking Rossi, and the board basically kissed his feet at our meetings.

But it was a big job. He had to travel, work much longer hours than a typical office drone, and his moves were always being watched and reported on by journalists—local and national. If he and Saoirse were delaying their family because I'd forced him into a life he'd never wanted, I wouldn't be able to live with myself.

"You're going to worry yourself into a heart attack like Dad." Reaching forward, Luca snagged my hand and gave it a tight squeeze. "The job is mine. I've made it my own. It doesn't own me like it did when I first took over. The fact is, I'm just not ready to share my wife full time yet. Call me a fiend, but I like being able to get her naked—"

I yanked my hand away. "Whoa, all right. Gross."

He laughed. "You know I have sex, right?"

"Yes. Obviously. But knowing it in an abstract way and thinking about it are two different things." I waved my hands in front of me. "Don't worry, I've learned my lesson about asking when you're having kids. I won't be doing that again."

"Huh. I'm going to remember this when Mom guilt-trips me for not giving her more grandkids."

I arched my brow. "You're going to tell our mother you have sex?"

He winced, falling back in his chair like I'd shoved him. "Hell no. I'd rather have bamboo shoved under my fingernails. Forget that."

I folded my arms at my middle. "I suppose one of the good things about the dissolution of my marriage is not having the pressure to procreate looming over me."

"For now. I have no doubt our mother is going to start fixing you up with her friends' nice, divorced sons as soon as she thinks you're ready."

I shuddered. "Horrific."

"Almost as bad as when you tried to set me up with your friends. They were basically clones of you."

"They weren't." His chin lowered, and his brows rose. I sighed. "Fine. My former friends weren't exactly your type, but you found Saoirse before you were subjected to any blind dates. I'm never marrying again. I'll have no cover when Mom decides my mourning period is over."

"Mourning period?" He scoffed. "Is that what she calls ridding yourself of your stiff-necked, boring, unhinged—"

"I know who Miller was. There's no need for you to describe his finest attributes."

Talking about my ex wasn't my favorite activity, which Luca was aware of. After all, he'd been the one to uncover exactly the kind of person Miller Fairfield actually was—and it wasn't at all the man I'd thought I'd married. Those rough first days of realization, Luca had held me while I utterly fell apart. Then Nellie came, and I'd had no choice but to put myself back together.

"All right." Luca smoothed his hand over the side of his hair. "I came in here to talk to you about the meeting with Motor Zone next week. I went through the initial proposal last night. On paper, it sounds good, but I want to hear your thoughts."

Just like that, I flipped from sister to COO of the largest manufacturer of motorcycles in the United States. This conversation wasn't in my schedule, but I mentally shifted things to make room for it.

There were few things I enjoyed more than having nitty-gritty, nuts-and-bolts discussions with Luca about Rossi Motors—and not just because this business was an integral part of my life. It was sharing this responsibility with my brother, having my opinions valued and my point of view honored even when he didn't agree. It was the freedom to express all my thoughts with him, unfiltered, unlike what I offered the rest of the executive team. It was the excitement we shared to move Rossi forward—to grow and expand what our great-grandfather had started before we'd even been a twinkle in the sky.

This was why I loved my job.

Working with my brother, as annoying as he was capable of being, was something I'd never trade.

Chapter Four

Clara

Sitting in traffic on my way home, I cursed Luca's name.

His visit had thrown me off track the rest of the day. I'd been late picking Nellie up from day care, and that meant she was starving for dinner and our time together had been cut by a half hour. It might not have sounded like a lot, but our hours were already so limited thirty minutes was precious to me.

It also meant once she was in bed, I'd be in my home office finishing the tasks I'd left undone instead of vegging out on the couch with a glass of wine and a smutty romance novel.

I relied on those books and an hour or two of laziness to get me through the week.

Damn Luca and his distinct ability to lure me into long conversations. He was too good at saying the exact thing I needed to hear to be distracted.

"I'm hungry, Mommy."

I glanced at Nellie through the rearview mirror. "I know, honey. I'm trying to get us home as quickly as I can. What would you like for dinner?"

"Noodles." She kicked her feet to punctuate her excitement for this particular food, which made up at least fifty percent of her diet.

"You had noodles last night. Let's think of something else."

Her little brow furrowed in consternation. "But I want noodles. Marina can make them."

"Marina's off the clock. Mommy can make you dinner."

She mumbled something that sounded a lot like, *"Not as good as Marina."* While it was objectively true, it still smarted. *Jeez, kid. Take that knife out of my back.*

I drummed on the steering wheel, ignoring the growling in my own stomach. That smoothie I'd sucked down for lunch hadn't done the trick. I'd have to make myself a double helping of noodles tonight.

Tomorrow, when we weren't running late, I'd fight for variety in Nellie's diet. Tonight, I—

"Mommy, the lights are flashing." Nellie twisted around in her car seat, trying to look out the back. "They're blue and red. So pretty, Mommy."

I checked my rearview mirror, already knowing what I'd find. That didn't stop the wave of dread from sweeping through my empty stomach when I confirmed it.

"Oh shit."

Those pretty lights belonged to the police car right behind me. I knew I hadn't driven over the speed limit—and not because I was a stickler for the rules. This damn traffic wouldn't allow it.

I couldn't think of anything I'd done wrong, but the cop was on my ass, not giving up.

Fortunately, I was able to pull into a shopping center parking lot. I didn't want to be the cause of traffic becoming any more dismal.

"The lights are coming with us," Nellie singsonged.

"They are. Mommy has to talk to the policeman for a minute, then we can go home for noodles."

I rolled my window down, keeping my fingers crossed this would be quick. Nellie was being as patient as any three-year-old could be, but I knew my daughter. We were reaching the end of her sweet little rope.

The officer bent down, sweeping a serious gaze over me then back at Nellie.

"Hi!" she burst out. "I'm going home to have noodles. I like your lights."

His no-nonsense facade broke. Lowering his mirrored sunglasses, he chuckled. "Thanks for that, little miss." Then he brought his attention back to me. "Are you aware both your brake lights are out?"

My mouth fell open. "No. What? Both? Isn't that—no, I wasn't aware." I hit the heel of my hand against my forehead. Another task to add to the list. I couldn't help thinking if I had a husband, he would have been on top of this. Well...not Miller. He wasn't much of a car guy. But if he'd been around, I might have had the bandwidth to pay attention to things like brake lights, oil changes... "Shit. I'll have to get that fixed."

"As soon as possible." He shook his head. "I can't let you drive home like this. It's not safe."

"Not drive home...? What do you mean?"

"You'll have to get the lights replaced before driving anywhere."

I hadn't cried since Nellie was born. It took a lot for me to become tearful. But this drive, my yearning for home, the gnawing hunger in my gut—I was so close.

"I just need to get home," I pleaded weakly.

With a sigh, he cocked his head to the side. "You're lucky you pulled over where you did. There's a Motor Zone on the other side of the shopping center. Go in there, buy new lights, and someone should be able to help you pop them in." He patted my door. "I'll follow you over there to be safe."

And to probably make sure I didn't drive away like I really, *really* wanted. Obviously, I wouldn't have, but maybe…

"Thank you, Officer," I murmured.

"I want the lights," Nellie announced, blissfully unaware her mother was about to crack.

"You got it, baby doll," he drawled before sauntering back to his car.

He gave us the full police escort treatment across the parking lot, lights flashing, siren booping. And while I wanted to melt into my seat, it tickled Nellie to death. I hadn't done anything wrong, and his presence behind me made me feel guilty and deeply embarrassed—especially with all the lookie-loos stopping to watch.

Thankfully, once I parked, he drove away. I exhaled a shaky breath.

"Why are we here, Mommy?"

I turned to smile at her. "We have to run into this store for a minute. My lights aren't working, so we have to fix them."

She tilted her head. "Do you know how to fix lights?"

I rounded my eyes and puffed up my cheeks. "No idea. I was hoping you would do it. You know how, right?"

"No," she squealed. "I'm only three!"

I snapped my fingers. "Oh, that's right. I forgot you aren't a car expert. Well, let's hope someone inside knows more about cars than us, right?"

"Right!"

I got myself and Nellie out of the car, handing her a granola bar from my emergency stash as we walked in. I hated giving her snacks so close to dinnertime, but desperate times called for desperate measures.

Inside the door of Motor Zone, I came to a standstill. I had never stepped foot inside one of these shops, and I was immediately overwhelmed. Considering it was bright and organized, with rows upon rows of supplies to maintain and repair vehicles, it wasn't any fault of the shop's. There was just *so much*; finding two little brake lights was like a needle in a haystack.

Fortunately, a young Black man in mechanic's overalls tied at his waist and a nametag reading "Dante" clipped to his shirt approached us with a friendly smile.

"Can I help you, ma'am?"

"I hope so."

"The policeman talked to Mommy," Nellie informed him. "He had pretty lights."

Dante shot me a polite smile. "Let me guess, do you have a light out?"

I nodded. "Both brake lights."

He hissed. "That's not safe. It's a good thing you came in. Let me see if I can help you find your lights."

He led us to the opposite side of the store, walking down a row with what seemed like thousands of different lights. Undaunted by the intense variety, he homed in on the ones I needed.

"Here you go, ma'am." He pressed the small boxes into my hand.

His arm braced on the shelf beside him, waiting while I studied one of the boxes. Nellie nibbled on her granola bar, dancing from foot to foot.

"Are you hungry?" she asked him.

He pressed his hand to his stomach. "Yeah, I could eat. That granola bar looks good."

"You want some?" She waved her snack at him like we hadn't all witnessed her sucking and drooling on it the last five minutes.

"That's okay, you eat it. I have a burrito calling my name at home."

"What's your name?" she asked.

"Dante."

She nodded. "Your burrito is saying, 'Daaanteee! Time for dinner!'"

He cackled, and I lost track of what I was doing from the overpowering need to squeeze my daughter's body into my side. Her sense of humor had definitely come from Luca. Her precociousness too. Luca had emerged into the world winking at the nurses...or so our mother had said.

Finally, I found what I was looking for, confirming they were the right lights, and Dante escorted us to the cashier.

"If there's anything else I can do..." he said, making the offer as he started to walk away.

I glanced at the lights on the counter, and he stopped. I must have looked helpless. "It might come as a surprise to you, but I'm not well versed in installing brake lights. Would you be able to help me? Or someone else?"

He rubbed the back of his neck and pulled his phone from his pocket to check the time.

"Any other night, I would, but I'm about to clock out, and I have plans." He glanced from me to Nellie, then back. "But lemme go check in the garage. I'm sure there's someone who can do it. It won't take long."

I pressed my hands together. "Thank you so much, Dante. You've been a huge help. If your manager's around, let me speak to him or her about giving you a raise. You deserve it."

He shuffled his boots, offering me a sheepish grin. "Thanks, ma'am. Just doin' my job." He jerked his head toward the direction of the garage attached to the store. "I'll send someone out to you."

Nellie waved to him. "I hope you like your burrito, Dante."

If my flattery hadn't been enough to get Dante moving, Nellie's cuteness had done the trick. At this point, I didn't care who fixed my brake lights. I just wanted it done quickly so I could get home, pour myself an oversized glass of wine, and kick off these heels.

CHAPTER FIVE

Jake

I wiped the grease off my hands with a stained rag and gave my shoulders a roll. I'd been under a hood all day, and I was feeling it. It was time to get out of here, grab some food, and go home.

This week was coming at me hard and fast, and it was only Monday. I never left the garage without cleaning my tools, though, so I got to work polishing the ones I'd used.

"Anyone have ten minutes to spare to change a couple brake lights?"

I looked up from my tools, finding the kid—Dante—swiveling his head left and right. The mechanics scattered around the shop, pointedly *not* looking at him. Dante's voice carried. No doubt he had been heard, everyone just had full plates, and they weren't looking to add another thing that would slow them down.

I wasn't the only one looking forward to crashing at home.

"Dante," I called, motioning him over.

He jogged toward me, but it was so slow he should have walked. "What's up, boss?"

I cringed at the title. To me, "boss" would always be my dad. "It's just Jake." Dante nodded, but he didn't appear convinced. "I was about to ask you the same thing. What's up with you trying to pass off work?"

"No, no." He waved his hand. "It's not like that. I was on my way out, but there was a customer who needed help, so I stayed to assist her. She's pretty clueless about her car. No idea how to change out the lights. I told her I'd ask if anyone could do it. I would, but I really do have to blow out of here."

I tossed the rag aside. "I'll do it, no problem. Good job helping the customer."

He cocked a grin. "She said she was going to tell my manager I need a raise."

I chucked. "Keep going the extra mile, and I can see that happening. Where is the customer?"

He nodded toward the attached store. "In the front, wearing a red dress. She's got a little girl with her. Chatty as hell. You can't miss 'em."

"Got it. Get out of here for whatever you're chomping at the bit to do."

Dante hightailed it the moment I'd finished talking. If I were a betting man, I'd put money on him having a date.

I stopped to wash my hands. There was no scrubbing off the gray stains from beneath my nails, but I managed to get them relatively clean before heading to the front.

The woman in red was easy to spot, but Dante hadn't done her justice in his barely-there description. Her plump, heart-shaped ass and wide hips filled out her dress just right. Almost as well as—

Nah. Now wasn't the time to start thinking about my biker fantasy woman. Who knew if or when I'd see her again? Filling my head with thoughts of her very fine ass would only serve to drive me crazy.

"Excuse me, ma'am. I heard you need some help."

Her shoulders became rigid at the sound of my voice. If I hadn't been watching closely, I might've said they'd jumped with surprise, but no, it was a snapping of muscles.

Tension.

My attention was drawn several feet down to the tiny girl at her side waving up at me.

"Hi. Mommy's car's broken. I'm Nellie."

Wide brown eyes, silky chestnut hair, round little cheeks—Nellie was the picture of cuteness. Her big, bold voice belied her diminutive size. She must've been older than she looked.

"Well, let's see what I can do to fix it, Nellie. I'm Jake."

"Hi, Jake." She poked her mom's leg. "This is my mommy."

The woman slowly spun to face me, and I took my time raking my gaze up her softly rounded figure, the familiarity of it making my head fuzzy.

Then I got to her face. Same brown eyes as her daughter. Same silky chestnut hair. But her plush lips were the only round place on her face. The rest was sculpted. High cheekbones, pointed chin, straight, refined nose...

CeeCee was as gorgeous as the picture I held in the back of my mind, but this version didn't look like she'd step foot close to a motorcycle, let alone ride one to a biker bar.

Her cheeks flushed, stirring my gut. That part of her I recognized.

Alarm bells rang in my skull, and I went on high alert. "What are you doing here, CeeCee?"

"I—Jake?" She tucked her daughter slightly behind her, but Nellie popped right back out, her head swiveling between us, trying to discern what was happening.

"Yeah. Did you track me down?" I asked tightly.

We hadn't done last names or details. I'd allowed her to lead on that, but that wasn't to say I hadn't agreed. I was all about keeping complications low, and as good as she looked, her showing up at my shop wasn't what I'd signed up for.

She scoffed. "No. Does it look like I expected to see you?" She gestured to her pink cheeks and then to her daughter, who was wrapped around her leg. Her voice dropped, low and pissed off. "If I were to go hunting for a man, I would never involve my daughter."

My defenses softened. This wasn't ideal, but I believed her. CeeCee walking in tonight, the one day I worked here, was a coincidence. Whether it was a good one or not had yet to be seen.

"All right. I get you." I held my hand out, and she glanced at it. Horror melted her expression, and she scuttled back a step. I shook my hand at her. "The lights, mama. If you want me to change them, you're going to have to give them to me."

"Sorry, I—" She shook her head, taking a moment to compose herself. Once she had, she handed over the boxes, her eyes meeting mine. "I'm sorry. I obviously didn't expect to see you or get accused of stalking, so I'm a little thrown off. If you could replace my lights, that would be wonderful."

"No problem. It won't take any time." I nodded toward the door. "Lead the way."

"Thank you," she said firmly. Politely. As if we were strangers and I didn't know exactly what every inch of her body looked like. I probably deserved that, though, after, as she'd said, accusing her of stalking me.

I followed her out to her SUV, immediately taken aback when I realized it was a Porsche. I hadn't priced one lately, but from my estimate, it ran in the six figures.

I'd figured this woman had money. Her leather jacket was high quality, and the bag she carried was some designer I remembered an ex coveting. Plus, her skin, hair, and nails were well maintained—and not by some walk-in shop in a strip mall. Her wealth was in the details.

I hadn't taken the time to ponder the level of rich the woman in my bed had been, but now I wondered where she went to work in her little red business dress. What kind of power did she wield?

My dick twitched in my pants.

"I wanna watch!" Nellie yelled.

Right. Now was not the time to get hard.

"I could use an assistant."

I popped the back hatch, and Nellie held her arms up. Without thinking twice, I picked her up, plopping her down in the empty trunk space. Her mother made a gasping, choking sound, but I ignored it, getting to work on her lights.

I started to show Nellie what tools to use to remove the taillight then glanced over my shoulder to make sure CeeCee was watching too.

"You might want to pay attention, so if this happens again, you can do it yourself."

She shifted from one foot to the other. "My father takes care of my car maintenance."

"You should know how to take care of yourself so you don't have to rely on anyone else. Look where that got you this time."

Her mouth flattened. "Can you please fix my lights without adding your opinions on my personal life?"

Nostrils flaring, she looked at me like I was just some random mechanic here to service her. I wasn't a fan.

Had I met this version of her a year ago, I wouldn't have looked twice, and I certainly wouldn't have gone back to that bar, again and again, to spend the night in her sheets, devouring her from her pretty head to her soft, baby-pink-polished toes.

I gave her my bland customer service smile and tipped my chin. "That I can do, ma'am."

Turning my back to her, I went to work on the lights, Nellie my captive audience. Her mom might've been a snob, but it hadn't worn off on Nellie yet. She was sweet as could be and friendlier to a man she didn't know than she should've been. She was my kid; I'd be wary about how open she was with a stranger.

Not that I was a danger.

I liked kids well enough, and this kid was cooler than most.

Once I got the lights unplugged, I let Nellie use my screwdriver. For a small thing, she was pretty dexterous, getting the hang of unscrewing a bolt right away.

"All right, little miss. You're a natural." I held up my hand, and she slapped it eagerly.

Behind us, her mom huffed. "I appreciate you showing her the basics, but her granddad can give her lessons on the weekends if she wants to learn."

I glanced back at Uptight CeeCee. "Is this you telling me to work faster?"

She tucked her shiny hair behind one ear. "No. Well...not exactly. I'm telling you you don't have to worry about teaching her. You can just do the light and—"

"I hear you. You want outta here."

She didn't correct me or say I was wrong, and the fact of the matter was I wanted out of this situation too. Awkwardness wasn't my jam, and we were up to our ears in it.

Still, I'd promised Nellie I'd teach her how to change a bulb, so I narrated what I was doing. She sat on her knees, watching every step, nodding along like she understood.

It was cute as hell. I hoped her mom appreciated what a bright little girl she had.

Once I got through replacing both lights, I wiped my hands on the back of my coveralls and scooped Nellie out of the trunk.

I patted her head. "Nice to meet you, Miss Nellie."

"Yeah! I'm going to have noodles now."

Despite the thick air around us, I chuckled. "All right. Enjoy your dinner."

CeeCee stepped between us, taking Nellie by the hand. Her eyes flashed to mine, something resembling panic swirling through the deep brown of her irises.

"Thank you so much for helping us." She grazed her forehead with the tips of her fingers. "I just realized I only paid for the lights and not your labor. What do I owe you?"

My jaw went rigid, and I took a beat to inhale. "Don't insult me with a question like that." I tapped the roof of her vehicle. "Get your girl home. She wants her noodles."

Without sticking around for her reply, I strode back to my shop, where things made sense.

There was a saying about never meeting your heroes—they should have also said never meet your fantasy in real life. Disappointment weighed on my shoulders. How could a woman who burned so hot be so cold outside the bedroom?

If I'd had more time on my hands, I might have tried to find out who'd done her so wrong she'd grown that thick, icy facade.

That wasn't me, though.

I did not do complicated.

CHAPTER SIX

Clara

Our detour to Motor Zone had not been fruitful in lightening traffic. Only now, my head was pounding, and based on the whining coming from the back of the car, Nellie was minutes from losing her shit.

Take a number, kiddo.

Jake.

I saw Jake.

Jake had fixed my car and picked up my daughter. Jake was real. A mechanic. He worked in Colorado, so he must have lived here too, not some rugged ranch in Wyoming like I'd pictured.

The entire time in his presence this evening had been like an extension of the fever dream from last weekend. I couldn't recall anything I said, but I was left with the impression I'd acted like a mega-bitch—my defense mechanism of choice.

I pressed my foot down on the brake yet again, and Nellie let out a quiet little sob. Glancing at her in the rearview mirror, her reflection showed her pouty bottom lip and tears welling in her beautiful eyes.

That poky little lip got me every single time.

"I have an idea, Nell-Belle. What if we stop for chicken nuggets and french fries?" I pointed toward the fast-food restaurant ahead of us. "I don't think I can make it home without getting food in my tummy. What do you say?"

"Can I have apple juice too?"

"I think I can make that happen."

Her fists shot up in victory, and she started telling me about all the times she'd visited this restaurant with her grandparents—far more than I'd been informed of. I could almost hear my mother telling me it was her right as Grandma to spoil Nellie. Ironic since she'd never let anything processed pass my or my brother's lips when we were little.

Luckily for all of us, my apron strings were a little looser. That might've been because I had no choice but to roll with the punches. After all, necessity was the mother of invention, and the horrific ending of my marriage had forced me to reinvent who I saw myself as a woman and mother.

We parked, and Nellie practically leaped from the car when I opened her door. I grabbed her hand in mine, and we took off across the relatively empty parking lot and into the restaurant. A smattering of diners filled tables, and there were a couple people in line to order. Nellie and I got behind an older couple, and I stared up at the menu, even though I already knew I was going to order a grilled cheese and waffle fries.

"Jake!" Nellie exclaimed.

I nodded absently toward the dessert section of the menu. "We can split a shake if you eat all your dinner."

A low chuckle from behind me had the hair on my arms standing on end. "It seems my stalking claim might actually have some validity."

"Mommy, Jake is here," Nellie cried, like this was the most amazing development that could have taken place and not a scene from a horror film.

I swiveled around, shocked beyond reason to find *him*. Sucking in a deep breath, I gathered my composure.

"I might accuse *you* of stalking since we were here first."

His mouth twitched. "Nah, I just like the burgers. Never imagined I'd run into you twice in one night, much less in a place like this."

I gave Nellie's hand a squeeze. "To be honest, we don't come here a lot, but I didn't think Nellie—or me, for that matter—could make it home without gnawing a limb off."

His mouth lifted. "Now I need to know who was going to eat who."

"It was something of a self-cannibalism situation."

He winced. "It's a good thing you stopped then."

Nellie tugged on my hand. "It's our turn, Mommy."

I gladly turned away from Jake, relieved the opportunity to discuss cannibalism was closed. What was it about him that made me behave this way? First, I'd been a cold bitch. Now, I was a sputtering ingenue. At thirty-seven, I was well past my ingenue days. None of this was a good look.

Nellie and I placed our order and went in search of a table.

Well...I thought *we* had. When I looked down, Nellie wasn't by my side. Instead, she was bringing up the rear, dragging Jake by his index finger.

He seemed helpless to resist her, throwing out his free arm. "How do you say no to her?"

"With the knowledge, if I don't, I'll have to live with a monster," I replied.

He made a rumbling sound. "Smart mama. Hope you don't mind me joining you for dinner. The invitation was too forceful to pass up."

"Forceful?" I laughed as I settled my daughter into her seat and booped her nose. "Not my Antonella Lucia."

Nellie nodded up at Jake. "That's my big name."

"Yeah?" He slid into the chair beside mine. "Big names are cool. Mine's Jacob, but everyone's called me Jake for as long as I can remember."

Nellie scrunched her nose, not seeming to know how to reply. I took over. Jake calling me CeeCee when we were in our fantasy world was one thing, but him doing it in real life didn't feel right.

"My big name is Clara." Jake's brow winged at my admission. I went on. "No one has ever called me CeeCee. Not until you."

"Clara." He rolled the letters around on his tongue. "Yeah, I like that. Soft and classic. It suits you a lot better than CeeCee."

I smoothed my hands over my thighs before clutching them in my lap. There weren't many things that made me nervous—certainly not men—but my palms were sweaty, and I wanted to jump out of my skin. The Jake effect. He'd managed to get under my skin from first contact, and now, in a situation I never wanted to be in, I still couldn't stop my body's reaction to his proximity.

"I don't know why I didn't give you my real name."

"I do." His lids lowered as he looked me over. "You wanted there to be no chance for something like this"—he gestured between us with his straw—"to happen. Maybe you wanted to play a role too—to loosen up, forget who you are on the daily."

"Maybe all that's true," I admitted.

A worker brought our trays of food, interrupting just in time. I set Nellie's up in front of her while Jake put together the little junky toy her kids' meal had come with. Once she was happy, I dug into my own food, taking bigger bites than I normally would to slake the gnawing hunger and get this over with as soon as possible.

"I'm guessing you live in Denver," Jake said out of nowhere.

A waffle fry poised midair, I jerked my head in his direction. "I do. You too?"

He nodded once. "Outskirts. Can't live in the middle of the city. I'll go stir-crazy."

"I never took you as a city guy. I'm surprised you can manage the outskirts."

His shoulder went up. "Necessity. Have to be close to work and family. You two live in one of the downtown high-rises?"

I snorted a laugh. "No. That's not me. And my monkey couldn't survive without a yard."

Nellie gave us her best ketchup-rimmed grin. "I'm a monkey."

"That's right." I patted her head. "A wild, untamed monkey who needs green space in order to be properly civilized inside."

Nellie's response was gorilla noises.

"Who does the mowing?" he asked.

I chuffed. "Not me."

His brow went heavy. "Why not you?"

"Because my father is old-school Italian in a lot of ways. He'd rather I spit in his face than do yard work."

"So, your...husband takes care of the yard?"

My gut turned to ice, all the food molding into a frozen block. Nellie, busy playing with her new toy and eating her dinner at a snail's pace, hadn't heard Jake's question. It was the only reason I didn't toss a waffle fry at his crinkled forehead.

"Is this your way of telling me you're married?" I countered.

He sat back in his seat, releasing a puff of air. "Never been married. Have never wanted to be married."

Relief thawed the tightness in my belly. The last thing I wanted to be was a homewrecking floozy. Just a floozy I could live with, but I would never sleep with a married man. My mother would tell me to spit in *her* face before doing that.

"All right. Why would you think I am? After everything…" I shook my head, trying hard not to be insulted but failing miserably.

"Not a personal judgment, sweetness," Jake said coolly. "Just thinking about you heading all the way out of town to hook up. Maybe you have a reason for that."

Oh, now I wasn't just insulted; I was getting pissed at his double standards.

"Once a month, I take my bike out on a long drive. I've been doing this since I reached adulthood. It has nothing to do with the desire to hook up in secret and everything to do with the need to be on the open road." I lowered my chin, leveling him with my stare. "The hookup being out of town is a bonus."

He rubbed his thick stubble, contemplating me.

"Why? You don't have hookups stashed around the city?"

I snorted a laugh. Oh, how little he knew about me. "Contrary to the current situation, I don't bring men around her." I nodded toward Nellie, who was trying to feed a chicken nugget to her toy. "I don't advertise being a mother."

Since my dating was purely hypothetical, I should have said I *wouldn't* do those things. Jake was the first man I'd been with since the divorce, and what we did wasn't anything like dating.

"Gotta admit, Clara, seeing you today shocked the hell out of me, but finding out you have a kid didn't. I admire your not bringing men around her. Smart choice."

I flinched at his off-handed comment. "You could tell I'm a mother?"

Of course he could. Being Nellie's mother was worth everything, including sacrificing my former body, but damn if it wasn't a blow to my wobbly self-esteem to know this beautiful man had taken a look at me and read my story in the lines and scars I now carried.

"You're thinking too much," he accused gruffly. "What I'm saying is, I'm no expert, but I've been around long enough to know that scar just below your pretty, lacy"—he mouthed *panties*—"is from a C-section. Me noticing it and bringing it up now is by no means a judgment, just a fact."

I didn't know what to say, but that was okay because Jake wasn't done. Leaning into me, he brought his mouth next to my ear. "And I think you already know I have no complaints about what you have going on under your leathers."

He pulled back enough for his eyes to dart between mine. "Nod if you hear me."

I nodded.

We weren't in our bar or hotel room, but he'd managed to put me under his spell where I liked to do what he told me.

He reached under the table to squeeze my bare knee. "Good girl, Clara. Turn that busy mind off when we're having a friendly conversation. I'm not one to have ulterior motives."

"No?" Regaining some of my equilibrium and a smidge of the confidence I normally had with him, I arched a brow. "Then what are you doing right now?"

"Having dinner with a gorgeous woman and her cute kid, what else?"

Nellie's head shot up. "What's gaw-juss?"

"For a second, I forgot she hears everything," I murmured, making Jake chuckle. Before I could explain, he took over.

"Look at your mom," he ordered softly.

Nellie peered at me with squinty eyes. "I see her."

"See how pretty she is?"

She nodded so hard her hair went flying.

"Pretty isn't a big enough word, though. She's much more than pretty. She's gorgeous, isn't she?"

My little girl put her chin on both fists and scrunched her nose as she examined me. "Mommy, you're gaw-juss."

God, this kid of mine. She regularly reminded me about the beauty of life in her observations of the world, but she didn't often turn them on me. Never mind Jake teaching her that word. I couldn't even focus on that right now. Otherwise, I'd do something stupid like burst out crying or ask him on a date.

"Thank you, honey." I tapped her nose. "You're gorgeous too."

"I think I'm ready to go home now," she declared, pushing away her half-eaten food.

"Me too," I told her.

In the time it took Jake to clean up our trash, Nellie started to droop. I carried her nearly unconscious little body to the car and slipped her into her car seat. She settled in with the stuffie she kept in my car and closed her eyes. Shutting her door, I spun around, and

Jake was *right there*, eating up almost all my personal space, his hands in the pockets of his jeans.

"No point in driving an hour when we can enjoy each other's company right here in Denver." He pulled his phone out of his pocket. "Give me your number."

I shook my head. "No, I'm not dating. I have Nellie and—"

He interrupted me with a low laugh and a loaded look. "I didn't say anything about dating, Clara. I want to fuck you, and I want to do it locally. The way you've reacted any time I've gotten close to you tonight, I think you want the same. There's no need to play games. Only time I enjoy those is when you're naked and I'm winning."

I couldn't breathe. Air expanded my lungs, but I couldn't force it out. This man, slightly less than a stranger by a narrow margin, had the ability to control my body without even touching me. I couldn't decide if it made me furious or turned me on.

Probably both.

"Clara," he crooned. "It's not difficult. I'm not going to intrude on your life. When you're free and I'm free, we—"

"Give me your number." I couldn't allow him to say "fuck" one more time. If he did, I might've taken it as an invitation. I wasn't equipped to handle a man like him. The only time my ex had said "fuck" was when he'd stubbed his toe or accidentally worn black shoes with brown pants.

Interrupting Jake and shoving my phone at him had been my desperate attempt at catching my breath. I needed him to turn off his rumbly voice and look away so I could force my lungs back to a normal, functioning state.

He stared at my screen for a moment, the corner of his mouth hitching. "Cute as hell," he muttered.

"What? Oh." My wallpaper was a picture of Nellie and me dressed as pirates on Halloween. I hadn't been a sexy pirate either. I'd given myself gnarly teethe, a hairy mole on my nose, and had smudged dirt all over my face. My hair had been a rat's nest of tangles, and I'd stuffed a pillow down my tunic. Nellie and I had laughed our heads off at how silly I'd looked, but maybe it was time to switch my picture.

He handed my phone back, but before I could draw away, he pulled me into him and cupped the back of my head. It had gotten dark outside, making it easier for me to look at him straight on. Jake in the dark, I could almost handle.

"Like that you dress up goofy with your girl. You two look thick as thieves."

I nodded. "We are. We have family close, but most of the time, it's just the two of us."

"And I'm not looking to encroach on that." He dragged his lips down my cheek to the corner of my mouth. "I just want to fuck you until I get your teeth clattering again. And again."

I put my hands on his shoulders, intending to shove him away, but nothing happened. I didn't push, and he didn't go.

"I can't think when you're this close."

His mouth ghosted over mine. "Why do you need to think? I'm not asking for anything more than you've already given me."

He was right, yet I couldn't allow myself to agree. Meeting him by chance at The Tavern was one thing. It was removed from my real life with no chance of entanglement. This was different. We'd had dinner with my daughter, for Christ's sake. My personal boundaries had been trampled on, and I'd been the one to do it. I blamed Jake for smoldering at me the way he did. He'd confused me to the point I didn't know which end was up.

"I should go," I said with as much conviction as I could throw behind it.

His forehead creased, and he sighed. "I see."

"What do you see?"

He took a step back, nodding toward me then my car. "It's too real now. You drive a Porsche and dress like that. I've got grease under my nails, and you saw me in my coveralls fixing cars. I get it." He reached around me to open my door. "Hop in, Clara. Get your girl home."

My spine went ramrod straight, and I stiffly slid around him to put the door between us. "That's an ugly accusation, Jake. Really ugly. But I'm not going to bother arguing with you. I won't be seeing you again, so your opinion of me doesn't matter." I climbed into my seat, my grip on the door shaky and white-knuckled. "You can live the rest of your life thinking the snobby, rich woman doesn't want you because of your job and not because she's trying to protect herself from more devastation she can't possibly handle."

If he had anything to say about that, I didn't stick around to hear it. Door slammed and locked; I backed out of my spot and drove away.

Nellie was asleep in the back seat, blissfully unaware anything had happened. I was a little jealous. I wished I could've slept through the last five minutes. What Jake had said to me, he'd looked down his nose at me, was seared into my brain.

Fuck him. And not literally. He'd ruined his shot of that happening again.

I'd have to come up with a new fantasy to keep me warm at night. Jake, the motorcycle man, was no longer it.

CHAPTER SEVEN

Jake

Four out of five days a week, I spent working in an office. Instead of coveralls or jeans and a T-shirt, I wore suits. This had been the case the past three years, and I still felt like I was suffocating inside my clothes.

I didn't need a psychiatrist to analyze what that meant. If I didn't have my one day working in the shop, I'd lose my goddamn mind. Desks and meetings weren't my thing, but I wasn't the complaining kind. Besides, working alongside my brother wasn't bad.

Now, *he* belonged in a suit. He wore them like a second skin and carried the mantle of CEO like it weighed nothing. Jeremy had been made for this. Technically, it was in his blood.

Mine too, but nurture had beaten out nature in my case. Jer and I had grown up in different houses, me on a ranch in Wyoming, him in the heart of Denver. The beginning of our lives had been nothing alike, yet we'd both ended up in the same place, courtesy of Grandpa Hayes.

I slapped my hand on the frame of his office door. "Time."

He jumped in his seat, his eyes darting from his computer screen to me before dropping to his cell.

"Shit." He shoved his fingers into his hair. "Why didn't you tell me?"

I leaned against the frame. "This is me telling you. We need to head out in five."

"I need more than five minutes to prepare. I was working on—"

"Jeremy," I barked, snapping him out of the death spiral he was sending himself on. I didn't interrupt, he would sink into his neurosis, and this meeting would not happen.

"Yeah?"

"You're prepared. Overly so. Get your ass up, run a comb through your hair, splash some water on your face, and let's go." I held up my hand, spreading my fingers. "Five minutes."

"Five minutes," he repeated.

Jeremy was eight months older than me. We worked for the company our grandfather had started and left to us. Jer was the CEO, and I was his VP. Despite living apart, we'd been raised as brothers. Holidays, vacations, and summers had been spent together. By rights, we should have been a lot alike, but we couldn't have been more different. He was happiest when he was with his wife of two years, Anne, or commanding a boardroom. I'd never been married, and getting my hands dirty in a garage or outside filled me up.

Our differences had a lot to do with sharing half the same DNA. His mother, our dad's wife, was a nervous little woman, always fluttering and wringing her hands. Jer was her one and only kid, and, man, did she hover. My mother had been a free spirit from day one. She'd taken our dad to bed while he'd been passing through her town and ended up pregnant with me. I had three younger sisters from the man she'd married a few years later—a rancher who let her fly free.

Jeremy had inherited his mother's frail nerves and our father's business acumen. I was a lot lighter on the acumen, and my nerves were made of steel. This was why we worked well as a team. When he spiraled, I righted him. If the business had been left to me alone, I would have run it into the ground—more than likely on purpose to rid myself of a responsibility I did not want. Jeremy never faltered as the head. When he needed to pull his shit together, he did.

This was why I wasn't worried about today.

He strolled up to where I was waiting for him in the lobby of the Hayes building, loose and casual, proving me right. From the outside looking in, no one would ever guess the internal warfare he had going on. Jeremy Hayes put on a damn good show when it was time.

"All right?" I asked, clapping him on the shoulder.

"All set." He squared his jaw, scanning the wall of windows to the sidewalk beyond. "Car's here?"

"Car's here," I confirmed.

The ride to Rossi Motors wasn't long, but the silence stretched it out. Once Jeremy was in this mode, he did not like to be pulled out of it, no casual shooting the breeze for my brother. Not that he was much for it on a normal basis.

That left me with my thoughts, which inevitably turned to Clara—the same way they had since I'd had her pressed against her SUV last week. I didn't like to think about what had come after, where I'd been a jackhole and she'd rightly called me on it.

The feel of her downy skin under my lips and press of her tits against my chest was preferable to the way she'd dressed me down before driving off.

In hindsight, she hadn't been looking down on who she saw as a lowly mechanic. My past experiences had had me jumping to the wrong conclusion about a woman protecting herself.

I'd been thinking with my disappointed dick—and look where that had gotten me, with nothing and nowhere.

As a man who had most of my personal life locked down from outsiders, I got where Clara had been coming from. If what she'd said about not bringing men around her daughter was true, spending the evening with me had probably frazzled her. Hell, it'd affected me too. I didn't date, but even when I had in the past, women with kids had never been on my radar.

Having dinner with the two of them hadn't been a bad way to spend my evening, though.

I knew myself well enough to recognize that as the precise reason I'd ruined it.

Once we got through this meeting at Rossi, I'd send her an apology text—put a nice stamp on the end of what we'd shared over the last year so she wouldn't look back on those nights with regret.

§

The headquarters of Rossi Motors was impressive. Bikes I had dreams about on display. Classics, with chrome so shiny, it could have been mistaken for a mirror. Made me wonder if they'd ever been ridden. It'd be a damn shame if they hadn't.

Jeremy elbowed me. "I see you eye-fucking that machine."

"Can't help it. It's a beauty."

He shook his head. "You and your toys. If I get a call about your brain being splattered on the street, I'm going to be pissed."

"I think I'd have bigger fish to fry than your anger."

Needless to say, this was another of our differences. Jeremy had never had any desire to straddle a bike and take it on the open road while it pained me to go more than two weeks without riding mine. The winter months were close to torture.

We were shown up to the executive floor, where more Rossi machinery was on display like art on the walls. I didn't have the opportunity to look it over as Luca Rossi strode toward us, his hand outstretched. With him was a sturdy woman with silver hair wearing a fitted leather moto jacket atop a button-down and black dress pants.

"Welcome to Rossi. I'm Luca, and this is Sally Fink, our CFO." He took Jeremy's hand and clasped it like they were old friends before turning to me. "Jacob, right?"

"Everyone calls me Jake."

"Jake it is." He clapped my hand between his and offered a grin that looked sincere. I'd heard a lot about this guy, but only Jeremy had met him. From all accounts, Luca was forward-thinking and affable. He took his company's success seriously, but outside of that, he was laid back and quick with a joke.

So far, my impression was good, but we'd only just met. A lot of people looked good at first or even second glance. I was reserving judgment.

While Jeremy and Sally exchanged greetings and small talk, Luca nodded toward the wall in front of us. "I noticed you were checking out our art."

"I was. I've never seen a bike sliced down the middle and mounted on a wall."

He chuckled. "We're all a little obsessed with our product around here. There aren't many employees who don't ride. How about you?"

"I do."

"Yeah?" He faced me, tucking his hands in the pockets of his trousers. "What do you ride?"

If this was a test, I was confident I'd pass it. Economics and budgets weren't my thing, but I could run laps around anyone when it came to my knowledge of motorcycles and cars. I had curated a small but impressive collection of each.

"I have a Rossi Streamer for touring and a 1974 M50 Road Knight for special occasions."

His brows show up. "No kidding? My grandfather passed on his '73 Road Knight to my dad."

"Tell me he takes it out." Luca shook his head, and I felt his denial like a physical pain. "Does he at least allow you to take it out?"

"No. Sadly, it's sitting under a tarp. He's holding on to it for sentimental reasons, but I'm close to convincing him to give it to me." He pulled a pewter key chain from his pocket and twirled it on his index finger. "Close as I've gotten to it in a while."

He stopped the twirling to hold it out to me. A replica of an M50 Road Knight was parked on Luca's palm. The details were impressive, down to the exact shape of the tailpipe.

"Given to me by my wife," he added.

"Nice wife."

His grin crinkled the corners of his eyes. "No doubt about that. Are you married?"

"No. Marriage isn't something I'm looking for right now."

"You're young. You have time."

That made me laugh. "Unless you've had a killer face-lift, I suspect we're about the same age."

"Thirty-three. As you can see, I was a child bride."

Shit. I barked a laugh before I could stop myself, and a sharp look from Jeremy had me biting it back. This guy was funny, though. Not like any CEO I'd spent time around.

"I'm thirty, so I guess that makes me a toddler."

He finger gunned me. "Exactly." Then he checked the time on his wide-face watch. I recognized it from the Rossi-Rolex collection when they'd partnered five years ago. It was a beauty, but my hands stayed under the hood too much to be a watch guy. Looking at it on Luca, I questioned that decision. "Meeting time. We don't get in there, my sister will come hunting, and we don't want to piss her off."

Since Luca struck me as someone like me—who wouldn't keep to a schedule if it had been up to him—it made sense his sibling counterpart was more like Jeremy. I racked my mind for the COO's name. Surely that information had been in the dossier Jeremy had given me. I'd read it. Absorbed a lot of it. But not that.

I held out my hand. "Lead the way."

⚜

There were several people milling around the conference room. A good balance of men and women. Luca and Sally guided us to the front of the room, where Jeremy would be presenting our offer of partnership. My role was moral support, as well as answering questions about the operational side of the business.

As I pulled my chair out, I looked up, my gaze catching on the back of a woman in a fitted navy-blue dress.

This time, I wasn't fooled into thinking I was seeing a look-alike.

Before I could make sense of why *she'd* be here, Luca tapped her on the shoulder. "Clara, I'd like you to meet Jeremy and Jake Hayes."

She spun, a practiced smile on her plump lips, focusing on Jeremy. When her gaze swung to me, her smile slipped, replaced by a look of complete confusion that had to mirror mine.

"Jake?" she uttered breathlessly. Her lips rolled over her teeth as soon as my name was out, but it was too late.

From my periphery, Luca's head swung back and forth. "You've met my sister?"

Clara Rossi.

What a fuckin' time for the name of Rossi Motors' COO to emerge from the abyss of my memories. Would it have made a difference? I wouldn't have associated *my* Clara with an executive—

No. Not my Clara.

This was the last place I would have expected to run into Clara. She belonged at The Tavern, with her wild hair and leather pants clinging to every one of her soft curves. More recently, she belonged in her fancy SUV and pretty, starched dress with her cute little girl holding her hand—not at the head of the company my brother had deemed necessary for ours to continue to grow. Yet, here she was, looking right at home.

She recovered before I did. "Yes. Remember when I told you about my brake lights going out? Jake was the mechanic who so kindly stayed late to fix them. But I suspect Jake is a lot more than a mechanic."

Jeremy laughed tightly. "My brother likes to make sure his hands don't get too clean. He works somewhat undercover in a Motor Zone garage once a week. It helps him keep his finger on the pulse of things."

"Interesting." Luca nodded. "While I like the idea, I don't think they'll let me work at the factory. I'll just stick to riding our product."

"Quality control," Sally Fink deadpanned.

"That's right. If I don't make sure the new Triumph model runs as smooth as last year's, who will?" Luca smirked at his CFO, who shook her head, a wry smile threatening to break out on her serious face.

I raised a brow at Clara. "Your lights still good?"

She straightened her spine and raised her chin, washing away her previous confusion.

"I haven't been pulled over again, so I think so." She offered the stiffest smile she could. "Thanks for saving the day."

"Yes, thank you, Jake," Luca added. "I appreciate you going out of your way to help Clara."

I nodded. "Not a big deal. If I hadn't been there, I suspect she and Nellie could have charmed one of the other guys to do it."

Luca brightened visibly, almost bouncing on his toes. "That's right, you got to meet my niece. She has a way about her, doesn't she?"

"Cute kid," I agreed.

Jeremy sidled up next to me. "Family is important to Jake and me. Motor Zone has always been a family business, like Rossi."

Oh, Jeremy. While he was a good schmoozer, small talk didn't come naturally to him. Like now, he often steered the topic to work when it should have landed there organically. The excitement quickly drained from Luca, and Clara looked away, clearing her throat.

"That's right. We should talk about why we're all here." Luca swept a hand toward the front of the room. "Why don't we all sit down so Jeremy and Jake can do their thing?"

Clara took a seat between Luca and Sally, leaving no chance for me to sit beside her, and kept her eyes glued to her tablet. I felt like an asshole, getting frustrated over not having her attention when it wasn't the time or place, but I couldn't take my eyes off her. She looked good in another of her starched little dresses. Had me wondering if she always wore dresses to work.

Jeremy turned on the screen displaying his PowerPoint presentation. He loved making these. He'd made one when he was twelve and had wanted a higher allowance. He'd also used a PowerPoint to present to our father why he should have gone to Princeton instead of Columbia.

He'd gone to Columbia.

It was our father's alma mater, and no matter how convincing Jeremy's slides were, his college had always been a foregone conclusion.

A map of the US glowed on the screen, red dots scattered across the country.

Jeremy explained what he was showing us. "There are six hundred and six Rossi dealerships in the US. Of those, five hundred and sixty have on-site mechanics for repairs and service."

He flipped to the next map, which was superimposed on top of the first.

"The black dots on this map are Motor Zones. Currently, we have six thousand seven hundred eighty-two open in the US."

The following slide zoomed into the central US, where there were far more black dots than red.

"We noticed a dearth of dealerships in parts of the country where there are multiple Motor Zones, and it got us thinking, how can we both use that fact to our advantage?"

The next slide described a partnership between Motor Zone and Rossi. My gaze flicked to Clara, who had her head down, still tapping away on her tablet. In fact, she hadn't looked up the entire time Jer had been presenting.

All the work he and his team had done, the least she could've done was look up.

Jeremy went on and laid out his plan. Motor Zones would become an official partner to Rossi, and we'd carry certain genuine Rossi parts and accessories. In areas where there were no Rossi dealerships for more than a hundred miles, our service bay would offer express services, like oil changes, brake servicing, and tire replacement. Our mechanics would receive the same training as Rossi mechanics, and we would have access to proprietary Rossi tools.

When he started going over the money, Clara finally looked up, her eyes narrowed. I blamed her wariness on Jeremy using Rossi earnings as part of his presentation. He wasn't treading as lightly as I would have at an initial meeting, but then, he wouldn't have been Jeremy if he had.

When he came to the end, he looked around the room with a slight smile. "That's all I have for now. Does anyone have any questions?"

Clara wagged her stylus. "I do. I have some questions for Jake."

Her eyes landed on me. There was nothing flirtatious or coy behind her gaze. This was business Clara, who didn't blush or back down. Hard ass women didn't do much for me, but this one...knowing there was a sweet, molten core beneath it all...

Yeah, she did a whole lot.

I rubbed my hands together. "I'm ready. Bring it."

CHAPTER EIGHT
Clara

I had a list of questions I could have asked Jeremy Hayes. He would have given me a polished answer that told me nothing. If I wanted real and raw, Jake was where I had to turn.

Jake Hayes. Jake Hayes in a sleek, black suit.

What were the odds the man who wanted a considerable amount of money and assets from my family's company would be the same man I'd met in a cowboy bar and had taken to bed?

If I were more cynical—and I was already loaded down with cynicism—I would have suspected this was all some elaborate set up. But no, Jake's expression when he'd realized who I was couldn't have been faked. He'd been just as surprised to see me.

He'd flinched then, but he didn't now. I launched into my questions, and while he wasn't as smooth as his brother, I liked hearing his unpracticed answers. Jeremy chimed in a time or two, but I made sure to direct everything to Jake.

I wasn't interested in this partnership, and Luca was well aware of that. But my brother was less rigid and far more open to change. It was easier for him. He hadn't devoted his entire adult life to learning the ropes to keep Rossi alive for future generations.

Luca laid his hand on my arm, taking over. "This has been extremely interesting. You've given us a lot to discuss and think about."

Jeremy blinked hard and folded his hands together on the table. "Any thoughts you'd like to share today?"

Luca chuckled. "Not yet. I'm going to have to go over everything you presented and let it percolate. Speaking for Clara and myself, we don't pounce on every opportunity like this. We take our time, do our research, and have many discussions with our advisors. Above that, we'd like to get to know you and Jake. As you pointed out, we're a family company. Knowing who we work with is important to us."

Something rippled over Jeremy's placid expression before he could school it. "That sounds good, Luca. I'm open to all the conversations you need to feel comfortable forming a partnership with us."

Luca and Jeremy walked out of the conference room together, talking affably. If my brother put his mind to it, he could smooth a path over hell, so it didn't surprise me how easily he'd relaxed Jeremy.

I walked out of the conference room directly behind them, not giving Jake a chance to speak to me on his own. This had been awkward enough already; there was no need to prolong it.

Reaching my office door, I couldn't stop myself from peeking behind me down the hall. Jake had stopped just outside the conference room, his body turned in my direction, hands in the pockets of his black suit pants. He wore a suit just as well as he wore a leather jacket and pair of coveralls, but there was something unnatural about this particular man buttoned up in such a way.

The smirk playing on his lips, though? That *was* natural, the intensity of his stare too. If I'd been ice, I would have been a puddle on the floor.

But I was Clara Rossi, the second-in-command of a Fortune 500 company. So, like Jake was any other man walking these halls, I straightened to my full height, met his eyes, and lowered my chin.

His mouth parted, but if he had something to say, we were too far apart. Besides, I wasn't in the mood for chatting. I needed time to collect myself—out of his sight.

Shutting myself in my office, I collapsed on one of the seats across from my desk. They were leather and cushy and tied with my desk chair in comfort. There weren't many moments in my day where I relaxed. That was saved for home. Work was work.

But if I were to ever make an exception, now was the time. I survived that meeting without making a fool of myself in front of my colleagues.

God, would they have been shocked to find out how I knew Jake. I bet, if asked, most of my coworkers had never thought about me and sex in the same sentence. To be honest, I didn't mind them having that perception. I'd *felt* pretty sexless until Jake turned something back on inside me that had been shut down for three years. That part of me would never emerge at work, though. Being in an executive position was hard enough—especially due to nepotism. The last thing I wanted was anyone thinking I was sleeping my way to a deal with Motor Zone.

My phone alerted me to a text. I slipped it from the pocket of my dress, mindlessly checking.

"Ah!" I tossed my phone in the air then scrambled to grab it before it crashed to the ground. Why was *he* texting me? Had he even left the building?

Jake: *Let's talk. Dinner?*

Oh, he had to be kidding. We didn't talk, and aside from the fast food with Nellie, we didn't share meals.

Me: *No thanks. If you have anything you need to say, you can text.*

Jake: *You don't eat dinner?*

Me: *I eat dinner. Not with you.*

Jake: *We need to talk about how we're going to handle this.*

Me: *That doesn't require dinner. Besides, I think we handled it fine today.*

Jake: *Is that why you snuck off before saying goodbye? Did you need to go to your office and handle yourself, mama?*

Me: *Do you masturbate in your office?*

Jake: *I haven't, but today, I'm cursing my glass walls. Don't need our employees seeing me fuck my fist while picturing you in that dress.*

I should have been offended. Should have had his number blocked. Instead, my thighs were pressed tightly together, and I was calculating the number of hours until I could slip between my sheets and quell this ache he'd created with my vibrator.

He kept going, texting me without waiting for a reply.

Jake: *Do you always wear dresses like that? It's a good look for you.*

Jake: *Can't decide if I like you in tight jeans and a leather jacket or your uptight little dresses.*

Jake: *Naked. It's naked. When you're letting me touch all that softness...yeah, that's my favorite.*

Jake: *But I need to see you in another dress to be sure, so meet me for dinner.*

Me: *Aren't you going to promise it'll be strictly professional?*

Jake: *No. The one thing about me you need to know is I don't break promises. There's no reality where I can be in your presence and think strictly professional thoughts.*

Me: *How will we work together if this deal goes through?*

Jake: *We need to talk about that over dinner.*

I closed my eyes and exhaled, my phone resting on my stomach. I didn't have to be facing forward during the beginning conversations with Motor Zone, thereby avoiding this situation with Jake all together.

Dating him was out of the question—if that was even what he was after. And I couldn't possibly sleep with him again.

So why was I vacillating?

Why was I tempted to say yes to dinner? Or more?

Jake: *Take the day to think about it.*

Me: *I don't need to think about it. The answer is no.*

Jake: *You're disappointing me, Clara. If you dig deep, I bet you're disappointing yourself too.*

I tossed my phone on my desk and groaned at the ceiling.

He wasn't wrong. A part of me wished I was the kind of woman who could throw caution to the wind, but that would never be me. I'd never been that way and had far too much to lose to change now.

CHAPTER NINE

Clara

I did not indulge in much, but there were a few luxuries I had long ago deemed necessary for survival. Biweekly pedicures with two of my best friends were on the top of that list and had a special, nonnegotiable place on my calendar.

Today, I was four minutes late. Needless to say, by the time I settled into my massage chair between Bea and Shira and dunked my feet in the warm water, I was a frazzled mess.

"I thought you died," Bea intoned.

"No." I smoothed my hand over the top of my head. "I'm alive, but my assistant might not be for long. He was supposed to interrupt my call with—"

Bea put her hand on my arm, drawing my attention to her. She shook her head, her perfect blue curls bobbing. "I do not care."

"Bea!" Shira whisper-shouted from the other side of me.

Bea leaned forward, her brow raised. "Do you care about her phone call with her client?"

Shira worried her bottom lip with her fingers. "It isn't that I don't care. It's the text you sent earlier..."

"Right, the text." I nodded.

"The one about you sleeping with a random biker in a bar," Bea added helpfully, paying no mind to the three women working on our feet or other women scattered around the salon.

I pressed my hand over my chugging heart. "Let me take a breath before I spill my guts."

"Take as long as you need," Shira said softly.

"Not too long," Bea added sharply, making me laugh under my breath.

Shira had come into my life several years ago when she'd married one of Rossi's board members, Frank Goldman. Half his age, and a resting bitch face that could cut with just a look, most people had steered clear of Frank's child bride. But something about her had compelled me to get to know her. I'd discovered she was painfully shy and one of the sweetest humans on the planet. Since losing Frank last year, she'd been making a valiant effort to keep his company running, but my friend wasn't having an easy go of it.

Sweet wasn't a descriptor that had ever been used for our darling Bea. We'd met through mutual friends over a year ago and clicked for reasons still beyond me. She was a decade younger than me, snarled at strangers, had blue hair and a septum piercing, and worked in catering. On the surface, we had nothing in common, but the three of us had clicked. Our differences jibed, guaranteeing there was never a dull moment when we were together.

Before Bea and Shira, I'd never had girlfriends I could say anything to without worrying I'd be laughed out of the room.

I hadn't told them about Jake, though. I had no fear of judgment. That wasn't why I'd been reticent. It was that I was inexplicably possessive of our encounters. They belonged in that dark hotel room.

If I spoke them aloud into the light, it would change how I viewed them.

Then yesterday, when Jake turned out to be Jake Hayes, heir to Motor Zone, everything changed.

"Okay." Opening my eyes, I glanced back and forth between my friends. "I'm going to tell you everything. Let me get it all out before you ask questions, okay? I just need to say it."

They both nodded in agreement, keeping quiet to show me they understood.

"A little over a year ago, I took my bike out on the road and ended up riding with a mixed pack out to Skyridge. I stopped there, got a room, and walked around a bit. There was this biker bar near my hotel, and something compelled me to go in. I guess...I wanted to see if anyone would look at me. It had been so long since I'd been looked at like a living, breathing woman I wanted to remember what it felt like. Then, a couple guys tried to buy me drinks, and I almost ran out of there. I didn't, though. The same urge that had compelled me to enter the bar kept me glued to my seat. It didn't take long for another guy to take the stool next to mine without asking if it was free. He got the bartender's attention, ordered a beer, then looked at me and asked me what I was drinking."

I shivered at the memory of experiencing the slow, sensual slide of Jake's full attention for the first time, of his leg touching mine and not moving away. His eyes on me, never leaving.

"One beer. That's all I drank with him before I stood up, held my hand out, and asked if he was in or out."

Shira gasped.

Bea was grinning like a proud papa.

I covered my face with my hands. "I don't know where I'd gotten that line or how I'd managed to actually say it, but Jake was in. We went to my room and"—I dropped my voice to barely above a whisper—"fucked all night. I have never done anything like what we did. I've never been touched that way or spoken to like that."

"Like what?" Shira murmured.

My exhale came out in a whoosh. "Like he owned me. Like my body was the answer to every single one of his problems. Like he was grateful to be with me and had to make sure I understood that." I shook my head. "I've never had a one-night stand, but I don't think they're supposed to be like *that*."

"They're not," Bea assured me.

"He took me over and over. All night long. And in the morning, he was still sleeping, and I just...left."

Shira blinked a few times. "You left?"

"I left. I thought that was it and didn't want to ruin it with morning-after awkwardness. A couple months later, I got restless and took another ride, ending up back in the same bar. I didn't think there was any chance he'd possibly show up, but an hour or so later, there he was."

"Was it just as good?" Bea asked.

I scrunched up my face. "It was somehow better, which I wouldn't have thought possible. We didn't exchange numbers, though, so I thought for sure that was it."

"But you got restless again?" Shira guessed.

"Two more times. We met up twice more, and each time was better. I almost asked for his number the last time, but I didn't. I told myself I could have him if I left it to chance. I'm not dating, so I won't pursue anyone. Jake was my exception."

"Why are you using past tense? This sounds like the perfect set-up," Bea said.

I groaned. "It was. Until I ran into him in town. He lives here, and I had Nellie with me."

"Oh no..." Shira sighed.

"Oh yes. But that isn't the worst of it."

Bea chuffed. "Has anyone ever told you you're a terrible story-teller? Stop edging us, or I'll lose interest out of spite."

I narrowed my eyes at her. "No you won't, and Nellie says I'm the best storyteller ever."

"That's because she knows five people." Bea wasn't wrong. "Plus, she's nice and doesn't want to hurt your feelings."

"Bea has no problem doing that, though," Shira said with a little laugh.

I poked my chest. "Don't worry, my invisible safety suit is lined with iron. None of this is penetrating."

"Clearly." Bea rolled her eyes. "Considering you still haven't told us the worst part."

This was why I loved Bea. She never pulled punches, but she wasn't mean. I could take her teasing, no problem. She was more careful with Shira, our tenderhearted friend.

Laughing, I waved my hands in defense. "All right. The worst part? Jake is the VP of a company we're considering partnering with. He showed up in our conference room yesterday in a suit and tie, looking like my own personal devil." I cringed. "I can't ever see him again."

"Oh *no*..." Shira repeated. "Was he just as surprised to see you?"

"What are the chances he didn't know?" Bea asked, ever the doubtful one.

I turned my head to look at her. "That's what I'd thought, that this was some elaborate set up to soften me toward the deal. If that had been their angle, it was a terrible misstep, considering I'm much more reluctant to even consider their offer now." I shook my head. "But I don't think he knew who I was. I'd told him my name was CeeCee, and unless he followed me to Denver from Skyridge, he couldn't have known where I was from or where I worked."

"CeeCee is cute," Shira said.

"Mmmhmm. I want to meet CeeCee. Is she a ditzy little flirt?" Bea shimmied her shoulders, a sardonic grin curving her lips.

Taking on Bea's usual tone, I deadpanned, "CeeCee is dead."

"And Clara's not interested in VP Jake?" Bea filled in.

"If only. That would make all this so simple." My fingers curled around the padded arms of my pedicure chair. "I told him I'm not dating, and he said he's not after me for a date."

Shira whimpered. "He just wants—"

I nodded. "He wants to continue our arrangement...but do it here."

"Even after the meeting?" Bea asked.

"Well, I don't know." I picked at the stitching in the arm of the chair. "He asked me to dinner to talk about the situation. I obviously turned him down—"

"Obviously?" Bea pressed. "Why wouldn't you want to talk about it? You're a talker. It's how you figure out important decisions. You talk and talk until it makes sense."

"Why does that feel like criticism?"

Her huff of a laugh told me to stop being silly. "It's an observation. Some of us internalize when we're making a big decision. You go external."

"It's true," Shira agreed. "Which is why I'm shocked you didn't tell us about Jake sooner."

"Well, there was never any debate about him," I replied. "What we were doing worked for me. But now it can't possibly continue, which is so damn disappointing."

"It could, you know." Bea poked my hand. "You need an outlet. A grown-up outlet that has nothing to do with being a mom."

She knew me too well. If she hadn't added the last part, I would have brought up the Mommy and Me paint class Nellie and I took and our weekend morning hikes, which were steadily getting longer as she grew.

"Maybe, but it can't be him." This, I was firm on. Seeking out someone nearby for a casual arrangement was one thing, but Jake was off the table. Things were too tangled now with the potential Motor Zone deal. But the thought of any other man touching me like Jake had held no interest. Quite the opposite, it actively repelled me.

"*Maybe* is a big step for you," Shira observed. "I know you feel guilty any time you leave Nellie, but if you were married, you wouldn't feel that way."

"But I'm not." My nails dug into the cushy arm. "Because of me, Nellie doesn't have a father. I messed up by choosing poorly, and now—"

"Oh, come on. That's such bullshit," Bea declared. "Nellie doesn't have a father because your ex was an undercover psycho. You can't possibly take the blame for his actions."

"I should have known," I protested.

"No one knew," Shira said. "My point is, you have a village of people who love Nellie almost as much as you do. There's no reason for you to feel guilty about letting her hang out with us, or her grandparents, or her aunt and uncle, or her nan—"

"Okay, okay." I smoothed a hand over my hair, offering her a smile. "I'm Italian. Feeling guilty is in my DNA."

Bea crossed her arms. "Screw that. Go to dinner with Jake. Talk it out."

Shira nodded. "At least then you'll be able to get on the same page, you know?" Leaning into me, she dropped her voice to whisper soft. "What's the bright side of this?"

"Of Jake?"

She nodded. "Yes."

This had been Frank and Shira's thing when he was alive. No matter how shitty their day or the situation they were in, they'd ask each other what the bright side was. When he died, Bea and I had continued it with her. Through her darkest, most miserable days, we'd ask her to tell us the bright side, and she always managed to find it. A couple months after she lost Frank, she took the reins again, and I had never been happier to let them go. Even Bea, our little angsty, grumpy friend, didn't mind finding the bright side for Shira.

"The bright side is..." I rubbed my lips together, flashing back to him kissing me, taking care of my new body, making me feel like something more than a mother like I was sexy and worth noticing. "Being with him brought part of me back to life."

Shira sighed. Shockingly, Bea did too.

"And you're going to give that up?" Bea asked incredulously. "Tell the truth, is Jake secretly ugly and you're too ashamed to take the chance of being seen with him in town?"

I sputtered a laugh. "God no. If anything, he should be ashamed to be seen with me. He's so far out of my league and definitely younger."

Shira gasped. "You didn't mention he was younger. How much?"

"I don't know. We never talked about things like that; it's just a sense I have." Bea flicked her long nails. "Younger, older—who cares? What I care about is you claiming he's out of your league. Unless you're talking pro sports, no one is out of your league, Clara. You're rich, incredibly successful, and, last but not least, astoundingly hot."

While she was singing my praises, I Googled Jake Hayes and clicked on a picture, promptly shoving it in her face.

"Care to eat your words?" I quipped.

Bea studied him carefully, a little line forming between her perfectly arched brows. "He's handsome in a flashy, obvious way, I'll give you that. But not hotter than you. Have you seen your ass lately? And your angel face? You have fewer wrinkles than I do."

"Blood of virgins," I said as I showed the picture to Shira. "And my ass has dimples in it."

Shira whistled softly. "He's hot, yes, but he's obviously seen your ass dimples and liked them."

"Who doesn't like dimples?" Bea added. "We're allowed to have them on our face cheeks but not our ass cheeks? I do not agree. Ass dimples are just as cute."

Laughing, I covered my face with my hands. "I can't stand you, Beatrice."

"Yes, you can. You'd be insufferably boring without me in your life," she replied smugly.

"True." I peeked from between my fingers. "Let's be done talking about me for today. I'd rather find out what's going on with you."

"Bea caused a car to run into a light pole yesterday," Shira reported.

Bea shrugged. "I can't help if someone chooses to watch me walk down the sidewalk instead of paying attention to the road."

This was one of the many, many reasons my pedicures with my girls were nonnegotiable. Bea made me laugh, and Shira focused on the bright side. I never failed to leave my appointments with pretty toes and a refreshed outlook.

That must have been why, as soon as I was back in my car, I opened my text thread with Jake and typed out what I did. If this blew up in my face, Bea and Shira were definitely getting the blame.

Me: *If the offer still stands, I'll have dinner with you.*

It took less than a minute for him to reply.

Jake: *The offer stands. Didn't think I'd hear from you. I'm free the rest of the week. You?*

Me: *I can make arrangements. Friday? Somewhere relatively private.*

Jake: *Come to my place. I'll grill. Private as it gets.*

Me: *I don't know if your place is a great idea. We're only talking.*

Jake: *I'll keep you on the deck, away from any soft surfaces so you're not tempted.*

Me: *Trust me, I'll be fine.*

Jake: *Yes you will.*

Me: *Please don't make me regret saying yes to this.*

Jake: *Have I ever not treated you right, Clara?*

Me: *Okay, text me the address and time. Thank you for volunteering to cook. I look forward to it.*

Jake: *There's my buttoned-up little businesswoman. Sexy.*

Me: *Jake...*

Jake: *Bet you're blushing.*

I was. He was supremely capable of controlling the blood flow to my cheeks. One flirty word, and it came rushing to the surface.

Jake: *That's okay, you don't have to tell me. I'll see for myself on Friday. Until then, be good.*

I tossed my phone onto the passenger seat. Yeah, this was almost certainly going to blow up in my face. Hopefully Jake was a decent cook, so my meal would be worth it.

CHAPTER TEN

Jake

Clara was sitting in her car in my driveway. She had been for the past ten minutes. I'd been watching her for the same amount of time, amusement growing with each passing minute.

First, she'd fixed her hair and swiped on lipstick.

Then she'd put on a jacket and taken it right back off.

Now, it looked like she was either talking to herself or singing.

It was cute as hell, but I was ready for her to come inside. Opening the front door wide, the light from inside spilled out onto the dark driveway. Clara's head whipped in my direction, her mouth forming a startled *O*. I tipped my beer at her. Her lips clamped shut, and she turned away, rummaging around while I took a long pull.

Finally, she climbed out of her car, shrugging the strap of a compact leather purse over her shoulder.

"I was still deciding whether to come in or not," she announced as she walked up.

"Yeah, my patience is finite, and we both knew you were coming in." I stepped back from the doorway. "Get in here before I come out there and retrieve you myself."

Heels clicked on the stone steps leading to my front porch as she got closer and closer. As soon as I could, I reached out and snagged her hand, guiding her inside. By the time I closed and locked the door, she'd taken off her heels and set her purse on the entry table. Her hands were tucked in the back pockets of her jeans as she scanned the foyer, which opened into the vaulted living room.

"Wow, the wood beams are stunning," she said.

"The woodwork was what sold me. That and the location."

"You said outskirts, but you should have emphasized the 'out' part." Her gaze finally landed on me. "Won't you show me the rest?"

"I'll show you some more." I walked up to her, placing my hand on the small of her back. "You'll have to let me lead, though."

A shiver ran through her, and I was gratified to feel it since she did a damn good job hiding it.

"I have no problem with that."

I took her around the well-used living room to the game room. She ran her fingers along the blue felt of my pool table.

"Do you use this a lot?"

I moved behind her, reaching around her to stroke the felt the same way she had. "Not as often as I should for how much I paid for it. You play?"

"Not since college." She spun, and her chest skimmed mine. "I think I remember the rules."

I smirked. "Maybe we can play a round or two after dinner."

Her shoulder lifted. "Maybe." Then she slid out from between me and the table to continue the tour.

In this case, I didn't mind walking behind her. Tonight, she'd left her conservative little dresses at home, trading them for dark, flared jeans and a silky black top that dipped low in the front. A long gold necklace disappeared into her exposed cleavage, tempting me to follow it.

Not the kind of outfit a woman wore when she wanted to draw lines with a man. This was an outfit meant to drag him over poorly constructed boundaries by his dick.

She twirled a handle on the foosball table and threw a magnetic dart at the board on her path through the room.

"This is a fun space," she remarked. "I'm surprised you have an entire room devoted to games."

"You don't think I'm fun?" I asked dryly.

The glance she shot me over her shoulder was coy as hell. "You told me more than once how much you don't like playing games."

"And yet I keep allowing you to play them with me."

She stopped walking and spun around to face me, her jaw dropping. "You're allowing me?"

Eating the space between us, I curved my arm around her waist and yanked her against me. She grabbed on to my shirt at my waist to steady herself but didn't let go once she had her balance.

"Let's face it, Clara, if I didn't like your style of doing things, I wouldn't have continued showing up at The Tavern, and I damn well wouldn't have texted you after the meeting at Rossi. Let me clarify for you, though. You teasing me is cute as hell. You running when we both know you're not going anywhere *isn't*. Let's cut that shit out now. You're here because you want to be, and I'm pleased you made that decision."

I dipped down and brushed my lips over hers. "Are you hungry? If you play sous-chef, dinner can be ready faster."

Only a brief hesitation before she nodded. "Yes. I'm hungry."

The corner of my mouth quirked. "You have to let go of my shirt if you want me to cook for you, sweetness. At least for a little while."

She looked down at her fisted hand. "Oh." Fingers unfurling, she dropped the fabric and stepped back. "I didn't even realize."

"I know you didn't." I pecked her again. "I like that. You grabbing on to me without thinking about it. It's sexy."

"You yanked me into you. I was keeping my balance, not trying to be sexy."

"Exactly. You don't have to try."

Her cheeks blazed brightly for me, and I wondered who had neglected this woman. Her reactions to compliments were too violent for her to be used to receiving them. If I'd been married to a woman like her, I would have never failed to remind her how valued she was. Then again, there was a reason she was divorced.

***

Clara knew her way around a kitchen. I didn't let her do a lot since she was my guest, but her confidence was obvious. She wielded a knife like an assassin, cutting vegetables like she was going to be graded on precision.

While I went in and out to tend to the grill, I caught her singing along to the tunes playing from my speakers, and when she didn't know I was looking, swaying her hips to the beat.

Slowly, the woman I'd met at The Tavern emerged from her icy shell, relaxing, muscle by muscle, right under my gaze. The full glass of wine had probably helped, but I liked to think I had something to do with it. She was getting comfortable with me again.

Maybe it was being in my space, letting her see something real about me. I liked her here, and that said something. I kept my privacy closely guarded, yet I hadn't hesitated in inviting Clara to my home. There hadn't been another woman here in years, but she looked good in my kitchen and at my pool table.

We ate our steaks and grilled vegetables out on the deck. With nothing but trees behind my house, it gave a vast sense of privacy.

"God, it's nice back here." Clara lifted her glass of wine and relaxed back in her cushioned chair.

"Yeah. I like it." I considered her. Where she might live. "You have a yard, right? Plenty of green space?"

"Nothing like this, but we have a nice fenced-in yard," she replied. "Nellie lives out there most of the year. My dad is going to buy her a swing set for her next birthday."

"She'll love that. Mama might find herself swinging back there too."

Clara huffed and swirled her wine. "If she wants me to, you know I will, but I was always more of a slide girl."

I could almost picture the two of them spending a sunny day on a playground. Nellie was a pipsqueak, but I could see her convincing Clara to swing with her. It probably wouldn't be too hard. In the little time I'd spent with them, it was patently clear Nellie was Clara's world. That was a good look on her, being a mother like that, with the kind of job she had. Pretty fucking impressive, actually.

"Where is she tonight? With your parents?"

"No." She shook her head. "They would have asked too many questions. Our live-in nanny, Marina, is home with her."

"What kind of questions would your parents have asked?"

She blew out a puff of air. "They'd want to know where I was going and with whom."

My brows popped. "Oh yeah? They're controlling like that?"

"No, not at all. They want me to start dating. If I told them I was going to have dinner with a man on a Friday night, they would get too excited, and I'd have to come up with a way of explaining why this isn't a date—"

"How would you have done that?"

She sipped her wine, watching me over the rim of the glass. "Thank god I don't have to come up with an answer. I can't think of anything that doesn't involve casual, anonymous sex. My father had a heart attack a few years ago. He can't take another shock."

I chuckled at that. "You did the whole marriage and baby thing. They're not satisfied?"

"Never." She placed her glass on the table. "Not until they have more grandchildren than their arms can hold. They'll have to look to my brother for that."

"No more kids for you?"

"No." She waved the question away. "Even if I began dating someone now—which is out of the question—by the time we got married and started trying for a baby, I'd be much too old. Nellie's it for me, and she's more than enough."

I narrowed my eyes at her. "You're going to date for ten years before you get married?"

She sputtered softly. "No. Where did that number come from?"

"I'm trying to figure out how you think you'd be too old to have kids sometime in the next couple years."

She arched a brow. "Is this you asking me how old I am?"

"Sure. You have me curious." I couldn't care less how old she was. I imagined she had a couple years on me, but that didn't make any sort of difference. Life was life. It came at you no matter your age.

"How old are *you*?" she countered.

"Thirty," I replied. "You?"

She shielded her eyes and moaned like I'd told her something tragic. "Thirty? That's—"

"Old enough," I stated. "Old enough to own this house. Old enough to run a business. Old enough to take what I want. Old enough to fuck you to sleep. Is that what you were going to say?"

"No," she croaked. "It's young. I feel silly sitting here with you."

Wrapping my fingers around her wrist, I lowered her hand, giving her no choice but to see me.

"The only thing silly here is you saying shit like that to me."

"I'm thirty-seven, Jake. We're from two different generations."

"We're not."

"I know," she muttered. "I *feel* old, though."

Releasing her wrist, I cupped the side of her neck. "Now see, that's your problem, and it has nothing to do with the year you were born. Last few years have been heavy on you?"

Sharp eyes met mine. "Have you been reading about me?"

"No. If you want to tell me about Nellie's dad and what split you up, you'll tell me. I can't say I haven't picked up on rumors and murmurings, but that's just from living in this city. People don't keep their mouths shut."

I grazed her throat with my thumb as she swallowed.

"No kidding."

I moved to stroking the unbearably soft skin under her chin. "You feel old because you went through a birth and divorce in the last few years. But sitting here, looking at you, I see life. I have seen you since the very first time I spotted you on your bike. Life and freedom. It's why I walked into The Tavern after you and took a seat beside you. Why I can't get you out of my head even when I need to."

Her lids lowered, thick lashes brushing her high cheekbones. "That's right. We do need to stop thinking about each other as anything other than a professional acquaintance."

I shook my head, and she slapped my knee. Her haughty look did it for me. I knew just how hot she was beneath that ice.

"It would be careless for me to get mixed up with you when Rossi is in discussions with Motor Zone."

I shrugged. "I guess you're careless since we're already mixed."

"Jake...you know what I mean. This is why I came here tonight, to talk about how to handle ourselves going forward."

She raised her chin, her professional face smoothing into place. The one that didn't pinken when I teased her. She looked gorgeous. And serious. I decided to go along with her so she felt satisfied in saying what she'd intended to with coming here.

"How do you picture this going, Clara?" I asked.

"Like I said, professional acquaintances. What happened between us in Skyridge will stay there. In Denver, we're potential colleagues, nothing more."

"What do you think will happen if it's more?"

Her exhale was heavy with frustration. "It won't be. Hypothetically, though, it would make negotiations awkward, and if the deal doesn't go through, we—"

"Is that a possibility?"

Jeremy would shit himself. MZ needed this. In a world where electric cars were slowly taking over, shifting our primary focus was vital to staying alive. Whether Rossi was the answer had yet to be seen, but Jeremy believed it was.

"This is what I mean. I can't talk about work with you or give you the inside track to our decision. You understand that, right?" She blinked a few times before her eyes met mine, imploring me to say yes, I understood.

"Sure. We've spent the last couple hours together without mentioning work and talked more than we ever have. I'm on board with leaving work at the door, but I don't agree with the need to stop seeing each other on occasion." I leaned forward into her space. "If that's what you want, though, after tonight, we'll go back to being strangers."

Saying that didn't feel right, but I wasn't going to argue for a place in her life when I had no intention of finding a place for her in mine. What we'd had in Skyridge was good. I'd been looking forward to more of it with her in town, but I wasn't a man to beg. If she wanted that too, she'd have to come get it.

Her shoulders rolled forward like she was disappointed I hadn't fought her. Only for a moment, though. Then she squared them, sitting up straighter.

"I'm glad we're in agreement."

For the time being, at least.

After we finished eating, Clara tried to help me with dishes, but I refused. "I'll get them later."

She twitched, and I laughed.

"That bugs you?"

"So much," she whispered.

"All right." I crossed my arms over my chest before I could do something stupid like swatting her ass for being cute. "Let's make a deal we can both live with. Guests in my home don't clean up."

She tried to protest, but I cut her off with a sharp shake of my head.

"My house, my rules, mama." I filled her empty wineglass to the top. "Take this to the game room. While you're in there getting the pool table warmed up and checking in with your nanny like I know you want to, I'll get the dishes. Deal?"

Her brow furrowed, and her bottom lip pushed out like she wanted to pout. After what looked like a bloody internal battle, she finally relented. "All right, Jake. It's a deal—so long as we continue staying professional."

"Mmm. Give me a few minutes and I'll be with you." I twisted toward the sink and flipped on the water, getting busy.

If Clara noticed I didn't agree with her, she didn't call me on it.

That was a good thing.

I never made promises I couldn't keep, and I didn't plan to start now.

Chapter Eleven

Clara

I wasn't as lousy at pool as I'd expected, given how long it had been since I'd played. If I thought about when I'd cut myself off from a game that had once been a favorite, the timing aligned with Miller entering my life.

Just another piece I'd whittled away to fit perfectly beside him.

Jake wandered behind me as I lined up my shot, and I glared at him over my shoulder, finding his eyes pinned to my ass. I should have told him off for ogling me, but his indecent perusal made me feel sexy and desired. Besides, there was no harm in looking, was there?

Except...with him standing behind me, I couldn't concentrate.

"Go stand over there and wait your turn."

His chuckle was deep, scuttling across my skin. "I'm just watching your game. Pretty sure I've been played."

He stopped on the opposite side of the table, leaning on his stick. *Devastating.*

This version of Jake, comfortable in his home and skin, was otherworldly. His hair was unstyled, softly flopping over his forehead instead of slicked away from his face. The cotton of his shirt hugged his chest and skimmed his flat abdomen and narrow waist. And his worn jeans were slung low enough when he tucked a hand in his pocket, a slash of bare, golden skin emerged, and the deep grooves at his hips rippled when he moved.

Before tonight, I'd been incredibly attracted to Jake. Now that he was off-limits, it was as if his attractiveness had grown exponentially.

But I'd made so damn many smart decisions with Miller, and everything had still gone wrong. I could give myself tonight. I needed some kid-free fun, and Jake was offering that without any strings. All I had to do was lean into it and let go.

One night of fun.

Smirking at him, I bent over the table, my chest nearly skimming the felt, and lined up my shot. Muscle memory was saving me. My arms and hands remembered how to do this, where to stand, how hard to hit the cue. I wasn't playing a perfect game, but Jake had been waiting a while for his turn.

"Boom," I whispered, sinking a ball in the corner pocket.

"Yep. You're a sly little shark." He looked me up and down with obvious interest, his teeth digging into his plump bottom lip. "Never would have thought Miss Clara Rossi would take me for a ride playing pool."

Spinning around, I grabbed my wine and raised the glass toward him before taking a long sip. With the drinks I'd had with dinner, I'd already resigned myself to ordering a rideshare, and since Marina was in charge of Nellie for the night, I didn't have to be home anytime soon, so I decided to indulge a little more.

It seemed I did a lot of that in Jake's presence.

"I'm no shark." I wound my way around the table, looking for my next shot. He didn't move when I had to pass him, so my ass brushed against him and one of his hands gave my hip a squeeze. "I didn't think I'd be any good at this anymore."

"I have a feeling you're good at anything you put your mind to."

"Maybe." I lined up another shot. It went wide, the balls bouncing off the side. "Damn."

Jake took over. Competent and confident, he sank shot after shot. Without gloating, he prowled around the table, looking for the best angle, and I leaned against the nearest wall, taking in the show.

My panties were stuck to my wet skin. Sipping my wine, I pressed my thighs tightly together to help ease some of the ache low in my belly, but I wasn't sure that was the answer.

When he sank the eight ball, Jake strode over to me, stopping so close our toes touched.

"Congratulations," I said softly. "I'd demand a rematch, but I think you have the advantage since you live with the pool table."

His huff grazed my lips. "The pool table is in no way loyal to me. I got through that game quickly to relieve your boredom."

"My boredom?"

"Yeah." He rested his forearm on the wall beside my head but didn't allow any of himself to touch me. Not even a little bit. "You looked bored over here. Maybe pool isn't doing it for you. What about a round of darts, Clara? Would that do it?"

I tipped my chin, meeting his dark eyes. "Maybe. We'll have to play to find out."

⚘

My head fell back with a groan. "I've never been this terrible at anything."

Jake chuckled from behind me. "I'm surprised at just how bad at darts you are. I think we've found the one thing you can't conquer."

That raised my tipsy hackles. "I can conquer darts. It's just a dumb game. Give me time, and this dartboard is mine."

"I knew you'd be competitive." He reached around me, stopping me from tossing my dart. "Let me help. We'll work on aim."

I nodded. "I think aim might be the most important part of this game."

"Think you're right."

He was behind me now, his chest pressed against my shoulders. The room had become almost unbearably warm. My free hand twitched with the urge to unbutton my blouse to cool off. But one button wouldn't do, not with Jake so close.

"Here." He circled his other arm around me to splay his hand on my stomach, pressing below my belly button. "Hips and shoulders back. Look where you want the dart to go. Focus on that and nothing else around it."

His hand around mine, we flung the dart toward the board. It didn't strike the bull's-eye, but at least it hit—a huge improvement over my last try.

"Yes!" I bounced on my toes in celebration. "I did it!"

Jake hissed and pressed harder on my stomach, which brought his groin to the top of my ass. There was no mistaking the thick ridge pressing into me. Without thinking about the consequences, I bounced on my toes again.

"Fuck, mama," he barked. "Watch yourself."

I leaned my head back on his shoulder to look at him. "You can wrap yourself around me, do that growly talk in my ear, touch me how you want, but I can't even move?"

He inhaled sharply. "Are you saying I'm turning you on?"

"What do you think?"

His eyes slammed closed, and he released a shuddering breath. "This is why I don't make promises."

His fingers went to the snap of my jeans, pausing there. This was the moment to tell him no and go home. Nothing had happened. It would have been so easy to walk out of here.

No—not easy, possible.

Instead, I arched into his fingers, and he took that as my consent. Unbuttoning my jeans, he slipped his big hand inside, completely bypassing the band of my panties, and cupped between my thighs with a sigh.

"Molten," he whispered harshly. Shoving my panties to the side, he parted my lower lips and let his fingers glide between my folds. "Yeah, Clara, you're turned on."

His lips closed over the side of my neck, and I melted against him. Sliding his free hand up my torso, he molded his fingers around my breast, kneading firmly.

I'd missed his command of my body. His confident touches and heady kisses. I'd missed being held by him, my skin stroked, being the sole object of his attention.

He removed his hand from my jeans and spun me to face him in one smooth motion. There was no time to protest the absence of his touch before his mouth was on mine, his tongue parting my lips to plunge inside.

I gripped his shoulders and kissed him back. God, had I missed *this*. Before Jake, no one had ever kissed the hell out of me. Taking my breath, giving me his. The scratch of his facial hair rough on my lips and chin, abrading my tender skin with each deep skid of his tongue along mine. He'd mark me for days. I'd have to wear makeup over the raw skin he'd leave behind. But in secret, I'd wipe the makeup away and look at the red to remind me.

My head was swirling. I barely noticed when my feet left the ground. Jake carried me back to the pool table, resting my butt on the edge. My thighs immediately parted for him, and he stepped between them like he was taking his rightful place.

Gripping my hips, he pulled me to the edge, aligning the thick ridge of his erection with my seam. Through my jeans and his, our bodies reached for each other. He cupped my neck as he ravaged my mouth. There was no other word for it. He was rough with me in the way he'd come to know I liked because he'd shown me. His teeth nipped at me, tugging my delicate skin, then he replaced them with his tongue, lapping at the stings of pain before plunging into my mouth to steal my breath.

I grappled with his shirt then his warm skin, digging my nails in to find anchor, urging him closer and closer even though there was nowhere to go.

"Jake," I moaned against his kiss.

His hold on my neck flexed. "If you say my name like that again, I'm going to have to eat your needy little pussy. There's nothing for it."

Oh, I like the sound of that. I want that. Yes.

His lips latched on to my racing pulse as he rolled my nipple through my shirt.

"*Jake.* Please." I moaned again, pleading for something to relieve this ache.

Jake wasted no time. Taking the waistband of my jeans in both hands, he yanked, and I helped by lifting my ass. With barely any effort, he had them off me, along with my panties.

Before I could remember why this wasn't a good idea, he dropped to his knees and spread my legs wide. We both went utterly still as he stared at me in the bright lights of his game room. My lungs seized. My fingers dug into the expensive custom felt covering the table.

"Gorgeous woman," he murmured, moving to kiss the soft skin of my inner thigh. His lips trailed to my apex, and he inhaled deeply, his eyelids fluttering as he took in my scent. Without any more delay, he buried his face in my pussy, sucking my drenched flesh. Biting my outer lips until the pressure was so great I had no choice but to scream at the ceiling.

"Yeah, sweetness," he urged. "Give me that voice."

I'd never been a screamer. I used to think women only did that in porn, acting out men's fantasies. But that was all it had been—acting. Not something that happened in real life, and most definitely not my life. In fact, before Jake, my experiences in bed had been largely silent.

The first time he'd made me scream, I'd covered my face with a pillow to stifle it, and he'd stopped immediately to throw the pillow to the floor.

"Never hide your reaction from me, sweetness," he'd growled.

He'd meant it, and I'd wondered how I'd ever been silent in bed. Jake made me moan and cry, pant and scream. Now, he had me pleading. Begging for him to give me the release burning bright in my belly.

Fingers tangled in his hair, I lifted my hips to ride his tongue. I felt him smiling against me, but he never stopped licking me, sucking me, biting me. Then he slid a finger along my center and beyond, wedging between my ass cheeks to find my opening. My belly tightened at the feeling of him rubbing my own wetness there.

When he pressed a finger inside me, my hips flew off the table, and the sound I made when he pushed in farther was inhuman. He flattened his palm on my belly, forcing my hips back to the table. I fought him, but he kept me there with firm pressure, fucking my pussy with his tongue and invading my ass with a second finger.

It was too much and not enough. I needed more to get over that final hurdle. Reaching down my sweat-misted torso, I needed to rub my clit. If I could touch it, roll it a few times, I would have what I needed.

As soon as my hand started past Jake's, he knocked it away.

"Mine." His voice was muffled from how deep he had his face in me, but the message was clear.

"I need to come," I whined. "I can't take it anymore. Let me? Please?"

"Mmm." His rumble sent shivers down my spine, but it wasn't an answer.

I got that when he pulled his fingers from my body, took me by the hips, and flipped me to my front. Then his mouth was on me again, wildly lashing from my ass to pussy. If my nails were longer, I would have shredded the pool table to ribbons. There was nowhere for me to hold, and I desperately needed to. Otherwise, I would fall...or float.

His fingers drove into my ass and curled at the same time his lips wrapped around my needy, swollen clit.

"Too much," I cried, lying through my teeth. It wasn't too much, but it was more than I'd ever had. "Please, Jake. *Please.*"

He sucked and thrust, sucked and thrust, and I felt him everywhere. Like he was kissing me, licking my nipples, and nibbling my toes all at once.

That wasn't what sent me over, though. No, the guttural groan of pleasure that rumbled through him was the final shove. My eyes opened wide, and the rest of my body tensed as I burst apart, regathered, and burst again. He stayed with me through it, holding my thighs, nuzzling me with his lips and nose between them.

When I was boneless and satisfied, he pulled me with him to an armchair and placed me in his lap. He was still hard as a rock but made no move to seek his own gratification.

"Jake," I sighed.

"Mmm." He rubbed up and down my arm, his nose in my hair. "Like when you say my name like that too."

"What about you?"

"What about me?"

I moved my leg over his erection. "This."

"I didn't do that to get anything from you, Clara. That's not what it was about."

Opening my eyes, I met his soft gaze. He meant it. He'd let this moment go with just me getting off, and he'd be happy about it.

"I know you didn't." Wiggling out of his hold, I took my turn dropping to *my* knees. "But there's no way we're leaving this room until I get to have my way with you."

Kneeling before him, he'd gone heavy-lidded, his knuckles grazing my cheek, his mouth tipped in a half grin.

"Do what you need to do, mama."

Keeping my eyes locked with his, I lowered his zipper to free his beautiful, smooth cock and wrapped my fingers around it. He shuddered, and I gave him a leisurely pump.

"I need to make you cry my name the same way I did yours."

"Mmm." He rocked his hips. "Have at it."

Dropping my head to his lap, I closed my lips over his wide head. That was all it took to elicit a moan from him. With my mouth full, I smiled.

I'd have him forgetting every name but mine before we left this room.

This *was* the game room, after all, and I had every intention of coming out victorious.

Chapter Twelve

Clara

This had to be a dream.

A really good one where I was coming without any effort on my part. I was asleep, after all. In Jake's bed, where I'd spent the night after we'd wrung each other dry in the game room and then again in his shower.

This mattress must have held special powers. I'd had the best sleep of my life, and now, I was on the verge of orgasm—

The rough chuckle against my pussy startled me awake. This wasn't a dream, and the head between my thighs was unmistakably Jake's.

That was all it took. Knowing this was real, and it was Jake, sent me into oblivion. Spine arching, I came quietly in the space between sleep and fully awake, but no less powerfully. Goose bumps blossomed across my skin, and my limbs vibrated as Jake kissed up my belly, pausing to lick my C-section scar and rub his beard against the soft swell below my navel.

Rolling me to my side, he fit his much longer body behind mine, and I raised my leg, allowing his cock to slide between my folds.

"What time is it?" I rasped, starting to remember there was a world outside this man.

"Early." He kissed my earlobe then beneath it, making me shiver. "I set my alarm. We have time before you need to get home."

"Smart man." I tipped my head back to nuzzle his beard.

"I'm a man who needs to fuck his woman as many times as he can in the time he's allotted."

Rearing back until we were aligned, he pushed into me. Our groans matched, and his mouth came down hard on mine.

"I need a condom," he murmured against my lips. "Last thing I want to do is pull out of you, but I—"

Maybe it was because I was only half-awake or because this man made me stupid, but I tightened around him to keep him inside.

"I haven't been with anyone but you, and I have an IUD."

He sighed, his head falling on mine. I knew what regret sounded like.

"Like that more than you can know, sweetness, but I gotta have a condom to keep us both safe. Shouldn't have gone in without one. You're too damn tempting, I couldn't help myself."

He rolled away to grab a condom from his bedside table, and a niggling of disappointment filled my gut, but he made quick work of putting it on, not allowing my doubts to overtake my desire for him. He pushed back into me, forcing the rest of those nagging thoughts away, and wrapped himself around me, one leg between mine as he held me from behind.

Cupping my breasts, he kissed my neck and shoulders. We moved together at a slow, languid pace, so different from all our other times. Maybe if I'd stuck around for him to wake up in my hotel room, this was what it would have been like. Or maybe now that we knew each other a little better, it was safer to express something other than desire.

What that was, I couldn't name, I just knew I'd never experienced anything like it.

"Need to wake up with you more often," he gritted out. "Best way to wake up."

He hooked his arm under my knee and raised it high, driving in deeper. My mouth fell open, and I gave myself over to his thorough fucking. Skin slapping each time his hips hit my ass, he groaned in my ear and mumbled how sweet I was. I threaded my fingers through his on my chest and bit his jaw when I began to tremble.

"Wait for me, Clara. Wanna come with you."

"Hurry."

"Chasing you over the edge, baby."

He gripped my hip and pulled me back into him, making our collision a cacophony of pleasure. It was almost impossible to hold back, but I bit down on my lip, waiting, waiting...

"Mmm...there." He plunged in as deep as he could and held. "There, Clara. Let go."

And I did.

His pulsing length and strong hold on my body sent me into a bone-shaking orgasm. My jaw quivered, making my teeth clack together. Jake's warm, rough hand closed around my jaw, holding it still while his lips dragged along my shoulder.

We eased together, relaxing into each other, muscle by muscle. He had to pull out to get rid of the condom, but stayed wrapped around me. I was drifting back into my sleepy space when he gave my shoulder a smacking kiss.

"My alarm is going to go off soon. I'd keep you here all day, but I know you want to get back to your girl."

"Mmm. You're right."

I scooted away from him, stretching out on my back. Without him draped over me and out of the moment, I suddenly felt very, very naked and grabbed the sheet but only managed to yank a corner of it over my middle. Raising my head, I looked down at myself, almost glowing in the bright morning light streaming through his blinds. Worse than my pale skin, though, was the stubble glistening along my legs.

I purposely hadn't shaved last night, so I wouldn't end up...well, here. But Jake had a way of making everything fade away when he put his mouth on me. Even my hairy Italian genes.

"I hear a lot of thinking happening over there." He propped himself on his elbow and tapped my forehead. "Are you coming up with reasons why this can't happen again? Before you even leave my bed?"

"No, that's definitely not what I'm thinking about." *Even though I should be.* "I'm sorry I didn't shave. If I had known we were going to do that, I would have, but—"

"You didn't shave?" He ran his hand over my exposed thighs, his forehead crinkling. "Yeah, you didn't. You're all fuzzy."

I covered my face with my hands. "I'm mortified. I never do this. I—"

"Clara, come on. It's hair. We both have it. Besides, did it seem like I was turned off by any part of you?"

Slowly lowering my hands, I peered at him warily. "No. You seem to be into me."

He chuckled. "Yeah. Glad you didn't miss that. I'm not a little boy. A little hair isn't going to deter me from getting to the treasure underneath it. Get that shit out of your head. Whoever programmed you with the need to be perfect all the time deserves a lesson or two."

My chest tightened from memories of Miller turning me down if my legs were the slightest bit prickly. Him refusing to go down on me unless I'd waxed everything off. Even then, it was hit or miss. Over the years, I'd preempted his criticisms by making certain I was nothing less than perfect when around him.

My mouth opened to tell him it was my ex's doing, but before I could get a word out, a loud sound came from the front of the house. A door slamming into a wall perhaps.

Jake shot out of bed, and I sat up, pulling the sheet to my chest. He started toward the bedroom door, yanking on a pair of sweats.

"Honey, we're home!"

A woman's voice echoed off the walls from the direction of the foyer, followed by a shushing sound and two murmuring voices.

Jake whirled around, none of the panic displayed in his frantic actions reaching his stony expression. He pointed at me. "Stay here. Keep the door closed. I'll take care of this."

He stalked out of his bedroom, firmly shutting the door behind him.

I didn't know what was going on. The one thing I did know was I wasn't going to sit in his bed naked, waiting for him to *deal with* the woman in his foyer with a key to his home who was close enough to him to call him honey.

As quickly as I could, I shoved my clothes on. Shame settled in as the seconds ticked by. I knew next to nothing about Jake, and the truth was, I hadn't asked anything aside from whether he was married. For all I knew, he could have been in a serious relationship.

If he was, I wouldn't be a party to keeping his secret, and there was no way in hell I'd follow his orders.

Jake's low, unhappy voice was the first thing I heard when I quietly swung the door open. "...need to call first," he gritted out.

"I did, Jacob. It isn't my fault you didn't answer." The woman's voice wasn't as low, and there was a teasing lilt to it. "Why are you getting so hot and bothered about—ohhh, you have company, don't you?"

I peered around the corner to find Jake standing in the foyer with a pretty, leggy blonde in leggings and a crop top, his arms crossed over his bare chest, which she poked the center of.

Jake grunted. "It's nothing."

"She must be something if you have her here. You're seeing someone and didn't—"

He swiped a hand through the air. "I said it's nothing, Carly. Jesus. It's just satisfying a bodily need."

She laughed. "Oh my god, are you embarrassed right now? How young is she?"

He shoved his fingers through his hair and chuffed like a raging bull. "Opposite. She's older and knows the score. I give her attention, she lets me in. Nothing more than getting off and getting gone."

My heart stopped, twisted, and plummeted to my feet. *Wow*, that stung. Worse, he wasn't wrong. Despite the front I'd tried to put on, I'd let him in awfully easily.

I had to get out of there, even if that meant passing them. Had my purse and shoes not been by the front door, I might have jumped out a window to avoid the awkwardness.

Then I remembered I'd done nothing wrong. Jake was the asshole ordering me around and bad-mouthing me to the gorgeous woman with a key to his house. He'd have to deal with me walking by him. I would not sit still and be quiet.

Sucking in a deep breath, I strode toward them. He noticed me immediately, turning his hardened gaze my way. The blonde twisted to see what he was looking at, and I was struck by how stunning and *young* she was.

"If you'll excuse me, I'll grab my shoes and purse so I can get gone."

Jake made a choking sound, and the blonde offered a sympathetic smile while stepping aside to make way for me. I slipped between them, my eyes trained directly in front of me. With my back to them, I stuffed my feet in my shoes and grabbed my purse.

"Clara," Jake gruffed.

I waved over my shoulder. "I can see myself out." Of course I fumbled with the lock, slowing down my escape, which had been going oh so smoothly until now. With my insides a trembling mess, I'd actually been impressed with how cool I'd played it. *Why wasn't this lock coming undone?*

In those few seconds—which felt like an eternity—it took to yank open the door, another layer of Jake's secrecy revealed itself.

"Dad! I forgot my field hockey stick!"

Jake Hayes was a father.

And he never thought to mention it.

Chapter Thirteen
Jake

Sage came barreling down the stairs, waving her field hockey stick, oblivious to the fuckup I was in the middle of. And this was a *big* fuckup. I hadn't even begun to wrap my head around it and couldn't, so long as my kid was here.

Clara threw herself out of my house as Sage skidded into the foyer.

"Whoa, who was that lady?" Sage's eyes went wide, and she scurried toward the door to press her face to the sidelight. "She's got really tall heels on. How does she walk so fast in those shoes? Mom, do you have heels that high?"

Carly laughed and joined our daughter at the narrow window, both spying on Clara. "You know I trip when I'm barefoot. She makes it look easy, though, doesn't she?"

"Yeah," Sage breathed before twisting to look at me. "Who is that?"

This was why I didn't do this. I didn't bring women back to my house, and I sure as hell didn't let my kid get a look at them. Explaining a no-strings hookup wasn't my idea of a good time. Then again, that didn't sound like the right way to describe Clara either.

Carly took over for me, as she should have. They weren't supposed to be here at all, so this was partially her fuckup too.

"That's Dad's friend. They're both early birds, so they had a quick coffee this morning, but she had to get home," Carly explained.

Sage's brow furrowed as she glanced back and forth between us. Thirteen and whip-smart, she probably wasn't buying what we were selling, but she was still young and sweet enough not to have a list of other possibilities readily available in her mind.

Sage scanned me, crossing her arms. "Coffee without a shirt on?"

Yeah, this kid was way too smart for me. "Spilled it all over myself. Had to take it off, or I would have gotten a third-degree burn. You don't want me burned alive, do you?"

She rolled her eyes. "You're exaggerating."

I nodded toward the stick in her hand, intent on veering the subject away from Clara. "Did you forget your field hockey stick—the key component to playing field hockey? Really?"

"Yeah, but I remembered before it was too late, and that's what counts." She frowned. "I guess I interrupted your coffee friend meeting or whatever. You should tell the lady to come back. Mom and I have to go."

A swell of feelings for my girl rocked me back on my heels. "You think I intend on missing your first game of the season?"

Sage chewed at her bottom lip, uncharacteristically unsure. "Well, it's Mom's day with me."

I raised a brow at Carly. "Mind if I go to Sage's game?"

She raised her palms, playing along. She knew it had always been my intention to be there. "I have no objections."

"Then it's settled. You two go ahead. I'll meet you there once I'm cleaned up."

My daughter's eyes pinched. "With a shirt on please."

"Yeah, Sage, I'm well known for showing up at your games shirtless."

She snickered. "Just making sure."

I drew her in for a quick hug and kiss to the top of her head. "Do your best on the field. Be a good sport, but don't be afraid to throw some elbows."

Carly stepped in and took our daughter away from me. "Enough of you two. We were in a rush, you know," she reminded Sage. "Let's hit the road."

I saluted Carly and winked at Sage. "See you on the field, tiger."

She giggled at the nickname. "Bye, Dad. Don't forget your shirt."

"I won't," I promised to the back of her head as she ran out the door.

Carly lingered for a moment. "I'm sorry. If I'd had any idea you'd had someone over, I would have...well, done something other than barge into your house."

"I appreciate it. I doubt I'll be in a situation like that any time in the near future, but you not barging in would be a welcome change." I nodded toward the door before she could register her displeasure at that statement. "You better get going."

She rolled her eyes. "Fine. I'll see you at the field." She started for the door, then spun around with a gasp. "We're supposed to bring oranges. Shit, I completely forgot. What am I going to do? I have to get to the—"

I raised a hand. "I'll pick up oranges."

She grinned. "You're a lifesaver, Jacob. See ya!"

If Carly's head wasn't attached, she'd forget it. Lucky for both of us, she had herself together when it came to taking care of Sage. We'd been teens when she was born, and while I'd walked around in a daze the first couple weeks of my little girl's life, Carly had stepped right into her new role like it had been as natural as breathing. I'd gotten there eventually. Wouldn't trade my girl for the world. But I hadn't even been eighteen when Sage had come squalling into the world.

Now that she had entered her teen years, I was right back to that same place, wholly unprepared, but this time for my little girl to start growing up. Hell, she'd be in *high school* next year, only a couple years younger than I was when she'd been born. Crazy to fathom, and if I thought about it too often, I'd go apeshit.

I ran up the stairs and grabbed my phone, right on the verge of texting Clara an explanation or at least an apology. I wish she'd stayed in bed like I'd told her to, but then what? There was no future for us, not when we both had kids we were protective over. I wasn't about to introduce Clara to Sage only for her to disappear from both our lives.

Tossing my phone aside, I walked into the bathroom and turned on the shower, letting it heat up. It was better this way, and with how reticent Clara had been to go there with me again, I was pretty sure she'd agree.

I took a quick shower, ignoring the claw marks on my thighs and sides of my ass. They'd fade, just like this heat between Clara and me. It'd been good, but I was letting it go.

We'd play things how she wanted.

Easy.

Uncomplicated.

This would be better for both of us.

CHAPTER FOURTEEN

Clara

Lunch with Luca was next on my calendar. My brother hadn't informed me which restaurant we'd be going to, so when it was time to go, I knocked on his office door, my stomach growling. Hopefully he'd made reservations at Green Station. I dreamed of their salads on particularly sad, lonely nights.

This past week had been full of those. I'd heard nothing from Jake, not even a "fuck off, loser," and I would not be the one to break the silence. We were very obviously done, but the least he owed me was an explanation.

I wasn't holding my breath on getting one. In fact, I was actively working on forgetting him entirely.

"Come in," Luca called.

I swung the door open and couldn't quite comprehend the scene in front of me. I blinked a few times, and even still, it didn't make sense.

Sitting on the floor atop a checkered picnic blanket was my brother and his wife, Saoirse, with Nellie between them, munching on a baby carrot.

She waved. "Hi, Mommy."

I closed the door behind me, frowning at the grinning trio. "Hi, honey. I didn't expect to see you here," I managed to squeeze out through raw panic.

"We helped her escape from behind bars," Luca explained.

Saoirse lightly slapped his knee. "Also known as signing her out of preschool."

They were both on my official approved pickup list at Nellie's day care, but I never imagined they'd use that permission to do...this. The only times they'd picked her up was when I was running late at a meeting—when I'd *asked* them to.

Luca wiggled his fingers. "Surprise!"

When I didn't move, Saoirse rushed out, "Don't worry. I'll take her right back after lunch."

My sister-in-law truly was wonderful. Tall and honey blonde, she was so gorgeous. At first glance, a lot of people were intimidated or expected her to be a bitch. The fact was, she was more down to earth than anyone I knew and would give the shirt off her back to a stranger. I reminded myself she was an incredible aunt and I trusted her with Nellie.

Taking a deep breath, I tried to tamp down the whirling, whipping emotions cycloning in my chest.

Luca's brow dropped. He must've seen something in my face I didn't want him to.

"Hey," he said gently. "We just wanted to surprise you. I'm sorry if it was an overstep."

I shook my head, willing myself to snap out of my frozen state. "No. It's a nice surprise. Just..." My eyes locked with his, and if my next words were desperate, I couldn't help it. "Promise never to leave this building with her without asking me first."

He instantly became solemn and nodded. "Of course, Clara."

"I promise too," Saoirse said with as much gravity.

"I promise too, Mommy," Nellie declared. "Sit with me please."

When she said "please," it sounded like "peas" and never failed to make me smile. Today was no exception.

"All right, all right." I kicked off my heels and dropped to the blanket, kissing the top of my baby girl's head. "What are we eating for lunch?"

Once we were all done eating and Nellie was busy listening to her aunt Saoirse tell her about the horses on her family's ranch, Luca leaned closer to me.

"I wasn't thinking," he uttered.

I shook my head. "It's been three years. I should be over it."

"No, you shouldn't be. I should have thought it through. You know no one else can take her out of that day care, right? Saoirse had to give a drop of blood and a chunk of her hair before they'd even let her through the first door."

I snorted. "Hyperbole."

"A slight exaggeration. My point is she's safe. I'd never take her from you, and if I did, you know I'd be giving her back within twelve hours. What am I going to do with a three-year-old?"

That finally broke me out of my sour mood, and I laughed. "I'm pleased to know the one thing keeping you from absconding with my daughter is having no idea what to do with her."

"Mommy's laughing," Nellie observed.

My stomach sank. I sometimes forgot how much my daughter noticed these days. I couldn't always hide when I was worried or panicked, but I would much rather she saw me laughing.

"That's because Uncle Luca is really silly."

She smiled, and even with grape jelly smeared around her mouth, it melted me.

"I like silly Uncle Luca. Can I ride a horse?"

I swung my gaze to Saoirse. "That's on you, Aunt Sershie. I know nothing about horses."

Saoirse held up four fingers and wiggled them. "When you turn four, we'll go to the ranch and put you on the sweetest horse we have. How does that sound?"

Nellie nodded hard. "Okay. I can ride a sweet horse."

"Yep." Saoirse smoothed a hand over Nellie's unruly hair. "A sweet horse for a sweet girl."

"I think Mommy needs to get on a horse too," Luca chided. He knew my aversion to them. Their mouths had always given me the creeps, and I *loved* animals.

It was the teeth. They were just so damn big and blunt. Absolutely horrifying. "I'm not a horse girl. They're just so...large."

Nellie bounced on her knees. "Mommy, please. You can ride a sweet horse too."

I shot daggers at my brother. He might've been a married man in his thirties, but he still liked to wind me up like only a little brother could.

"We'll see," I hedged, unable to fully deny her since she'd said, "peas."

Saoirse saved the day. "Actually, I bet your mom would love to watch you, Nell-Belle. She can't do that when she's riding, can she?"

Nellie took that logic in and finally relented. She'd be okay with me watching her ride a sweet horse with Aunt Sershie. Luca was lucky he'd married such a gem. Otherwise, I might've gone to the board to oust him and stage a hostile takeover just to spite him.

The four of us had a nice lunch together—seeing my daughter and sister-in-law in the middle of my workday really had been a treat—but I didn't truly exhale until Nellie was back where she belonged. Most people might not have understood, but I felt more at ease witnessing her day care's security measures. No one could waltz in, claim to be her grandmother, and scoop her up.

On the elevator ride back to the executive floor, my fingers twitched at my side. The week I'd gone back to work after having Nellie, Miller's mother had shown up at her day care and demanded entry, which, for some inexplicable reason, she'd been given. Had I not been watching the parent cameras at that exact moment, I shuddered to think what would have happened. As it was, sprinting two blocks to her day care had taken years off my life. Mrs. Fairfield was not a stable person, and what little sense she'd had left after her only son was sent to prison.

My reaction had been swift and extreme, but if I couldn't use my wealth and power to keep my daughter safe, what good was it? That was why I'd overseen the construction of the Rossi day care center. Now, I was assured Nellie was in the safest place she could've been, and the rest of the Rossi employees were able to take advantage of a top-of-the-line facility as well.

A win-win, and any whispers of me having lost it after everything with Miller had been squashed.

I returned to my office, annoyed at myself for still being so on edge. If I were honest, I'd been tense ever since I'd run out of Jake's house.

So, maybe I wasn't doing such a great job of pretending he didn't exist, but I'd never had a vivid imagination. I'd always been one to deal in facts. My kindergarten teacher had had to call my mother. Informing her that while the rest of the class had done the assignment of creating their own colorful monster out of paper plates, feathers, and tissue paper, I'd read a book. What she didn't know was that I'd been told I wasn't allowed to draw Mrs. Payton, our mean old neighbor, and she had been the only monster I could think up.

I hadn't gotten in trouble, though. My mother had kissed my cheek and said, *"It takes all kinds of people to make the world go 'round. Some of us make up monsters, some of us see them in the real world."*

If only I'd seen my husband for what he was.

My assistant, Thomas, poked his head into my office, and I raised a brow. "Do you have the Salt Lake City numbers?" I asked.

"I don't." He slumped in my doorway, dramatic as always. Over the five years he'd been working with me, he'd gotten comfortable enough to let his true personality show the last four. "I've been hassling Greg Thorne's admin for days. She's a real cunt. She won't put me through to him, and I have a feeling she's not passing along my messages either."

I rolled my eyes. "Greg should have fired her years ago." Then I wagged a finger at him. "Not that I condone you calling a woman a cunt."

"She deserves it." Thomas flipped his flop of blond hair off his forehead.

"True, but let's keep the cunt talk to a minimum at the office."

He cocked his head. "You've now said it more than I have."

Resting my chin on my woven fingers, I smirked. "Whose name is on the building?"

He huffed. "Rub it in."

I laughed and glanced at my computer screen then back to my assistant. "I need the Salt Lake City numbers. Get Samantha on the phone for me, please?"

Straightening, he tapped the doorframe. "On it, boss."

Just like that, I returned to what I understood best: facts and figures. Men and monsters were still a mystery to me, and since my imagination was far too underdeveloped to figure them out, they'd likely remain that way.

Chapter Fifteen

Jake

Jeremy strode through the restaurant with his usual confidence. This was his domain—the place where he conducted his *outside the office* business and felt like he had the upper hand. It was why he'd suggested meeting the Rossi execs here.

Rossi had been serious about getting to know us before making any decisions. They hadn't even begun their SWOT analysis of Motor Zone. It seemed Jeremy and I were still being weighed and measured.

I feared my fuckups would lead to them finding us wanting, something I sure as hell should have thought about sooner. As we approached the table where Clara was already seated between a pair of suits, I was reminded of how I'd gotten here in the first place.

She glows in candlelight.

Laughing, smiling, leaning in to speak lowly to one of the men, likely lawyers or analysts. My fists clenched at my sides. Logic knew no place when I looked at her. Each version of her sent me reeling, and I wasn't familiar or comfortable with that feeling.

Luca stood first, smiling amiably at Jeremy and me. We'd chosen not to bring a team with us. Jeremy had reasoned, when it boiled down to it, we were reminding the Rossis we were a family business. I couldn't say he was wrong, but faced with the Rossi siblings and *their* team put me on my back foot.

Luca took my hand and patted me on the shoulder. "Nice to see you again, Jake." He turned my hand over in his, inspected it for a beat, then chuckled. "Just seeing if you'd spent time in the garage today."

Forcing a grin, I shook my head. "No, Mondays are my garage day. That's all the time out of the office I can afford."

Jeremy had worked his way around the table to Clara. He shook her hand gently, barely gripping her fingertips, and I somehow knew she wouldn't like that at all. I followed his lead, forcing myself to stop and greet the men between us, whose names I immediately forgot, before holding my hand out to her.

"Clara. It's nice to see you again." Under different circumstances, I would have added how gorgeous she looked, her black dress flowing over the silhouette of her body.

Her gaze swept over mine, but it was unreadable in this fucking lighting. I'd have to speak to Jeremy about the location of his business dinners. Candlelight did not make good company when trying to get a bead on an associate or potential partner.

Business partner.

She slipped her soft hand into mine, squeezing it firmly. "Jake."

How she'd made Jake sound like, "fuck off," I had no idea, but she'd managed it. It made me want to toss her over my lap and spank the sass out of her. Instead, I did what was right and let go of her hand.

Jeremy naturally took the seat beside Luca, putting me across from Clara. She made sure not to look at me again. Not when I spoke. Not when I ordered. Not when I accidentally bumped my foot against hers beneath the table.

"So, Jake," Luca began, gaining my attention, "how did you get your start as a mechanic?"

It wasn't natural for me to talk about myself. Not with people I was close to, and especially not with those I barely knew. But this was part of the game, becoming *friendly* with the Rossis so they'd come to see us as trustworthy.

"Grew up on a ranch and something always needed fixing. When I got tired of waiting around for someone else to do it, I taught myself."

Luca's brow dropped, and he leaned forward, intrigued. "You grew up on a ranch?" He glanced at Jeremy. "And you grew up in the city?"

"We have different moms," I explained. If anyone did the math on our ages or our dad's marriage, they'd know he'd stepped out on his vows and I'd been the product of his weakness. It wasn't my favorite topic, but I'd shucked the yoke of shame a long time ago. Dear ol' dad's misdeeds were not mine.

Jeremy hadn't gotten to my stage of enlightenment yet. Then again, he cared a lot more about others' opinions. Sitting next to him, I felt his discomfort, so I pressed on the gas, moving us right past my being Johnathon Hayes's bastard son.

"Jer spent summers with me on the ranch. He's been known to change a battery or two in his day."

Jeremy chuckled, disguising every bit of his unease. "It's been a while, but I think I still have it."

Luca held up his hands. "That's about all I know how to do." He returned his attention to me. "Do you get to weld when working on vehicles?"

I shook my head. "Not these days. But like I said, back on the ranch, I taught myself how to fix things that needed fixing, so welding wasn't out of the question."

The lawyer beside Clara spoke up. "Are you still making those steel mobiles, Luca?"

"I am," he replied. "I don't have as much time to devote to art as I'd like, but I find a way."

Clara's shoulder pressed against the lawyer's. "You should see the fixture hanging in my entry. Luca made it custom for the space. It looks like the weeping willow we used to lie under when we were kids, staring up at the leaves and branches. It's stunning."

Lawyer Boy rotated toward her and lowered his voice. "I'd love to see it sometime."

"Maybe you will," she practically breathed back.

"I'd like to see it too," I replied more sharply than intended. "I bet you have a picture. We can all see."

Clara didn't look at me, but waves of annoyance blasted in my direction. Yeah, she was not liking me tonight, but I wasn't particularly enjoying watching her flirt with the suit next to her either.

She turned her attention on me, her haughtiness on full blast. "I don't think I do."

"Too bad." I prodded her foot, and she quickly jerked it away. Her inattention was driving me mad, forcing me to resort to childish games. I liked playing with her, but not like this. "Luca probably does."

"Uh, yes," Luca answered, "I probably do. However, I don't like to take my phone out during dinner. Why don't I email it to you later?"

Jeremy elbowed my side hard, but I couldn't stop myself from throwing one final jab. "That'd be great. Maybe email him too"—I jerked my chin toward the lawyer—"so he doesn't have to go out of his way to Clara's house."

Luca's gaze pinched, his eyes going between me and Clara. I kept my expression as impassive as I could while Clara laid her hand on the lawyer's forearm and murmured too softly for me to hear.

Jeremy swooped in, saving the situation. "Luca, I hear your wife rides horses." Luca nodded, confirming this. "My wife, Anne, grew up riding in England. She's still getting used to riding western style. Maybe they can meet up and Saoirse can give Anne some pointers."

The rest of the night, Jeremy kept the topic of conversation firmly in his grasp, barely allowing me to speak unless answering a direct question. That was fine by me. If I was honest, it wasn't too far off from our usual dynamic. Jer talked, I listened.

Tonight, I wasn't doing much listening either. I was too distracted by the pinhole of light streaming between Clara's arm and the lawyer's. He couldn't have been out of his twenties and, how stunning she was in all black, looked seconds away from coming in his pants. If she was trying to convey a message to me, she was torturing the man beside her at the same time.

I touched the tip of my shoe to hers.

She kicked me in the shin.

I grinned at her show of violence, and her eyes narrowed.

There was no explanation I could come up with for my reaction—not when I'd been firm in my decision to cut things off with her and hadn't wavered. Of course, this past week, I'd had Sage, so seeing Clara had been out of the question anyway. I could've picked up the phone to apologize, but I'd chosen silence as the period at the end of our...situation.

Yet, here I was, feeling very much not done with this woman. I did not like her involving someone else to make me jealous—or whatever her intention was—and I would let her know in no uncertain terms. But first, we had unfinished business that needed taking care of.

As soon as I could get her alone, we'd do just that.

Chapter Sixteen

Clara

My hands shook as I climbed into the back of the limo Luca had ordered for me. It was ostentatious, but after that dinner, I couldn't possibly drive myself home, and the last thing I wanted to do was make small talk with a driver or anyone.

As soon as the door shut, it was yanked open again, and a man slid into the back seat.

Leather and wind.

He wasn't wearing any, and as far as I knew, he hadn't been riding, but Jacob Hayes smelled like the road anyway. I'd know him with my eyes closed.

Infuriating.

"Why are you in my car?"

"Look at me then I'll answer you." He commanded my attention like he had a right to it.

I turned my head, focusing on a spot beyond him. "Remember the last time you ordered me to do something? How did that go for you?"

He breathed a laugh. "Not well. I had a spitting-mad woman storming out of my house—"

"I didn't storm. I left calmly," I clarified.

"Don't deny being spitting mad?" he teased.

My nostrils flared at his amusement. There was nothing entertaining about his asshole behavior.

"I don't like being told to stay like I'm a dog. And while being blindsided by your...I don't know—*girlfriend? Wife?*—showing up with your child, whom you never mentioned, was an absolute blast; let me tell you, the things you said about me...that was beyond the pale."

"I get that, but I didn't lie. That was the first time I ever woke up with you. Before that, you let me get in then *you* got gone."

I finally had to look at him. He was speaking like what he was saying made sense and wasn't the most obtuse way to look at everything that had happened between us.

"That was private. Me spreading my legs for you was *private*. Staying the night with you happened because I was beginning to think I could trust you." I scoffed at my idiocy. "I should have known. I have no sense of danger."

There was a long pause, and I was finally able to avert my gaze to my fingers twisting in my lap.

Then, like feathers floating in the wind, Jake spoke. "I'm no danger to you, Clara."

"Okay." I did not agree. Any man able to cut me the way he had was definitely dangerous.

He groaned, and I slanted my eyes toward him in time to see him dragging his fingers through the sides of his hair.

"All of that was a fuckup. I should have handled it differently, but I hadn't expected them to show up—"

I scoffed. "Obviously."

He groaned again. "Clara, come on. Do you honestly think that was my wife or girlfriend? You think she would have been laughing if she'd walked in on her man with another woman?"

Of course I didn't think that, even though it had been my knee-jerk reaction at the time. Still, there had been a woman with a key to his house and his child. A woman he'd felt comfortable enough to share how easily I'd spread my legs for him.

"I don't want to talk about this anymore. That night shouldn't have happened in the first place. Now we can both move on like we should have done in the first place."

He twisted sideways on the bench we shared, his arm draping over the top. "Does moving on involve you flirting with that guy barely out of law school?"

I sniffed, slightly embarrassed at being called out so blatantly. Since I hadn't the first clue how to flirt, it hadn't been conscious, but I might've played it up just a little once I saw Jake's grumpy reaction.

Not to make him jealous, though.

I didn't like the implication I was some scorned woman, trying to get back at him.

"It's funny you're calling another man young." *There. That'll show him.*

He leaned toward me. "Age isn't all about the number, Clara. I'm talking about who he is as a man. I got the impression that suit would let you lead him around by the ear like a little boy. Poor guy's probably going to have blue balls for a week from you touching his arm."

I rolled my eyes. This was ridiculous. "I highly doubt any of that is true."

"You didn't see his tongue wagging any time you looked away."

I was never going to flirt again. I had to work with Trevor, and if what Jake was saying held even a fraction of truth, I was going to feel incredibly awkward the next time we had a briefing.

"Jake…" I sighed. "Let's stop this. Say what you need to in order to clear your conscience and we'll both move on."

He exhaled, long and rough. "Look, I'm sorry about the way that morning went down. I'm not a big talker, and sometimes I say shit I don't mean when I'm put on the spot. The way I handled myself isn't a reflection of my respect for you. That was me trying to close the subject as quickly as I could."

"Okay. Thank you for apologizing."

"Clara," he bit out, "don't give me that haughty little attitude. I know you better than that by now. That's not you."

Incensed, I pinned him with a hard look. "I think it's been proven we hardly know each other. You have a *child*, Jake. At no point did you think you should have mentioned that? Like, possibly when you sat down to dinner with *my* child?"

In hindsight, it made sense. The truth was there in the details. He'd been so damn good with Nellie, comfortable lifting her, speaking to her in an age-appropriate way, putting together her kids' meal toy like a professional. I hadn't had the correct information to unscramble all those details into a picture, but looking back, it was so clear. Jake was good with Nellie because he'd done all that with his own daughter.

"Didn't think I'd see you again." He reached across the inches of space between us to put his hand on my knee. "I get you're protective over Nellie. I'm the same way with Sage. I don't bring women around her."

I pointed to the ground like he'd done that day and imitated his gruff voice. "Stay here please. That's my daughter, and I'd rather her not see you." I tipped my head, switching back to myself. "Do you think you could have said something like that?"

He squeezed my knee. "Like I said, I was on the spot, and it came out wrong. She wasn't supposed to be home until Sunday. And if you would've stayed like I told you—"

My jaw went tight. "I don't follow orders."

Letting go of my leg, he cupped the side of my jaw and turned my face so we were almost nose to nose. "And I'm sorry for that too. Can you put yourself in my place? Imagine it was Nellie coming through the front door? My daughter needs protecting more than you or me. Just like Nellie."

I hated myself for it, but hearing him talking about his girl softened me toward him. Part of me wanted to see him in girl-dad action, but a bigger part still found it difficult to believe he was a father. Big, rough biker Jake Hayes didn't strike me as the paternal type. Yet he was.

I sighed and wrapped my fingers around his hand, lowering it to my lap.

"I understand your instincts. I don't think it's an excuse for saying what you did about me, but I respect your fierce protectiveness."

I cut myself off from asking about his daughter...and the woman. It wasn't my business.

He chuckled. "That's it?"

I tried to pull my hand away, but he held on. "Yes. That's it. You apologized, I accepted, we're good."

"*Did* you accept?"

"Internally, yes."

"How about some words then, sweetness?"

"Why does it matter?"

His thumb moved over my knuckles as his eyes scanned my face. "I'm not sure. All I know is I don't like the idea of hurting you how I did, and I need to know you're okay now."

I raised my chin. *Haughty*, as Jake called it. "Of course I'm okay."

He shook his head. "I know you are. You've got that spine of steel. No one could topple you. What I mean is you're okay with me. That you get why I said what I did, know it wasn't about you, and those words aren't spinning around and around in your head. That you know my opinion of you is a hell of a lot higher than I let on. That how I treated you isn't going to be a setback. I know you're still trying to move on from whatever it was Nellie's dad did to you, and I would hate thinking I had any part of kicking you off the path to healing the hurt he left behind."

My lips parted, and a soft gasp passed between them.

"I don't know," I said with as much honesty as I could muster since he'd just given me all...*that*.

"All right. Then we'll get you there."

"How?"

His nostrils flared as he inhaled. "This was supposed to be over."

"It is," I replied, though it didn't feel nearly as honest as what I'd said before.

He gave me a long look that made my head fuzzy and my body list toward his. What was it about this man? I had never understood *"like a moth to a flame"* until him. His brightness and heat attracted me, but I refused to burn. I *couldn't*. I had Nellie. What good would I be to her if I allowed myself to fly into what I already knew had the potential to ruin me?

He brought his hand up to cup the side of my neck. "Go on a date with me."

"What?" My eyes flicked to his, and the surprise I felt reflected back at me. Had he not meant to say that?

"Yeah." His brow furrowed as he nodded to himself. He was coming up with this idea on the fly. "Have dinner with me. Take a walk with me. Go see a movie. It's your choice. So long as you give me some time. If you want me to make the choice, I can do that. I'd like to see you in candlelight again. When you're not flirting with another man."

"Date?" We didn't do that.

"Yes, Clara. We're going to date. You and me. We'll see where this goes."

"But..."

"It's complicated. We both have kids we need to protect. But I think we could understand each other and this could be good. I feel that."

He was barreling on about the complications of us...together, and I was stuck on him wanting to date at all. This was the last thing I'd expected him to say.

"I'll have to think about it," I replied. "I don't have a lot of spare time and give what I have to Nellie—"

"What time does she go to bed?"

I frowned. "Seven thirty, usually."

"Fine. We go out at eight, after you put her to bed. You're not missing any time with her, and I get your undivided attention without you feeling guilty."

"What about you? Won't you be missing time with...Sage?"

His mouth hitched. "She's with her mom every other week. I can fit you into my life away from her if this works out. And, sweetness, I think it could."

"I don't know..."

The car slowed. Outside the tinted window was familiar. Relief unfurled in my belly. This ride was almost over. Soon, I'd be able to breathe air that didn't remind me of danger and hot, hot nights. Maybe then I could think properly.

"Yes you do," he crooned roughly.

We stopped in front of my house, and my hand shot toward the handle as my heart leapt into my throat. Part of me didn't think he'd let me go.

"This is me," I said.

"I see that."

"I'll see you later. The driver will take you back to your car." His hand was still on my neck and showed no signs of dropping. "Good night, Jake."

He slowly shook his head, his eyes never leaving mine. "You haven't said yes."

"I'm not going to. Not tonight." Leaning forward, I touched my lips to his. I'd done it so suddenly he didn't have a chance to take more before I moved away again.

"Clara..." he growled.

"I have plans this weekend, and you probably have Sage next week. We can take that time to reevaluate whether we actually want to see each other again. You know, when everything isn't so fraught. If you take a pause, I think you'll most likely find you're in this limo to prove a point, not because you actually want to date me."

"What point?" he asked, a jagged edge to his tone.

"That I want you more than Trevor—"

"Who the hell is Trevor?" His hand on me was as gentle as ever, but his question carried a sharp bite.

That made me grin. "The lawyer boy. Trevor."

He scoffed. "Trevor doesn't stand a chance with you."

"You think you do?"

"Yeah, sweetness, I do. I'll give you the next week to take a breather, then I'm coming for your yes."

A wave of desire shot to my core at his cockiness. It should have been a turnoff, but I'd found there were few things about Jake Hayes that turned me off. Right now, I couldn't name any. Not with my thighs pressed together and him inching toward me. As he got closer, I tipped back until I hit the door.

Then there was nowhere to go.

He spoke to me in a low, private tone, just for me, even though there was no one else around. "One thing you need to know? When you say yes, you're going to be safe with me. I want you to think about that. Think about the first time you took me back to your room, how your instinct guided you into trusting I wasn't going to hurt you. You were right then, and when you say yes, you'll be right again. You take all the time to think about that. I'm for damn sure going to be thinking about you—and it'll have nothing to do with that pipsqueak *Trevor*."

As quickly as he'd advanced, he retreated, leaving me alone against the door, my chest heaving, lips tingling from the kiss that never happened.

It took me a moment to collect myself, and all the while, Jake watched, satisfaction tugging at the corners of his mouth.

"Don't be smug," I murmured as I grabbed my purse and opened the door.

"When you look at me that way, I can't help it."

Ugh. He had to stop. I was one heartbeat away from mounting him right here. Luca didn't pay his driver enough to bear witness to that, and my suburban neighborhood would be scandalized by the rocking limo parked on the street.

With those thoughts, I stumbled out of the car and scurried up my driveway. When I got the door open, I took a chance and looked back.

Jake was still there, the window down, gaze pinned on me. When I didn't move, he jerked his chin as if telling me to get in there. So I did. Only when I was locked behind the door did the car pull away.

He'd waited to make sure I was safe inside.

That was nice.

So nice.

I pressed my back against the door and groaned. This was supposed to be over. Jake Hayes shouldn't have even been a thought anymore. But he was a devious man. If he'd kissed me like I thought he was going to, I could have easily written all this off as physical.

Instead, he'd used his clever mind for evil, planting these...ideas that were already taking root.

What if we could date in a way that worked for us both? What if I didn't have to be entirely alone?

There was still the woman in his house and things he'd said showing me an ugliness I didn't trust.

Double *ugh.*

This called for Bea and Shira time. They might not know what to do, but they'd make me laugh, and I could use some comedic relief right now.

Chapter Seventeen

Jake

Carly gave Sage a shove toward me. "Your girl-child demands braids."

Sage chewed on her bottom lip, blinking her pleading eyes at me. "Please, Dad? Mom does them too loose. They always fall out midgame. I know it's last minute, but—"

I stomped on the metal bleacher in front of me. "Yeah, it is last minute, so get yourself over here."

It was a good thing I'd shown up early to her field hockey game, but this wasn't my first go-round. I'd had a feeling I'd be tapped in for hair duty, and I hadn't been wrong. Sage sat between my feet while I got busy braiding her hair into two Dutch braids—one of her simpler requests.

We sat in silence while parents and siblings settled into the bleachers around us. Carly was off somewhere wrangling her youngest son, Dex, but her husband, Mike, and middle daughter, Cleo, had taken a seat with us.

Mike shook his head. "Don't know how you do it."

"All in the hands. I've got my rhythm down." I wrapped an elastic around the second braid and palmed the top of Sage's head. "Feel good, Sagie?"

She shook her head all around so violently I was afraid she was going to give herself whiplash. Then she hopped to her feet and flashed me two thumbs up.

"They're perfect. I don't think they're gonna come out for a week. Thanks, Dad."

"Welcome, baby. Go knock 'em dead."

"Oh, I will." With a wide grin, she thrust out an elbow, demonstrating exactly how she was going to knock 'em dead, then scampered down the bleachers to rejoin her team. Surrounded by friends, she said a few things then pointed to me. Ten tweens turned in unison to look at me. I waved, and they whipped their heads back around, giggling.

"Your fan club." Mike chuckled.

"So weird, man," I uttered.

"Carly thinks it's hilarious. I told her to wait until Dex is a teenager and his friends get weird about his hot mom."

I glanced at him. "That shut her up?"

"Oh yeah. For a little while anyway." He nodded toward the field. "The team's looking good this year."

"Sage eats them all up."

He took his hat off and swiped his forehead. "I was trying to be diplomatic and not brag about my stepdaughter being the best on the field."

"Leave it to me. I'll brag about her all day."

Back when I'd been faced with becoming a teen dad, I never could have envisioned my *Brady Bunch* future, but here I was, living it.

Mike and Carly had been together for a decade and married for six or seven of those years. Mike had come into the situation cool and secure, building a friendship with me while being nice to my kid and her mom.

At their house, with two younger siblings and two attentive parents, Sage had a full-on nuclear family. There were times when she came to my house for the week, I felt she'd gotten the short end of the stick, but she never complained. Besides, Carly and I lived less than a mile from each other. Sage could go play with her siblings and return to my house for peace and quiet when she wanted to.

It worked for us.

A few minutes before the game started, Carly climbed the bleachers with Dex on her hip and Jeremy and Anne in tow. Somewhere along the way, Anne and Carly had become friends, which was funny to me. Anne was very British and regal, and Carly was a loud and proud ATV-riding farm girl. But much like our family unit, their friendship worked.

I stood to kiss Anne's cheek and clapped Jeremy on the shoulder. "You made it."

"Just in time," Jer agreed. "Do you have any clue how many fields there are in this park?"

"We almost gave up and cheered for a random team," Anne added.

"Glad you found us. Sage'll be happy you came."

My brother settled his wife beside Carly then moved down the aisle to take the open seat beside me.

"I wouldn't miss my niece tearing up the field, would I?" Jeremy nodded toward Sage running onto the field, looking fierce as the devil for a girl who didn't have a mean bone in her body.

"You're a good uncle like that."

Once the game got going, he knew better than to try for my attention. All of it was on my baby girl. She was tough, but I couldn't help still being on the edge of my seat, dreading her getting injured. With the way she played, never backing down, getting in the other players' faces, it was bound to happen. I kept telling myself that, hoping I didn't lose my shit when it did.

She played for most of the first half before her coach subbed her out. Only then did I take a full breath and sit back.

Jeremy chuckled. "I've never seen you nervous like when Sage is playing."

"Girls are running after her with sticks."

"True, true." He rubbed his hands on his jeans. "So, what's going on between you and Clara Rossi?"

I went still before slowly turning my head in his direction. "What makes you ask that?"

"Your unhinged behavior at dinner last night. Demanding to see pictures of her art and acting jealous when she invited Trevor to her home. What the hell was all that?" He wasn't angry or shouting. My brother sounded genuinely confounded.

Welcome to the club.

I was the unrufflable one. Steady. Levelheaded. But something about Clara Rossi riled me in a way that was hard to control.

I didn't lie to my brother, and starting now wasn't an option, but he also didn't need to know everything. That was between Clara and me.

"I'm interested in her, and she knows it." Jeremy jerked back. "After dinner last night, I laid it on the line and asked her out."

"On a date?" he clarified.

"Yes, on a date."

He squeezed the bridge of his nose. "Did she accept?"

"Not yet."

"Why not?"

"She's thinking about it."

He exhaled, long and heavy. "Do you have to prove to her you're worthy of a date? Is she making you jump through hoops like her brother is doing to us?"

"That isn't what she's about, and I'd appreciate you not speaking about her that way." I folded my arms over my chest. "Are you unhappy with the Rossi negotiations?"

"There are no negotiations to be unhappy about. I'm starting to feel jerked around by Luca Rossi."

"I don't think it needs to be said we need them more than they need us."

His jaw rippled. "It doesn't, but we're also not looking for a handout. They'll profit too."

"We can do a few dinners, Jer. Let Anne go riding with Luca's wife. Dance the dance. Luca told us from day one he was going to take his time. That's what he's doing."

"Are you dancing the dance by going after the sister?" He asked this carefully, but he might as well have punched me in the face.

My hands balled into fists I kept tucked under my arms. I was not violent by nature, but right now, if my brother breathed wrong, I was liable to draw blood. This, however, was not the time or place for that, and under my sizzling anger, I knew I'd regret taking such action.

"My kid would be heartbroken seeing me toss you down the bleachers. That's the only reason you're still sitting beside me. Fuck off with that kind of question, Jeremy."

He nodded once then turned to the field. He'd heard me and hopefully understood how he'd insulted both me and Clara and would never misstep like that again.

"I'm sorry," he said. "That was unnecessary. Last night had taken me by surprise. You could have let me in on your personal relationship with her."

It was my turn to nod. He wasn't wrong. "It's complicated, but if I had thought there was something you needed to know, I would have told you."

He cast me a sidelong glance. "You like her?"

"I don't know." I shrugged. "There's a lot to like about her."

He turned more fully toward me. "I didn't think I'd hear you say something like that about another woman."

"I'm not marrying her, Jer. Get those stars outta your eyes."

That broke his serious demeanor, earning me a chuckle. "I'm just glad to see you moving on, even if it's with a surprising woman."

"Why surprising?" I was finding my hackles were quick to rise when the topic of Clara came up.

"Well, she's older and, from what I understand, has a child. I would think both would give you pause."

"Like I said, I'm not marrying her. I want to take her out to dinner where some guy in an ill-fitting suit isn't drooling on her."

He slapped his knee. "Poor Trevor. He thought he had a chance."

I chuffed, letting my arms fall. Jeremy wasn't my enemy, and I had to remember that when we disagreed. Threatening to toss him off the bleachers wasn't exactly brotherly behavior.

"I don't know if *I* have a chance."

"Knowing you, you won't back down." He tipped his chin toward the field. "That's where she gets it from."

Sage ran back on the field to finish out the first half, bringing the discussion to a close. It was a good thing too. I had another week before Clara owed me an answer, and talking about her might have made me lose my patience, which was unlikely to end well.

Something told me Clara Rossi wouldn't respond positively to being hunted down.

Chapter Eighteen

Clara

Bea nudged my arm. "Are you certain all this sunlight is good for us?"

"Yes."

"I'm not." She shoved her oversized sunglasses firmly up her nose. "You know I only blossom at night."

Shira huffed a little laugh. "That sounded extremely whimsical, Beatrice."

Bea wrinkled her nose. "Didn't it? That's what all this sunshine does to me. It turns me into a different person. Soon, I'll be skipping through a field of wildflowers. Can you imagine?"

I looked her over and shook my head. "No, I can't, actually."

We were at Saoirse's favorite farmers' market after having an early brunch. Nellie was happily hanging in her stroller, having a conversation with the handmade rag doll Shira had bought for her from a vendor. Shira, in her pale-blue linen dress, was on the other side of the stroller Bea had volunteered to push.

Shira blended. In my flouncy red dress, jean jacket, and white sneakers, I did too. Bea, on the other hand...well, it wasn't her blue hair that made her stick out. My friend wore a black babydoll dress, fishnets, Docs, and a black, wide-brimmed hat. Her lips were so deep red, they were almost black too. She looked like she belonged in a hipster bar in Brooklyn, not hanging out at a farmers' market with a three-year-old.

This was why I loved her. She gave no shits and did her own thing. Since becoming friends, I'd tried to absorb some of her attitude. Too much of my life I'd spent trying to be who I was *supposed* to be and had become unrecognizable in the process.

"I know what you need," I said.

"A dark room and a cup of coffee?" Bea deadpanned.

"No. You can have that when you go back to your lair. You need a honey stick. The honey guy has been pining over my sister-in-law for years."

"Have you seen her? I'm pining over her, and I'm pretty much straight," Bea said.

I laughed. "I know, which is why I feel terribly sorry for him and throw money at his business as often as I can to ease his aching heart."

We wandered over to the honey stall, and as soon as its owner caught sight of me, he stiffened. I'd been here with Saoirse often enough for him to know who I was. I really did feel bad for him. She'd been married for three years. He'd had ample opportunity to make something happen before that and never took it. Living with that sort of regret must have been terrible.

I greeted him with a big smile. "Hi, Joe. I promised my grumpy friend honey sticks."

For a moment, he was flustered, looking anywhere but me. Then Bea waved, drawing his attention.

"I'm the grumpy friend." Bea slid her sunglasses off and shot him a lazy grin. "What do you have to cure me?"

Joe's mouth fell open, and his cheeks blazed. "I-I-I...I'm not sure. Let me think."

He was a big, bearded farmer who handled bees for a living, but in the face of Bea, he'd turned into a blushing, stammering boy. I hadn't even seen him react this way around Saoirse.

"Oh no," Shira murmured.

"Now she's done it," I whispered.

Unlike Saoirse, who was classically beautiful and had men tripping over their feet, Bea had something about her that drove certain men out of their minds. For a year, Bea had had random yet continuous run-ins with a man she'd described as a mysterious billionaire. Since they'd never actually spoken, she didn't know his true identity, and while most people might've called it stalking, she was used to things like that happening and had shrugged it off as an annoyance.

By the time we left the stall, Bea had a bag filled with sticks and jars of honey she'd been given for free.

The four of us found a picnic table in the shade to sit down for a minute and suck on our honey sticks. I handed a strawberry-flavored stick to Nellie, dubious whether it was a good idea.

"Let Mommy hold your doll so she doesn't get sticky."

Nellie held it out toward Shira. "Shira holds it. 'Kay?"

Gently taking the doll, Shira cradled it in the crook of her arm. "Thank you. I'll take good care of her for you."

Nellie's eyes were on her honey, but she managed to answer. "I know that."

I laughed. "She believes in you, Shir."

Shira rocked the doll back and forth. "Thank goodness I think I can handle this. I'd hate to let her down."

"Did either of you ever have to carry around a baby in high school sociology?" I asked.

"Yes." Bea had replaced her sunglasses, but I sensed her eye roll. "My teacher strapped a five-pound bag of flour to a stuffed animal and made us lug that thing around for two weeks."

"How'd you do on that assignment?"

She twirled her honey stick between her fingers. "I turned in an empty flour bag."

Shira gasped. "Your baby bled out?"

"It was a slow leak," Bea quipped.

My hand flew to my mouth to hold back my giggles. "I'm picturing a trail of flour following you all over your high school."

"You wouldn't be wrong," Bea answered.

"Why didn't you patch it?" Shira asked.

"I thought it best to let nature take its course." Bea sucked on the end of her honey stick. "Good thing I'm planning to never have children."

"To be fair, I really doubt you'd let your own child slowly bleed out," I replied.

"You're right." Bea wagged her stick at me. "Too messy."

"I'm messy!" Nellie squealed, gaining our attention. For a girl who'd been left to her own devices with a honey stick, she wasn't too bad.

"Are you sticky?" I asked.

"Yeah, I'm sticky." She poked at her chin, which had gotten the worst of it. "I don't like that."

Bea hopped up before I could and fished the wipes out from under the stroller. Pulling a few out, she crouched down to Nellie's level. "Look at you, Miss Antonella," she cooed. "Did you like that honey stick, darling?"

"It was yummy," my daughter said. "But too sticky."

Bea gently wiped her face before moving on to each finger. For a woman who didn't want kids of her own, she was remarkably good with mine.

"Speaking of messy..." I tipped my stick toward myself.

Shira raised a brow. "You? You are immune to mess."

Bea glanced over at me. "Is this where you give us a J-a-k-e update? I've only been waiting all morning. It's about time."

Shira's eyes widened. "Oooh, J-a-k-e. Yes, please update us and tell us why you're messy."

Wording what had happened since the last time we got together in a PG way wasn't exactly easy, and my daughter heard *everything*, even if she seemed like she was in her own world. After one of our brunches, she started telling everyone she met how much she liked champagne. I had Bea to thank for that one.

"The update is: he has a thirteen-year-old daughter, and she arrived after we had an unplanned sleepover," I summed up as concisely as possible. "And now he wants to take me on a d-a-t-e."

"Did you know he had a k-i-d?" Bea asked.

I shook my head. "No idea. He must have had her when he was a teenager, which is just—"

"Whoa..." Shira breathed.

"We didn't get into the details. I'm not sure I want to know." I was curious, naturally, but unless I decided to allow him deeper into my life, I wouldn't go any deeper into his. "This is a bad idea."

"Why?" Shira asked.

"I don't have time, and his life seems even more complicated than mine." I paused for effect. "The daughter has a mother who has a key to his place."

Bea's brow winged. "And you know this...how?"

I lowered my chin. "She let herself in when I was there."

Bea booped Nellie on her now clean nose and returned to the table with us. "After being chased with a bat by an angry *baby mama*, I don't deal with men who have k-i-d-s."

"Only you, Beatrice." I laughed. "This one didn't seem angry. But do I want to get in the middle of whatever they are? I have a lot of doubts."

"One date won't hurt though, will it?" Shira chimed in with her voice of reason. "It might be nice."

"It might end in a chase," Bea added.

I laughed harder. "You guys were supposed to help me make a decision."

Shira cleared her throat. "I thought I was being helpful."

Bea shrugged. "You didn't put that in the job description."

I rubbed between my eyes, grinning. I was no closer to a decision, but at least I was smiling.

The four of us wove through the market until Shira and Bea stopped at a booth with handmade clothes while I went to look at the silver jewelry next door. Nellie was done hanging in the stroller, so I had her on my hip to look together.

The table was filled with necklaces and bracelets. It wasn't really my style, but I spied a pretty hand-hammered pendant Saoirse would love.

I held it up for Nellie. "What do you think? Would this look pretty on Aunt Sershie?"

Her eyes rounded dramatically. "Oh yes. It's so beautiful."

"Isn't it? I think she'll love it." I rubbed my nose on hers. "Can you keep it a secret if we buy it?"

Her little mouth twisted as she mulled that over. Then she touched her finger to my chin and gave me a very thoughtful, serious look. "Maybe."

I kissed her sweet, round cheek. "Thanks for being honest, Nell-Belle. I know how hard it is to keep secrets."

I gave the necklace to the clerk to wrap up and browsed while we waited. A young girl moved in beside me, her arm extended toward a bracelet hanging from a hook.

"Excuse me? Can you reach that for me?" the girl asked.

"Sure I can." I grabbed the bracelet and turned to hand it to her. "This one, right?"

She looked up at me, and her blue eyes struck me like a blow to the solar plexus. "Yes. Thank you." She paused, her pretty eyes moving to Nellie. "Your little girl is really cute."

"Thank you. This is Nellie."

Nellie waved. "Hi."

"Hi, Nellie. I'm Sage. How old are you?"

I froze when she said her name. The moment her eyes had locked with mine, I'd known, deep down, she was Jake's daughter, but this confirmed it. Our girls chatted like friends. Nellie even had me put her down, and Sage crouched so they could be at eye level.

It was very sweet.

It freaked me the hell out.

"Did you make a new friend, Sagie?"

Whipping around, I came face to face with the beautiful blonde from Jake's foyer. Her eyes flared with recognition.

"Hi," she said. "I don't know if you remember me, but—"

A nervous laugh burst out of me. "I do. That morning was pretty memorable."

"Right." She offered me a smile. "Well, we didn't properly meet. I'm Carly."

"Clara."

"Nice to meet you, Clara." She swung her head to our daughters. "Is this one yours?"

"She is. That's Nellie."

Sage stood up, holding Nellie's hand. "Isn't she cute, Mom? She's three like Dex, but I like her better."

Carly snorted a laugh. "Sorry, kid, you have to keep your brother."

Sage poked her lip out. "But he's always got food on his face—*and* he *jumps* on me. Nellie smells like honey, and I bet she'd never even think about jumping on me."

My reactions were impossible to hide. I wasn't prepared for any of this. Sucking in a deep breath at the mention of Sage's brother caught Carly's attention. Her gaze swept over me, and the corners of her lips shifted into a frown before her expression slackened, like something had dawned on her.

"Dex isn't Jake's if that's what you were thinking," she murmured, wiggling her left hand. Sunlight glinted off the diamond on her ring finger. "Ecstatically married to a man who is very much not him. Mike and I have Cleo and Dex together. Sage is Jake's one and only."

"Okay," I pushed out. "He's very...private."

She rolled her eyes. "That's one way to put it. I'm a talker. His two-word responses have always driven me up the wall. Don't get me wrong, I appreciate how he keeps Sage away from the more public-facing aspects of his life, and he has his reasons for being kinda skittish."

"We probably shouldn't talk about him." I rubbed my lips together. "I mean, if there are things he hasn't told me, I would rather they come from him."

Nellie took that moment to hold out the hem of her ruffled dress. "Do you like my dress?"

Carly didn't miss a beat, pressing her hand to her chest. "Oh my goodness, I don't think I've ever seen a prettier dress. I'll have to find one for Sage just like that."

Nellie tipped her head back to look at Sage. "You can wear this one next time."

Sage thanked her, then blinked at her mom. "See? Dex wouldn't even share a used tissue."

"Well, Nell-Belle talks a big game, but I'm not sure you'd actually be able to pry that dress from her hands when the time came."

My girl was an angel, but she wasn't perfect and sometimes got feral over her possessions. Plus, she tended to develop amnesia when it was convenient for her. Like promising not to take her water bottle to her room—after losing a hundred of them—or telling a new friend they could borrow her dress.

Sage grinned at me for a moment, then her eyebrows popped. "Hey, I know you. You're the lady with the tall shoes from my dad's house."

My smile barely faltered. "That's me. I'm sorry I couldn't formally meet you that day." I stuck my hand out. "I'm Clara."

Her handshake was firm and confident, something I admired immensely. "Nice to formally meet you, Clara. I can't wait to tell my dad about this."

Carly put her hand on her daughter's head. "Speaking of which, it's time to take you to his house. He's probably wondering where his cheese and daughter are."

Sage wrinkled her nose. "I bet he's thinking about the cheese the most."

"I bet you're wrong," Carly singsonged. "It was great to see you and meet Nellie. She's the cutest thing."

"Thank you. I can only hope she grows up with half the confidence Sage has."

A pleased flush spread across Carly's cheeks, then she leaned in and air-kissed each side of my face. Before pulling back, she spoke softly next to my ear. "That is the best compliment ever. I like you, Clara. Give Jake hell."

Moments later, mother and daughter disappeared into the crowd, and I had no idea what to think. That meeting had gone far better than I could have dreamed, but I also had never imagined meeting either of them. Now that I had, all of this had become *real*. Whether that was a good or bad thing, I hadn't decided. One thing I was almost certain of, I'd be hearing from Jake sooner than later.

Chapter Nineteen
Jake

The book in my lap had gone unread, and I'd barely taken a sip from the warming beer beside me, too busy mulling over the information Sage had been bursting to tell me when she got home this afternoon.

"Dad, you'll never guess who I met today at the farmers' market." She didn't pause for me to take a guess. *"Clara! And Nellie too. She's so freaking cute. Like, way cuter than Dex. Almost cuter than Cleo, but Cleo's not a baby."*

"Nellie's not really a baby," I said.

Her eyes went wide. *"You've met Nellie? You didn't tell me Clara had a daughter. Don't you think that was pertinent information?"*

"Before today, you didn't even know her name, so no, I didn't."

She huffed, putting her hands on her hips. *"Yeah, well, now I know her name. I got a good look at her too, and she's so pretty. I know she's like a coworker or whatever, but have you noticed how pretty she is?"*

"It's hard not to notice," I hedged. If I said no, she'd see through me. Only a blind man wouldn't notice how fucking gorgeous Clara Rossi was.

"Yeah. I'm surprised you have a friend like that."

"Like what?"

A wicked little gleam shone in her eyes. "Actually cool."

"'Cause I'm so uncool?"

She lifted a sassy shoulder. "You said it, not me!"

Lucky for me, Sage had a relatively short attention span. I'd been able to move the topic right along but had a feeling I'd be hearing from Carly, and she wasn't so easily distracted.

I couldn't decide if I was pissed off or quietly amused. There was no one to be angry at, except the universe for putting them in the same place at the same time. But, hell, maybe meeting my kid would sway Clara to my side.

Sage was a lot better at winning people over than I was.

I picked up my phone and flipped it in my hand. Sage was in her room for the evening, and from what she'd told me, Clara would have put Nellie to bed an hour ago. Since it had become apparent I wasn't going to get her off my mind anytime soon, I figured I might as well ask her directly how she was feeling about the meeting.

And if I was honest, I'd been jonesing for some more Clara since she left the limo Friday night.

Me: *Good day at the farmers' market?*

It didn't take long for her to reply.

Clara: *Great day. How's your cheese?*

This woman…

I'd already cracked a grin, and she'd only given me five words.

Me: *Already dug into. Sage and I made pizza for dinner. What'd you have?*

Clara: *Do you really care, or are you making small talk until you ask what you really want to?*

Me: *Both. I'm curious about what you get up to when you're home. What are you wearing?*

Clara: *I'm not sexting you! I wouldn't begin to know how, and you'd be terribly disappointed.*

Me: *Oh, sweetness, I really doubt you could disappoint me when it comes to you being sexy. But I'm more into the real thing, so get that out of your head for tonight. I want to know what you wear when you're at home.*

A couple minutes passed. I sipped my beer while I waited. The faint sounds of Sage moving around in her room, singing along to her favorite pop music, filtered in. I took another sip and realized I was relaxed. Connecting with Clara was all it took to ease my tension.

My patience was rewarded with a picture. She'd taken it in the mirror, her camera covering her face, but the rest of her was visible. White tank, black lounge pants, and a slouchy sweater, she looked sexy and cozy, especially with her hair piled messily on top of her head.

Like the thirsty man I was, I zoomed in on her tits to study the impression of her nipples in the fabric. *No bra.*

Me: *I thought you weren't going to sext me.*

Clara: *What are you talking about? I sent you a picture in my pajamas.*

I snapped a picture of the tent in my sweats and sent it to her.

Me: *That's all because of you, mama. Don't tell me you don't know how to be sexy.*

Clara: *You've proven me right since I don't know what to say now.*

God, she was cute. I imagined her being flustered, rubbing her flushed cheeks. As much as I wanted to lean into the direction we were headed, it wasn't all I wanted. Afraid she'd get spooked, I steered us back to safer ground.

Me: *Answer my earlier question: what did you have for dinner?*

Clara: *A very glamorous salad and side of Nellie's mac and cheese.*

Me: *Ah, mac and cheese, one of Sage's four food groups at that age.*

Clara: *She has your eyes, you know. Her mom's personality.*

Me: *Nah, she has a personality all her own. She had a lot to say about you and Nellie.*

Clara: *Good things I hope. I admit, I was somewhat shell shocked during the whole encounter. Luckily, she was smitten with Nellie, so I didn't have to try too hard.*

Me: *Good things. She liked your outfit and said she was surprised I was able to have such a cool friend.*

Clara: *Great. I nearly cracked my screen from laughing so hard. I should show her a picture of me when I was her age. I had chicken legs, braces, and the biggest, frizziest hair ever. Plus, I was captain of the math team. The epitome of uncool.*

Me: *What you're telling me is, you did what you liked and were good at it? To me, that's the coolest.*

Clara: *That's a nice way to see it.*

Me: *Now that I've softened you up, what do you think about going on a date with me?*

Clara: *I think...yes. I would like that, if I can find a free night.*

Me: *Bet you can if you set your mind to it.*

Clara: *I bet you're right. Good night xx*

Me: *Night, sweetness.*

When I put my phone down, I realized I'd been grinning the last couple minutes. I didn't know how this thing with Clara was going to go, but I had a feeling there was more goodness to come.

Chapter Twenty

Jake

A woman like Clara Rossi didn't quite fit in at a *seen-better-days-but-still-fucking-charming* bowling alley, but she didn't seem to care. Once she got over her surprise at where I'd brought her, her enthusiasm turned up, along with her competitive nature.

I did not mind being beaten by her. Not when I got to sit back and watch her wiggle her round, biteable ass in tight jeans as she lined up her shots. That was enough of a win for me.

Hell, having her here with me tonight was enough of a win. I'd been on edge all week, thinking she'd cancel on me. When she'd walked out her front door, a smile on her face, the knot in my chest had unfurled. She'd been just as eager as I had. As quickly as I could, I got her on the back of my bike, like I was getting away with a crime.

Clara spun around, her hands over her head, bouncing on her toes. I told myself tonight was about getting to know each other, not fucking, but when she made moves like that, it tested my resolve.

"Nice job, mama," I called. "How about you save some pins for everyone else? You're destroying them."

She sauntered over to me, a pretty flush in her cheeks, confidence in the sway of her full hips. "I can't believe how well I'm doing." She tapped her arm. "I guess it's muscle memory."

I got up and snagged her around the waist, pulling her into me. Her breath caught, and my heart stood still as she peered up at me. Pretty brown eyes wide with surprise...and something else. Something vulnerable.

"I can't think of many things better than seeing you win," I said. "Except when I beat you. That'll be much better."

Her haughty chin rose. "How would you know? You haven't done it yet."

A rumble of a laugh rolled out of me. "You got me there. I think I'm about to throw in the towel and admit defeat." My hand roamed down to the curve of her ass. "Can I buy you a treat for your prize?"

"You can." She smiled, pressing her palms to my chest. "Just so you know, I'm having a really good time."

"I am too."

Her teeth dug into her bottom lip. "I was nervous. I haven't been on a date since college, and those were more like casual hangouts. In a way, this is my first real date."

My brows rose. "Yeah?"

She nodded.

I tugged her closer and squeezed her ass. "I'm honored to have one of your firsts. That means I'm also your best. At least I won something tonight."

She laughed lightly. "You were already my best."

Closing my eyes, I let my forehead fall against hers. That admission was big, and I didn't even have to think about whether I agreed.

"Mine too, Clara. By a landslide."

We sat in a cheap plastic booth in the back of the bowling alley, both of us sipping on a milkshake.

"Tell me how it's possible you haven't been taken on a date."

Her lips were wrapped around her straw. They broke off, and she licked the drop of chocolate off her bottom lip.

"Pretty simple. I met my ex-husband in college. He was my first serious boyfriend. We hung out at parties and in each other's dorms. Once we were out of school, we'd go out with family or friends, but that was rare since we were both so busy at our jobs." She shook her head. "Time slips by quicker than it seems. One day, we're starry-eyed college kids, and the next, we're in our thirties, entrenched in work, and checking off the have a baby by thirty-five box."

I tried not to show how miserable that sounded to me, but Clara took one look at me and winced.

"It didn't feel as lonely as it sounds until I was out of it," she said softly.

"I get that. Like boiling a frog. The water temperature is raised by small increments, so the frog doesn't notice until it's too late. Now that you're out of the pot, you can see the bubble and steam."

"Hindsight is a bitch." She took another sip of her milkshake. "What about you, Jake Hayes? You give a good date, so you must be experienced in all this."

That eased a chuckle out of me. "I like that you think this is a good date."

"It is," she insisted. "Games and a milkshake, does it get much better?"

"Now I feel like you've laid down a challenge."

She leaned forward. "And I feel like you're not answering my question. This leads me to believe you've done *more* than your fair share of dating. Tell me."

With a sigh, I slid down in my seat, one arm resting over the back. I didn't have much interest in rehashing my dating history, but it was only fair since I'd been the one to broach the topic. And, as I'd learned over the years, my natural closemouthed state wasn't conducive to building any kind of relationship. I wasn't certain things were going to go there with Clara yet, but I knew damn well they wouldn't have a chance if I fell back on old habits.

"If I choose to be with a woman, I like to make her feel special." I drummed my fingers on the table. "When Sage was younger, I got it into my head I should settle down to make a conventional family life for her like she had at her mom's."

"Carly told me she has two siblings."

"Yeah. Dex and Cleo. Cute kids. Sage pretends they annoy her, but she loves having siblings."

"Carly seems nice," Clara hedged, her teeth digging into her bottom lip. I heard the question behind her statement—one she clearly didn't want to ask but needed an answer to.

"She is." I took a drink of my milkshake. "We grew up in the same town. Tried things out in high school but decided we were better as friends. A week later, she got a positive pregnancy test and made up her mind to keep it. At the time, I'd thought my life was over, but we had a lot of family support and worked it out. Managed to stay friends and co-parent pretty damn well."

Something in Clara eased as I explained my history with Carly. It hadn't been some love affair, just two dumb kids irresponsible with contraception. I liked that Clara cared, that she had been a little jealous, and that she was letting it go now that she understood.

"And Carly got married, so you decided you should try to do the same," she filled in.

"Yeah." I rubbed the back of my neck, feeling sheepish. So succinctly, she'd summed up my previous way of thinking. "I dated around. Found a woman I liked well enough to be my girlfriend. We were together for two years, but it didn't work out, and I haven't had much interest in going down that road again since."

"Was it messy?" she asked. "The break, I mean."

"Clean as could be." I swiped my hands together. "One day, she was there. The next, she was a ghost in the wind."

Her brow furrowed. "After two years together, she disappeared? How did Sage take it?"

Of course that was her first thought. She had a daughter too, and she was probably imagining what that would've been like for her girl.

"Devastated." I had to look away. Letting that happen to Sage still haunted me. Hearing her crying about it being her fault, saying she'd be better, quieter, nicer if Andrea came back, had permanently scarred me. "It took a long time for me to convince her she hadn't done anything wrong."

Casual flings were easier. Nothing serious, no ties, nothing close to a relationship, and Sage didn't get introduced to anyone. It wasn't a risk I could take, and frankly, I hadn't cared about anyone enough to be tempted.

With Clara, I was dancing a line I'd drawn for myself. This didn't feel casual, but the thought of allowing her into my life with my daughter put so much pressure on my chest it was hard to breathe.

Clara's pretty brown eyes went impossibly soft. "Poor Sage. With how friendly and open she is, I can see her getting attached quickly."

I nodded, needing to make sure she understood. "So, you get me when I say I need to keep this separate from her."

"I get you, Jake."

"We managed well tonight, didn't we?"

"We did. Luckily, I have Marina and won't have to ask my parents to babysit. Well...if we're doing this again, that is."

"We are." My foot nudged hers beneath the table. She didn't pull away this time and propped hers on top. "Keeping me a secret from your parents?"

"I guess so. I'd rather not tell them I'm dating." She wrinkled her nose. "They've been waiting for me to date since my divorce as if I don't work fifty hours a week and have a small child at home."

"You make it sound impossible, yet here you are."

"Well"—her cheeks pinkened sweetly—"I wanted to be here, so I made it happen. I *don't* want to sign up for dating apps or go on terrible blind dates."

"Good thing you're not going to be doing either of those while I'm in your life."

She brought her milkshake to her lips. "Good thing."

I cocked my head, sweeping my eyes over her. All I wanted was to join her on her side of the booth and feel her soft, warm body against mine. But this wasn't bad. The talking. Listening to her confident, slightly husky voice. Hearing about her life.

"Your ex doesn't see Nellie?"

Her entire body tensed at my question, her shoulders bunching around her ears. The lightness she'd carried since eagerly emerging from her house dimmed almost fully, and I wanted nothing more than to snatch the words out of the air and shove them back in my mouth.

"You really don't know?" she rasped.

I slid my hand across the table to hold hers. "No, I don't. I see I stepped in it by asking about him, and I'm sorry. If you don't want to tell me, we can leave it at he's not in her life—"

"He's in prison. So, no, he doesn't see Nellie. He never has." She balled a napkin in her fist and wiped something invisible from the table. "Anyway, it's getting late. We should probably go."

She slid from the booth before I could wrap my head around what she'd said.

Fuck.

Clara dumped her milkshake in the trash and waited for me facing the exit, giving me her back. I followed her, tossing my trash and coming up behind her. She wasn't asking me for anything, but my gut urged me to give her something anyway.

All I had was myself, so I wrapped my arms around her and pulled her into the wall of my body. She was stiff for long seconds but didn't fight me. I hugged her tighter and curled around her, resting my head on top of hers.

"I'm so fucking sorry for bringing that up," I murmured into her hair. "I feel like I ruined something good—"

"No, it wasn't you. It was him. Even locked up, he's screwing me over."

"The last couple minutes don't take away the last couple hours." I lowered my face to touch my lips to her temple. "I've never had a better date, and I haven't even kissed you on your front porch yet."

Her shiver vibrated through my bones, loosening my hold just enough for her to turn in my arms to face me. "You're really good at this." Her palms slid up my chest and neck to cup my cheeks. "I'm glad one of us knows what we're doing."

"Don't worry, sweetness. You want me to lead, I will. I happen to really like being in control when you give it to me."

With a sigh, she melted against me, tension seeping from her in one solid whoosh. Her hands dropped from my face to circle around my neck, embracing me in return. I kissed her hair and temple a few times, earning contented little chirps from her. We stayed like that until she was steady again then walked outside and climbed onto my bike.

She wrapped around me a little tighter, snuggling a little closer than she had on the way to the bowling alley. I didn't say anything, but I felt it, and I liked it. This woman had so many responsibilities she shouldered in everyday life, a lot of them all on her own. When she was with me, I'd make sure that weight was lifted. She could hand it all over for me to carry, and I'd be happy to do it.

The drive back to her house was shorter than I would have liked. With anyone else, I would have taken the scenic route, but Clara had her girl sleeping under her roof and an early morning ahead of her. She needed her rest, and I needed to make sure she got it.

I parked in her driveway and helped her off the bike. "Gotta admit, seeing you ride your machine made me weak in the knees, but having you on the back of mine is something else entirely."

She stepped up on her porch and smiled at me. "I've only ever been on the back of my dad's motorcycle, and now yours."

I moved into her space, sliding my fingers into the side of her hair. "Let's keep it that way."

"Okay," she agreed without hesitation.

Damn, did I like this woman. Leaning down, I covered her mouth with mine, tasting her. Sweetness and vanilla milkshake—a combination that made my heart race and stomach clench.

She fisted my shirt as I backed her into one of the pillars holding up her porch. I couldn't remember the last time I'd kissed a woman for the sake of kissing her, and I couldn't get enough of doing it with Clara. Her mouth was pliant and giving, answering my calls with the swirl of her tongue along mine, sucking and nipping and moaning when I swept my tongue between her lips.

Unable to help myself, I snuck a hand up her shirt and groaned from the contact. Her skin was unreal. So smooth and soft, like she was made of rose petals. One touch and I wanted to sink into her, coat myself in her softness. I palmed her breast, and the scratch of her lacy bra brought me back to earth.

"Clara," I murmured against her lips. "I need to let you go inside."

"You do."

Her lips melded with mine, and her grip on my shirt tightened. The idea of her going inside without me felt so wrong. I pulled her even closer until there was nowhere for her to go.

Eventually, it was either fuck on the porch or break apart. Though the first option was incredibly tempting, I did the right thing, breaking our kiss. I rolled my forehead along hers as we both caught our breath.

"*Really* good night," I said.

"It was."

"I like what you're showing me. I want more of it. More talking and playing games together. The good kind."

She tipped her head back to grin at me. "Is this you asking me on a second date?"

"I hope I already made it clear I want more of you. If you need me to formally ask, I will. Clara Rossi, you gorgeous fucking woman, will you go out with me again?"

"Yep." She bounced on her toes. "I will. And I'll plan it this time."

"Well, all right. I'm looking forward to seeing what you come up with." I leaned down to brush my lips over hers. "Go inside now. Get a good night's sleep."

She finally unclenched my shirt and started backing toward her door. Before turning to open it, she stopped, worry pinching her brow.

"Jake?"

"Yeah?"

Her hand rose to cup her throat. "I don't want to tell it. I hate explaining everything. I think you should know, though, before we go forward. His name is Miller Fairfield. He was the CFO of Rossi. Look him up. I'm sure you'll find plenty of reading material."

I should've argued, told her it didn't matter, but it did. What'd happened with her ex had shaped who she was now, and I wanted to know her. I liked what I'd uncovered so far. I had a feeling I'd like her even more the deeper we got.

"All right. I'll do that." I locked my gaze on hers for a long moment, showing her I wasn't backing down. I took her seriously, and what she'd just given me meant something. "Best night, Clara," I said with a softness she needed right now.

"Yeah." Her lashes fluttered and there was the barest curve to her kiss-swollen lips. "Best night, Jake."

It was worse than anything I could have dreamed up.

I'd heard about commotion at Rossi a few years back, but that was before I'd taken the job as VP and the business page of the newspaper hadn't exactly been my daily read.

Miller Fairfield was a sick fuck. He'd become fixated on an elderly husband and wife who'd run a business blog with a readership of a few thousand. They'd been critical of Rossi Motors, which was what had set Miller off. He'd stalked them, harassed them, essentially terrorized them for months. He'd doxxed them online so strangers started appearing at their house looking for free puppies or kink hookups. Had sent pig fetuses and rats. A book about surviving the loss of a spouse. A fucking funeral arrangement.

The old man had been hospitalized from stress, and they'd had to sell their house to get away from the bombardment.

As if that hadn't been enough, he'd also embezzled over a million dollars from Rossi.

And this had all come to light days before Clara had given birth.

The scandal had done a number on Rossi's stock prices—it was written in black and white in the articles I read. What wasn't there was what it had done to Clara.

The woman I'd met at a bar in Skyridge, whose hands had trembled around her glass while she'd held her spine straight and proud, had survived this. Heartbreak and humiliation. The end of what she'd thought would be her life. And it had all happened in front of a thirsty audience, eager to see how the Rossi heiress had borne her world falling apart around her.

She and her newborn baby.

My hands balled into tight fists, violence flowing through my blood. There was no one to take the pure rage boiling in my stomach, though. Miller was locked up in federal prison, doing his time. He'd been sentenced to fifty-seven months, and it didn't seem like nearly enough.

Not with the wreckage he'd created and lives he'd destroyed.

I understood Clara's reticence. Why she'd always left at sunrise. Why it'd been so difficult for her to say yes to a date.

My girl was brave for opening herself up to me. She had every reason to keep herself cloistered and safe behind her walls for the rest of her life, but she didn't.

Her strength made me proud. And even more attracted to her. Something I wouldn't have thought possible.

Clara Rossi was a revelation.

No matter what happened between us, I promised myself I wouldn't become another reason for her to distrust men. I couldn't make any other promises, but she'd always have the truth from me.

Always.

CHAPTER
TWENTY-ONE
Clara

Thomas stuck his head in my office. "You must've done something right."

I huffed, looking up from my computer. This man couldn't just pass me a message and insisted on adding drama to everything.

"Why is that?" I asked, only playing along because he was a damn good assistant and I'd be lost without him. His injection of dramatics also kept my days interesting, but I wouldn't be telling him that.

He walked into my office, carrying a small flower arrangement in a Ball jar and a pink box. "Because these were just delivered for you." He placed them on my desk and put his hands on his hips. "Are you dating and forgot to tell me?"

My heart pitched to a gallop, but I wouldn't allow myself to get too excited. The way I'd left off with Jake last night, I wouldn't be surprised if I never heard from him again.

"They're probably from a client."

"You know, you didn't answer me." He tapped the envelope snuggled between the miniature roses and baby's breath. "That probably says who they're from."

"It probably does." I crossed my arms and leaned back in my seat. "But you'll never know."

He rolled his eyes and groaned at the ceiling. "I tell you everything about my dating life."

"Because I'm a captive audience—*not* because I asked." I grinned at him. This had to be driving him mad. "Besides, they're most likely from one of my managers. Don't excite yourself over nothing."

"Fine. I'll give you privacy, but don't think I didn't notice you not denying they could be from a date. I'm on alert now, Clara."

He stalked out of my office, throwing a dirty look my way before closing my door. As soon as he was out, I plucked the card from the flowers and tore it open.

Clara,

I want a rematch ASAP.

I'll let you win if you wear those jeans again.

Yours,

Jake

I brought a shaky hand to my mouth, surprised to find myself smiling like a fool. I wouldn't have expected Jake to write me flowery, romantic messages. This was his style, and to me, this was nothing but sweet.

Then I opened the pink box, and tears sprung to my eyes. A cookie decorated like a bowling ball with "*#1 Champion*" written in icing. I'd never been given anything so thoughtful, and that realization took me aback.

I'd been gifted huge, showy bouquets and flashy jewelry. At the time, it had been nice, but looking back, no real thought had been put into them. They were gestures made for other people to see and give Miller pats on the back for being such a loving, giving, wonderful husband.

While Jake…he'd sent this just for me. Our own little joke to make me smile in the middle of my workday. To tell me he was thinking about me and still wanted to see me.

I snapped a picture of myself with the cookie at my lips and sent it to Jake.

Me: *Why, Jacob Hayes, I had no idea you could be so adorable!*

It didn't take long for him to reply.

Jake: *You're calling me adorable when you send me the cutest picture I've ever seen? Christ, woman, I'm trying to work.*

Me: *Thank you, Jake. I mean it. You really brightened my day.*

My ringtone sounded as soon as the text sent. Jake was calling.

I put the phone to my ear. "Hey."

"Hey." His voice sent goose bumps rolling across my skin. "Are you having a bad day, mama?"

"Nothing out of the ordinary. I'm just in my head more than I like," I admitted. "Your gifts were exactly what I needed."

There was a brief pause, then, "You were thinking about me? Thinking something you did or said would turn me off?"

I almost laughed at how perceptive he was. "I told you I've never dated, and I put all my baggage at your feet last night. I was wondering if I scared you off."

"You got your answer?"

"Yes." I looked at the little jar of flowers and my oversized cookie. "You like me."

His chuckle was warm and comforting. "I do. Pretty sure you like me too."

"The cookie was a nice touch, but your note kind of pissed me off. You don't need to *let* me win. I can do that all on my own."

"Wear those jeans again and you sure can."

"Jake..." I sighed as I slid down in my seat like a melted puddle of wax.

"When am I going to see you again?"

"I don't know. I want to see you soon, but we should take this slow...right?"

"Right."

My stomach sank. Deep down, I'd been hoping he'd argue with me on that point.

"Lunch tomorrow," he said. "Do you have the time?"

I laughed. "Is that going slow?"

"Sure. I'm not stealing you away tonight when that's what I want to do."

"I kind of want to be stolen...but I'll wait. I have some bad news, though."

"What's that?"

"I won't be wearing those jeans you like so much."

He inhaled sharply. "That's all right. I like you in those sexy corporate dresses just as much."

I looked down at my staid navy-blue dress. "They're not sexy."

"I guarantee you have not seen yourself from the back in those dresses. Come to think of it, you must not be looking at yourself from the front either."

"Jake..." He kept stealing my ability to speak.

"I'll see you tomorrow, Clara. Wear whatever you want. I have no doubt I'll like you in it."

"Okay," I whispered. "See you tomorrow."

After I hung up, I carefully put my cookie back in the box, unable to bring myself to eat it. I would, eventually. Just...not yet.

Thomas popped his head into my office. "You have a visitor."

Even though I'd known Jake was on his way up since he'd had to check in with security, my stomach fluttered.

I stood up from my desk and smoothed my dress. "You can send him in."

He cupped his hands around his mouth and stage-whispered, "You look really hot today. Don't worry a single bit."

"Put your professional pants on, Thomas."

"They're on. Marc Jacobs." He stuck his long leg out like he was wearing an evening gown with a dramatic slit. "You like?"

My eyes flared. "Thomas."

"Oh, all right." He opened the door wide, switching to his cool, professional tone. "Ms. Rossi will see you now."

Jake thanked him and strode into my office. Thomas pulled the door closed behind him. Not knowing what was going on had to be killing him, but I didn't have time to worry about my assistant.

Walking straight up to me, Jake dug his hands into the sides of my hair and kissed me. My body responded immediately while my brain hurried to catch up. Jake ate at my lips like he'd been starving for them, then his tongue swept in, giving my mouth a thorough licking.

Moaning, I gripped the lapels of his jacket, giving myself over to him. In one fell swoop, he'd rid me of my nerves and doubt. This man had been chomping at the bit to get me in his arms again, and that was a heady, powerful feeling.

Our lips parted, and his forehead rolled on mine. Panting breaths passed back and forth until his fingers loosened in my hair and I let go of his jacket to slide my palms along his shoulders.

"Hey."

His lips touched the corner of my mouth before he pulled back and gave me a long, slow once-over. "Hey, gorgeous. You hungry?"

"I am."

"Then let's go."

Once we left my office, we stayed a respectable distance from each other. Thomas gawked, and I smiled at him. Had my head not been foggy from that kiss, I might have found a task to keep him busy and out of trouble while I was gone.

Jake further distracted me in the elevator, leaning against the wall and checking me out from head to toe.

"Sexy," he stated.

"I'm covered from my neck to my knees," I argued, even though I'd specifically chosen a dress he hadn't seen me in yet. The ruffled sleeves were feminine, and the cut had been tailored immaculately, skimming the outline of my body in the most loving way. The patent belt at my waist nipped me in just right, and the collar, though high, was wide, while the tops of my shoulders and collarbone were bare.

Jake reached out and dragged a fingertip along the skin at the base of my throat. "It's the peeks of what's underneath that makes it sexy. Then again, you could be in a sweat suit and make it work."

"I guarantee you'll never find out if that's true."

He laughed, the corners of his eyes crinkling. "I don't doubt it."

We ended up at a crowded sandwich shop a couple blocks from my office, crammed in a booth barely big enough for us. Our knees tangled beneath the table, and any time either of us moved our hands to pick up our sandwiches or reach for a napkin, we inevitably brushed one another.

"Your assistant is interesting," he remarked between bites.

I snorted a laugh. "He's insubordinate and annoying. I would have fired him a hundred times if he wasn't so good at his job."

"As long as he takes care of you." He put his food down to shrug off his jacket and loosen his tie. Once he was free, he released a long breath. "Out of my costume," he muttered.

"Now you look more like yourself," I mused.

"I don't look good in a suit?"

"Oh, you look incredible, but it doesn't feel like *you*."

"Never thought I'd end up working in an office, wearing a suit." He shook his head. "But whose life turns out the way they thought it would when they were young?"

"Not mine," I said dryly. "How *did* you end up doing what you're doing?"

"Probably the same way you did. Familial obligation. A couple years ago, our grandfather had handed Jeremy the reins, and he'd wanted me by his side when he took over. He'd been raised to run the company while I'd watched from the outside."

"And now you're in an office four days a week instead of a garage or working on a ranch. That must be frustrating."

"It's like wearing a suit—doesn't fit right, but if I stop thinking about it, it's bearable." He picked up his sandwich. "I have to be an adult. Sometimes that means giving up how I thought it was going to be. It's worth it to me to be there for my brother."

"I understand that, probably more than anyone else. It bothers me for you that you have to fit yourself into a mold that's just *bearable*, though. Seems there are other positions that would better suit you—"

He cut me off. "It is what it is, Clara. I'm not exactly miserable, and Jeremy and I are a team."

There was something he wasn't saying about his relationship with his brother, but we weren't in a place where I could push for answers. Maybe one day he'd open up and explain why he was so adamant he was where he needed to be.

"All right, Jake." My knuckles brushed his. This time, on purpose. "It's funny how our positions are reversed. I've always known I would work at Rossi. Luca had lived in denial. If he had his druthers, he'd be a professional artist and freewheeler."

Jake chuffed. "Wouldn't we all be professional freewheelers?"

"Well"—I folded my hands primly on the table—"not *all* of us. Some of us were math nerds who grew into business nerds and thrive in a corporate environment."

"Yet Luca's the CEO."

I nodded. "He is, and he's much better at it than I would have been. Despite him raging against the dying of his life free of responsibilities, I always knew he'd thrive in that position. And he does. My brother is incredibly smart and has brought his creative mind to the table. Our shareholders love the hell out of him, and he's made me excited about my job all over again. Plus, you know, I get to see my brother a lot more than before, which has been the best part."

Jake reached across the narrow table and swiped his thumb over my bottom lip. "I like the shape of your mouth when you talk about someone you love."

"That's...I don't know how to respond when you say things like that to me." I bit down on my bottom lip. "That was really nice."

"There you go. You responded."

"I did." I rubbed my warm cheek. "I didn't think I was still capable of blushing."

"Oh, Clara," he rumbled. "If me complimenting you makes you blush, get used to being pink. I say what I think, and these days, I'm thinking a lot about you."

"I am too. Thinking about you, that is."

"Good." His eyes trailed over me. "That's exactly what I want."

Strangely, I believed him.

Chapter Twenty-Two

Clara

Jake walked me back to my building after lunch. As easy as it was to be with him, he also made me flustered, like I was a young, inexperienced girl. In a way, I was. I'd only known one man, and since Jake was nothing like Miller, everything he gave me was brand new.

I was thankful for it too. I'd had quite enough of that life.

At the front of my building, I stopped, intending to say goodbye, but Jake caught my fingertips and pulled me along.

"Nope. It's door-to-door service."

"You really don't have to walk me back to my office."

"I really do," he insisted. "You haven't asked me out on our second date, so I don't know when I'm going to see you again."

Laughing, I walked with him through the lobby, swiping my pass at the executive elevator.

"This wasn't a second date?"

"No." He eyed me seriously. "You told me you'd plan it. This was lunch."

"But there was a kiss," I reminded him.

"And there's going to be another one before I leave you." He crossed his arms. "Still not a date."

I stepped into the elevator and whirled around to tease him. "Well, you would know since you're the dating expert with your vast experience."

He walked right into my space, backing me against the wall. Luckily, we had the elevator to ourselves, but I had a feeling Jake might not have cared either way.

"My vast experience, huh?" He cupped the back of my neck and bent so we were nose to nose. "Funny, I don't remember any of it."

"That *is* funny." I wet my lips with the tip of my tongue. "You're too young to have memory troubles."

"And you're too smart to taunt me in a confined space." His lips touched mine in a barely there kiss. "Be good, Clara."

My thighs clenched around the ache between them, and my breath seized in my chest. How was this man capable of being sweet one minute and melting my panties the next?

The elevator came to a stop, and Jake retreated as if nothing had happened. It took me a moment longer to pull myself together and scrape myself off the wall. As soon as the doors opened, I took a deep breath, straightened my back with my head held high, and exited the elevator. Jake chuckled under his breath as he escorted me to my office, as promised.

Except we didn't make it there. Luca stepped out of his office, pausing when he caught sight of us.

He scratched the side of his head and shot us a sheepish look. "Did I forget to put a meeting on my calendar?"

Jake put his hand on the small of my back. "Not with me, you didn't. I'm here to bring Clara back from our lunch."

"Lunch?" Luca echoed, his gaze following where Jake's arm had disappeared behind me. "Ah, I see. That's where I'm headed now. Unfortunately, mine is business and not...friendly."

"You should go. You don't want to be late." My eyes flared, signaling for him to go away and end this awkward encounter. I planned to tell him Jake and I were dating at some point, but not yet. Not until I was certain it would amount to more than a dinner or two.

"You're right. I should." He reached out to shake Jake's hand. "Nice to see you again."

Jake closed his hand around my brother's and gave it a firm shake. "You too, Luca."

Luca gave me a pointed look I interpreted to mean, "*We're talking about this as soon as humanly possible.*"

I had little doubt he'd let this drop; I just hoped he'd give me time to formulate an explanation.

Jake escorted me to my office and closed the door behind us. Once we were alone, he didn't ravage me like I thought he might. Instead, he prowled around the room, inspecting my art and what I had on my desk.

What I had on my desk...oh no.

Picking up the cookie box, he lifted the lid. "You didn't eat it." He raised his eyes to me. "Do you not like cookies?"

I patted my round hips. "I obviously like cookies, and that one looks and smells delicious, but—"

He took it out of the box, sniffed it, and turned it over on his palm. My stomach tumbled. This was about to be embarrassing.

"It does smell good. You want to share it with me? Give me a little bite of your cookie?"

He held it between his fingers, just about to break it, but I couldn't let that happen. I wasn't ready.

"Wait!" I rushed to him, snatching the cookie away. Only when it was safely back in the box did I remember I had to face him and explain why I'd just done that.

He chuckled. "Guess you don't want to share."

I looked up, my lips rolled over my teeth. "It's not that. I would share anything with you."

His head tilted as his eyes darted around my face, thoughtful in his examination of me.

"But not the cookie."

"Not that one. It's so...cute. And you ordered it for me. You had to explain to someone exactly what you wanted it to look like and what it should say. I just want to keep it and look at it for a while. I'm not ready for it to be gone."

God, I sounded like a lovesick teenager, not a thirty-seven-year-old mother. This was truly humiliating, but I couldn't help being honest with him. His gift had touched a long-neglected part of me and made me feel special in a way I never had.

"There's that sweetness I can't get enough of," he crooned.

One moment, I was dying of embarrassment. The next, I was in Jake's arms, being kissed to within an inch of my life. He groaned as he tangled his fingers in my hair, keeping my mouth locked against his. Not that there was a chance I'd pull away.

He kissed me until the burn in my cheeks spread across my body like wildfire. Then he lifted me onto the edge of my desk and situated himself between my spread legs. Shoving my dress to the tops of my thighs, he stroked my bare skin and panted against my lips.

"Eat the cookie, Clara. It's not going to be the only one I send you." One hand moved to graze my cheek. "You were neglected for so long, weren't you? You're starving, and I'm going to be the one to feed you—fill you up until you forget what it's like not to be cared for."

My breathing stuttered, and I let my head fall against his chest. "We've only gone on one date. You can't promise me that."

"It's been over a year. You've been in my head since the first night at The Tavern. You're not going anywhere, and neither am I. I intend to see this through, wherever it goes."

"Okay."

He pried me from his chest and tucked his knuckle under my chin so I had no choice but to meet his gaze. It was warm, playful, belying the curves at the corners of his mouth.

"Okay." He kissed my temple. "Go for a ride with me Friday night? Unless you planned your date for then."

I shook my head. "I have an idea, but it's not for a couple weeks."

"Well, I'm not waiting that long." He gave my chin a shake. "Say yes. Go for a ride with me."

I nodded. "I'd love to."

"Good." He touched his lips to my forehead and backed up, carefully replacing my dress over my thighs. "Eat the cookie."

I nodded. "I will."

I would have walked him out, but my knees weren't quite working after he'd melted my bones, so I sank into my chair and watched him go. When he was out of sight, I picked up the cookie box. I'd never been sentimental, and it was silly of me to have saved this. Before I could talk myself out of it, I broke a piece off and slipped it into my mouth.

Vanilla. Of course it was delicious.

I ate it slowly, taking little bites between replying to emails. A quarter of it was gone when Luca arrived, sauntering into my office with a smirk.

"Is there something you want to tell me, my dear sister?"

With a sigh, I rested my elbows on my desk. "Jake and I are dating."

He folded himself in the chair across from me. "I gathered that. I caught the vibe at dinner last week." He rubbed his chin in thought. "Looking back, there was a vibe at our first meeting too, if I'm not mistaken."

"There was a vibe," I confirmed. "I like him."

The explanation I'd wanted to drum up fell away. In its place, I chose simplicity.

"He seems like a good guy. I can't say I'm not surprised at the pairing. For one, I thought you were content leading the nun life. For another, Jakey is younger than both of us. Never thought you'd rob the cradle."

I shot him a murderous glare. "Never, *ever* say anything like that again, or I'll steal Clementine and give her to Nellie."

That made him laugh and hold up his hands. "No, no, don't take my cat. I'm only kidding. I don't care about your age gap. It's no big deal. Not like you're some withered prune. You've got a few years yet."

I flipped him off. "You have the same genes I do."

"True. And they're damn fine genes at that." He leaned forward, his elbows on his knees. "Seriously, I'm happy you're getting out there. You deserve to have someone take care of you, you know."

Jake's promise echoed in my head, and I smiled. "Thank you. I'm happy too. Cautiously so, but still."

"No one would blame you for being cautious." He tapped the edge of my desk. "Did you tell Jake we're moving forward with Motor Zone?"

"No. I thought about it, but I'd rather not have our business dealings overlap our personal relationship. He'll find out through his lawyers or brother."

"That makes sense. It's a good idea to keep it separate. Hopefully it will remain possible."

Moving forward didn't mean the deal was signed. That was still months away. Next would be the SWOT analysis, then our lawyers would meet with their lawyers to draw up terms, and we'd sign a memo of understanding once we agreed. Anything could happen in the following months. Deals fell through all the time. Luca's meaning rang loud and clear. If something happened and we couldn't seal the deal with Jake's company, I could only hope it wouldn't affect our personal relationship.

"One of the many reasons I'm cautiously optimistic," I returned.

"You always were the smart one in the family." His gaze fell on the pink box on my desk. "Aren't you going to offer your brother a bite?"

On instinct, my hand shot out to pull it closer to me. "No."

"Rude." He reached for it, and I swatted him away, making him laugh. "Come on, Clara. You're seriously not going to give me any? It's a huge cookie. What does it say on it?"

With a sigh, I turned it toward him. I'd eaten around the words, leaving them there.

"Number one champion...of what?" he asked.

"Bowling. Jake had this made for me after I beat him," I rushed out, hoping he'd leave me alone now that he had an answer.

Something about Luca loosened, and the corners of his mouth curled into a soft smile he usually reserved for his wife and my daughter. It was...tender. Sweet, even.

"I think I like this guy." He stopped trying to steal my cookie and met my gaze. "Remember, Saoirse and I are happy to babysit and keep Nellie overnight. All you have to do is name the date. All right?"

I nodded, a wad of emotion lodged in my throat. Without Luca's support, I wouldn't have survived my divorce and becoming a new mother. I was on my own two feet now, but he was still there for me, never allowing me to feel like I didn't have backup.

"I remember."

It was only later, when I was replaying our lunch in my mind, I realized Jake hadn't mentioned my ex at all. I didn't believe there was any way he hadn't gone home and looked him up.

He saw my scarred underbelly, my heavy, beat-up baggage, and hadn't been scared off. If anything, he'd drawn himself closer to me, making really lovely promises.

Moving forward with him terrified me down to my core.

But I'd been brought up with the confidence to face difficult situations and survive in boardrooms filled with men who would always look down on me because I was a woman.

If I could do that—with style, might I add—I could crack open my heart, just a little, and allow Jake inside. Being closed off and alone wasn't a good example to set for Nellie. I had to take this chance.

If it blew up in my face...well, at least I could say I tried.

CHAPTER TWENTY-THREE

Jake

If I couldn't have Clara wrapped around me on the back of my bike, I was content to eat her dust as she flew past me on hers. Nothing sexier than a woman who knew how to handle the powerful machine between her legs and wasn't afraid to show off.

Since the first time I met her for lunch at her office, we'd gone riding together once and had had a few more lunches when our schedules allowed. Mine was a hell of a lot more flexible than hers, but it was by design. I didn't thrive under rigid routines, but I understood Clara lived and died by her calendar. No one worked their way as high as she had, family business or not, by not being dedicated.

Now, it was Sunday, and after having Sage home for a week, she'd gone back to her mom's. Clara and I had the rest of the day and night to play on the road and whatever else we decided to get into.

This wasn't a date, though. She hadn't planned it, so I wasn't counting it.

It was just a day out with my girl, letting the fresh air and sunshine soak into my bones while drinking my fill of her. The sips I'd gotten over the past two weeks had been delicious, but they hadn't been enough to sustain a man.

We rode on back roads, twisting and winding until we found the biker bar we'd been aiming for. I pulled into the spot beside Clara and paused to watch her climb off her bike.

The helmet came first. She tugged it off and tousled her hair like she was in a shampoo commercial, letting it swish around her shoulders. Then she shrugged off her leather jacket and raised her arms over her head, giving her back a long, thorough stretch. A swath of soft ivory belly peeked from between her jeans and top, and her tits strained the thin cotton fabric. Once she was done, she turned toward me, finding me watching. A grin as wide as a mile stretched across her pretty face.

"Are you going to get off or stare at me all day?" she teased.

"I was hoping to do both."

She circled around her bike and sidled up beside mine, taking my hand in hers. "Get your ass off that bike and flirt with me then. We'll see what happens."

I climbed off and wound my arms around her waist, pulling her against me. "I've been watching that glorious ass of yours all spread out on your seat for the last hour and a half, mama. I'm barely standing. If you think I have enough brain cells left to flirt smoothly, you obviously haven't taken a look at your ass lately."

"You're right, I haven't. But I must say, that was very smooth, Jake Hayes." She tapped my chest and flashed a sassy little grin. "Keep it up. For now, I'm parched and could use a drink."

"Then by all means, lead the way. Can't have my girl going thirsty."

The bar was little more than a shack with three open sides. All types of bikers, from grizzled and old to fresh hobby riders, were scattered around, having a drink and shooting the shit with like-minded folks. Most of their heads would probably explode if they knew they were now in the company of motorcycle royalty.

Clara leaned her middle against the bar, and I lowered my mouth to her ear. "The queen of Rossi is in their presence, and they have no idea."

She tipped her head back and lowered her lashes. "The queen, huh? I think I prefer being the king's advisor. We both know they have the real power."

"Are you saying you have power over Luca?"

She chuffed. "Not quite. But he respects what I have to say and is always open to listening to me."

"Love that for you, sweetness."

The bartender slid two cold ones in front of Clara, and she turned around to pass me mine.

"Jeremy doesn't listen to you?"

I clinked my bottle against hers. "We don't have the kind of relationship you and Luca do. I'm at MZ to pick up the pieces Jer can't juggle and support him when he needs another voice on his side. Make no mistake, one person is the head of MZ—and it's not me."

"Hmmm." She sipped her beer and said nothing else, even though it was obvious there were a hundred things on the tip of her tongue.

"You can say anything to me. I don't get offended easily."

She waved me off. "Nothing. It's just...I don't see you as a support-and-be-quiet man. You're smart; you know your way around your product and your shops. It seems to me your insight would be invaluable."

She was treading into uncomfortable territory—a place I didn't like to think about existing because, at this stage, there was nothing I could do about it.

"Thank you for your confidence in me." I dipped my head to trace my lips along the side of her graceful neck. "It is what it is. It's not forever, but it is where I need to be right now. Get me?"

She leaned into me, fisting my shirt. "I get you. I don't know how you and Jer work, but if you say it's how it needs to be, I'll believe you." Her palm flattened, settling over my heart. "I want you to be happy, Jake."

I slid my hand down, squeezing her plump ass. "I'm happy as a clam right now. Can't think of anywhere I'd rather be."

That was the god's honest truth. I'd been sinking fast for this woman, thinking about her more often than not, wondering what she was doing when we weren't together, wishing she was beside me in my bed when I went to sleep.

I would never resent my daughter, and I was still steadfast in my resolve to keep my relationship with Clara away from her. My resentment toward Andrea, on the other hand, had been renewed. If Sage hadn't been hurt, devastated, destroyed...if we hadn't gone through what we had, I might've been able to bend—to have the kind of time with Clara I craved, where it didn't feel so much like getting away with a crime.

We drank our beers and moved over to the jukebox, picking a few tunes we surprisingly agreed on. Clara swayed her rounded hips to the easy beat of the first song she'd chosen, her focus solely on me.

"Come here, Jacob. Dance with me for a minute or two."

I glanced toward the open space in front of the jukebox. It might've been intended as a dance floor but more likely served as standing space for when this place got crowded. That might've been due to the fact that Clara was one of four women in the bar and these men weren't the type to dance with each other.

If I didn't dance with her right now, she wouldn't have to look far for someone else to partner with her. The little shit who'd been checking her out by the bar. The grandpa with the white beard down to his chest and gleam in his eye as he watched her. The table of yuppie city boys who must've recognized Clara for the fine, upper-class woman she was and wanted a piece.

The kicker was, she had no idea. Clara was all about me. Smiling at me. Holding her hands out to me. Swaying those sexy hips in my direction. Her laser-focused attention was a powerful thing. It filled me with confidence in her feelings for me and fed my ego just the right amount. To have a woman like her all about me meant I was doing something right, and I fully intended on continuing so I could have more of this.

Hand around her waist, the other holding hers, I staked my claim. Our boots touched, side to side, as I slid my thigh between hers. She let me lead, giving it to me naturally. I wasn't an experienced dancer, but I could wind my girl around the dance floor so long as I had her soft body moving against mine.

The warmth of her core seeped through her jeans into mine. Knowing her pussy was resting on me was enough to thicken my cock, but that was all I'd allow. There were too many eyes on her—on *us*—for me to touch her how I wanted. No one else got to see what she gave me. That would come later. For now, it was about closeness and our rhythm.

She laughed in my ear, and lightness filled my chest like helium. Then we were singing along together, moving our lips in time to the lyrics, smiling as I rocked her, turned her, took her with me. This was our first, second, third dance together, but it easily could have been our hundredth for as in sync we were. That might've been because she trusted me enough to follow me, and I knew the movements of this woman's body well.

When our songs ran out, we didn't have to discuss whether it was time to go. We just walked hand in hand out of the bar. I held Clara's leather jacket out for her, and she slipped her arms into it, then I zipped it to the top.

"You look good in leather, mama." I ran my hands down her arms and my nose along hers. Her lips tempted me more than anything ever had, but if I kissed her now, I wouldn't be able to stop. "Need to find someplace to be with you."

She nodded, our noses bumping more. "I need that too."

"I'm going to lead."

"Okay," she whispered. "Take me where you want me."

Oh, I will, sweetness. I will.

CHAPTER TWENTY-FOUR

Jake

There was a spot by the side of a covered bridge hidden from the main road—a term I used loosely since it was little more than a one-lane path, rarely traveled by anyone. I'd found it a while back when I'd needed to pull off to adjust something on my bike. It was a fine spot to watch the sunset and even finer to get my girl alone where no one would be coming by.

I was off my bike first, pouncing on Clara as soon as she came to a stop. Her helmet and jacket were discarded quickly, then I had my hands on her, under her shirt, inside her bra, squeezing her perfect tits, trailing along the softness at her middle.

"Here?" she panted. "Outside?"

"I've got you." Lifting her top, I exposed her breasts to the cool dusk air. "No one's going to see you. This isn't a well-traveled road, and we're hidden from sight. I'm not sharing any of this."

That was all the reassurance she needed. Her mouth sought mine, immediately opening for me and letting me take over. I slanted her head so I could kiss her deeper, slaking a fraction of my hunger for her. She balled my shirt in her fist like she was holding on to me to keep herself from floating away. I loved that her instinct was to cling to me—to keep herself attached to me.

I kissed down the column of her throat to her chest. Taking her breasts in my hands, I plumped them together and licked a line across them. Her skin was so damn smooth and silky, giving under the press of my hands and mouth, tasting distinctly like Clara mixed with a day of wind and sunshine.

Taking her pebbled nipples in my mouth was a drip of her flavor. A tease to my tongue. It only made me want more. An ocean of Clara might not have been enough, even if I drowned in her.

Her zipper came down in one smooth motion, and I toyed with the lacy band of her panties with my fingertips.

"I'm going to put my mouth on you."

She nodded, her eyes bright, lips puffy and red. "Okay."

"Lean over the seat of my bike." I took her hand, leading her where I wanted her. She bent forward with barely any hesitation, the glassiness of her eyes telling me her arousal was clearing the path of resistance. She lay across the seat of my bike, looking like something out of my dreams, her eyes closed, head resting on her folded arms, waiting.

For me to do with her what I wanted.

My mouth watered as I grazed my hands over her unreal shape—the plush bends and curves that drove me to distraction.

Hooking my fingers in the waist of her jeans, I yanked them down as far as they would go, catching on her boots at her ankles. That left her in pale-pink lace barely covering the globes of her ass. I got on my knees behind her to take a good, long look at what she was offering me, cupping her cheeks in my hands and squeezing.

Her skin was so pretty and well taken care of. The finest velvet brushing against my palms, making me want to be covered in it—in *her*. When we were apart, and I hadn't touched her for days and days, it became hard to believe she was as lush as the memories I held, but she *was*. She was even better.

I slipped her panties down to keep company with her pants, baring her pretty ass and just a peek of her pussy between her thick thighs.

I tapped the outside of her legs. "Spread as wide as you can for me, sweetness. Let me see what I'm about to have."

With a soft sigh, she listened, her boots sliding in the grass, giving me just a little more. It wasn't enough. Not even close. I spread her wide with my hands, feasting my eyes on her hidden parts, the valley of her ass leading to two of my favorite places to bury myself.

"Jake," she moaned. "Why are you looking at me like that?"

"I'm admiring what's mine. You're pretty everywhere. Did you know that, Clara?"

I didn't wait for her answer, nor did I need it. What I needed was my mouth on her, her taste coating my tongue, her moans in my ears. I leaned in, nuzzling one cheek then the other, before sinking my teeth into the bottom curve. She tensed, jumped, and sighed as I licked the small mark I'd left.

It was enough to activate the primal part of my brain urging me to make a bigger claim on this woman—to make her and everyone else understand she was unequivocally mine.

Carrying her scent on my beard was a start. I buried my face in her, licking from her clit to her ass and back again. Once I started, I didn't stop, lapping up every sweet drop of her, drowning just like I wanted to, living off her flavor.

Needing more, I thrust two fingers into her pussy, her slick arousal easing the way. She tightened around me, moaning my name into the darkening sky. I twisted my hand to roll her pearly clit under a finger and moved my mouth higher, laving her puckered hole with the flat of my tongue.

Clara keened. Her legs tried to close, but I was too deep between them for her movements to make any difference. I was where I wanted to be, and nothing would deter me. There was no part of her I didn't want to know the taste and feel of. No part that would be closed to me.

And she knew that.

She was aware of how much I liked the secrets she kept locked away from everyone but me.

She liked it too. Her pussy fluttered and tightened around my thrusting fingers. Her hips bucked against my mouth. It wasn't long before she was moaning my name, her feet shuffling, knees bending, melting. But I had her, holding her up until I had my fill of her—until her scent and taste firmly clung to my lips and beard and lodged inside my mind.

Then I was on my feet behind her, smoothing my hand up her spine to cup the back of her neck. There was a riot inside me, a need setting fire to my blood. "You ready for me, Clara?"

She nodded, and I knew she didn't get it. Couldn't feel me practically vibrating for her. I needed her to want it as badly as I did.

"You need to use your words. I'm not feeling quite myself, and I need to take you hard. You ready for that?"

"Yes, Jake. Fuck me hard," she rasped. "I want it."

That was what I needed. "Then I'll give it to you."

My jeans down, cock out, condom rolled on in a flash; I took her hips in my hands and aligned myself with her hot flesh, nudging her opening. Her body welcomed me, and I accepted the invitation, driving into her until my hips slammed against her ass.

She reared back and cried out, but it wasn't in pain. My sweet Clara liked it rough.

I got lost in her, taking her body with brutal force. Our skin collided, the sounds echoing off the open sky. She moaned and begged, and I told her how good she was, how I wanted her to feel me for days to come, that she was precious and I wanted her to carry my marks for as long as possible.

I was deep in her, but it didn't feel like enough. Grabbing a fistful of her hair at the base of her skull, I pulled her toward me so I could devour her neck and jaw. I pulled her lobe between my lips and whispered words for only her. Hot devotions. Promises of pleasure on top of pleasure. She quivered and moaned, trying to nod but finding she couldn't with the grip I had on her. Her "Yes," came out in broken syllables, and I fucked her little fluttering cunt. Nothing was more important than this. Her and me. Not even breathing. My world had whittled down to our connection.

"Clara." I breathed against her damp temple, nuzzling her tenderly. "Can't get enough of you."

"Jake," she moaned. "Please. I need it."

"You'll have it. I've got you."

Releasing my hold on her hair, I pushed her forward, planting my palm in the center of her back. She clamped down on me as her cries grew more frantic, desperate. I knew she was at the precipice, and I followed her, giving and taking. Losing my pace, my rhythm, my mind as I plunged us both into oblivion.

Falling, falling, barely breathing. She reached back to hold my wrist, and I moved my hand to thread our fingers together. If we fell, it would be together.

It took a long time to hit solid ground again. Only when my knees were steady and my feet level did I pull out of her, dispose of my condom, and hitch up my pants. Taking Clara in my arms, I brought us to the grass and cradled her in my lap. She looped her arms around my neck and thrust her face under my jaw.

Stroking her back, I calmed my breathing and hers. She smelled so good, like fresh air and her signature floral scent. I shoved my nose into her silky hair and took a deep whiff.

Dusk had turned to night. Crickets chirped, and grass and bushes rustled in the gentle breeze. I couldn't think of many places I would have rather been than in the grass next to my bike with this woman in my arms.

"I can't go that long without you again," I murmured. "I lost it on you."

"I didn't mind that at all." She drew herself upright and stroked my beard with her fingertips. "It'll be an adventure riding all the way home with this ache you left behind, though."

I winced. "Shit. I clearly wasn't in my right mind. I should have considered—"

"No, Jake. Come on. I asked for it just as much as you wanted to give it. I'm mostly kidding."

I cupped between her legs, studying her for any signs of pain. She blinked back at me, a smile curving the corners of her mouth.

"All right. I'm going to trust you're telling the truth, but I'll be more cognizant next time—"

"You fuck me on the side of the road?" she filled in.

I gave her ass a little smack. "Next time, I want to fuck you like a madman, *Clara*."

She snorted a laugh and looked down at herself, her pants around her ankles, my hand holding her pussy. "I think you should take me home."

"I intend to."

Her hand covered mine. "What do you think about staying the night?"

My stomach lurched. I'd been dreading dropping her off, but she had Nellie, and we'd agreed that was a no go.

Before I could decide how to answer, she said, "You could leave early. Sneak out through the patio off my bedroom. No one would even know you'd been there. No one but me, that is."

"You're sure?"

She nodded. "I wouldn't have asked if I wasn't. That brief morning we had together was nice. I'd sort of love to fall asleep and wake up with you again."

Closing my eyes, I let my forehead fall against hers. She'd been through a hell of a lot more trauma than I had, yet here she was, being brave—asking for what she wanted, telling me exactly how she felt. Her confidence was so fucking sexy and attractive, my head went foggy.

"You know? I'd really love that too."

I took her hand in mine, and we made our way back home. Dread didn't pool in my gut as we drew closer to her house. Our near-perfect day wasn't over. We didn't have all the time in the world, but we had hours more than expected.

All because Clara had taken a risk and reached for what she wanted.

I wasn't going to forget this.

Chapter Twenty-Five

Clara

It was a shame how quickly life sped by when things were going well. A month passed in a blink. Thirty-one days full of stolen moments at lunch, sweet kisses, and long, sweaty nights. I was so caught up in the whirlwind of falling for him, I hadn't savored it as much as I should have, but neither of us was going anywhere.

Not when we had it so, *so* good.

I opened my eyes, squinting at the light streaming through a crack in my blinds. Nellie must've dug her fingers into them the day before, leaving them in enough disarray for the sun to sneak through. I tried to be annoyed, but that lasted all of fifteen seconds. It was impossible for me to take issue with my little girl any longer than that.

I rolled over, expecting a warm body, only to be met with lukewarm sheets. Sitting upright, I peered around my bedroom and turned toward the en suite bathroom. It was dark.

Had Jake already left? He never left without kissing me goodbye. And it was usually difficult to pry ourselves apart.

I checked my phone. No messages from him.

Huh.

He wouldn't have left the bedroom, not with Nellie and Marina out there. At least, I didn't think he would have.

When he came home with me the first time, I'd introduced him to Marina, so that wouldn't have been a problem, but Nellie hadn't seen him since the night they met over fast food. Part of me thought it might be time for a slow introduction, but we hadn't talked about it…

Not that that mattered. Jake probably had to get to Sage or something and hadn't had a chance to text me. He knew I liked to sleep in on Sunday mornings. If not for the sun peeking in my room, I would have been asleep now.

Climbing out of bed, I pulled on my robe, needing to figure out what was going on. After a stop in the bathroom, I padded out to the living room. A smile stretched across my face at the sound of Nellie's laugh, only to droop when I turned the corner.

Nellie was dancing to the music show she loved so much, with Jake right beside her, grooving along. If I hadn't been so distressed at him going against my wishes, I would have stopped to admire how cute they both were. I never would have pictured Jake as the kind of man who boogied down to a kids' show, but he was shaking and wiggling without restraint. For a fleeting moment, I wondered if this was how he'd been with Sage when she was little. Then I remembered I was pissed.

"Mommy's awake!" Nellie spotted me first, and her little legs carried her to me at top speed until she crashed into my knees. "Good morning, Mommy. Jake's here."

I smoothed my hand over her tangled hair and took a deep breath. The last thing I wanted to do was get mad in front of her, but my blood was boiling.

"I see that, honey. What a surprise. Do you remember him?"

"Yep." She nodded hard, her little head bobbing around. "Jake fixed Mommy's car."

"You have the memory of an elephant. Wow."

I took a time-out from my anger to be impressed. Nellie didn't meet tons of people, and we certainly didn't have fast-food dinners with the ones she did meet, but that had been nearly two months ago. For a three-and-a-half-year-old, it might as well have been a decade.

"I'm not an elephant," she cried. "I'm Nellie."

"Oh, right." I laughed, though I didn't feel it like I normally did. "I forgot for a minute."

"Okay." She let go of my legs and swiveled around. "I'm gonna go dance now."

During our conversation, I'd refused to look at Jake, not quite ready to deal with him yet. But once Nellie was immersed in her show again, he came striding in my direction, and I had no choice but to deal.

"What are you doing?" I hissed.

He took me by the bicep and led me toward the kitchen, stopping just outside Nellie's range of hearing while keeping her in view.

"I know you're not happy, but let me explain."

The gruffness of his voice in the mornings was still there. I loved waking up to him saying my name and touching me wherever he could. Today, though, I wasn't so pleased to hear it.

"Go ahead."

He cupped my elbows, keeping me within reach. "Marina knocked on the door this morning. Her daughter was in an accident on the way home from her shift, and she needed to get to the hospital to be with her—"

"Is Cassie okay?" I pressed my hand to my forehead. "I should check with her—"

"She's okay." He tucked my hair behind my ear, stroking his knuckles along my cheek. Steady as a rock, like always. "Marina said she bumped her head and they were checking for a concussion. She's conscious and nothing's broken."

A breath whooshed out of me. Cassie was a nurse, and Marina always worried about her driving home after long shifts. Now that I knew she wasn't seriously injured, I refocused on the subject at hand.

"Good. That's good. Now, can you tell me how you made the decision to hang out with my kid without running it by me?"

He remained calm in the face of my unhappiness. "You were sound asleep, and Nellie had crept up behind Marina. She saw me and remembered my name." Another stroke of his knuckle, soothing me. I must've looked as conflicted as I felt. "I get it, Clara. I do. But she already saw me, so I figured the jig was up. I made her a waffle and cut up some fruit, and we watched her favorite show. I think she'll recover if she never sees me again."

He lowered his forehead to mine, and it was impossible not to soften. If only by a fraction. "I hope that's not the case. I'm getting tired of sneaking out. I could use some lazy mornings with you, and I don't mind watching a cartoon or two."

My lips twitched, almost smiling. "You looked like you were enjoying it."

He chuckled. "I can't help it. When a Rossi girl asks me to dance, I dance."

I took a step back—the only amount of space his hold would allow. Sighing, I glanced toward my daughter in the other room before bringing my eyes back to him. "Sage is lucky to have you as a dad."

"I'm lucky to have her as my daughter." He nodded toward Nellie. "She reminds me a lot of my girl. Always moving and grooving. She hasn't met a stranger."

I snorted a laugh. "That's Nellie. With her in tow, I can't run a quick errand. She's always trying to have conversations with people she thinks look interesting."

The corners of his eyes crinkled as he took my face in his hands. "If you're okay with it, I don't mind being her buddy. We'll go slow, and I swear to all that's holy I'll be careful. The last thing I want to do is hurt either of you."

"I know that. If I had any doubt of your intentions, you wouldn't be in my home." I sighed. "But sometimes things don't work out as we intend."

"No, they don't." His hands dropped to my shoulders then slid down my arms before letting me go. "It's up to you, Clara. If you want me to go, say the word."

My stomach swirled like a storm in a bottle. There was no manual for parenting. Everyone had their own ideas on when kids should be introduced to their parents' boyfriends or girlfriends. And when I put my shock and anger aside, seeing Jake and Nellie dancing had felt...right. He wasn't here to be her daddy, but he could be her friend. And I could have some cozy mornings with my favorite people.

"I want you to stay." I circled my arms around his middle. "I'm sorry I freaked out. I do trust you. It's just—"

He kissed my forehead, then his eyes met mine again as he ran his fingers through the sides of my hair. "You've been through hell and back."

I chuffed. "Yeah."

Taking my hand in his, he kissed my knuckles. "Why don't you go dance with your girl while I make you breakfast? Waffles okay for you too? I'll pour you a cup of coffee first."

I blinked at him, wondering if this was real. The offer had rolled off his tongue like we'd done this a hundred times, but this was our first morning together, and he'd already made my daughter waffles.

"You're going to make me breakfast?"

His brow dropped low. "I'm here, and I'm not going anywhere this morning. Why wouldn't I make my girl breakfast?"

"I—" I felt stupid for being so blown away, but I was, and I couldn't quite hide my reaction. "Well, no one has made me breakfast since I was a kid. You took me by surprise."

"Clara," he growled my name with a vicious edge, "don't tell me shit like that when I can't do anything to go back and make it right."

Snatching up my hand, he pulled me fully into the kitchen and pushed me against the wall. I leaned my head back, and he cupped my throat. Anger crystallized in the blue of his eyes, and though I knew it wasn't directed at me, my stomach swooped and knotted. I had never seen him that way. Jake was the most even-keeled man I'd ever met. For him to snap...

"You were mistreated and neglected for a long time. I'm seeing that now. I fucking hate you being surprised over something small like me wanting to make you breakfast."

"I hate it for myself too," I whispered.

He stroked his thumb over my throat as I swallowed. "Expect me to take care of you now that you've let me in. You can lean on me. I *want* you to. It makes me feel good to be that for you. Everything I'm going to do for you is my pleasure because you're mine and you're important to me. Keeping you happy is important to me. That means feeding you, talking to you, making you smile, protecting you, tucking your soft body under the covers after making you come on my tongue and cock…"

That made me grin. "You had to throw that in there."

His answering smile wasn't quite as bright as mine, but it was there. Some of his anger had slipped away, unfurling the knot in my stomach. "Had to. It's just as important as the rest."

My eyes met his. Honest and clear, he hid nothing behind his gaze. I'd never known this man to say anything he didn't mean. My instincts told me to lean on him like he wanted. He would be there. As steady as ever.

"Jake."

"Clara," he rumbled.

I pushed up on my toes and touched my lips to his. "I would love breakfast. Thank you."

"You're welcome. Now"—he gave my butt a smack and a squeeze—"go dance so I can cook you a waffle before it's lunchtime."

"Well, all right. You don't have to be so impatient."

He squeezed my butt again. "Always playing. Wait until later when I play with you."

"Cards? Battleship?" I raised my brows. "Another round of bowling?"

He took me by the shoulders and spun me away from him. "Get out of here."

I squealed like a kid and ran before he could land another smack. This man made me feel all kinds of things. Right now, I felt younger and happier than I'd been in a long time.

I'd *squealed* for heaven's sake.

Nellie looked up when I got close, studying me with her big brown eyes that didn't miss much. "I like when Mommy's smiling."

I dropped down to the floor next to her and kissed her plump little cheek. "Jake made me laugh."

She reached out and tapped my chin. "I like Jake."

I couldn't resist pulling her into my lap to nuzzle her fuzzy hair. "I do too, Nell-Belle. I do too."

Chapter Twenty-six
Clara

Jake cupped my face and lowered his hips between my thighs. "We had a good day, didn't we?"

"We did." My eyelids fluttered closed. I didn't know how he expected me to have a conversation when he was naked on top of me like this. I slid my feet up his thighs, and his cock slipped lower, nestling at my seam.

He groaned, rocking slightly. "What are you trying to do, mama?"

"The same thing you were trying to do when you got in this position."

"Not the same thing." He pecked my nose. "I just want to talk to you for a minute and tell you I liked hanging here with you and your girl."

That opened my eyes and flipped my heart. We'd had a regular day. Nellie went full speed, showing Jake her favorite park, every corner of the yard, her treasured dolly. We ran errands and ate lunch and dinner together. Jake listened in on our bedtime stories and made lion and dragon sound effects when they were needed.

It was a regular day.

A really, *really* good one.

"Are you sure you weren't bored?"

He chuffed. "When would I have gotten bored? Don't think I sat down for more than a few minutes other than mealtimes."

Laughing, I shoved my face in his neck. "She did have you running, didn't she?"

"Yep."

One word, but there was so much meaning behind it. He liked the way Nellie had kept him running. Had enjoyed it. While that made me immeasurably happy, it also frightened me. Days like today would be too easy to get used to. And I couldn't do that. Nellie and I were a unit. Jake was a guest star in our little life. We were excited to have him here, but it wasn't a permanent position.

"Sage must've trained you well."

"You say that like she doesn't keep me running now." He rubbed his nose along mine. "Thank you for opening your world to me."

I looped my arms around his neck. "I like having you here. Especially this part—in my bed, leaving your scent on my pillows."

He peered down at me. "You like smelling me after I'm gone?"

"Why wouldn't I? You smell delicious."

Head cocking, he smirked. "Then why am I the one always tempted to eat you alive?"

My thighs tried to clamp together, but with him wedged between them, I only succeeded in drawing him closer. His cock brushed my clit, making me arch toward him.

"Jake, I want you inside me."

"That's gonna happen." He rubbed his length back and forth over my clit, getting so close to where I needed him. "Let me grab a condom."

He made quick work of it, expertly rolling the latex over his erection. I liked watching him handle himself, rough and efficient. Then his hands were on me again, and there was nothing efficient about it. He took his time running his palms down the length of my thighs before slipping them under my ass and yanking me into him.

"Come here, sweetness," he rumbled, lining up his cock with my entrance.

The first stretch of being breached never failed to take my breath away. He slid into me slowly, pushing past my flexing walls until he found home and stilled, as deep as he could get. We sighed together.

"Christ, do you feel good." This guttural utterance spilled from his mouth like he couldn't hold it back. He moved slowly, barely pulling out before he shoved back in.

"It feels incredible to me too." I trailed my fingers along his biceps to clutch his shoulders and raised my head to kiss his chin. "Maybe we can ditch the condoms once you get tested. I would love to have you raw inside me."

His head dropped, and his exhale was shaky as he rolled his forehead along mine. "Clara...it's not about that."

"Okay." He was stopping, and I didn't want him to. We'd talk about this later. "That's okay. I don't care. Just fuck me, Jake."

He hesitated briefly before he groaned and started moving. Kissing me. Fucking me until neither of us could breathe. He let me draw in some air, then went after me again, his tongue deep in my mouth, cock even deeper in my pussy.

We clung and clawed at one another, rolling around the bed like we were fighting. He gave me the top, then took it back, driving my body into the mattress. Like he was trying to reach a point I wasn't even aware existed but he was determined to find. I held on and gave back, our skin slapping and sliding.

He wrung me out—out of orgasms and energy. I almost lost my voice from crying out his name and pleading with him for more, less—everything. Finally, he collapsed beside me. Once he got rid of the condom, I curled into him in a space between bliss and sleep.

Then he spoke softly. "I always wear a condom, Clara. After one accidental pregnancy, I don't want to risk another."

I lifted my head from the crook of his shoulder so I could look at him as we spoke. "That makes sense. I have an IUD, though. The chances of a pregnancy are really slim. Less than one percent. But I understand if you're not comfortable."

His brow furrowed. "You think I want anything between us?"

"I don't know." I rubbed the center of his sweaty chest. "But, so you know, I was tested after I had Nellie, and I haven't been with anyone since. If you think you might want to forego a condom, get tested, and we—"

"Got a clean bill of health at my physical last year. A month or two after we met the first time." He tugged on the end of my hair. "You really want to go bare with me?"

"God yes." I kissed his pec. "If you want it, too, get a recent test and we can talk about it more—or skip the talking and go straight to the fucking."

His grin was halfhearted, and his brow was still furrowed. "Told you I'm in the clear."

"Well...yeah, last year you were. Since then..." I trailed off, having no desire to say he'd obviously been with other women and we couldn't be too careful.

"Since then...what?" He sat up and tugged me with him, situating me on his lap so we were face to face. "Clara, you're the only woman I've been with for over a year."

"What?" I breathed. "How?"

"You were there that first night. You felt it too, didn't you?"

I knew what he meant. I wasn't experienced outside of my ex-husband, but what happened between us was nothing short of electric. It was why I returned to The Tavern again and again. Two strangers shouldn't have lit the bed on fire the way we had. To me, my hours with Jake in that hotel room had been something special. The universe's reward for going through hell and surviving it. I hadn't realized he'd felt even close to the same way.

"I felt it, Jake. I just assumed...since it was so long between our meetings and neither of us really knew if there even would be another meeting..."

"I knew you'd be back." He rubbed his thumb along my bottom lip. "It's why I paid the bartender to call me as soon as you walked in the door. Lucky me, you only showed up on nights I was free to hightail it there."

I pulled back in shock. "You *what*?"

He shrugged. "You think I wanted to leave seeing you again to chance? I sure as hell didn't. You wouldn't give me your number, so bribing the bartender was my master plan. Look how that worked out."

I thought back to the times he showed up at The Tavern and swept me away. He'd always gotten there after me. I'd sat at the bar long enough to have a drink or two, a little over an hour.

The amount of time it took to drive from his house to the bar—if he was breaking a few speeding laws.

"You're serious," I said aloud as I realized this inside my head. "You bribed the bartender."

"Yeah, mama. I want something, I take it."

I licked my lips. "For a year, I was the only one you wanted."

"Mmm." He tenderly tucked my hair behind my ear. "And that remains true."

His touch and honest declaration warmed me from my chest outward, reaching the top of my head to the tip of my toes. I wasn't a young woman. I'd been married and divorced. I had a child and the scars to show for it. I'd worked my ass off to get where I was in my career. Generally, I'd made peace with where I was in my life, content with what I had and never dwelling on what I didn't. But now, I had *this*—a man who had wanted me for a whole year despite not knowing if or when he'd see me again. He'd wanted me so badly, he'd bribed and broken laws to have me. It was nearly impossible to believe, but it made so much sense; it had to be the truth.

"For me as well," I whispered.

"Glad you agree. Even more glad you walked into my garage."

My mouth curved. "I think we like each other."

He smiled back at me and dug his fingers into my hair. "You're just now figuring that out? I like the hell out of you, Clara Rossi."

There wasn't much else that needed to be said after that. Jake rolled us onto the mattress and gathered me close. He'd done everything he'd promised me today—feeding me, talking to me, making me smile, then ended the day by tucking me in under the covers.

It was perfect.

A beautiful, lovely day.

Even so, my quiet yet persistent inner voice couldn't help reminding me not to get used to any of this.

Chapter Twenty-Seven
Jake

There was no hiding from my kid. It wasn't her day with me, but I never turned down some extra Sage time. She just happened to show up, wanting to chat about her day when I was finally getting ready for the date Clara had planned.

Now, she was sitting on the closed toilet seat, watching me trim my beard, suspicion furrowing her brow.

"You never trim your beard at night."

I met her gaze in the mirror. "It was looking a little unruly, don't you think?"

She shrugged, still scrutinizing me. "You don't usually take showers at night either. Are you going somewhere?"

"You're pretty nosy today, Sagie."

She shook her finger at me. "And you're avoiding the question, Daddy. What gives?"

I placed the trimmer on the counter and grabbed my beard oil. "You're right, I do have plans."

"What kind of plans?"

"I'm catching a movie."

I tried to keep it light and easy, not wanting to arouse my little detective's suspicion. It had been easier to date when she was younger. She didn't ask questions when I went out for the night other than if I'd be home when she woke up. There was no getting anything by her now, though. I wasn't even sure if I *wanted* to get this by her or be straight up and tell her I was seeing someone. I hadn't decided, and I was hoping for time to consider it.

Her head tipped to the side. "Can you cancel? I want you to come to dinner at our house. Mom's making meatloaf and mashed potatoes, and I *miss* you so much."

Fuck. I could've passed on dinner, but not my daughter missing me. Guilt swept in, knocking me back a step. I'd been looking forward to tonight for days, and I would've given anything not to miss it. But not to the detriment of my girl...

Turning to face her, I crossed my arms over my chest and looked her over. She'd shown up bouncy and happy, in her typical good mood. She hadn't acted out of sorts. I tried to assess how serious this was.

"You're coming back to me tomorrow afternoon, sweetheart. We'll have all week together. You're going to be sick of seeing me."

Her eyebrows popped. "Sooo...you're saying even though your beloved daughter misses you, you really don't want to cancel your plans?"

"I will if you really need me to." I took her chin in my hand, tilting her head left and right. "I'm just trying to decide how serious you are. Is something going on? Something happen at school or your mom's house?"

"Nope." Her mouth curved into a devious little smirk. "I was testing you."

"How so?"

"Well, you'll drop anything for me, so I wanted to see how disappointed you'd be at the possibility of canceling." Her smirk morphed into a full-wattage grin. "You have a date, don't you?"

Ah, damn. I knew Sage was smart, but I hadn't expected her to be able to manipulate me so easily. This girl was going to be trouble if she chose to use her powers for evil.

"What would you think if I said I did?"

"I'd say I hope she's cool and treats you nice."

"She is, and she does."

Sage gasped. "So, you've been on more than one date with her?"

I nodded. "A few."

"And you didn't tell me?"

"No. Didn't think you'd be interested in a couple old people going out, doing boring things."

That earned me an eye roll. "Oh, please. Of course I'm interested. What's her name? Does she like kids? Do you think she'd like me?"

Looked like we were doing this. Lying to Sage wasn't in my wheelhouse. She was old enough to get straight answers. And I guessed telling her about Clara and letting her get attached to her were two very different things.

"Do you remember Clara?"

She shot to her feet, her hands flying to her hips. "You're not dating Clara."

I had to laugh at her adamance. "Why not?"

"She's too cool for you, obviously."

I ruffled her hair. "Sorry to break it to you, but she happens to think I'm cool enough for her."

She huffed and stalked out of the bathroom. Worried she was genuinely upset, I followed her into my closet where she was riffling through my shirts.

"What's up?" I asked from the doorway.

She didn't bother looking back at me. "Your clothes are too boring for Clara. Do we have time to go shopping before your date?"

This kid. She was a roller coaster. One second, she had me thinking she felt one way, then she flipped and showed me a whole other side. Sometimes, I didn't know which way was up, but damn was it a fun ride.

"I was thinking I'd wear a T-shirt and jeans. We're not going anywhere formal."

The sigh she gave me could've knocked down a skyscraper. "Oh, Dad. Clara wears fancy high heels and has super shiny hair. Do you really think she wants you wearing a T-shirt and jeans on a date?"

"Well, that's what she wears half the time I see her, considering she rides a motorcycle too."

That got her attention. She spun around, her eyes bugging out of her head. "She rides a *motorcycle*? But...she's...she's so fancy."

"She is fancy, but she's multifaceted. Want to know something really cool? Her last name is Rossi. What kind of motorcycle do I have?"

Her mouth twisted as she thought over my question. "You have a Rossi—oh my god, did Clara's family make your motorcycle?" When I nodded, she stumbled backward and pretended to faint, going starfish in the middle of my closet. "Dad, that is *so* cool."

"I think so too."

She pushed herself up on her elbows. "Just in case it's not obvious, I approve. Don't mess up, okay?"

With a grin, I shook my head. "I'll try not to."

Chapter Twenty-eight
Jake

Clara's big date was a movie in the park. She'd asked me to pick her up in my car so she could wear a dress, and fuck if it wasn't a treat. We were late because I'd had to pin her against the passenger door and touch her through the thin fabric of her sundress. I'd done the same when we'd arrived at the park, sucking on her neck as I stroked her smooth thighs and toyed with the elastic of her panties next to her pussy.

Getting enough of her seemed impossible. Since Nellie had found me at the house two weekends ago, I'd slept at Clara's most nights I didn't have Sage. Each time I saw this woman, my heart jammed itself in my throat—and that wasn't me.

Except...with Clara, it was.

I laced my fingers between hers and led her through the rows of people on blankets and in lawn chairs. *Back to the Future* had just started playing on a big screen set up for tonight. We found a good spot to spread out our own blanket by the trunk of a grand old tree with widespread gnarled roots. Marty McFly wasn't much more than a speck from back here, but we both knew the movie well enough it didn't matter if we couldn't see every detail.

I sat with my back against the tree and made room for Clara between my legs. She leaned against me, her head on my chest, and all was right with the world. I could kiss her temple and forehead and stroke my fingers along her soft stomach and sides.

"I didn't plan this well, did I?" she whispered.

"I think you did all right. I'd rather be back here, alone with you, than stuck in the middle of everyone. This is nice."

"Yeah," she sighed. "It is, isn't it? Peaceful."

A movie in the park hadn't been on my radar, and I'd been dubious when Clara suggested it. But fireflies darted here and there in the dark, and my girl was curled against me while a classic movie played. The air was cool, and she was warm. Peaceful was one way I'd describe it. Even with hundreds of people around us, we were in our own quiet bubble. Quiet was rare for us, with our kids and jobs. This...this was needed, and I intended to feel every second of it.

"Mmm." Her hair smelled like oranges mixed with sunshine. I nuzzled the side of her head, breathing her in. "I told Sage I'm seeing you."

She turned her head and tipped it back to look at me. "Did you? I'm surprised."

"She pushed the subject, and I found I wanted her to know."

"What did she think?"

"That I need to wear fancier clothes to keep up with you. My own daughter would choose you over me in a heartbeat, and I don't even blame her."

That made her laugh. "She doesn't even know me."

"Yeah, and you think it'd change if she did? You're incredible. Plus, you're a Rossi, and Sage dreams of having her own motorcycle. She probably thinks you'll hook her up."

"Ah, a motorcycle girl. I love her already."

She didn't mean it in a real way, but those words coming from her mouth had me holding her tighter and pressing a kiss to her lips.

"Think you'll let Nellie ride a motorcycle one day?" I asked.

"Hmm...if she wants to. I'd be a big hypocrite otherwise. I'll teach her how to ride responsibly, the way my dad had with me. He drilled safety rules into my head until I was saying them in my sleep." She shuddered in my arms. "I can't think about letting my baby drive away on a bike."

"It goes fast. Feels like Sage was born yesterday, and she's a whole teenager now."

"Do you think you'd have more kids if you found the right person?"

I froze. A hundred thoughts whirred in my head, all too jumbled to grasp the right thing to say. There was no right answer to a question so out of left field.

"Clara, what the fuck?"

She shot up and twisted around, alarm evident in the drop of her jaw and brightness of her eyes. "What is it?"

I rubbed my forehead, taking a breath. "You're asking me about meeting the right person when I'm holding you in my arms. You don't think that's something I'd take offense to?"

She blinked at me as rapidly as my heart stuttered in my chest. "I didn't mean to offend you. I—"

"Just don't take me seriously, do you?" I reached around her to grip her hair at the base of her skull. "Because I'm a few years younger than you? Is that still a hang-up? Tell me what it is so I can demolish your reasoning."

"I take you seriously, Jake. I wouldn't have you in my bed or around my daughter if I didn't. But I know most things aren't forever, and you and I already have a lot of obstacles and baggage between us. It isn't crazy for me to think you and I are part of each other's story but won't be at the end. That doesn't mean I'm not into you or don't want to be with you. I do."

I shook my head. "I thought I was a pessimist. Jesus, that's some dreary shit to have in your head. Can't we ride this out and see where it goes without thinking about the end?"

"Jake..." She touched my face, stroked my beard. Then she gently described the hell she'd gone through. "The way you're protecting Sage from being hurt? I have to do the same for myself. You wouldn't have recognized me three years ago. I was utterly decimated, and I mean that in a true sense. Everything I thought I knew was false. The life I'd planned was gone in a blink. *Breathing* was difficult—and that was automatic. Doing anything I had to put thought into was impossible. Nellie was the *only* reason I kept going, and even that was touch and go. I can't go through that again. I know myself, and I won't survive it. My heart was pummeled far too hard. It can't withstand another round. The damage was far too catastrophic."

This was the first time she'd truly opened up about her ex and the wreckage he left behind, but it wasn't the first time I felt violent toward him. What he'd done to this woman was a crime in itself. We couldn't even have a night out without his shadow darkening it.

I was not that man. He might've destroyed her trust, but she had to see we were not the same. It wasn't her fault, but it still pissed me off. What he'd done had colored how she saw the world—including how she saw me.

I slid my hand from her hair to her throat, cupping her beneath her jaw. "I can't make promises of forever. I *can* promise, no matter what, I'll never lie to you, and I'll always be gentle with you. I'm not *him*. I won't add more scars."

"I know you're not him. I swear, I know that." Pushing up to her knees, she held my face in her pretty hands. "I do feel safe with you, but I can't help protecting myself. There's nothing you need to do to prove yourself to me. I don't know if I'm stuck like this or need more time."

I got her. She was coming from a place close to where I'd been—blindsided and left behind. Hers was on another level of hell, but I still got it. If we'd tried this a few years ago when my guard had been at full strength, we would've never gotten past the bedroom. Putting my ego aside and truly thinking about it, Clara was being a lot more vulnerable and open than either of us gave her credit for.

"We have time, sweetness. I can be as patient as you need me to be."

She swallowed hard against my palm. "Thank you for that. But if I say stupid shit, call me on it. The last thing I want is for you to think I question your integrity or motives."

"I have no problem calling you on your shit. I think you know that by now."

That broke the tension around us. She snorted a little laugh. "I guess that's true. You don't have trouble speaking your mind."

"Even when I'm wrong."

She giggled. "Especially then."

With a growl, I grabbed her around the middle and yanked her into my lap. Lowering my face to her neck, I nibbled and licked while she squirmed and dug her nails into my hands locked at her belly.

"Jake," she breathed, "stop eating me in public."

"No one's watching." I touched my lips to the side of her neck. "Your skin is the finest feast I've ever had, you know that? After our first time, I thought about your skin for months."

"Thank you...so long as you don't plan to make a suit out of me."

I kissed her neck again then put my lips to her ear. "You never know."

That got her giggling again, and the sound made my chest fill. This woman might've thought she'd been torn up and put back together wrong, but with a laugh like that, light as an afternoon breeze and carefree, she was just right.

After a minute or two, she turned her head, her mouth grazing my cheek. "Should I get off you?"

My arms tightened. "Never."

"But"—she moved her soft ass over the bulge in my jeans—"you're hard. This can't be comfortable."

"Mmm."

"That's not an answer." Leaning forward, she reached behind her and flipped open my button. Then her hand snuck inside my jeans and wrapped around the head of my cock.

"Jake." My name was a plea. A request for an unmet need. Asking permission. A sigh of desperation.

"Do what you need to do." She should've known I'd always give her what she needed, no matter where we were or who was around.

Shifting, she unzipped my fly and freed my cock so it was nestled between her thighs. If anyone glanced at us, they'd see her sitting on my lap, her skirt spread across her legs, nothing else. But no one was looking, not when the idiotically villainous Biff was chasing Marty on the big screen.

Clara sat like that for a minute then she slid her panties to the side, and I held my breath as she slowly took me inside. Fully seated, she leaned against my chest, and we exhaled together. Her pussy held me in a snug, hot embrace, and her body was soft and relaxed in my arms.

"Like that?" I murmured next to her ear.

"Yes," she breathed. "Is this okay for you?"

I laughed softly. "Being inside you is always more than okay."

I felt her smile more than saw it. "I mean, we're in public. Anyone could see."

"No one's going to see." I kissed her temple. "You feel so fucking good."

She hummed in agreement, nuzzling my beard. "I could stay like this all night. The connection I feel to you...it's more than this. But this..."

Her fragmented sentences made sense to me. I got it. I felt it too. "I know, Clara."

Our bodies' physical connection was an outward mirror of the deep, visceral emotional bond we shared. Both were pleasure. Bliss. Something neither of us had discovered with anyone else. She didn't need to say it for me to know that was true. If I'd had anything like this before, I would have moved heaven and earth to keep it.

Her fingers stroked my arms in a hypnotizing rhythm, lulling me to another plane where only we existed. Sometimes, she wiggled or shifted, and it made me jump inside her, but for the most part, we were still in each other's arms. Simply together.

We stayed like that until the characters got to the school dance. The happy ending was approaching, and as much as I would've liked to stay until the end, my patience was at its limit. An hour of being deep inside Clara had been exactly what I needed, but now, I needed more.

Hand in hand, we ran to the parking lot, our blanket abandoned under the tree. I'd parked in a fairly dark area, but at this point I didn't give a damn about privacy. My need for her was so strong I might've taken her under a spotlight.

As soon as the door was closed and locked, Clara straddled my lap, taking me deep again. We didn't stop to savor it. I gripped her by the waist, holding on to her as she fucked herself on my cock. She drove down hard, bouncing on me with the same frantic desperation strumming through my veins.

It didn't hit me until that moment we weren't using a condom, and it barely gave me pause except to acknowledge how incredible her skin felt sliding over mine. Raw, without a barrier between us...just like it should've been.

And holy fucking Christ was I going to come fast. Clara was taking what she needed, moaning my name, riding me like I was the answer to every question she'd ever had.

"Oh, Jake," she moaned. "I'm—I'm—"

"Me too," I gritted out. "Take it. I've got you."

"Yeah. You do."

The second she got there, her head fell back, and she vibrated in my arms. I followed her over, pulling her pliant body to my chest and releasing the groan of a man so near death he could taste it. That was what it felt like when I fell into the abyss of pleasure and came inside her tight, perfect pussy. A death and rebirth. I wouldn't be the same after this. After *her*. Something clicked and shifted within me. I couldn't pinpoint it yet, but when my mind was straight, maybe I'd be able to.

What I knew with certainty? Being with Clara had changed me, and it was undoubtedly for the better.

Everything was better with Clara around. I had no idea where the road was going to take us, but maybe it didn't matter. Like Doc Brown told Marty McFly, maybe where we were going, we didn't need roads.

CHAPTER TWENTY-NINE
Clara

My mood was sour as could be, but I was attempting to go with the messed-up flow of my day. Luca and I were in the middle of a video conference while I flew to Utah to deal with a mess at one of our factories.

The joy of having a Rossi jet meant I could fly in and out during work hours without Nellie being any the wiser. That didn't mean I was happy about having to take this trip.

"Give Greg my salutations when you see him," Luca teased.

I held up my middle finger. "Is this what you mean by salutations?"

"Now, now, Clara. Is that how a representative of the Rossi family behaves?"

I rolled my eyes. "As if you haven't been pictured stumbling out of clubs with a different model every night."

"Pffft. That was years ago—before Saoirse. You can't hold me accountable for anything I did in my twenties."

Back in the day, my brother had been a star of the gossip rags, so it was funny for him to now care about the Rossi image, even in the context of a joke. We both knew I wasn't going to be flipping anyone off but him. The image of our family's company was safe for another day.

"How convenient." I clicked on my inbox, horrified by how many emails I had to get through. "Is there anything else we need to discuss? I am going to need the rest of this flight to make a dent in my inbox."

He exhaled and shifted around as if uncomfortable. "Actually, yes. One of the emails is the preliminary financial report for Motor Zone."

"Oh?" If he was about to give me bad news, I understood his discomfort. "Are they not doing well?"

"I'm still going over it, but there was something that stood out to me. Up until last year, the company had been divided between Jeremy, Jake, their father, and a few family members. Grandpa Hayes left Jeremy fifty-one percent and scattered the rest around the family."

"Okay. What happened last year?"

"Jeremy sold ten percent of his shares to an investor—Roman Wells. It obviously brought in a huge flux of cash."

I sucked in air between my teeth. I recognized that name. Roman Wells had a reputation for sweeping in, investing in failing companies, then riding away with his profits once he turned it around—or sold his shares off to the highest bidder.

"Okay. How is the company doing overall?"

"The year before, they closed a hundred stores, but seem to have stabilized since Roman was brought in. It'll be interesting to see the reports from this fiscal year."

I chewed on my bottom lip, mindlessly clicking the end of my pen. "Are you considering backing out of the deal?"

He paused. "I'm not there yet. What do you think?"

I measured my answer carefully. Up until now, I'd been able to mentally separate my relationship from this potential business partnership, but now I found myself thinking about how my answer would impact Jake. "I'm not sure I should be the deciding factor. There's no way I can give an impartial answer here."

He raised his brows. "Are you recusing yourself?"

"This isn't a jury selection." I huffed a laugh. "But yes, I suppose I am. Keep me informed, but I'd rather not be one of the decision-makers unless absolutely necessary."

He nodded. "Second-guessing mixing business with pleasure?"

"No, I'm not."

That made him smile. "Wow. I'm all sorts of happy about that answer. Saoirse and I should have you two over for dinner soon." He pointed at me through the screen. "Not this weekend, though. I'm cutting out after lunch to head to the ranch for her nephew's birthday."

"Is he taller than you yet?"

He made a disgruntled sound. "He's getting close. I don't know what they feed their kids up in Wyoming. There's no reason an eight-year-old should be five and a half feet tall. No reason at all."

I laughed. "Don't get in fights with children."

"I won't if you promise to be nice to Greg."

That wiped away my smile in one swoop. I couldn't make any such promises. "Bye, Luca."

My meeting in Salt Lake City went as well as expected. Greg Thorne lived up to his name as the ultimate thorn in my side, and his assistant, Samantha, lived up to her reputation of being a cunt.

Greg danced around giving me the numbers I needed then hedged on allowing me to speak to workers on their break. As if my name wasn't on his check and all the parts fabricated at the plant he managed. As if he wasn't replaceable at the snap of my fingers. As if he could readily find another job at this level in fucking Utah.

When I reminded him of all this, his overgrown head filled with so much blood, I feared an explosion. There were pulsing veins in his forehead, eyeballs, neck...a nightmare.

Shira always found a way to look at the bright side of her days, so I followed her lead and did the same. In this case, the bright side was I now had the ammunition I needed to fire Greg. As soon as our lawyers completed the paperwork and we had a plan for his successor, it would be done.

Thomas would be pleased to know cunty Samantha would be going with her boss.

I leaned back in my seat on the plane and closed my eyes. There were a million things I needed to do, but it wasn't often I had the chance to just relax in the middle of the day. Once we took off, we'd be home in under two hours, and I would hit the ground running. After my torturous meetings, I decided I deserved a little rest before getting back to work.

I let myself drift...

Someone tapped on my shoulder, and my eyes flew open. I was disoriented at first, forgetting where I was. I expected to see Nellie, but the face of the flight attendant filled my field of vision.

"We're about to take off, Ms. Rossi. You'll need to buckle up, please."

"What?" My brows drew together, and I looked out the window. We were still on the ground, which was strange since I felt like I'd slept for quite a while. "What time is it?"

"Just past four." She smiled, her ruby lips curving over snow-white teeth. "We were worried we'd be grounded until tomorrow, but the storm over Denver passed in time for us—"

"It's past four?" I sat up in my seat. "I've been asleep for over two hours? How could you let me—how is that possible?"

She stutter-stepped backward, eyes wide with alarm. "You seemed so peaceful, and since we weren't going anywhere, I thought it best to let you get some rest. I'm sorry if that wasn't the right choice. I—"

I waved her off, too filled with worry to be polite. "I have some calls to make."

She nodded. "Of course."

"We'll be taking off imminently?"

"Yes. As soon as we're given clearance."

If we left right now, we'd be getting back to Denver at six—the same time Nellie's day care closed. I'd thought I had given myself plenty of padding in my schedule to get back in time, but it seemed I had been wrong.

I went to Luca's name in my contacts, intent on asking him or Saoirse to grab Nellie from day care, then I remembered they were already on the road to the ranch for the weekend. My parents would have picked her up in a heartbeat, but they were on a two-week

Mediterranean cruise. And as stupid luck would have it, Marina was off for the week, staying with her son's family in Idaho.

Panic banded around my chest, squeezing tight.

I told myself this was okay. I might be a little late to pick her up, but her day care wouldn't abandon her. They'd make me pay a hefty fee, but that was fine.

I made a call to the day care, giving them the heads-up on my situation, then exhaled a heavy breath, attempting to calm down. But every minute that ticked by and the plane didn't move, my heart rate picked up.

The flight attendant kept checking on me, promising we would be leaving any minute. We were only waiting for clearance, but an hour passed before our wheels moved.

I couldn't be an hour late picking Nellie up.

My thumb hovered over the contact on my phone. I did not want to make this call, but I couldn't think of another solution. She'd be safe with Jake, I knew that, but would he agree to do this, or would I be crossing a line even asking? And if he turned me down, would I be able to forgive him?

Despite my fears, I pressed the call button. This was for Nellie. My fears could take a hike.

"Hey, mama," Jake answered smoothly. "It's a nice surprise to get a call from you."

"Jake, I—"

"What's wrong? Did something happen?"

"Yes. I've been in Utah for the day and my return flight has been delayed. I'm not going to be back in Denver before seven. I hate asking you to do this. I know you have Sage. It's just...there's no one else I can ask."

"You need me to get Nellie?"

"Yes." A gust of breath burst from my lungs. "I'm sorry for asking you. My brother and parents are out of town—"

"You don't have to apologize, Clara. I promised to take care of you, and this is part of that promise." He shifted modes, getting down to brass tacks. "Text me the details for her day care. I can send my assistant out for a car seat, but they've changed so much since Sage was little. I need to know the brand and style I should buy."

Tears welled in my eyes from relief and disbelief he was so willing to go the extra mile for me.

"I'll text you in a few after I contact her day care. They're incredibly strict, so I might have to send in a blood sample for them to okay it." I was only half-joking, but I wasn't laughing. I bit down on my bottom lip so I didn't cry. "Thank you, Jake. I didn't know what else to do."

"You did the right thing by calling me. I've got it handled. The only thing you need to do is text me those details and get yourself home safely."

I nodded, but he couldn't see me, so I squeezed out the words. "Okay. The plane's finally moving. It looks like I should be back by seven."

"Don't worry about a thing. Between Sage and me, we'll keep Nell-Belle entertained and happy until her mama shows up. I'll let you know when I have her, all right?"

"Yes. Thank you."

"I've got you, Clara."

"I know."

When we hung up, I finally let the tears escape my eyes. As the plane took off, I cried from my overwhelming mix of emotions.

From Jake's easy caretaking and my difficulty believing it *could* be so easy, from feeling like a failure of a mother, for not being home for my daughter. And hating myself for carrying guilt over things outside of my control—the weather, choosing an unworthy partner to have children with.

I hadn't cried in a long time. After Miller went to jail, I'd cried gallons of tears. So much, my sobs became dry, hacking things, only producing clouds of salty dust. I hadn't let myself dwell on what I'd lost since Nellie was born and I'd pulled myself together, focusing on the riches I had instead. It had been the only way.

But Jake...he sliced straight through the binding I'd kept around my bucket of tears, letting them spill freely. The flight attendant took one look at me and offered me a glass of wine and chocolate. I turned down the wine, though it would have done a world of wonder for my shaking hands, but gladly accepted the chocolate.

Sometimes, chocolate cured everything. This wasn't one of those times, but at least it provided the distraction I needed to get me through the rest of the flight.

Chapter Thirty
Clara

Everything that could have gone wrong had. Once we touched down at the private airport outside Denver and I finally got in my car, traffic was an utter nightmare. Detours from downed trees caused by the earlier storm sent me well out of my way, so by the time I pulled up to Jake's house, it was eight o'clock, past Nellie's bedtime. I crossed my fingers she wasn't being a grumpy beast for him. He'd sent me updates and pictures from the time he picked her up to about an hour ago, but I was nervous about what I was going to walk into.

I walked up the steps to his porch and peered through the picture window beside it. From my vantage, I could see the back of Jake's head and Sage sitting catty-corner from him on their sectional sofa. I tapped lightly on the door, and Sage hopped up, waving at me through the window.

She swung the door open, allowing me in, and pressed her finger to her lips.

"They're sleeping," she whispered.

"Nellie?"

She nodded. "And Daddy. It's the cutest thing I've ever seen."

She led me into the living room, and my heart skipped several beats. Jake was kicked back on the sofa, his feet up on the ottoman. Nellie was sprawled on his chest, her arms and legs hanging limp on either side of him. Her little lips were pursed, cheeks rosy, hair a fuzzy mess. She was sacked out. When I tore my eyes from her, I grinned at the sight of Jake, his head back, mouth slightly agape, just as asleep as my daughter. Even in sleep, though, he had a hand on Nellie's back, keeping her safe.

Affection flooded me, washing away the day's worries, and a thick knot formed in my throat. I didn't know what to do with this feeling.

Sage tugged on my hand, taking me into the kitchen. "Aren't they cute?" she asked, a little louder now that we were away from the sleeping beauties.

I nodded, getting ahold of myself so I could answer her. "I was worried Nellie would be a grump when I got here."

"Nope." She hopped up on the counter. "My dad and I took care of her all afternoon. She likes our yard, so I showed her how to play soccer out there. Then we had dinner and watched *Finding Nemo*. Right in the middle, Nellie climbed on my dad and fell asleep. He was a goner a few minutes later. I stayed up because I knew you were coming soon and wanted to see your reaction."

I smoothed a hand over her silky hair. She really was the sweetest girl. "Thank you, sweetheart. I appreciate you and your dad taking care of Nellie tonight. I don't know what I would have done without you guys."

She shrugged. "We liked it. My dad is good with kids. Sometimes he watches Dex and Cleo for my mom and Mike, so he has a lot of experience. We can babysit Nellie again if you want."

I smiled at her offer. "We'll see."

"Are you hungry? We made extra spaghetti for you."

My stomach heard food and decided to growl for attention. Sage and I laughed, and I placed a hand on my middle. "I guess that answered that question. I am hungry, but I should probably get Nell-Belle home and into her bed."

"I'd rather you stay."

I jumped at Jake's low rumble coming from the doorway. I turned, finding him leaning his shoulder against the wall, his arm crossed, hair disheveled.

"Hey. You're awake."

He nodded. "Your girl knocked me out. She's like a little heated blanket."

That made me smile. "And maybe she ran you just a little bit ragged."

"Maybe."

His eyes crinkled, and he reached for me, pulling me close to kiss the top of my head. He'd kissed me like that in Nellie's presence. It hadn't fazed her, but I was surprised he wasn't being more circumspect around *his* daughter since she was very much aware of what was going on. If he was fine with it, though, then I wasn't complaining. I needed a hug after the day I had.

I peered beyond him to the living room. "Where is she?"

He slipped his arm around my waist and pulled me into his side. "Passed out on the couch. She didn't even stir when I moved her. I think she's down for the count."

Beeps from the microwave pulled our attention to Sage. "I'm heating up spaghetti for Clara. She's starving."

Jake raised his brows at me. "You're starving, huh? No one took care of you today?"

"No. I worked through lunch, but I hadn't expected I wouldn't be home for dinner. All I've had is chocolate and an obscene amount of coffee." I glanced back at the living room. "I really should get us home. It's getting late, so—"

"It's getting late, so you should stay here. Tomorrow's Saturday. You don't have to go to work. No reason you can't stay over," he said lowly, even though Sage was very much attuned to what her father was offering.

"Are you sure?" My eyes darted between his, trying to get a read on him. "I know this isn't what we agreed on."

He kissed my forehead. "You look beat. I don't want you out on the road like this. You're staying the night."

His tone was firm and final. Obviously, I could have taken my child and run, but I didn't want to. I liked being in the kitchen with Sage and Jake, his arm around me, her fussing over my dinner. After hours of panic, they were *my* warm blanket.

⚘

We tucked Nellie in on a twin air mattress at the foot of Jake's bed. Sage had wanted her to sleep in her room, but I worried Nellie would wake up scared in the middle of the night. I promised Sage she could have a sleepover with her in the future, but the words felt like dust on my tongue since I didn't know if they were true.

Jake stepped into his en suite bathroom and stood behind me while I brushed my teeth. His hands slid over my hips and around to my stomach, holding me as he watched me in the mirror. I leaned forward to spit out my toothpaste and rinse my mouth, incredibly aware of his body aligned with mine. Even though he wasn't hard, I felt him through the flimsy fabric of his pajama pants, and my core tightened.

Straightening, I leaned back, and his arms wrapped around me fully. We looked at each other in the mirror. I was wearing one of his old T-shirts, which was tight around my chest and hips while barely covering my butt.

"I don't have pants," I whispered.

"You don't need pants."

I eyed his bare chest, saliva pooling in my mouth. "Together, we make a full outfit."

He breathed a soft laugh. "Seems like we make a good pair then."

"Seems like it." Sighing, I turned my head to nuzzle the underside of his chin. "I don't know how to thank you for today."

"You already said it. You don't owe me anything else. What you asked of me wasn't a burden at all. Sage was in heaven having her here, and I can't say I wasn't too."

My throat swelled, and I hid my face deeper in his neck so he didn't see the emotion on my face. "You like my daughter," I murmured against his warm skin.

"I do. She's a part of you, and there's no part of you I don't like."

Oh, how my chest ached, heavy with emotion and the scars of past heartbreaks. There were many parts of myself I wasn't fond of, but I found myself believing Jake meant what he said. After all, he took one look at the parts of me I considered flaws and got on his knees to worship them.

"You can't say such beautiful things to me. I don't know how to take them."

"Take what I say as me telling you the truth. That's what it is." He gathered the hem of my T-shirt and slipped his hands beneath to cup my breasts. "I like every little and big thing about you, Clara. Inside and out."

"Jake..." He weakened my knees. I braced my hands on the counter in front of me. "What are you doing?"

"Touching my pretty girl." He nudged my face with his, turning my head toward the mirror. "Look at you."

He pulled my shirt above my breasts and held them in his rough, wide palms. His arms and hands were tan from the sun. Calluses lined his fingers, and a little motor oil darkened his nails. We were a study in contrasts, but his skin on my paler, softer flesh looked right.

"Look at us," I said. "How do we fit so well?"

He shook his head. "I'm not one to question the good things in my life. We just do, mama." He dipped to drag his lips along the side of my neck. "We just do."

Releasing my breasts, he put pressure on the center of my back until I folded at the waist. Then he slid my panties down and nudged my legs apart. From behind, he delved between my legs, rubbing those rough fingers through my folds until he got to my swollen clit. I was already wet, so he glided over me, making circles around my most sensitive part. He had me panting in a minute, and I had to bite down on my lip so I wouldn't cry out.

"So wet," he murmured. "I need to be inside you."

"I'm ready. We just have to be quiet."

He bent over me, his mouth latching on to my shoulder. "I can do quiet, so long as I get to have you."

"Please," I whimpered. "I want you."

He slid into me slowly, stretching me open as he took the place he'd claimed as his in my body. I forgot to breathe, too caught up in watching him in the mirror. The tendons in his neck strained, and his biceps flexed, his complete focus on where we were joined.

He held his control like the edge of a cliff. One slip would send him plummeting. But knowing Jake how I did, he wouldn't let go until he was ready.

It made it easy for me to completely unwind, letting my troubles slip away as I sank into his possession.

He looked up, meeting my gaze in our reflection. "You're so fucking beautiful. You know that?"

I couldn't look at myself—only him. Looking at my tits swinging, my stomach rolls and scars, the lines in my face...would take me out of the moment.

"You're the beautiful one," I uttered.

"No." He wrapped his arm around me to hold my chin. "Look at yourself. Don't you see what I do? You're made of silk and flower petals, sweetness. You're soft and lovely all over."

He trailed his knuckles along my cheek and down my chest to cup my breast. "I dream about these. Your rosy nipples in my mouth, pressed against my chest, the cream of your pretty skin bouncing in my face. Silk and flower petals. Cream and sugar."

Sliding my hand over his, I held my breast with him, trying to see what he did. My silk and flower petals.

It didn't work. I couldn't think of myself that way. Knowing Jake saw my body as something like poetry was enough for me to appreciate it and understand why he liked it.

And I...I liked him. If he wanted me—to look at me and touch me—I would willingly hand myself over.

I watched him watch me with pure desire in his gaze as he thrust into me, deep and smooth. Colliding and parting, again and again, until my belly ached and filled, until I had to cover my mouth with my hand and bite down on my palm to stifle my cries. Warm lips on my shoulders and back and hot licks along my spine dragged me past the point of no return. I came around him, shuddering and shaking, falling limp on the counter.

Jake held on to my hips, plunging into me through my orgasm, and after, when I was sated and barely standing. He kept going, his deep strokes over my tender, sensitive flesh sending aftershocks through my limbs.

"Oh, fuck, Clara," he groaned. "Look at me. I need those eyes on me right now."

My eyelids sprang open like they were on a string and he was my puppet master. Our gazes locked. His bottom lip was clamped between his teeth, and he watched me like he was afraid I'd disappear if he blinked.

"Come on, Jake," I whispered. "Fill me up, baby."

My words were the tipping point. He drove in to the hilt and fell over me, groaning through his release. Then he gathered me in his arms and walked us to the tub, sitting on the edge with me in his lap. I rested my head on his shoulder, and he buried his nose in my hair. We sat like that for long minutes, our breathing steadying, my eyes growing heavy.

"I had a wreck of a day," I murmured. "You turned it around."

"Happy to," he gruffed.

I touched my lips to his throat. "Are you sure this is okay? Us being here with you and Sage?"

He hummed, his fingers slipping through my hair. "I wouldn't have told you to stay if it wasn't."

"We can talk about it more tomorrow," I reasoned.

"There's nothing to talk about." He tilted my chin up with his knuckle. "Are you ready for bed?"

"Yeah. I should probably put some clothes on, though."

His smile was soft, tender. "Probably."

We got redressed and tiptoed into the bedroom. Nellie was sound asleep on the air mattress, unaware of anything outside her dreams. Down the hall, Sage was sound asleep too. I curled up in Jake's bed, my head on his shoulder, his arm around me, holding me close.

He turned so his mouth grazed my temple. "Got all my people under my roof tonight. I'm going to sleep soundly."

My heart thumped, and I snuggled closer.

"Me too."

Chapter Thirty-One
Clara

I woke to an empty bedroom and the sound of giggles coming from the living room. Stretching my stiff limbs, I smiled. What a lovely way to wake up.

Once I snagged a pair of Jake's sweats, I ventured out to the living room, surprised at what I found. Sage was sitting on a chair, and Jake was standing behind her, braiding her hair in two plaits. Nellie was perched on Sage's lap, facing her, watching Jake's hands with rapt attention.

"Good morning, everyone." I walked over to Jake and kissed his arm. "Seems you've been hiding a secret talent from me."

"Morning, sweetness." Jake leaned over to kiss my head. "I've got a line formed. If you want a braid too, you have to get in the back of it."

I poked my bottom lip out, pretending to pout about waiting. "That's fair, I guess."

He chuckled. "No pouting in this house. It's a rule."

"Hi, Mommy," Nellie chirped. "I'm gonna get a braid like Sagie."

Sage tried to turn toward me, but Jake held her head steady. "Daddy watched a bunch of YouTube videos to teach himself how to do my hair. He's way better than my mom. He can even do fishtail braids."

I cocked a brow. "Fishtail, huh? That isn't in my repertoire."

"Marina braids my hair," Nellie said.

"That's true. I'm utterly inept at anything more complicated than a headband or ponytail."

Jake leaned into me again. "You never said whether you want a braid too."

I glanced at Sage, who was trying to nod despite her dad holding her head, then at Nellie, who was copying Sage.

"Well...I'll feel left out if all the girls are doing it. One braid, please."

Sage clapped. "Yesss. You guys have to come to my field hockey game so everyone can see us."

Jake's movements stilled for less than a heartbeat, but it was long enough for me to notice. Last night, he'd said there wasn't anything to talk about. Today was a new day, and we absolutely had to discuss how we were going to handle our kids going forward. But we couldn't have that discussion in front of them, and I got the sense from his hesitation he wasn't ready for us to play happy family at Sage's game.

"I would love that, honey, but I had a really long day yesterday and there are things I need to do at home." Her shoulders slumped, and I quickly thought of how I could cheer her up. "What if we take pictures together when we're all done? How's your dad with a camera?"

She wrinkled her nose, and Nellie copied her. It was so adorable I had to stop myself from squeezing them both.

"He doesn't get the right angle," Sage replied. "Selfies are better anyway."

Jake huffed under his breath. "Can't be good at everything." Then he patted Sage's shoulder. "All right, Ms. Critic. You're done. Next victim."

I knew Jake was patient. After all, he'd dealt with my reluctance without breaking a sweat and had waited for me to finally see what he already knew—that we'd be incredible together. But watching him do my wiggle worm's hair, never getting angry or annoyed when her silky strands slipped from his fingers from her constant movement, made me understand his level of patience was near godlike.

He gave Nellie two little braids in the front that crisscrossed into one large one trailing down her back. For only three and a half, she had a lot of hair, and he'd had no trouble taming it. When he was finished, she ran to the bathroom to see herself. Jake lifted her up to stand on the counter, and she gasped, her little hands pressing to her cheeks.

"Oh, I love it," she cooed. I swore, Jake melted at her "wuv it." He met my eyes in the mirror and shook his head. But I didn't miss his little grin or the way he let her examine her reflection for as long as she wanted before putting her back on the ground.

When it was my turn, his hands were firm but gentle, brushing through my bed-tangled strands until they were smooth. He braided the front from ear to ear, forming a headband. It wasn't my usual style, but he'd done it for me, so I loved it and would wear it like that all day.

When I got up from the chair, my limbs were loose and relaxed. I leaned into his chest and sighed. "Maybe I want all my hair braided. And when you finish, you can take them out and start all over."

He chuckled. "Liked that, did you, mama?"

"Yes. You have magic fingers."

He dipped to whisper in my ear. "Think you already knew that."

I shoved his chest, my cheeks aflame. "Shut it, you. There are children around."

He glanced over his shoulder. Nellie and Sage were packing up her duffel bag for field hockey, paying no attention to us.

"This was a good morning," he murmured.

"It was. I loved all of it."

"We'll do it again."

I nodded. "Nellie would love another sleepover."

He slipped his arm around my waist. "And her mom?"

I pushed up on my toes to graze his lips with mine. "I would love it too."

He kissed me firmly. "Then we'll make it happen."

منهم

"He braids." Bea stared at me, almost angry, like I was lying to her.

"He does!" I took out my phone to show her the selfies I took with the girls over the weekend. "See? Aren't we cute?"

"There's no proof Jake did this," Bea pointed out. "But yes, all of you are very cute."

Shira took the phone, murmuring how adorable we all were. I leaned over in my pedicure chair to scroll back a couple photos. I'd captured some action shots, which I was now happy for since I apparently needed proof my boyfriend was multifaceted.

"Okay, there's no denying this," Shira said, passing the phone back to Bea.

Bea hmphed. "Fine. He's incredible. I admit it."

I snorted at her dour tone. One day, a man was going to excite her when she least expected it, and I could not wait to see Bea all gooey and smitten. I wouldn't admit that to her, though, since I valued our friendship.

"He is." I smiled at the screen for a moment before sliding my purse away. "Which is why I'm terrified something's going to go wrong."

"It might," Shira said.

I nodded. "I know."

"You also might be struck by lightning," Bea added. "Does that stop you from using an umbrella in the rain?"

"Well, now I might." I had to laugh. "Thank you for putting things in perspective. Both of you."

Shira reached over and squeezed my hand. "It's okay to be scared. It's what you do when you're afraid that matters—and look at you. Moving on right alongside everything that scares you. It's there, but you're not letting it stop you. Take it from a woman who hides from her own shadow; you're doing great."

"Don't talk about my friend that way," I admonished gently.

She shrugged, giving me a small smile. "I think I'll get sky blue on my toes today."

"Nice choice, Shir." Bea fluffed her blue hair. "And brilliant change of subject, no segue or anything."

Shira shook her nail polish. "Pretty, right?"

I laughed. Shira was very shy, but if you paid attention, her personality shone, and she was terribly funny in her own low-key style. Not enough people gave her a chance, and it was a damn shame.

"Lovely," I agreed. "I'm going blue too."

Bea pointed to us both. "One time, friends. I'll allow it once, so long as you remember blue is mine."

"Sure, Beatrice," I agreed. "Have you run into your billionaire lately?"

"You mean besides you?" she drawled.

"Obviously."

She studied her nails. "There was an incident last week with a corkscrew."

Shira hissed. "Did you stab him?"

"No. He was in one piece as far as I could tell. His car, on the other hand..." She flicked her fingers. "I was walking Benjamin in the park"—her gray Staffy who was more hippo than dog—"and we came across some boys attempting to open a juice box with a corkscrew."

"As one does," Shira murmured.

"Mmhmm. If they'd been teenagers, I wouldn't have intervened. Because, let's be honest, most teen boys deserve a little humbling via bloodletting. But these boys couldn't have been older than ten. So, I helped them, properly stabbing the juice, then confiscated the corkscrew."

"I bet they loved that," I said.

"Oh, they did." Bea smirked. "But since I was saving their lives, I decided to commit to the act and tossed the corkscrew into a trash can on my way out of the park."

"And then...?" Shira raised her brows expectantly. None of Bea's stories ended so merrily when it involved her mysterious billionaire.

"Then the corkscrew ricocheted off the inside of the trash can and flew into the road, piercing the tire of a limo idling at the curb," she deadpanned.

Shira gasped. "Was it *his*?"

She nodded. "His driver got out to inspect the damage. I didn't stick around for his assessment."

I snorted. "Well, he *is* worth billions. Surely he can afford a new tire."

She pointed to me. "Exactly my line of thinking."

"Wait—you recognized the driver?" Shira asked, incredulous since Bea hadn't actually seen the billionaire from the front.

"Of course. We're old friends. Formally met six or seven months ago, after a guy on a bike told me I was dazzling then crashed into a woman carrying a tray of coffees. They went flying through the air and landed on the windshield of the limo waiting at the traffic light." Her nonchalance was truly a thing of beauty. "The driver's name is Igor, by the way."

I narrowed my eyes. "You never told me this story."

"It wasn't that exciting." She let her head fall back and sighed as her technician massaged her calves.

I exchanged glances with Shira, laughing silently at our friend. We could have both used a little more of her *laissez-faire* attitude. It was probably what had drawn us to her in the first place.

If only being carefree was contagious. My work life required me to be as careful and methodical as possible. Unfortunately, I'd allowed that to spill over to my real life, and I was sick of it.

My phone alerted me to a text. I smiled when I checked the screen.

Jake: *Dinner tonight. I'll bring the beer. You bring your pretty face.*

Me: *I like how you invite yourself over.*

Jake: *I like it too, so I hope there's no sarcasm behind those words.*

Me: *None at all. I like you wanting to see me.*

Jake: *Always. Tell Nell-Belle I've got a special drink for her.*

Me: *Not beer, I hope.*

Jake: *Haha, nope. Found her some lavender lemonade. She told me her favorite color is purple. Has that changed in the last couple days?*

My breath caught, and I had to pinch my nose so I didn't do something stupid like cry in the middle of the nail salon.

Me: *Not yet. It's still her very favorite. She'll love that.*

Jake: *All right. Can't wait to see her smile. See you tonight, sweetness.*

I closed my eyes and sank down in my chair, my heart a wild, throbbing thing.

If I could have, I would have channeled some of Bea's fearlessness. Then, I wouldn't have been so afraid of tumbling head over heels for Jake Hayes since that was exactly what I was doing.

Chapter Thirty-Two
Jake

I t was strange to see Roman Wells leaving my brother's office.

Not that the man was out of place at the MZ offices. With his impeccably tailored suit and sharklike movements, he looked like he went where he wanted and took ownership. The thing was, there was no discernible reason for this man to be visiting Jeremy. As far as I knew, they weren't friends or associates. Jeremy didn't tell me every detail of his life, but I was aware of most of it.

Roman strode toward me, where I had paused on the way to my office. His grin wasn't exactly friendly, nor was it threatening.

"Ah, the other Hayes brother. It's about time we met." He held his hand out to me. When I frowned at it, he introduced himself. "Sorry, I shouldn't assume anyone knows who I am. Roman Wells."

I shook his hand out of obligation. "Jake Hayes, but you seem to know that."

He chuckled, but it was perfunctory more than a reaction to something humorous. "I would expect I do. After all, we're partners, aren't we?"

I did not let my shock show. My molars might've ground to dust, but I managed to keep my expression neutral.

"Nice to meet you, Roman. I need to get back to work."

He nodded at the bag in my hand. "Working lunch?"

I'd been looking forward to the sandwich I'd grabbed from a deli down the street, but now the idea of eating made my stomach roil.

"Something like that," I answered. "Have a good day."

I beelined to Jeremy's office, knocking once before letting myself in. He was at his desk, surprise crinkling his forehead when he saw me.

"Hey. I thought you were out to lunch with Clara."

"Mmm. That had been the plan, but she called when I was on my way to cancel."

This was my week with Sage, so we only had lunches to spend together. We both guarded them like flames in the wind, but sometimes things came up. Today, it was an emergency meeting about Rossi's Utah factory.

"Ah. That's too bad." He folded his hands on his desk, blinking up at me. "It seems like something's on your mind. How about you sit down so I'm not breaking my neck looking up at you?"

Bracing my hands on the edge of his desk, I leaned forward, putting my face a few inches from his. "I saw Roman Wells, Jer. He introduced himself as my partner. Let's not beat around the bush—you scheduled whatever meeting you just had when you thought I'd be out of the office. What the fuck is going on?"

He swallowed hard, but that was his only tell. Otherwise, he was cool and composed, gesturing for me to take a seat. I finally gave in. Me being in his face like I was didn't do either of us any good.

Once settled, one ankle braced on the opposite knee, I nodded. "Go on. I want to hear what you have to say to me."

He flattened his hands and sighed heavily, dropping them to his lap. "When we had to close those stores two years ago, I knew we needed to do something drastic. We can't keep closing stores and expect to be around long term."

"I know this," I stated. "It's why we're going after Rossi—to breathe new life into MZ."

"That's this year. Last year...well, to be frank, things weren't getting better. Dad suggested taking out a loan, but the last thing we needed was to bleed out paying back loans. Then I met Roman at a charity golf tournament. His reputation precedes him—"

"For sinking money into failing companies and sucking them dry when he's done. Yeah, I've heard of him."

He exhaled slowly and rubbed the center of his forehead. "That's categorically untrue. Roman revives failing businesses."

I blinked at him. "You think we're failing?"

He leveled me with his gaze. "No. But it was where we were headed. So, I talked to Roman, and he'd been willing to buy ten percent of my shares. It'd been exactly what we'd needed. And with his money, he brought ideas. The new branding was from his team. The Rossi deal? All Roman. And—"

"You didn't think this was something I should have known? You brought me on to support you. How can I support you when you're keeping secrets?"

"I knew you wouldn't be happy about my decision. Honestly, I was afraid you'd offer up your own shares so you'd have a reason to leave."

I chuffed. "Since when do we avoid tough talks? I'm sitting here in a suit because you asked me to be. There's nothing you can't say to me. If we're in trouble, we figure it out together. You don't plan underhanded meetings with the vampire of Denver and make me look like an idiot when it's plain to see I have no idea what's going on with my own company."

Heat rose up his neck to his cheeks. "Sometimes I have to make tough decisions, Jake. Granddad handed MZ to me. If it fails, *I* fail. I won't let that happen."

"You think I want it to fail?"

"I don't think it would devastate you. This all disappears, you go back to being a car guy, living the life you always wanted. Maybe with a little less money, but you have your very own heiress now."

"Fuck off with that, Jer." I stood over him again, jabbing at his desk. "That's the last time you bring up Clara."

He leaned back to look up at me. "You're right. That was low. I shouldn't have said that. I'm stressed, and you've got me cornered. Lashing out was wrong, though."

"A whole lot is wrong in this scenario." I'd walked in here pissed off, hoping he'd have a logical explanation for me. Now, I was more fired up. Angry. And more than that, disappointed in my brother. "I am here because you asked me to be. I would do a fucking backbend for you. If you're not willing to see that and do the same for me, you're spitting in my face. Don't tell me losing MZ would be no skin off my back, as if I don't care about you, about our family's legacy."

"I believe you care about MZ, and I would never question that you care about me, but...you didn't grow up being told all this rested on your shoulders. It's a heavy load to carry. If I don't turn this ship around, it's not just me going under. Thousands of livelihoods will be lost. You may not agree with me bringing Roman in—"

"You didn't give me a chance to agree or disagree."

His lids lowered as he took a deep breath. "Maybe that was a mistake, but like I said, this rests on *my* shoulders, which means there will be times I make a unilateral decision."

"That's fine." It didn't feel fine, but he was right. In the end, our grandfather had left control of the company to the legitimate heir. I stood at his side, but the yoke was his alone.

"I'm glad you agree," he intoned.

I moved my jaw side to side, no less pissed than when I'd walked in here. "You're the boss, Jer. I get that. But if you keep secrets concerning MZ from me again, I'm out of here."

His nostrils flared—the only sign he was getting mad too. "You say you care about MZ and me then threaten to leave in the same breath."

"It wasn't a threat. I've drawn my line in the sand, and there's no reason for you to cross it."

He lowered his chin. "We'll talk about this later."

I straightened, shoving my fists in my trouser pockets. "You don't keep secrets, we won't need to have another conversation like this."

"I hear you."

I walked out on my brother, but I didn't feel any better. If he'd punched me in the gut, I would have been less winded. What he'd said to me in there, the way he'd looked—that wasn't the brother I knew.

He had me thinking maybe there was a side to him I didn't know at all.

Crickets chirped outside my open windows, a cool breeze rustling the curtains. Sage was tucked in her room, probably reading one of the books in her many stacks. I was in bed, TV on, but I couldn't focus.

Picking up my phone, I texted the one person I wanted next to me.

Me: *Hey, mama. You in bed?*

Clara: *Hey, baby. Not even close. I'm working in my office. What are you up to?*

Christ, I liked when she called me "baby." Never thought I'd be into that, but coming from Clara, it was the sweetest thing.

Me: *My girl works too hard. I'm lying in bed, thinking about you. After my wreck of a day, I'm wishing you were here.*

Clara: *I'd rather be there with you too. Want to talk about it?*

Me: *My brother...it's a lot. You're working. We can talk about it another time. Just wish I could hold you for a minute. That would make it all go away.*

I waited for a reply, but seconds turned to minutes and nothing came through. She was probably caught up in what she was doing. I'd hear from her when she had the chance.

Settling against my pillows, I picked up the remote and flipped to a movie I'd seen a few times. Nothing I needed to pay close attention to. Exactly what I needed since my mind was scattered and worn out.

My eyelids were drooping when my phone pinged with a text. I picked it up, rubbing my eyes as I read it.

Clara: *Are you still awake?*

Me: *Yeah, I'm here.*

Clara: *Good. Come outside for a minute.*

Heart thrashing, I vaulted out of bed and jogged for the front door. I threw it open, and there she was, bundled in a fuzzy sweater, leaning against my porch railing.

"You're here." I felt like I was dreaming.

"Of course I am." She held her hand out, beckoning me to her.

I stood in front of her, ghosting my hand over her hair. "You're here," I repeated.

"I am." Her arms wrapped around my middle, and she pressed her face to my chest. "I missed you, and when you said you wanted to hold me for a minute, I thought that sounded like the best idea I'd heard all day."

I clutched her tight, burying my face in her hair. "You came here because I wanted to hold you?"

"Mmmhmm. I particularly like being held by you, Jake Hayes."

I laughed, but it was wet and thready. She had me choked up like an idiot. This woman turned me inside out.

"You're the cure, Clara," I murmured to the top of her head. "You make it all fade."

She kissed the center of my chest and stroked my back in slow, steady drags. Bit by bit, I curled around her as the tension drained away.

We stayed like that for a while before sitting in one of my rocking chairs. Clara settled sideways in my lap, her feet tucked under one of my legs. She was in her pajamas—a tank top, floral pants, flip-flops on her feet.

I ran my hand along her leg, smiling at the cute little flower pattern. "You rushed over here, didn't you?"

"A little. I stopped to ask Marina to listen out for Nellie. Maybe driving in my PJs wasn't the best idea, but—"

"No, it was. I can pretend I'm going to take you inside and put you in my bed in a little while."

"Wouldn't that be nice?" She sighed. "At least we have this."

I slid my fingers through her silky hair, studying the way the shadows played on her face. In the dim porch light, I couldn't see nearly enough of her, but beggars couldn't be choosers.

"Thank you for coming over. I hadn't expected it, and you're exactly what I needed tonight."

She slowly stroked my beard, her eyes darting between mine. "Did something happen?"

"Yeah. It did." I held a strand of her hair between my fingers, rubbing my thumb back and forth over it. "Jeremy sold part of his shares of MZ last year and never told me. He purposely hid it from me. I didn't find out until I ran into his investor today."

"Shit," she muttered. "Roman Wells."

Closing my eyes, I nodded. "I guess your lawyers' due diligence had turned that up."

"Yes. I never would have guessed you didn't know, though."

"Before today, I wouldn't have either. Never would have guessed my own brother would accuse me of wanting MZ to fail so I could go back to my old life."

"That's harsh. Wow."

"Yeah. Messed me up to hear that from him."

She leaned into me, gliding her hand from my beard to wrap around my neck. "He must know the sacrifice you made to be there with him instead of doing what you want. Every time you put on a suit instead of coveralls, you're showing how committed you are despite it bringing you no joy. He knows that, doesn't he?"

"I don't need my job to bring me joy."

"It would be better not to be miserable, I think."

I cracked my eyes open. "'Miserable' is an overstatement. I want to be there with Jeremy."

"I know you do. You made a sacrifice for him, but it doesn't sound like he really appreciates it."

"Doesn't matter if he does. It's what I have to do."

"But why?" she whispered.

"Because I had a really good life where I could be whoever the hell I wanted. When I got Carly pregnant, my family rallied around me and promised we'd make it work. That was how it always was. But my brother—my own *brother*—didn't have that. Where I had warmth and acceptance, all he got was cold and discipline. If he messed up, it was his obligation to fix it. Neither of us had done anything to earn the families we were born into. It was the luck of the draw, and his hand lacked in every way."

There were a lot of reasons our grandfather gave Jeremy MZ and not his own son, our father. The main one, which went unsaid because we all knew it: Martin Hayes was a piece of shit. An angry drunk, a neglectful father, irresponsible with his money, he was no more capable of running a large corporation than a child. Jeremy had been molded for the position from his youth. Our grandfather had plotted his schooling, hobbies, and even the clubs he joined.

"You feel guilty," Clara surmised.

"Yeah, I guess. But that's not my biggest driving point. I'm there with Jeremy because he's never faltered in being there for me. He could've hated me for everything I had, but he didn't. He never turned on me or became resentful. He was at the hospital when Sage was born. He read baby books and helped me change diapers. Even now, he rarely misses one of her games. He's there for me, so I'm gonna be there for him."

"Okay."

Her acceptance wasn't easy. Her doubts rang out in her questions, but she chose to let it go. It was obvious she didn't agree with my point of view, but it was just as obvious my mind was made up.

"Clara..." My lips touched her eyelids and the tip of her nose. "Thank you for letting it go. Don't know how to say how much I appreciate you letting my reasons stand."

"I didn't come here to argue with you, baby." She nuzzled my throat and jaw, sighing against my skin. "I like understanding you. I don't have to always agree with you so long as I understand."

"And you do?"

"Yeah," she breathed. "I'm sorry your day sucked."

I kissed her temple once, twice, three times. "I honestly don't remember what made it suck so bad anymore. Not with you here."

"I'm really, really glad I could be here for you."

Something told me Clara would always be there when I needed her. It was who she was, what made her *her*.

We rocked for a while longer, content to be in each other's arms without a lot of talking. When she had to go, it wasn't easy. It never was. But these days, watching her drive away was becoming harder and harder.

Something had to change.

And it was up to me to figure out what that change would be.

CHAPTER
THIRTY-THREE
Clara

The honey guy looked incredibly disappointed Bea wasn't with me today. He handed over our honey sticks with the glummest expression I'd ever seen on a man. It would have been funny if it weren't a little sad.

As we walked away, Jake slid his arm around my waist. "What was up with that guy? He always looks like someone peed in his cereal."

I snorted a laugh. "No. I think he was looking for Bea. Poor guy doesn't know he's better off she's not here. She would chew him up and spit him right out."

He chuckled. "I think that's very true."

Jake had been introduced to Bea and Shira during brunch at my place a few weeks ago. To me, it had been interesting to see three distinctly different people get to know one another. Jake had been gentle with Shira, and once he'd gotten the feel of Bea, he hadn't let her give him any guff.

Before they left, Shira had said she liked him very much, and Bea had shrugged. *"He's nice to Nellie, and he's smart enough to see your value. So what if he's chronically good-looking? Not everyone can be perfect."*

From Bea, that was the highest of praise. Had she ever met Miller, she would have laughed him out of the room. Then again, if Miller had still been around, I would have been a different person and truly doubted I would have been open to a friendship with Bea or have grown as close to Shira.

I would never voluntarily choose to go through everything I had because of Miller, but deep down, I knew it had been worth it. *Look what I have now.*

"Jake!" Nellie called from her stroller. "Out, please?"

"Peas," I murmured.

Jake grinned at me. "She'll start saying it the right way far too soon."

"Don't remind me. I can't think about her being Sage's age."

Jake unbuckled Nellie from her stroller and put her feet on the ground. She shook her head, holding her arms out to him.

"Up, please," she demanded sweetly.

He scooped her up without hesitating. "Like this or higher?"

She kicked her feet excitedly. "Higher. I wanna go up."

Jake had the dad maneuver down, plopping her on his shoulders like he'd done it a thousand times. Knowing him, he'd probably had Sage up there until she'd gotten too big and independent. Thinking about that made my stomach twist wistfully. For what, I wasn't sure.

We strolled around the farmers' market, buying fruit and veggies for the week and looking at craft vendors. Jake bought Nellie a doll matching the one Shira had given her since she'd claimed she needed it and me a bouquet of flowers he'd claimed *I* needed.

By the time he got to the cheesemonger, he'd slipped Nellie off his shoulders and into his arms. She was getting tired but refused her stroller and frankly wanted nothing to do with me when she could have Jake. Her head rested on his chest, and her little body was nestled firmly against him. He carried her around like it was no big deal, but my heart was a wild thing, wanting to leap out and claim this man as our own. The pit in my gut echoed with panic though, because he wasn't ours to keep.

"Daddy?"

I turned around from examining the choices of cheese to find Sage and Carly almost upon us. Carly was smiling and Sage had a perplexed expression.

"Hey, Sagie." Jake held his arm out to his daughter, pulling her into his side as soon as he could reach her. "What a nice surprise, kid."

"We came to buy you cheese," she stated.

I tapped my head. "I guess great minds think alike, huh?" I reached into my bag slung on the back of the stroller and pulled out a few honey sticks. "Have you hit the honey stand yet? We practically cleaned them out. Want one?"

Carly plucked a stick from my hand. "I love these." She leaned in and air-kissed my cheeks. "Thank you. Long time no see. Jake's been hiding you guys."

It sort of felt that way too. Since the emergency sleepover at his place, we hadn't seen Sage, and that had been over a month ago. Jake's walls were firmly in place, and it bothered me at times, but he'd been patient with me so I could give him the space and time he needed. I just hoped he'd feel safe enough to crack open his world sooner rather than later.

Carly tickled Nellie's arm. "Hi, sweetie. You look sleepy."

"She is," I answered for her. "The fresh air always knocks her out."

"Sage is here." Nellie lifted her head with great effort and waved at her friend. "Hi, Sagie."

Sage tugged on Nellie's foot. "Hi, Nellie. Is my dad comfy?"

"Yeah." Nellie flopped against Jake's chest. "My Jake."

Carly laughed, light and carefree. "Well, I guess she's claimed you, huh? Too cute." She patted her daughter's head. "Want a honey stick, babe?"

"Oh." Sage's brows were drawn together. "Yeah, sure." She carefully chose one from me, her eyes flicking to mine. "Thank you, Clara."

"No problem."

Jake still had his arm around his daughter, but she pushed away from him a little, giving herself room.

"I can't believe you're here," Sage said. "It's weird. I didn't think you even knew where the farmers' market was."

"Your dad knows a lot of things," Jake joked. "But, really, this is my first time. It was Clara's idea. Turned out to be the best idea ever since I get to hang out with you. Want to show me all the cheese choices?"

She lifted a shoulder. "I guess I could do that. If I leave it to you, you might pick a bad one."

Carly and I fell back and found a seat on a bench, letting them have a moment together. Well...with Nellie too, since she was firmly attached to Jake. But she was halfway to falling asleep and didn't have many opinions about cheese, so she'd probably be a pretty silent companion.

"Sage says she never sees you guys," Carly said.

I smoothed my hands over my linen pants, uncertain of how much I should say. "That's true. We mainly hang out during the weeks she's with you."

She nodded. "Obviously, he and Nellie have bonded."

"Yeah. They're buddies." I opened and closed my fingers. "To be honest, I'm flying blind here. This is my first time dating as a single parent, and I'm not sure I'm doing it right. It feels like it, but then Jake's doing the complete opposite, so—"

She put her hand over mine. "Jake dated a real bitch who fucked him up. Excuse my language, but that's the truth."

I laughed. "Your language is fine. I'm glad you don't beat around the bush."

"Never." She laughed too. "Push him a little. He's got to get over that experience, and I can tell you're the real deal. Push him. Tell him you want more and he needs to get off his ass to provide it to you. If I trust you around my daughter, there's no reason for him not to."

My brow winged. "You trust me?"

"Sure. You're a mom, and you're just as sweet to my girl as you are yours. Jake probably does too, you know? The fact is, Sage is good. She bounced back in no time after the bitch left. Jake was the one who was flattened. Not that she was any great love; he'd just been blindsided by it all—that she could be there one day and gone the next. I don't think that's you. Even if it doesn't work out—"

I shook my head. "I was blindsided too. I'd never do that to anyone else."

She squeezed my hand. "I'm sorry that happened to you. I bet you had people who pushed you, didn't you?"

My brother, sister-in-law, parents, Bea, Shira, even Marina. They had all pushed me to move on. To reach for happiness with both hands.

"Yes. A whole team of people."

"Good for you, girl." She nudged me with her shoulder. "Don't worry. I'm going to push his stubborn ass. Obviously, his team hasn't been after him enough. I'm on it now."

"Does anyone say no to you?" I asked.

She grinned. "Not if I can help it."

When we got back to my house, I put Nellie down for a nap and joined Jake on the deck, his feet kicked up on the rail, his hands clasped at his middle. I tucked myself beside him on the padded bench, resting my head on his shoulder.

"Do you know I love Carly?"

He let out a startled chuckle. "Do you? Why's that?"

"She's just so blunt yet peppy. She reminds me of Saoirse."

His eyes narrowed on me. "What were the two of you talking about?"

"You."

He took my chin between his fingers. "Don't know if I like you teaming up with her. It could be dangerous."

"Considering I only see her at random, I don't think you have to worry about us forming a team. We'd have to see each other far more often for that."

His eyes swept over me like he was looking for something. Up and down, left and right, he examined me.

"You want to see Carly more?"

"It's not that." I pressed my lips together. "I think…I would like to be let in to your world a little more. Only having every other week with you is becoming more and more difficult for me."

His eyes darted with what I feared was panic, so I hurried to amend and backpedal.

"I'm not asking for a massive change, and I would never want to interfere with your time with Sage. I know how important that is to you. But maybe, when you're comfortable, we could have a dinner or two together, the four of us. Or maybe Nellie and I could come to one of her games. I want to know that part of you and not feel like you're living a completely separate life I'm not privy to."

His jaw rippled with tension, but he kept his hand on my face, cupping it with tenderness.

"I know things have to shift." He nodded like he was agreeing with himself. "And as glad as I am to have my girl with me during her weeks, I miss the hell out of you and Nellie."

"We miss you too," I said softly.

"Something was up with Sage today, seeing us like that. I need to talk to her and think this over." His lips grazed mine with a sweet little kiss. "Is that enough for you?"

"Yes." If I pushed him too hard, he'd retreat. "I'm not going anywhere, Jake, whether you like it or not."

Groaning, he hauled me onto his lap and buried his face in my neck. "Oh, I like it, mama, and you're right. You're absolutely not going anywhere, not unless I'm with you."

I wrapped my arms around him, melting into his embrace. There was a twinge in my chest that took me a moment to identify.

Hope.

It might take time, but maybe this was going to work out after all.

CHAPTER THIRTY-FOUR

Jake

S age was back with me the day after the farmers' market. She went about her normal business, but she did it quietly. Sure, she still had stories about what Cleo and Dex had gotten into over the past week, but she wasn't bursting to release every word. There was something pensive about her, which was unusual. That wasn't to say Sage wasn't a thinker. My girl just did most of her thinking out loud.

I let her have space. If she had something on her mind, I trusted she'd come to me with it.

That finally happened over dinner. We made pizzas together with the cheese we'd bought the day before. Once they were done, we brought our slices out back to the deck. I felt her staring at me as I took my first bite. She nibbled at her own pizza for a minute or two before putting it down with a sigh.

"Dad?"

"Yeah?"

"Can I ask a question?"

"Always. Anything you need to ask."

She scratched her cheek, her eyebrows furrowing. "Maybe it's not a question so much as something I figured out."

I put my plate down on the table beside me and turned to face her. "All right. Shoot."

"When I saw you with Clara and Nellie yesterday, it made me feel weird. I had to think about it for a while because I couldn't really understand why my stomach ached. Last night, in bed, I realized it was because you hang out with them when I'm not around, maybe do fun stuff with them, and I don't know anything about it. If I hadn't run into you at the farmers' market, I wouldn't have known you were there."

"I get that. You can always ask me what I do during the week. I'll tell you."

She had her T-shirt bunched around her fist like she was nervous. I hated her feeling that way around me, but this was pretty new territory for both of us.

"You hang out with Clara and Nellie a lot? Like, you don't just go on dates with Clara; you see her daughter too?"

I nodded. "Not every day, but a few times a week the three of us have dinner. Sometimes, I'm there for breakfast too."

"And you go out on the weekends?"

"We're not going to amusement parks, Sagie. Nellie's little. We take her to parks or on short hikes. She usually just tags along with Clara and me."

Her hands clutched at her stomach, and she turned her head, not looking at me. "I felt weird when you were holding her. But I didn't feel weird when she fell asleep on you at our house."

God, this girl. So bright, too wise for her ol' dad. She was so good at expressing herself, even when the feelings and concepts were bigger than her.

I treaded carefully with my sensitive soul. "Why do you think that is?"

She shrugged, but she knew. With a deep breath, she let the words out. "I'm jealous, Daddy."

I took her hand in mine, holding it tight. "That makes sense. You know I love you and you're always my priority."

"I know." She sniffed and turned back to me. "I like Clara and Nellie. I want you to have them; I just...why can't I be a part of it too?"

That hadn't been where I'd thought this was going. Not at all. She could have smacked me in the face, and I would have been less surprised.

"You...want to?"

"Yeah," she whispered. "Why don't you want me to? Or does Clara not want me around?"

My laugh was choked and ragged. I had to take a breath to swallow back my emotions. The last thing I wanted was for Sage to feel like she wasn't a vital piece of an important part of my life. It's what I'd been protecting her against. Yet, here we were, exactly where I hadn't wanted to end up. All because I was an idiot too shortsighted to see the forest for the trees.

"Not at all, baby. We both want you around. In fact, Clara was just asking me yesterday if the four of us could start having dinners a couple times a week."

Her eyes brightened like a whole different kid was sitting next to me. "Did you tell her yes?"

"I told her I needed to talk to you. We have to take it slow this time around."

Her brow knitted. "Why? I mean, you've been dating Clara for ages now. It's not like she's a stranger or anything."

"No. She's not a stranger. I trust her very much, and I would like you two to get to know each other. But I'm being cautious. I can't forget how sad you were after Andrea disappeared on us. You thought it was your fault, and I swore I'd never put you in that situation again."

She rolled her eyes at me. "That was a long time ago, and I was a little kid. I understand if Clara breaks up with you, it'll be because you messed up." She wagged her finger. "Don't mess up, Dad, and we won't have to worry about it."

I threw my hands up. "I don't like how this has all gotten turned around on me."

"Well, you tried to put the blame on me, so I guess we're even."

Her casual accusation was a shot to the solar plexus, sending me falling against my chair. *Fuck.* She wasn't wrong, and it stung to admit I'd used my own daughter as a scapegoat. Not that Sage hadn't had her heart broken back when my ex left, but I'd hung on to that faded memory with such a tight grip, it was in tatters now. Now that my eyes had been opened by my too-wise daughter, I had to admit my own hang-ups had been a big part of me holding back.

If I screwed up and lost Clara, it wouldn't be an easy recovery for me. My heart was fiending to be hers, but I'd kept it restrained. Because I knew, *knew* once I fully gave in to this, allowed her to become an integral part of my life, I would never be the same.

I was still kidding myself, though. The days without seeing Clara felt unfinished and off-kilter. It didn't matter that I'd still had walls up when I'd opened a gate to allow her in. This final step, this arbitrary space I was keeping between us, was my last feeble attempt at self-preservation.

Sage continued talking. "Besides, Clara's a mom. She wouldn't just leave me in the dust if she got tired of you. Moms like her wouldn't do something like that."

That was a simplistic way to look at things, but the kid was only thirteen. And she wasn't wrong. Even if I couldn't keep Clara, she'd be gentle with Sage. It was who she was and why I'd fallen so fucking hard for her.

"She wouldn't," I agreed. "So, you think we should invite them over for dinner this week?"

"I do. And they could sleep over if you want." She picked up her pizza. "Nellie could sleep in my room this time."

"Maybe." I smiled at how eager she was to finally get her sleepover with Nellie. "Let me talk to Clara about it, see what she says."

"Ask her if I can come to her house too." She swiped a hand in front of herself. "But don't tell her I asked, okay? 'Cause that's probably rude. I just bet she has a really nice house, and I want to be able to picture where you're spending your time when you're over there without me."

I cupped the back of her head and leaned over to kiss her forehead. "How did I ever get so lucky to have a kid like you?"

"Don't know. You must've done something right." She smirked. "I can't think of what that could be, though..."

"Are you mouthing off to me while in noogie position?" I brought my fist to the top of her head. "Are you asking for trouble, Sagie?"

"Nooo," she squealed, pulling away from me. Her arms went over her head to protect herself. "I hate noogies with the passion of a thousand burning suns. Besides, I'm too old for them."

"Nah, you're never too old for a noogie. Sometimes, I put Uncle Jer in a headlock and rub the hell out of his head. He loves it."

She giggled. "No he doesn't. I don't believe you."

My brows winged. "Oh, so when he's calling me an a-hole, you think he means it?"

That earned me a groan. "Oh my god, Dad, you're such a weirdo. *No one* likes noogies. That's a scientific fact."

"It's a scientific fact I love you."

Her cheeks flushed with rosy happiness. "I know."

My head tilted. "And...?"

"I love you too...obviously."

⚘

After two successful dinners during the week, one at my place, one at Clara's, Friday night was our first intentional sleepover. Nellie was crashed out on Sage's trundle bed, and Sage was reading on her e-reader.

Sage whispered good night to me with a big grin on her face as I eased into the hallway. My girl was pleased as punch to have her little friend with her. Nellie had been just as thrilled to sleep in a "big girl bed" next to Sage.

Something settled inside me, having everyone under my roof, just as it had the first time. This whole week, my mood had mellowed. I'd even found it easy to move on from the argument I'd had with

Jeremy. That was how I knew this was right. Taking this step with Clara was what we were supposed to be doing.

I walked into my bedroom, spotting Clara in the en suite bathroom, the door open. When she heard me approaching, she turned around, body butter in one hand, face wash in the other.

I leaned against the doorframe and crossed my arms. "What's happening, mama?"

"These are the things I use." She held up the skincare. "At first, I thought it was a coincidence that my face cream was here, but then I looked through the drawers and in the shower. Everything's the same. It's all my stuff. How—?"

I went to her, hooking my arm around her waist. "I took notes. Wrote down everything at your place so you'd have it here too."

Clara took care of her skin, and with what she used, I'd known it came with a hefty price tag, but *damn*, I hadn't been prepared. That didn't mean I skimped. In fact, I bought double of her body butter. That was for me as much as it was for her, though, since I got to run my hands over her supple skin after she lathered it with thick lotion.

Her blinks were rapid, and her pretty mouth was parted in an *O*. "But why?"

"I like having you under my roof, like falling asleep and waking up with you. I want you to be comfortable here so you'll come around often. That means making it so you don't have to pack a bag like you're on a trip." I ran my nose along hers, and her breath caught. "I want you to feel just as at home here as you do at your place."

Her mouth opened and closed before she sighed and leaned into me. "This was incredibly thoughtful, baby. Thank you so much. I love being here."

"You're very welcome." I plucked the tub of body butter out of her hand. "Did you put this on yet?"

"Not yet. I got sidetracked looking at everything."

"Let me do it for you."

"Okay." She bit her lip. "In here?"

I took her hand in mine. "Nope. On the bed. Pajamas off, sweetness."

Coming to a stop at the foot of my bed, we faced each other. Clara pulled her T-shirt over her head and shimmied out of her sleep shorts and panties. I cupped one of her heavy breasts, lifting it to my mouth to suck her beaded nipple. Her fingers delved into my hair, holding me there as my lips traveled over one creamy globe to the other. I'd never get enough of the feel of her—not even if she was in my bed for the next hundred years.

"Lie face down."

The act of her climbing onto my bed and crawling to the center almost undid me. The sway of her hips and generous ass lit me from the inside out.

Once she was on her belly, I kicked off my pants and joined her, straddling her legs. With a scoop of lotion shared between my hands, I rubbed it into her back in slow swirls, starting at her shoulders and working my way down. Her soft moans urged me to keep going. I took my time on her, massaging her muscles, making sure every inch was well-lathered and cared for. When I reached her ass, I used more lotion to knead her soft, addictive flesh, my erection resting at the valley between her cheeks.

Soon, I would get to bury myself there, but not yet.

Her hips rocked back and forth like she was seeking something more than I was giving her. She'd have it. I never left her wanting.

I lifted off her to smooth my palms down the back of her thighs, getting them nice and evenly coated. I worked my way down to her feet, digging my thumbs into the soles, earning more moans from her. A different kind, but no less potent.

I gave her ass a tap. "On your back, beautiful. Let me see the rest of you."

She rolled over, her arms lazing above her head, her legs falling open. My mission was almost sidetracked by her glistening pink slit, needy for my tongue and cock, but I managed to keep my head on.

With lotion on my fingertips, I drew lines over her breasts and rubbed it in with my palms. I got lost in what I was doing, molding her soft flesh, tweaking her sweet little nipples. Eyes closed, her lips parted to let out a low moan.

With reluctance, I moved away from her breasts to her sloped tummy, giving it some much-needed attention. Her breath caught, muscles clenching as I caressed around her belly button before moving lower, over the outer curve of her hips to the small scar above her trimmed thatch of dark, silky hair.

"Beautiful," I murmured, running my fingertip over that little line. When I raised my eyes, Clara was watching me, her lower lip caught between her teeth. "You're beautiful."

She released her lip, and her tongue peeked out to wet it. "What are you doing to me?"

"Taking care of you like I need to."

Driving us both out of our minds. But we had all night. Our worlds were here, inside these walls. There was nothing for us to worry about.

Finally, *finally*, we had the time to get lost in one another.

Chapter Thirty-Five
Clara

I'd been lotioned and caressed from my collarbone down to the tips of my toes. Jake had rubbed every muscle and touched every inch of me. I had never felt so utterly cared for. Or as turned on and needy.

Jake had endless patience. If not for his thick erection bobbing against his taut stomach, angry and weeping, I would have thought this wasn't affecting him the same way it was me. He hadn't paid any attention to it, though, too intent on making me feel as good as he could.

He'd succeeded. Now, I just needed him.

"Come here please." I opened my legs to him and used two fingers to spread my lower lips—something I never would have done before. He'd turned me brazen. He made me want to show and give him everything—and that meant my body as well.

"I'm coming for you, mama," he gritted out.

Instead of falling between my thighs and driving into me, he took me by the hips, flipped me over, and buried his face in my pussy and ass. He wasn't neat and tidy as he laved me with his tongue. He was wet and messy, licking me with abandon. I clawed at the sheets and muffled my moans in the mattress. He'd worked me up so thoroughly, all it took was a swipe of his tongue over my clit for oblivion to shine like a beacon behind my eyelids.

Then he pressed his index finger against my tight ring of muscle, slipping inside easily with the aid of my arousal, and I detonated. White light went off like a million flashes inside my head as he fucked me with his finger and licked my aching clit until I couldn't take it anymore. My orgasm wrung me out yet left me hollow. I needed him to fill me.

He didn't keep me waiting long. His chest to my back, legs bracketing mine, he plunged into me from behind. Slow and intimate, he moved in and out like all we had was time. As he fucked me, his lips barely left my skin. Kissing my shoulders, the side of my face—anywhere he could reach. Reverence and desire blended into the perfect mix, making me feel cherished and wanted. God, I couldn't remember ever feeling like this. Not even close.

He made it impossible to hide any part of myself. Even the pieces I'd thought were shut off forever had been pried open. He had me. Fully. Completely. My trust, my heart, my thoughts—they were all his.

"God, Clara," he murmured next to my ear. "I don't think I'll ever have my fill of you."

"You better not."

"Never," he vowed. "This pussy, this body, your voice, that little smile you're giving me...it's all too sweet. I'm so stuck on you."

"Jake, please," I whimpered. "Please, I need you."

"You have me."

And I did. He was touching me everywhere, surrounding me, covering me, and so deep inside me I could barely breathe. Then he put his lips on mine and exhaled, giving me the oxygen I needed. I held his breath inside me, little pieces of Jake mingling with pieces of me until they merged, becoming one.

His air was mine, and mine was his.

He kissed me and fucked me long into the night. Flipping me over, driving into me again and again while he stared down at me and held my face in his hands. I cried his name, and he swallowed it with the sweep of his tongue between my lips. When I was dizzy from him, from the pleasure he gave me, he fucked me in earnest. Long, deep strokes plunging into me until he groaned and coated my inner walls with hot spurts of cum.

He fell to the side, and all I could do was sprawl boneless on his heaving, sweat-misted chest.

As I came back into myself, I giggled softly. Jake picked his head up to look at me with a slight frown.

"What's so funny?" he gruffed.

"I was thinking I'm glad you're the one who bought that body butter. If I'd paid for it, I would have cut you off in the middle of your massage and asked you to switch to a less expensive one."

He huffed a laugh, drawing me tighter into his arms. "You could buy this town, but you're a cheapskate with your lotion?"

"I prefer economically minded." I grinned happily at his teasing. And Jake in general. "I don't think I've ever been quite this mois-turized. I appreciate your efforts."

"Glad to be of service." He nuzzled my forehead, and I felt his smile against my skin. "I now understand why you feel the way you do."

"I'm economically minded with rich tastes and the desire to not look like a prune anytime soon."

He ran his hand along my abdomen and hip, releasing a low grunt of satisfaction. "I don't think you have to worry about that. You're all ripe and lush. No pruning here."

"You make me feel really good, you know."

"I'm glad me telling you the truth about yourself makes you feel good. Seeing you smiling in my bed makes me feel a thousand feet tall, so I think we're square."

We snuggled for a while longer, then got out of bed to clean up and get ready for sleep. I'd gotten used to brushing my teeth beside him at my place, but it was a novel experience at his. I kept catching him watching me in the mirror, grinning at me when I had toothpaste all over my mouth, so I flicked water at him with my fingers. Then, when I leaned over to rinse my mouth out, he stood behind me and felt up my backside and breasts. I may have stayed in that position a little longer than necessary to give him ample time to touch what he needed.

Once we returned to bed, I lay on the pillow Jake had dubbed as mine. Not only had he bought all my beauty products, he'd gotten me the same pillow I had at home—the one I'd told him I'd bought for my neck, which occasionally got sore ever since my car accident when I was pregnant with Nellie.

Jake faced me, his eyes tracing my features. "You look right at home here."

"I feel it. This has been my favorite week since we met."

His forehead crinkled for a moment before smoothing. "I was gonna argue with you that we've had a lot of weeks I've considered the best, but you're right. Every step I take toward you feels like I'm headed in the right direction, and the calm that came over me this week proved that. We're doing the right thing."

"It feels that way to me too." I chewed on my bottom lip for a moment. "I haven't trusted my instincts for some time. It's been difficult for me to fully let go of my worry, but I think I'm almost there."

He cupped my cheek and brushed my chewed-up lip with his thumb. "We'll get you there."

I leaned forward to graze my lips over his. "I don't doubt that at all."

Chapter Thirty-Six
Clara

Thomas strolled into my office, his hands tucked in his pockets. I looked up from the budget I'd been reading over and raised a brow. The day was almost over, and I knew Thomas wanted to get out of here as much as I did, so I was surprised at the interruption.

Not surprised he waltzed right in, though.

"You don't knock?"

He snorted. "When have I ever?"

"It's never too late to start."

"I'll take it under consideration." He perched on one of my chairs. "So, there's a small child on the phone for you. She says you're friends, which I find odd since I wasn't aware you were making friends with children."

I opened my mouth only to close it. If I were anyone else, Thomas would have been fired ages ago, but I'd always considered his irreverence a breath of fresh air in this buttoned-up corporate environment. Right about now, I was questioning my decisions.

"Did she tell you her name?"

He tapped his temple. "It was Mage. No, that's a mystical occupation. Paige? No—wait, Sage! Her name is Sage. She sounds sassy."

I groaned and reached for my phone. "That's Jake's daughter, you jackass."

"Oh, right. She did mention that."

I tossed a pen in his direction. "Go back to work."

He stood and saluted me. "Aye, aye, captain."

As soon as he left, I pressed the speaker button on my phone. "Sage?"

She sniffled. "Hi, Clara. I'm sorry for calling you at work. I don't have your cell phone number or I would have texted. I'm really sorry."

Her voice was wobbly and wet. Alarm bells sounded in my head.

"You don't have to apologize for calling me, honey. And I'll make sure to give you my cell number when I see you so you can get in touch with me whenever you need to."

"Thank you." She huffed a ragged breath. "Um, I would have called my mom, but she's on a trip for work. I thought I was just having a bad stomachache, but then I went to the bathroom...and it's not that. There's blood, so I guess...I guess I'm having my period."

I held my gasp in, but just barely. This was not what I'd been expecting to hear. Sage and I had certainly become friendly over the last couple weeks of getting to know one another, but this was a big leap.

"Are you at home?" I asked.

"Yes. My dad will be home soon, but I don't want him to know. It's just gross, and my stomach hurts really bad. I wish my mom was here. She'd know what to do. My friend said I should stick in a tampon, but I don't have any idea how to do that. Do you think you could help me, Clara?" Her question was so small and unsure, it nearly broke my heart.

"Of course I can, but your dad can help too. I promise he won't be grossed out."

"Okay." Her sob was muffled, but there was no mistaking it. "I'm sorry. I guess I should just wait for him."

"No, Sage, honey, I'm coming. I have to grab Nellie from day care and stop to get you some supplies. Can you hang on for an hour?"

"Yes," she said quickly. "I can hang on."

"Good girl. When we hang up, call your mom and tell her I'm going to come help you, okay? I'm sure she'll want to know what's going on, and even though she can't be with you, it'll make you feel better to talk to her, I promise."

"I'll call her."

"I'll be there soon, Sagie. We'll get you all fixed up."

Once we hung up, I sat there for a solid minute, frozen in fear. Not that I was afraid of periods or helping Sage. My fear was I'd screw this up for her—a momentous moment in a girl's life. She'd look back and always remember her dad's incompetent girlfriend who'd made it weird.

I quickly snapped out of it by making a list of what I needed to do. First, text Jake, then grab all the work I needed to complete tonight and pick Nellie up from day care. I lined up everything one by one, so I knew exactly what I was going to do.

My calm and confidence were in the details.

Centered now, a game plan laid out in my mind, I was on my way to Sage.

Jake opened the door for me, worry creasing his brow. "Hey, sweetness." He took my hand and pulled me into his arms. Since Nellie was on my hip, she was part of our embrace, which made her giggle.

"Hi, Jake," she squealed.

Plucking her out of my hold, he balanced her on his arm. "Hi, Nell-Belle." He smoothed a hand over her messy hair. She was always a wreck when I picked her up from day care. "You look like you had a wild day. Want me to braid your hair?"

"Two braids, please," she asked sweetly.

"Of course."

His eyes met mine, and they were full of concern. I'd texted him to tell him what was going on, so he'd hurried home from work, but Sage hadn't wanted anything to do with him. Surely, it had stung, but I understood her. When I'd gotten my period around her age, I'd been mortified my mother had told my dad and brother.

"Where's our girl?" I asked.

He blinked a few times. "Uh—she's in her bathroom. She refused to come out and asked me to leave her alone until you got here."

I held up my bag of supplies. "Don't worry about a single thing. I've got her covered. Are you okay to hang out with Nellie while I take care of Sage?"

"Yeah. Of course." He palmed Nellie's head. "I've got my work cut out for me with this munchkin. We'll keep busy."

I leaned in and kissed him. "Don't worry," I said softly, "I'm well seasoned at this. I'll get her through it."

He held my gaze for a long beat. "I would never doubt you."

After showing Sage how to use a pad, I got her to shower and change into fresh clothes, then settled her in bed and placed a heating pad on her abdomen. Reaching into my bag of supplies, I pulled out a chocolate bar and a bottle of ginger ale.

"This is my magic concoction. Chocolate doesn't fix everything, but it certainly helps."

She took the treats, but her shoulders remained slumped, and her mouth was turned down in a pitiful frown.

"Thank you." She blinked up at me. "Do you think you could sit with me for a few minutes? I don't really want to be by myself."

"I'd love to." I took a seat on her full-size bed, propping up against the headboard. She curled onto her side to face me, and I helped her adjust the heating pad. "Do you feel better now?" I asked.

"I think so." She bit down on her bottom lip. "I feel kind of stupid too. All my friends have their periods already. I've been wanting mine to come for a long time, but now that it's here...I don't know, I guess I'm a little sad. Why do you think I'm sad, Clara?"

"There could be a lot of reasons."

I slowly reached out, wanting to stroke her hair but unsure she'd accept it. When she didn't move away, I smoothed my palm over the top of her head and ran my fingers through the ends.

"It could be something as simple as your hormones making you emotional. To be honest, that's probably a big part of it." I scooted down a little, bringing myself closer to her level. "I was around your age when I got my first period. It happened at school, and I bled through my pants. Luckily, someone told me before everyone saw, but guess who that person was?"

Her mouth twisted. "I hope it was a teacher with a quiet voice."

I shook my head, my eyes going wide. "It wasn't. It was the boy I'd been crushing on since the start of middle school—Brian Kegan. 'You've got blood on your butt' were the first words he'd ever spoken to me."

Rolling her face into her pillow, she groaned mournfully. "Nooo. Did you drop out of school?"

"Unfortunately, my parents wouldn't let me. They wanted to celebrate my 'becoming a woman,' as they'd put it, by taking me out to dinner. My mom made me a chocolate cake with *congratulations* written on the top, and I was totally devastated by all of it. I cried and yelled that I wasn't a woman and didn't want to be. That I was still a kid, and they couldn't make me accept being a grown-up. Thank goodness I have a really patient, understanding mother."

"She didn't get mad when you yelled?" Sage asked.

"Not at all." I lifted her hair, rubbing my thumb over the silky strands. "She held me in her lap—something she hadn't done in ages since she's a tiny woman and I'd already been taller than her by then—and told me I would always be her little girl."

She gave me a dubious look. "Do you think that's true?"

"Yeah. My mom would totally hold me in her lap now if I'd let her." I scooted down even farther to lie beside her. "A few years ago, I went through something really sad. My mother tucked me into bed with her, fed me chocolate, and promised me everything would be okay."

"I'm glad you have a mom like that," she whispered.

"Me too." I brushed her hair off her forehead. "Getting your period is part of your body growing up and a step toward you becoming a woman, but that doesn't mean your girlhood is over. It doesn't mean you aren't your dad's girl anymore or your mom's baby. You are, and I think you always will be."

She nodded. "My dad seemed really worried about me."

"He definitely was."

Her nose wrinkled. "I just felt so gross. I didn't want him to be grossed out."

I poked her shoulder. "He changed your diaper, honey. Believe me, there's nothing that can gross him out now."

"Oh no," she moaned. "I didn't even think about that. How can my dad even look at me? I've seen Dex's diapers, and they're—" She gagged as dramatically as a girl with tears in her eyes could.

"That's how much he loves you."

Her shudder shook the mattress. "It has to be a whole lot to get past that."

I chuckled, but what I wanted to do was give this girl a big hug. She really was something special. But then, she had Jake and Carly as her parents, so that made sense.

"When you're feeling up to it, I know your dad would love to see you with his own eyes. Nellie too, for that matter."

Her eyes brightened, and she wiped away the few tears that had escaped. "Nellie's here? Really?"

"She's my sidekick. I don't go many places without her. Your dad's tackling her tangled rat's nest while you and I hang out."

She gave me a wobbly smile. "I was thinking, at least I didn't bleed in front of the boy I like."

I snorted a laugh. "Girlie, that happened more than twenty years ago and I still think about it. For your sake, I'm relieved too. No one needs that kind of trauma."

"Did you ever talk to him again?"

I solemnly shook my head. "Not in middle school. The little twerp had spread it around to everyone."

Sage gasped. "Oh no. That's the worst."

"It sucked, but guess what? When we grew up and I started working for Rossi Motors, I happened to see him there for a job interview and looked at his résumé. He wasn't at all qualified for the job he wanted, so I took the opportunity to tell him Rossi doesn't hire dipshits."

Her mouth fell open. "No. That's epic."

I laughed. "Okay, not really. But I did tell him we weren't interested in hiring him, and that made up for all the mortification I went through because of him."

She stared at me, her eyes alight. I could practically read the millions of thoughts bouncing around her mind. Perhaps it hadn't been the best story to tell her, but it was one of my favorites.

Her brows waggled with mischief. "You got your revenge."

"I did. You don't judge me for being petty and holding a grudge?"

"No way. That guy had it coming. He didn't have to spill the tea way back then, and he had some nerve applying for a job he didn't deserve. Sounds like he was an all-around tool."

I tapped her nose, pleased at her read on the situation. It had been ages since I'd had a conversation with anyone Sage's age, but I found her exceptionally easy to talk to.

"You're absolutely right, honey."

Sometime during our conversation, she'd rid herself of the last vestiges of sadness. Her eyes, which were so like her father's it would have been eerie had they not been so gorgeous, were clear, and her mouth was tipped up at the corners. I matched her expression, returning her smile.

"I'm so glad you're here," she said.

I cupped her smooth cheek and let her see the emotion stirring in my gaze. "You know, I was just thinking the same thing."

Chapter Thirty-Seven

Jake

Clara walked out on the deck with a glass of wine and an ice-cold beer she handed to me as she dipped down to give me a kiss. When she went to pull away, I caught her by the nape and covered her mouth with mine, drinking in her flavor. The sweetest of sweets, my girl was.

When I finally let her go, it was only so she could curl up on the padded bench beside me. She hadn't been prepared to sleep over and was wearing one of my T-shirts and a pair of shorts she'd left here. Neither of us had questioned whether she and Nellie were staying over tonight. It was a given.

She'd taken care of my baby like she was her own. I'd peeked in on them as they lay together, talking quietly, only picking up on half the words they exchanged. But I could see Clara soothing Sage, giving her the love and care she'd needed today. My heart had done a wild dance, thumping and thrashing for this beautiful woman and my little girl who was growing up faster than I was ready for.

"How are you?" she asked. "Shell-shocked?"

"Nah." I trailed my knuckles along her thigh, easing into the comfort of having her beside me. "I would've been lost if you hadn't been here. You made my job a hell of a lot easier."

She sighed, taking a sip of her wine. "I'm pretty honored she trusts me enough to call me."

"That's because you've always treated her like she matters to you."

There was no hesitation when she replied, "She does."

"Yeah, I know." Closing my eyes, I rubbed my nose against her cheek. "I'm in love with you, Clara."

She leaned into my touch, making a soft, high hum. "I had a feeling you were."

"Yeah?" I dug my fingers into the back of her hair, my forehead to hers. I could've been patient, waited for her to say it when she was ready, but that wasn't me. I laid my heart out for her, and I needed it back from her. I knew she was there with me, but I had to have the words. "What about you? Think you might love me?"

"Oh yes. I most assuredly love you, Jake. Very much, in fact."

There we go. Knowing and hearing it were distinctly different things. I grabbed her very Clara-like declaration and tucked it in the space in my heart I'd made solely for her. When I took it back out to remember this moment, I'd think about her flowery-fresh scent, the solid weight of her in my arms, her warm breath exhaling across my lips. In my memories, I'd find her arms around my neck and her forehead pressed to mine, and relish in the feeling of never having felt so close to another person besides my child.

I clutched her to me, my fingers digging into her waist. "You didn't bother telling me."

She giggled, and the happy sound landed right in my chest.

"I don't remember you saying a word either."

I chuffed. "It's really something the two of us ended up together."

"Why? Because we're so locked down, we can't even name our own feelings, much less identify someone else's?"

I swatted her ass. "You're using present tense, mama. You and I are changed people."

She raised a brow. "Oh, are we?"

"Obviously. I knew you loved me, and you knew I loved you before either of us got brave enough to name it. But we did, didn't we?"

"Yes, we did, but I'm not convinced we're completely changed. Do you believe we're no longer affected by our pasts?"

"What past?" I gave her ass another smack. "I don't remember existing before seeing you on your bike, riding like the wind."

"Then you might be surprised to learn you have a thirteen-year-old daughter."

I snapped my fingers. "True. I do remember her. Everything else is vague and blurry."

More sweet giggles. "If only life were truly like that. There are quite a few things in my past I'd like to blur out."

I thought about it for a minute. There'd been shitty times in my life too. Things I'd love to shove to the back of my mind and never think about again. But in the end, if I was offered a pill to make that happen, I wouldn't take it. Not when everything led me to this.

To her.

"Nah. I'm not going to wish away anything that got me you." I pecked her lips. "But if I come across a selective memory wiper, I'll pass it your way."

She groaned. "I can't use it now that you're being so principled. Just destroy it."

I grinned at how miserable yet adorable she was. "If I find a fictional memory wiper, I'll keep that in mind."

That made her laugh again. "You know how I know I've still got work to do? Being this happy with you makes me nervous. Like I'm waiting for the other shoe to fall."

That hurt me to hear. I didn't take it personally, though. This woman trusted me with her daughter, so it wasn't me who made her feel that way. She'd been done so wrong, even secure with me; she was bracing for the bad to show up anyway. This wasn't the first or last time I hoped her ex had an unfortunate and very painful accident in prison.

"It'll take time, and we've got that. One day, you're going to realize you're not waiting anymore."

"At least one of us is patient."

My mouth tipped. "That's why we work so well. Between us, we're one emotionally healthy person."

Her laugh was melodic, making my chest tight. "Do we really need any more than that?"

"Nope." I kissed her forehead and gave her ass a squeeze. "I've got all I need right here."

CHAPTER
THIRTY-EIGHT
Jake

The other shoe dropped.

After living in a dream with all my girls, growing closer to Clara, watching her bond with Sage, getting all the cuddles I could possibly handle from Nellie, I was flying high. Dinners and sleepovers and dancing to cartoons had me armed to the teeth, so when I walked into my office Tuesday morning, I wasn't as on edge as I normally was. I didn't love this job and never would, but what I had outside these walls more than made up for it.

The thing about finding happiness was it existed on a razor's edge. Without balance, it could have been sliced into ribbons. Lucky for me, and Clara, we *did* balance each other. It was outside forces we had to worry about.

The woman on the other end of the phone meant less than nothing to me anymore, but she was the last person I'd needed in my ear today—or any day in the future.

"Hello, Jake. Nice to hear your voice."

A chill rattled my spine. I hadn't heard from Andrea in years. Had never expected she'd call me at all, let alone at work.

"Why are you calling me?" I gruffed.

She chuffed. "Straight to the point. Aren't you going to ask me how I am? I'd love to know what Sage is up to."

There was a time I would've taken advantage of this situation to tell Andrea she was a coward who'd broken a little girl's heart, spitting all the vitriol I'd carried around with me for too long, but I had none of that in me anymore. I didn't care about this woman, and she certainly wasn't going to get the gift of hearing about my daughter. As far as I was concerned, she was a stranger and Sage was none of her damn business.

It was easy to keep my voice level. I wasn't mad or upset at this phone call. Why it was happening was all I needed to know, then I'd be hanging up and going back to forgetting she existed.

She. Did. Not. Matter.

"I don't see any reason to chitchat. What do you need to talk to me about?"

"Well"—she cleared her throat, probably trying to gather her composure after I'd shut her down flat—"a story that pertains to you landed in my lap. Actually, Motor Zone, to be specific. My editors are badgering me to run it now, but since we have history, I thought I'd give you a few days' heads-up."

My gut clenched. Andrea reported for *Denver Times*. Last I'd known, she was writing for the entertainment section, but that'd been years ago. She could've switched up to the business section in that time. What story she could have possibly had, though, I had no idea.

"Are you going to tell me what it is or make me play a hundred questions?"

"You know, Jake, you'd think you'd be a little nicer since I'm doing you a favor."

I pinched the bridge of my nose, summoning my patience. "If you expect me to do a little dance for you to spill your supposed story, you're barking up the wrong tree. Either tell me or don't."

"Oh, you'll want to know."

"All right. Then spill."

She did. Like an oil tanker in the sea, covering everything good with thick, deadly sludge. I fell back in my chair, covering my face with one hand as everything we'd worked for got shoved to the precipice of a cliff. One word from Andrea, one article in her paper, would send us over.

I made myself play nice for the rest of the call. Told her Sage was fine. Everything was fine. Even thanked her for her call. When she asked if Jeremy or I would give her a quote, I bit my tongue to stop myself from laughing at her sheer audacity. By the time I hung up, my head was throbbing, and I had blood in my mouth.

I did not let any of that stop me from vaulting from my chair and storming down the hall to Jeremy's office. What did stop me was the sight of my brother in a meeting with two of our lawyers, our head of PR, and Roman fucking Wells.

Jeremy was always put together. Suits immaculate, hair neatly combed, ties tucked neatly at his throat. Today, he looked like he'd been through the wringer. At least a day's worth of stubble on his jaw, hair everywhere, tie loosened. And when he looked up at me, it was with wide-eyed panic.

I fell back a step, recoiling from the scene like I'd been shot. "You know."

He shot to his feet. "Jake, wait. Join us. I'll explain what's going on."

"Funny, I just found out and came to tell you." I gestured to the others in the room. The lawyers, I got. PR too. But Roman Wells? There was no reason for him to be privy to this, not when I wasn't. "I see you didn't extend the same courtesy to me."

"I was going to tell you today." Jeremy stood in front of me, his hand on my shoulder. "I needed to figure out how to get ahead of this."

How did we get ahead of a recording of MZ's spokesperson for the last five years, country singer and all-American dad Dallas Fox, saying some of the most racist, misogynist, vile things I'd ever heard? There was no spinning this as "locker room talk." And I wouldn't be a part of a company that tried.

I shrugged him off. "When did you find out?"

"Yesterday. We've been working on a plan. How to distance ourselves from this so the Rossi deal doesn't fall through."

The one we were supposed to be signing at the end of the week. Jeremy was practically salivating to put his signature on the contracts. His desperation had me on edge, making me wonder if there was a lot more he wasn't telling me.

"You can't be serious, thinking about the Rossi deal. Dallas Fox needs to be removed from MZ swiftly and decisively." I crossed my arms over my chest. "Andrea Wallace has the story."

"Fuck." He was the one to fall back a step this time. "She called you?"

I nodded once. "She's holding the story as a courtesy to me, but there's no stopping this from running. It's going to come out."

"Okay, okay." His head bobbed somewhat maniacally. "We can handle this. As soon as we sign the deal, we'll fire Dallas."

"No. That doesn't work for me. We're not entering a partnership by deceiving them."

Roman approached us like he had a right to be part of our conversation. "Jake is right, Jeremy. We'll have to handle the Dallas situation before we can sign with Rossi. If you don't disclose this to them, they'll have you in court faster than you could say the word."

I turned on him, my jaw tight. "Why are you here?" Swiveling to Jeremy, I asked, "Why is he here?"

Roman did not wait for Jeremy to speak. "I was in a meeting with Jeremy when he received the news, and I've promised MZ the use of my PR team. They are well versed in handling crises and working on a plan as we speak. By the end of the day tomorrow, we will go to the press with a statement disavowing everything Dallas had been recorded saying and end our professional relationship with him."

I didn't like his use of "our," like he was part of MZ, but he was. He owned a large portion of this company. His dog was very much in this fight.

I chose not to ask why I hadn't been brought in yesterday. It didn't matter. The betrayal was absolute. Wrapping my head around my brother knowing where my line in the sand was and stepping it over anyway would have to come at another time. Once we were through this, I'd have to decide what that meant for us—for me. But not until we managed this crisis.

"When are you planning to tell Luca?" I asked.

Jeremy shook his head. "Not until we know our next steps."

"After our statement comes out," Roman stated in a tone brooking no argument. Except, I was feeling a hell of a lot like arguing.

"I think he'd appreciate hearing it personally," I said.

"He will. I'll call him," Jeremy assured me. "I can't go to him now. Not with everything up in the air. We need to have a solid plan so he understands this is under control."

"I don't think that's a good idea." Dread clawed at my throat. "Delaying leaves room for anything to happen."

Roman inserted himself again. "I agree with Jeremy."

My jaw rippled. This fucking guy. As far as I'd been aware, there wasn't a third Hayes brother, but he sure acted like there was. "I'd rather keep this professional between us, so I'm asking you to step back and let me speak to my brother."

He held up his hands. "I'll leave you to it."

Roman rejoined the rest of the team across the room. We didn't have much privacy, but it was better than him interjecting every other sentence.

"Roman knows what he's doing," Jeremy started.

"That's comforting," I intoned. "When this is over, we're going to talk."

He nodded once. "I know. Give me a day. I need to get a grasp on this."

"One day," I warned.

He put his hand on my shoulder again. "That means you can't tell Clara about this. It has to stay between us, just until tomorrow."

Funny enough, my focus had been so single-minded, Clara's part hadn't occurred to me. Now that it had and he was asking me to keep it from her, a bitter taste blossomed in my mouth.

"I don't lie to Clara."

"It's not a lie," he hurried out. "It's a delay. One day, Jake. I know you're mad as hell at me, and maybe I've lost you, but I need this.

MZ needs it. I'm asking you, as my brother, to give me this. One day to get ahead of it."

It was on the tip of my tongue to tell him no. But then I thought of him, solid by my side while I told our dad I was becoming a father at seventeen. I thought of when he'd started staying summers at our ranch, the way he'd shrunk away from physical contact and loud noises because he'd been used to cold and quiet. Then I thought of him being sent back alone to the cold after living in the warmth with me for two months. He'd never held it against me. Had always had time for me. Had looked out for me when our father was on the warpath.

I couldn't say no. Not when he rarely asked for anything. This, one day...it didn't seem like much.

"One day." There was finality in my statement. I would not back down from it, no matter what happened in the next twenty-four hours. This concession was the length my brotherly loyalty stretched. It would go no further.

"Thank you, Jake." He squeezed my shoulder. "If you want to sit in on our meeting, I—"

I shook my head. "I want nothing to do with this. Any of it," I spat in disgust. "Just excise Dalla Fox's poison from MZ. That's all I need to know."

"It'll be done."

I believed that. But at what cost?

Chapter Thirty-Nine
Clara

Jake wasn't a talkative man in general, but tonight, he'd been quieter than normal. He'd laughed with Nellie, danced to her favorite cartoon, but in between, he was a million miles away, caught up in his thoughts.

My propensity for pessimism reared its ugly head with thoughts I couldn't tamp down.

He's tired of us.

He realizes I'm too old for him.

Too damaged.

Too much baggage.

He met someone else.

He's hiding something from me.

He's leaving me.

All evening, I tried to get a read on him, but it was impossible. The walls he'd knocked down had been resurrected in record time. Just this morning, we'd been thick as thieves, and tonight, I wasn't sure what we were.

I might've been mistaking a bad day for disaster on the horizon. That was distinctly possible. But I'd ignored my instincts with Miller for months while he'd been terrorizing an old couple. If I'd spoken up sooner, I might've saved them some heartache at the very least, if not myself too.

Jake was propped on my bed when I entered my bedroom after tucking Nellie in. He put his phone down when I approached him, tipping his head back to look up at me. I slid my fingers through the top of his thick hair, and he closed his eyes, leaning into my touch.

I refused to let this go on a second longer. "So, what is it? Bad day, or are you sick of me? Either way, I'd like to know now."

His eyes sprung open. "Sick of you? How could you think that? That's not possible."

"It's easy to think that when you've barely looked at me since you got here. You've said maybe ten words and were a million miles away anytime Nellie wasn't climbing all over you. So, I'm asking you to tell me now if you want to leave or are unsure whether you want to move forward. Don't drag it out, please."

He stared at me with an open mouth and furrowed brow as if he didn't comprehend what I was saying to him.

He didn't refute my claim or reassure me. Instead, his arms shot out and grabbed me by the middle. Whirling around, he threw me on the bed and climbed on top of me, straddling my legs. His clenched fists landed on either side of my head, and he glared at me with a tense jaw.

"I love you, Clara."

I swallowed hard, unable to speak from the intensity rolling out of him in thick, cloying waves.

"I'm not done with you. I'm pretty certain I never will be," he gritted out. "If I haven't made it clear how completely in love with you I am, that's my fault. I love you down to the core of me. It came on slow and steady, like a summer rain shower, and before I knew it, I was drenched. My love for you goes so deep it's a part of me now. Even if I tried to carve myself hollow, I wouldn't be able to rid myself of it."

He pressed his fists deeper into the mattress, his nose almost touching mine. "I'm not trying. I *won't* try. I never want to stop loving you. Being in love with you is the easiest thing I've ever done, and next to having my daughter, the best. So no, I'm not leaving you, and I'm damn sure I want to move forward with you. I. Love. You."

My breath froze in my lungs. Jake might've been on top of me, but *he* was the vulnerable one. His feelings seeped from his pores as his mouth put them into words I'd never forget.

"Jake..." I wiggled to free my hand so I could touch his tight jaw, "I love you too. Very much. That's why I can't sit by and watch you get lost in your head without feeling concerned. Maybe you need space, I don't know. It's just...I'm so messed up; when you don't speak to me, I think it's my fault."

His sigh was so heavy he deflated, his forehead lowering to touch mine. "No, Clara. Not your fault. I'm really sorry for putting that thought in your head when it's the opposite of the truth. Spending time with you and Nellie has been the best part of my day."

I stroked his jaw, from his ear to his chin and back again. "Then what's going on, baby? You can talk to me."

He collapsed onto his side and pulled me with him, not leaving any space between our bodies. Those beautiful blue eyes of his were brimming with worry and something that looked a lot like pain. He was so good at this, letting me see his emotions, it made it easier to trust him and impossible not to love him.

"Jeremy and I...well, I'm going to have to make some decisions soon. He crossed a line with me I can't get over. I would've said he broke my heart, except you've fortified it so well it's pretty damn solid. He did put a dent in it, though, and I don't think I'm going to be able to forget that."

"What happened?"

He shook his head, his eyes closing. "I'm not ready to talk about it. Soon, I'll tell you everything. I just really need to hold you tonight. Need you in my arms."

"You don't have to ask. I'm here."

For a while, that was all we did. Jake had buried his nose in my hair and trailed his fingers up and down my back. I'd slipped my hands under his shirt, needing to feel his warmth under my palms.

As he held me, trickles of belief pooled inside me. The trail of his fingers on my spine and shoulders told me he loved me. His lips touching every place he could reach proved he wasn't tired of me. The murmurs of my name and soul-deep groans as he tugged me closer and closer, even though I was flattened against him, were echoes of his need for me. Soon, I was filled with belief in Jake and me, my previous doubts floating away with my sighs.

He'd had a bad day. That didn't mean impending disaster. He was human. He could be grumpy and quiet so long as he gave me this and worked through it with me when he was ready.

"Clara." It was an exaltation—a declaration of desire and love wrapped up in the five letters of my name.

I opened my eyes, finding his already there, locked on me. "Jake."

His answer was a kiss. Long and deep, his tongue plunged into my mouth, laving me, tasting me. Fingers braced on the back of my skull, he held me where he wanted me and took and took and took.

What I'd said to him that night in The Tavern still held true. I liked a man who took what he wanted. Well...certain men who took certain things. Jake was that certain man, and this kiss was that certain thing.

I was breathless and still didn't try to pull away. Even dizzy, I kissed him back, gripping his neck like he might disappear if I didn't.

In between removing my clothes and his, his lips found mine. Each time he kissed me, it was like it was the last time. As if he was leaving for battle in the morning and I might not see him again.

The room spun, and my heart twisted and twirled as his kisses traveled over my skin, devouring me inch by inch. He settled between my thighs and brought me to another planet with his tongue. The obscene yet wholly erotic sounds of him lapping my soaked flesh filled the room, but the volume of my moans nearly drowned everything else out. Jake made me come and come and come. If he'd been determined to wring me out and leave me boneless, he'd succeeded, yet I couldn't ask him to stop. He kept at me until I lost track of my orgasms and sense of self. I'd been condensed into a being who only knew pleasure and love for the man who gave it to her.

I opened my eyes when he crawled over me and pulled me to my side. He moved me how he wanted me, draping my leg over his hip with the rest of me snuggled as close as he could have me. In one long, slow plunge, he entered me and stayed there, rooted at the end of me. Our breath mingled, neither of us blinking or looking away.

"Clara," he murmured.

"Jake," I whispered back.

He moved inside me, only retreating slightly before returning to the place he'd claimed as home. My body was languid, responding to his with rolls of my hips and high, ragged sighs. Jake was as tireless as he was gentle, holding me while he made love to me.

I watched him at times, and he looked at me with such intensity and adoration I almost felt like I was intruding on a private moment. That might not have made sense, but very few of my synapses were awake, so I closed my eyes and let him have his time with me. I didn't need to see him anyway because although my mind was drifting, my skin was alive and aware of *everything*.

The prickling of Jake's chest hair on my sensitive breasts.

His strong thighs intertwined with mine.

Hot breath on my shoulder.

Strong fingers clamped around my hip.

Thick cock sliding into me until I couldn't breathe, only feel.

Impossibly, my belly grew taut and full. Gripping his shoulders, I panted and keened as another orgasm rippled through me. My inner walls clamped and fluttered around his cock, making him groan and push in harder.

"Clara."

"Baby," I whimpered.

He flipped me onto my back and drove into me with force and purpose. "Look at me. I need your eyes on me right now."

I forced myself to focus on the man above me. He'd given me so much; it was now time for him to take. He was beautiful and fierce, tendons like ropes in his neck, a sheen of sweat on his brow.

"I see you," I said.

"You do. Always." Ragged and broken, he groaned as he pounded me with abandon. Our skin slapped, and I slid up the mattress from the force of it, the headboard stopping me from falling off the end. I braced myself, arms over my head. Jake's eyes dropped to my bouncing breasts then back to my face. He licked his lips and released a feral growl.

Through that, his ferocity and desire, he stroked my hair and touched my face with the reverence he never forgot.

"I love you," I told him.

"Love you so fucking much," he gritted out.

"Come for me, baby." I raised my leaden legs, allowing him a deeper angle. "Fill me up, Jake. I want your cum all over me."

"You'll have it. All over my girl."

He pressed my leg back to my chest and fucked me hard. There was fire in his icy eyes, flames licking to the surface, spreading to his burning skin. Soon, he thrust deep for a final time and stayed there, coating my inner walls with liquid heat. My neck arched with pleasure as he pulsed inside me.

Time passed, the world spun, our breathing slowed. Jake stayed planted, holding me, brushing my hair from my eyes, leaving light kisses all over my face. It was tender and perfect.

"You're making me feel adored," I slurred.

"That would be because I do adore you, Clara. Completely. You know that, right?"

"Mmm." My eyes fluttered open. "I might forget sometimes, but you don't let it go on for long. When you kiss my forehead, I fall right back into the softness of your feelings for me. I can't tell you how much I love being yours, Jake."

"Same way I love being yours." His eyes darted between mine, then he grabbed me, yanking me tight against him. His arms were steel bands around my shoulders. We were so close his thrashing heart pounded through his cage, rattling mine too.

In the back of my mind, I noticed something frantic about how tightly he held me, something unsettled about him in general, but I brushed it away. He'd had a bad day. If he needed me close to soothe himself, I would give him me a hundred times over.

Hopefully, tomorrow would be better for him. If not, I'd be there for him anyway.

CHAPTER FORTY
Clara

Mornings on the executive floor of Rossi were normally quiet. We all locked ourselves in our offices to fully wake up over cups of coffee and answer emails that couldn't wait. At least, that was what I did.

This morning, Thomas had flagged me down before I could make it past his desk.

His eyes were wide, and for once, he didn't beat around the bush. "Meeting in the conference room starting as soon as you get in there."

I dropped my bag on his desk, grabbing my phone and tablet out of it. "What's going on?"

"No idea, but a team of lawyers went in there with Luca and Sally right before you got here."

I did not like the sound of that. Nothing good could come from an emergency meeting with lawyers at eight thirty in the morning.

I strode into the conference room, scanning the sea of suited men and women. Luca caught my eye and nodded toward the seat beside him. With a curious look, I sat down.

He didn't keep me waiting long. While the others were in the midst of quiet conversation, he leaned over to fill me in.

"We're canceling the deal with Motor Zone."

I almost jumped in shock. "What? Why?"

As far as I knew, it was a sure thing. I'd kept my distance from the intricacies, but of course I was up to date with the proceedings. We were scheduled to sign contracts later this week. Everything was set.

"One of our investigators turned up a recording starting to get some attention."

I nodded, on tenterhooks. Luca was terrible at telling stories. He conveyed snippets and paused for drama. If we were alone, I might've flicked his forehead.

"What is it?" My impatience wasn't very well hidden, but Luca was unfazed.

"Motor Zone's spokesperson, Dallas Fox, is a racist piece of shit. The recording is of him talking about the type of women he likes and the type he...doesn't. I'm not going to go into detail, but it's ugly and disgusting."

I swallowed hard to keep the bile from working its way up my throat. This wasn't what I'd expected to hear. Otherwise, I might've skipped the coffee. My stomach gurgled from the implications of Luca's revelation.

"I don't need those details." That was where the devil was, after all.

Steepling his fingers, he took a deep breath. "Look, I know this might put some strain on your relationship, but there's no way we can go forward with this deal. You know how long it took us to recover from the hit we took after Miller's crimes came to light. We can't take a chance on anything scandalous blowing back on us."

"Of course," I answered immediately, trying not to allow my guilt over my ex-husband's misdeeds and the way it affected our company seep in. Now was not the time for that. "There's no question the contract can't go through."

He covered my hand with his. "I'm glad you agree."

"I'm glad our investigators picked this up before it was too late."

"The owner of the recording is shopping it around and not being quiet about it." His jaw moved back and forth like there was something he wasn't saying. Then he lowered his chin, his eyes locked with mine. "I doubt we're the only ones who know about this."

It only took a moment for his meaning to dawn on me. "You think the Hayes know."

His shrug was slight. "I don't know anything for a fact, but if I were in possession of a recording like that and wanted money, I'd take it to the company that couldn't afford for it to get out. Whether they found out overnight like we did or days ago, I don't know, but I'd bet my suit collection Jeremy Hayes is at least aware."

Luca was careful with his words, but they still knocked me back. My chest went tight, and the possibilities of who else might have known ricocheted around my skull.

I sat through the meeting, gathering myself to be as present as I could be. I told myself this was about someone else and had nothing to do with potentially being deceived by a man I loved once again.

If there was an upside, we were at least ahead of the scandal this time and would be able to remove ourselves from the narrative. The lawyers were already drafting a memo to end the negotiations with Motor Zone they would be sending before the end of the day. A crisis team was working on our response in the case that we were mentioned in the circus sure to begin once the recording was out there for everyone to hear. I felt confident we would get through this without much damage.

At least, Rossi Motors would.

I wasn't sure I would fare so well.

Even though I hadn't confirmed the worst was true, my gut knew it was. Jake's bad day couldn't have been a coincidence.

As soon as I was in my office, I texted him, unable to bear hearing his voice right now.

Me: *Did you know about the recording last night?*

It took a minute for my phone to ring. I declined it, but he called back three more times before texting.

Jake: *Pick up the phone, Clara.*

Me: *It's a yes or no question, Jake.*

Jake: *Nothing is that simple.*

To me, it was. His unwillingness to answer was an answer in itself. He'd known. He'd come to me knowing. I'd shared my bed and body with him while he'd been deceiving me.

God, how could this be happening again?

I'd been so careful. I'd gone slow. I'd been wary of every step. Yet, here I was, back where I'd already been—the place I swore I'd never be again.

A drop of water fell on the papers on my desk. I touched it with my fingertip as another fell beside it. *Oh, those are tears.* I hadn't even realized I was crying. For the longest time, I'd thought I was out of tears. I supposed I'd been wrong about a lot of things.

I had no idea how long I sat there—watching my teardrops dent my papers—until a scuffle and muffled voices outside my office drew me back to the present.

Without warning, the door to my office swung open, and Jake stormed in. Thomas tried to stop him, but Jake slammed the door in his face and locked it.

He stood there, chest heaving as he stared at me. I looked back, too sad to summon my anger, even though it would have been nice right now. Anger, I could have used. Sadness did nothing but bog me down, leaving me immobile.

"You're crying," he uttered.

"Well, of course I am. You've broken my heart." As soon as the words left my mouth, I wished I could take them back.

The speed at which he circled my desk and dropped to his knees in front of me stole my breath. He took my hands in his, holding them so tightly I had no hope of freeing myself.

"I found out yesterday, and I was going to tell you today. I had no intention of deceiving you—"

"But you did. You told me you'd had a *bad day* while knowing something that would affect not only you but Rossi too. You chose not to tell me. How is that not deception?"

He shook his head. "It wasn't going to go that far. Jeremy asked me to give him a day to put a plan in place. That was it, one day. I told him I wouldn't give him more than that."

"I don't believe you," I stated.

Mouth agape, he fell back on his heels. "I'm telling you the truth. I would never lie to you."

"I don't believe you."

"Clara, sweet—"

"I don't believe you," I repeated with more force. "I can't believe you, Jake. I trusted you and look where that left me. Our team is scrambling to put out fires before everything blows up when you could have given us the knowledge and time we needed yesterday. Why does Jeremy get that courtesy but I don't?"

My Jake was always confident and self-assured. He walked around like he'd found his place in the world and knew exactly what he was doing. The man in front of me was deflating before my eyes. That spine of steel was melting, curling him forward over my lap.

"He's my brother, Clara. I explained our history, and I...I made a mistake giving him that time. I see that now. If I'd thought any harm would come to you or Rossi, I wouldn't have done it."

My nostrils flared, my anger fighting its way to the surface. "I don't believe you."

His head shot up, panicked eyes latching on to mine. "I'm telling you the truth. I would never hurt you. You have to know that."

I reached out to take his face in my hands. "It's funny; you just reminded me of my ex-husband. The two of you couldn't be any more different, but he'd said almost the exact same thing to me when he was arrested. He'd poured out this emotional apology, said what he'd done to those people had had nothing to do with me. Said he'd never hurt me on purpose and loved me very much. Isn't that laughable?"

His fingers wrapped around my wrists, lowering my hands from his face. "I get you're mad and hurt right now, but I'm nothing like that son of a bitch. When you take a step back, you'll see that."

"Will I? I don't know, Jake." I tipped my head back to stave off the angry tears threatening to spill. I was so goddamn sick of crying. "The thing is, I don't trust myself. My gut is a liar, but I thought..."

I rolled my lips over my teeth, biting down to distract myself with pain, but I only succeeded in matching my outside to my inside. Bright, stinging hurt I couldn't ignore. This wasn't supposed to be happening. This wasn't us. It shouldn't have been.

I sucked in a breath lined with broken glass. "After everything, you were supposed to be safe for me. How could I have gotten this so wrong?"

"You weren't wrong, Clara. You were right to trust me. You, Nellie, and Sage are my world."

Oh, this man. He was saying all the right things now. If only he'd done the same thing yesterday.

"That's pretty, but I *don't believe you*. You chose Jeremy and MZ over *us*. You lay in my bed and told me you'd had a bad day. That was only a half-truth—another word for a lie."

He winced, but he didn't deny it. "And I'm so fucking sorry for making that choice. In my head, I was doing right by you and my brother, but I know I fucked up. I'm human. Sometimes, I'm gonna do the wrong thing. Mess shit up. I'm here to fix it and remind you we love each other."

"You think I forgot I love you?" My chin wobbled, and I felt utterly pathetic. "God, if only. This would be so much easier if I hadn't let myself fall in love with you."

"I know, mama. I know." He released my hands to wrap his arms around me and press his face to my belly. "You don't have to forgive me today. I'm going to put in the work to get us back to where we need to be. If we have to start from the beginning, we will. I promise you I'll never keep anything from you again."

I wished I could let myself feel what he was saying. If I hadn't gone through what I had with Miller, I would have caved to Jake's desperation and beautiful promises. My instincts screamed for me to believe him, but they had led me astray one too many times.

I touched the top of his head. "History is repeating itself."

"It's not." He raised his head, and my breath caught. His face was flushed, eyes glassy. He looked as ravaged as I felt, and it hurt me. It hurt so badly, but I couldn't be the one to comfort him. Not when he'd put us in this position.

"I'm not letting you go, Clara."

I shook my head. "You made your choice, and it wasn't me."

"No. *No.* You can be mad at me and disagree with what I did—hell, I disagree with myself—but you are my first and only choice."

I leaned forward, meeting his pleading gaze. "I don't believe you."

"I know. I am really fucking sorry I gave you any reason to doubt me."

"Me too." I turned my head toward the door. "I'd like you to leave."

A deep gust of breath punched out of him. "That can't be it. This isn't it."

I shook my head. "I'm at work. I can't do this now."

"Right." He smoothed his hands up and down my thighs. "We'll talk more tonight. We'll work this out."

"No. I—I need some time."

He took my chin in his hand, turning me back toward him. "What kind of time?"

"I don't know. Enough for me not to be so in the thick of this. My thoughts are too jumbled. I can't sort them out."

"We'll sort it out together, Clara."

I squeezed my eyes shut and let out a hysterical laugh. "I can't sort out my feelings for you *with* you. I need you to give me space to think about this. If you don't give that to me and force me to answer you now, then we're o—"

His hand slid up to cover my mouth. "No. Don't say it. Those words don't leave your mouth."

I nodded, fresh tears slipping past my lashes. He swiped them away with his knuckles, so gentle and sweet.

Then, for the second time in a very short period, my office door swung open. It wasn't Thomas on the other side, but Luca.

He took a second to assess the scene—me crying, Jake on his knees pleading—then sprang into action. Closing the distance between the door and my desk, he motioned for Jake to get up.

"You need to leave. I'm not having you in my building upsetting my sister." Luca was a thundercloud, looming and dark. "Get up, Hayes."

For his part, Jake barely acknowledged Luca, his attention focused on me. "I'll give you some space, but you can't go silent on me." There was an edge of panic to his plea, and I understood it, but I couldn't promise him anything right now. "The only way we get through this is if we keep talking to each other."

Luca chuffed, his hand landing heavy on Jake's shoulder. "Should've thought about that yesterday. Too late now."

Ice melted in Jake's gaze. "Tell me it's not too late."

Luca's fingers dug in. "Get up and leave, or security will physically remove you."

Finally, Jake rose, but he went slowly, like his bones were old and creaky. As soon as I was free of him, I spun away. I couldn't bear watching him leave. Couldn't bear that it might have been for the last time. I couldn't have that in my memories.

I felt his presence, though. It lingered as my brother grumbled.

It took several long, drawn-out moments before Jake spoke with a clarity and sureness he hadn't possessed until now. "I love you, Clara. To my bones."

Of course it was that. A dagger to my brittle heart.

"Come on," Luca said with a bit of softness. "Let's go, Jake."

After Jake's heavy, plodding footsteps faded, the door clicked shut, and I was left alone with nothing but silence.

CHAPTER FORTY-ONE

Jake

It was the silence that did me in.

I was a man who had never minded solitude, like those quiet weeks between having Sage home. Clara and Nellie had cured me of that. They'd filled my home and life with dancing and laughter. Passion, joy, and so much love. Now that it had nowhere to go, my chest was near bursting.

The week wore on, and I didn't hear anything from Clara. No matter how many times I called and texted, I got nothing but silence in return.

I would've borrowed her words and said history was repeating itself, but nothing in my past compared to the stark absence of the love of my life and the little girl I'd been starting to think of as mine too.

Days of nothingness went by. I didn't go into the office. Instead, I spent time in MZ's garages, losing myself in fixing cars since I couldn't fix what I wanted to.

I was giving Jeremy as much silence as I'd been getting from Clara. I'd seen the news stories. MZ came out strong in denouncing Dallas Fox, but we were still mentioned every time a story ran about him.

Jeremy had to be having a hell of a time, but I couldn't find it in me to want to help. He'd asked for too much from me. I'd known it. He had too. And he'd done it anyway.

I was the idiot for giving in to him.

In my days of silence, I had a lot of time to think and make decisions. When I thought I'd be able to look at my brother without punching him, I'd let him know what conclusions I'd come to.

For now, I had to pull my shit together. Sage came back home yesterday, and I couldn't have her seeing me losing it. She was just a kid, and she needed to know her dad had his shit together so she could rely on me no matter what.

I couldn't fail another person I loved.

***

It'd been a week since I'd spoken to Clara. I was getting close to going to her house and forcing the subject on her, but that didn't feel right. Not yet.

Sage sat across from me, her fork scraping her plate as she slowly ate dinner. She'd been too busy studying me to get much food in her mouth.

"Are we ever going to talk about it?" she asked.

I cocked my head. "What do you need to talk about?"

She dropped her fork with a huff. "I'm not dumb, Dad. We haven't seen Clara and Nellie this week. You haven't taken any calls from her or spent too much time smiling like a goon at your phone. Where are they?"

I blew out a heavy breath and set my own fork down. "Clara and Nellie are home, but she asked for some space, so I'm giving it to her."

Her brow furrowed. "Space from us?"

"Nope. From me. This has nothing to do with you, sweetheart."

Blood rushed to her cheeks. "What did you do? Did you mess up?"

God, I wished I was the type of man who could lie to his kid. If she hadn't asked me a direct question, I sure as hell wouldn't have told her what I'd done to get where I was. But she had, so here we were.

"Yeah, I did." I scraped my hand over my scruff. "I'm hoping it wasn't too big and Clara will be able to forgive me."

"But what did you *do*?"

"I kept something from her I shouldn't have. Something that had the potential to affect her family's company. She found out and asked for some time to think about what she wants to do next."

As I spoke, Sage's eyes turned glassy, and her lips rolled over her teeth. Her fingers dug into the table so hard, the tips turned white. It was hard to look at her, but I needed to show her what it was like to own up to my mistakes. I didn't know if I'd get Clara back, but Sage was stuck with me, so I had to be the best I could be for her.

"I can't believe you did that," she rasped. "She must be so mad."

"She is, but I think she's more sad than anything."

"Oh." Whimpering, she folded her arms protectively around her middle. "Do you think she might forgive you, or...or are we never going to see her again?"

It took a lot for me to keep it together. This was exactly what I'd been avoiding—getting back to the place where my girl lost another important person. It was all my fault we were here, and I was fucking furious with myself. With my brother. And if I were honest, with Clara too.

"I hope she can forgive me." I tipped her chin with my knuckle and caught her watery eyes. "I bet you'll see her again, though. You're important to her."

I really fucking hoped I wasn't blowing smoke and Clara kept her end of the bargain. She had every right to ignore the hell out of me, but Sage hadn't done anything wrong. She didn't deserve to be set aside and forgotten.

"You just have to keep telling her you're sorry and won't do it again." She nodded like she agreed with herself. "We can't lose her, Dad. She's important to us too. You can't give up on winning her back. You can't."

"I'm not going to, Sagie." I left my seat to wrap her in my arms and kiss the top of her head. "I know it's hard, but I'd like for you to try not to worry about this. I want to enjoy my Sage time this week. If you're all mopey 'cause all you've got is me to hang around with, I'll call Dex to join us."

"Oh my god, no. Dad, you *wouldn't*."

I nodded, and for the first time in a long while, I grinned. "Try me, kid. If you mope or catch me moping, we're calling in Dex. He'll cure us."

She shuddered. "He'll spread diseases! He licks everything."

"I don't think you want me to tell you the gross stuff you did when you were his age."

Her hands slammed over her ears. "La-la-la, can't hear you."

Laughing, I kissed her again, relieved she was here with me. No matter how shitty life was, I always had this beautiful, perfect spark of joy I got to claim as my own.

And that was worth a whole lot.

I couldn't forget that.

Chapter Forty-Two
Clara

I t might have been the wrong thing to do, but throwing myself into work was about survival. I spent a week in Utah overseeing the new management at our plant there. Fortunately, Marina was able to come with me to watch Nellie when I was working, and the three of us went on adventures when I wasn't.

The distance helped. Being somewhere I hadn't shared with Jake seemed truly imperative to...well, breathe.

I couldn't decide if I was overreacting or if what Jake had done was as horrible as it felt. Forgiving him and brushing it aside certainly would have been the easy choice, and god, how I wished I could do that.

But it didn't feel right. What was to stop him from doing something like this in the future? He could tell me he would never keep anything from me again, but he'd made *so* many promises he could break just as easily.

As soon as we were home from our trip, a different kind of pain began. Nellie had run through the house like she was looking for something, then came trudging back to me, her little lip poking out.

"Where's Jake?"

"He's not here, honey. It's just us girls."

"Okay." She fished my phone out of my purse and handed it to me. "We can call him."

My stomach twisted into a barbed wire knot. "Not right now. What if we watch your show?"

She'd been distracted that time, but later, after her bath and bedtime stories, she brought him up again.

"I can call Jake."

"No. I'm sorry, but it's too late. He's sleeping."

"He sleeps at my house." Her chin bunched and quivered. "Sage too."

"Not tonight," I told her as gently as I could.

"Tomorrow?"

I smoothed her hair from her sweet face, wishing I could give her what she wanted. I wanted him too, but I didn't know how to get past this. Or if I could.

"We'll see."

She jerked her head away, clutched the dolls Jake and Shira had given her, and rolled over, giving me her back. Under her breath, she muttered, "Want my Jake."

The remnants of my broken heart crumbled into dust. I couldn't give her what she wanted, and it felt like it was my fault. All I could do was be present and remind her she was safe and cared for and that would never change. "I love you, Nell-Belle. Very, very much. I hope you have sweet dreams."

After a moment, I heard a quiet, "Wuv you too, Mommy," and for a very short span of time, all was right with the world.

It didn't last.

The next few evenings and bedtimes were filled with demands I couldn't fulfill and angry, mournful tears. How I'd kept myself together in front of my daughter, I could not say. It was a feat I hadn't known I'd had the strength to survive.

"Where's my Jake?" she cried, big fat tears streaming down her cheeks. "I need my Jake!"

"I'm sorry, Nell-Belle. We can't have Jake right now."

"No!" Her cry came straight from her heart. "My Jake! I call him. I need my Jake, Mommy."

I held her against my chest as sobs rocked her small body, hugging her tight. It was too much. More than I could bear. But I had to. I had to stand firm and be strong for her.

"I love you, honey," I crooned. "Mommy's here, and I love you."

She clung to me, even though I was certain she was furious with me for not getting her Jake.

"I need him," she whimpered. "My Jake."

"I know, Nell-Belle. I know."

That night, I'd scrolled through his texts. Since he'd left my office, he hadn't failed to send at least one every day. So many times, I'd been close to replying, but I hadn't been able to bring myself to.

Fortunately for both Nellie and me, Shira and Bea came over the next night, giving us a much-needed distraction. Nellie was in hog heaven with all the attention from my friends and requested Bea put her to bed.

When everything was quiet, the three of us took large glasses of wine onto my deck and unwound.

They allowed me half of my glass before pressing about what was going on.

"Are you broken up?" Bea asked.

"I don't know," I replied honestly. "It's been two weeks, and I just can't get myself to even think about it."

"Why not?"

I shrugged. "It hurts, and whenever I try to sort out my thoughts, they get jumbled with my feelings about Miller. I...I'm confused. And so damn sad, I don't know how to keep moving sometimes."

"Don't you think speaking to him would help?" Shira asked.

"Maybe." I rubbed my forehead. "I'd planned on speaking to him, but I wanted to be more clear headed. I didn't think I'd be stuck in the same place two weeks later."

Bea hummed, and I raised a brow at her. "Please, speak freely. It isn't like you to hold back."

"I'm probably going to hurt your feelings," Bea stated.

I snorted a laugh. "Last night, my daughter pleaded and cried for me to give her Jake. I don't think my feelings could possibly hurt any worse."

"All right." She took a deep breath, gesturing in my direction. "This is very like you. The whole needing a clear head before you'll even have a conversation with Jake. You revel in the details and ticking boxes. It's what makes you successful at your job. But this...it isn't that, Clara. You're treating the fate of your relationship like it's a business deal and you won't go to the table without being fully prepared."

"Bea," Shira gasped. "That was—"

"It's true, Shir," Bea said. "Tell me what part is a lie."

Shira glanced from me to Bea, her mouth opening and closing, no denial forthcoming.

"Is that what I'm doing?" I whispered. "I don't mean to. But I can't just follow my feelings. If this were about how much I love him, I would've forgiven Jake immediately."

Bea sipped her wine, as calm and cool as always. "I'm not saying you need to forgive him now—or ever. But taking two weeks to gather facts when you already have them isn't going to get you anywhere."

My shoulders deflated. "I know, but—"

"Is it safer?" Shira asked. "This...in-between—is it safer for you, Clara?"

"What do you mean?" I asked.

"I mean...I was there when Miller went to prison. I saw what that did to you. If I'd been pressed, I would have said you'd never open up to anyone again."

"I would have said the same," I agreed.

Shira set her glass down to clutch my hands. "You did, though. You let Jake in and shared Nellie with him. That was huge for you...and it also terrified you, right?"

I nodded. I couldn't deny it. "Absolutely."

Shira wasn't a big talker, but she seemed determined to get this out. If it was important for her to say, I would listen, even if I didn't exactly want to hear it.

"You never stopped being terrified of having your heart broken again, did you?"

Pressing my lips together, I shook my head. At the very root of me, I carried a deep-seated fear I'd end up back in the dark place Miller had left me, and I couldn't go back there. Not with Nellie. I had to stay in the light for her.

Shira's big eyes were so gentle, steady on me as she imparted her thoughts. "If you let Jake go now, it's safer for you. That doesn't mean it's the wrong decision, but if you're choosing it because of that, I think it is."

I fell back against my chair's cushions. She might as well have taken a look inside me and mapped my neuroses out for me to clearly see. There was no question she was right. I might not have been aware of what I was doing, but I'd certainly allowed two weeks to go by because it was safer than facing what might happen if I confronted Jake head-on.

Bea held up her glass. "Yes. Shira put it much better and more kind than me. I agree with everything she said."

I looked up at the stars twinkling above me. "So, I have to decide if I can move on from this."

"Oh, you can," Bea said with assurance. "Whether you move on with Jake or on your own is what's up in the air. Do you want my vote?"

I rolled my wrist. "Sure. Why not?"

"I can't believe I'm saying this since I would tell you to walk away from ninety-nine percent of the men on this planet, but Jake...he adores you, Clara. And he's so sweet with Nellie. I can't, in good conscience, advise you not to at least have a meaningful conversation with him."

I blinked at my friend, who regularly chewed men up and spit them out. Not necessarily men she dated, but random guys on the street who tried to talk to her—which happened at a surprising frequency.

"You've gone soft," I said.

"Don't say that." Bea's nose crinkled. "It's the influence of the two of you. You know that, right?"

Shira let out a tinkling laugh. "Well, you've toughened me up a little."

Bea's brow arched. "Have I?"

Shira's cheeks pinkened. "You've made me *want* to be tougher. And for what it's worth, Clara, I love you with Jake. What he did was a betrayal, but I don't think it's unforgivable." Her long lashes lowered to brush her cheeks. "Then again, I haven't been through what you have."

"I hear you," I whispered. "I'm still scared."

Bea kicked my chair. "But you're a badass, Clara Rossi. You ride a motorcycle and make grown men cry."

"That happened once." I laughed through my welling tears. "I'm going to talk to him."

Bea tapped her chin, her eyes sweeping over me. "When?"

"I don't know. Soon."

Her eyes flared. "Soon could be next month, knowing you and how you overthink everything. Give yourself a deadline."

"By tomorrow," Shira added. "End of the day."

I crossed my arms over my chest. "What if I'm not ready?"

Bea put her finger to her lips. "Shhh. We're not humoring you anymore."

"Is this tough love?" I turned to Shira. "You too?"

Shira gave me her meanest look, which was not very mean at all. "End of the day tomorrow...or else."

I tried not to let the churning fear in my belly surface. My friends were right to push me. They'd done it when I'd needed it in the past, and I'd needed it even more now.

"All right. I'll contact him by the end of the day tomorrow."

First, I'd have to figure out what exactly I would say to him.

CHAPTER FORTY-THREE
Clara

I had been staring at my phone all day, yet the words refused to come. So far, I'd typed, "Hi." That didn't seem to be enough, and I had no clue what to say after that.

I'd read his texts, though. Over and over.

I'm sorry, Clara.

Don't forget how much I love you.

We need to talk to make this right. Everything's going to stay fucked until we talk.

Gotta know you're all right. Give me something. Anything.

Sage has been asking about you. This isn't fair to her. Not fair to any of us.

I miss you. Miss you so fucking bad, I can't breathe sometimes.

Last night, I heard Nellie's laugh in my dreams. Woke up with tears on my face. I'm breaking here, mama. Something's gotta give.

To tell you the truth, I'm pissed off you're doing this. I love you more than anything, but I'm mad at you too.

Just talk to me.

Not much work had gotten done. I'd sat through meetings and conference calls, spacing out during most of them. Fortunately, the topics weren't in my arena, and Thomas had been there to take notes in case there might've been anything I needed to know later.

I was once again staring at my phone when Thomas strode into my office, a puzzled expression on his face.

"I just received a strange call from security in the lobby," he announced.

I threw my phone down on my desk and straightened. "What was strange about it?"

"They said there's a young girl down there asking for you. A few weeks ago, I would have said Clara Rossi doesn't know any young girls, but given the phone call I fielded, I'm aware of one. Were you expecting a visit from your little friend?"

My brows drew together in confusion. "My friend...is Sage in the lobby?"

Smirking, he nodded. "Yep. What should I tell security to do with her?"

I pushed back from my desk and stood. "Tell them I'm coming. I'll be down there in a minute."

My mom instinct—which I trusted far more than my man instinct—sounded the alarms. How was Sage here? She should have been in school fifteen miles away.

The elevator went at a snail's pace. By the time it reached the lobby, I was frantic to get my eyes on Sage and make sure she was okay. When I found her behind the security desk, spinning on one of the guards' chairs, I nearly folded in half with relief.

"Sage." I gripped the edge of the desk. "Honey, what are you doing here?"

She stopped spinning and vaulted out of the chair. "Clara!" Then she was around the desk and throwing herself at me before I could brace myself. Luckily, she was light as a feather and didn't topple us over when I caught her in a hug.

As I held her, she started rambling. "I'm sorry for just showing up like this, but I haven't seen you in so long, and I really wanted to talk to you. My dad said you were taking space, but not from me, so I didn't think you'd mind seeing me. I know I'm not supposed to come to your job, and I'm sorry if I interrupted something important, but I couldn't wait another day."

"Sage" —I pulled back to look at her— "how did you get here? Shouldn't you be in school?"

"Well, yes, but this was important." She bit down on her bottom lip before admitting, "I looked up the bus routes last night. I had to take three to get here, but it was super easy. Public transportation is totally legit in this city."

"Wait, wait, wait—do your mom and dad know you're here?" I had a feeling I already knew the answer, but I needed her to confirm it so I could wrap my head around how much trouble she was going to be in.

"Um..." She dug her toe into the floor sheepishly. "Not really. I was going to tell my dad when I got home."

"Shit." I smacked my forehead. "Okay, here's what we're going to do; let's go sit down over there, have a treat from the coffee stand, and catch up. But first, we have to call your dad and tell him where you are."

I escorted Sage to one of the café tables near the stand in the lobby that served coffee, pastries, and sandwiches. My stomach was a roiling mess when I walked a few feet from her and dialed Jake. I hadn't heard his voice in—

"Clara?" he rasped.

"Hi, Jake. I—"

"Any other time, Clara—*any* other time...but I can't talk. Sage is missing—"

"She's not missing," I blurted out. "She's here."

"What? Where?"

"At Rossi. She's here with me in the lobby."

He was silent for a long beat, then, in an even tone, he asked, "What is she doing there?"

"She wanted to see me," I admitted quietly. Too quiet for all the background noise around me, but from his grunt, he'd heard. "Tell me what you want me to do. Bring her home?"

"No. I'm coming there. Give me twenty minutes."

"Of course. We'll be waiting."

He hung up without another word, and I returned to Sage. "Your dad's coming."

Her brow crinkled. "Is he mad?"

"I think he's mostly relieved." I nodded toward the cart. "Let's order something. We can talk while we wait for him."

Sage wanted a donut, and I decided I needed one too. We sat down at the small table with our treat, and I watched her dig in, getting chocolate frosting on her teeth and lips. My stomach panged. I'd missed her terribly over the past couple weeks and was just now realizing the magnitude of it.

So, I told her. "I missed you, Sage. I'm sorry I haven't called or texted. I should have, and I really regret not doing that."

She wiped her mouth with a bunched-up napkin. "I thought you would, you know. I guess I could have texted you first, but even though my dad said the space you were taking was because of him, I wasn't sure I believed it."

"He was right, though. You have quickly become one of my favorite people. Not many people know about Brian Kegan and Periodgate. I told you that because you're important to me."

Her stare was long and contemplative. "It doesn't really feel that way."

Oh, my heart. My poor, crumbling heart.

"I'm sorry. I was taking care of myself, and I neglected you."

"Yeah." She looked down at the napkin in her hand. "Are you breaking up with my dad?"

"I don't know what's going to happen with us, but I don't want you to worry about that. You have enough on your plate. Wait a good ten years before you start dealing with grown-up stuff. It's no fun, I promise you."

"Okay. I get that." She fluttered her lashes at me. "But just so you know, if you guys do break up, I'll probably be deeply traumatized."

A laugh snuck out of me. This kid knew how to dig the knife in and look adorable doing it.

"Wow, if I'd known I was going on a guilt trip, I would have brought my passport."

She snickered. "That's a good one. I'm writing that down."

"You'll have to credit my brother. He said that to me one too many times growing up."

After that, the vibe lightened. We were trading jokes when Jake stormed toward us, long strides eating the distance. Sage's back was to him, so she missed her father's tortured glare. It must've been the sound of her laughter that slowed his approach. His eyes met mine, and while his glare softened, the torture remained.

I had to hold on to the table to stop myself from going to him. He needed a hug, comfort, and it felt incredibly unnatural not to give that to him.

I interrupted Sage's story. "Your dad's here."

She whirled around, and Jake tore his gaze from me to peer down at his daughter.

"Don't be mad." She balled her hands up under his chin, giving that same fluttery-eyed look she'd used on me earlier. "Please, Daddy."

He chuffed. "Oh, I'm mad. Your mom and Mike are beside themselves. I can't even begin to fathom what you were thinking, but we're going to talk."

Her head bowed. "Okay. I'm really sorry."

The next moment, he grabbed her from her seat and pulled her into his arms, hugging her tight. His arms were shaking as he held her and murmured something I couldn't hear against her head. I imagined he was telling her he loved her and that she'd shaved at least a decade off his life today.

I couldn't tear my eyes off them—off *him*. I drank in the sight of him, wondering how I'd been able to go so long without seeing him.

Strangely, when Miller betrayed me, my love for him had shut off like a valve. One minute, it was streaming freely, and the next, it was cut off, the pipes dry as a bone. That wasn't the case with Jake. I loved him now just as much as I had before I found out what he'd done.

Still, I couldn't bring myself to stand or go to him. My feet were leaden with fear.

He took the choice out of my hands. Pulling back from Sage, he pointed her to a bench a good distance away and sternly ordered her to wait. Once she followed his orders, he closed in on me, taking the chair across from mine.

We stared and stared and stared. He had to be the one to speak first. My tongue was stuck to the roof of my dry mouth, and I couldn't think of anything more than his eyes, his lips, his hands, the beating heart inside his warm chest. Plus, I was afraid if I said something now, it would come out wrong. Desperate. I would latch on to him, not because I had gotten over what he'd done, but because the last two weeks had been hell, and I couldn't stand to let him walk away again.

"You made me a liar to my daughter, Clara."

I jolted, surprised by his growl and what he'd said. "What do you mean?"

"I told her you'd never leave her in the dust like my ex, but you did. You left us both that way." He pressed a hand to his head. "I don't care about me. But that little girl is all I have, and she's hurting. Isn't today proof enough for you?"

"Jake, I—" I licked my impossibly dry lips. "I apologized to Sage, and from here on out, I'll be there for her. I know I screwed up, but she and I made amends."

"Good." He nodded curtly. "If you want out of her life, you'll need to do that with compassion."

I shook my head. "I don't want out of her life."

He stared at me, his jaw working. "How's that going to work? You hang out with my kid without seeing me? Let's be real. I messed up badly, but I can't continue paying for another man's crimes."

My eyes flared. "So that's it? You're giving up on me?"

His brow dipped in confusion. "Don't you want me to?"

"No, I—" I sucked in a deep breath. "I was going to contact you tonight. I promised Bea and Shira I would. You're right; we need to talk. I've *wanted* to talk to you since the moment you left my office, but I'm scared. Even now, sitting across from you."

He shook his head. "You don't have anything to be afraid of when it comes to me."

My laugh was humorous. "I have everything to be afraid of. If this happens again…"

"It won't."

My eyes burned, which was just great. If I cried in the lobby of my office building, I would have to take early retirement.

"See? This is the part that's scary, Jake. To get past this, I'll have to take your word. And while every part of me is screaming for me to wrap my arms around you, I don't know if I can trust *myself*. I don't mean to make you pay for another man's crimes. A lot of the time, it feels like I'm the one paying for them. Until you. It felt like I'd served my time, and I was free."

His nostrils flared as he took me in. Remorse carved deep lines between his brows and tugged at the corners of his mouth. But his tenderness for me hadn't been erased. It was there in the sweep of his icy blues and the way his hands slid across the table, stopping just before they reached mine.

"Then I went and threw you back behind those bars."

I nodded slowly. "You threw me, but I pulled the door shut."

I waved him off before he said anything else. I couldn't do this here. It was too big to have over half-eaten donuts with nosy security guards pretending they weren't watching from their desks. "You should get Sage home. I'm sure Carly and Mike want to see her with their own eyes."

He gave me a good long stare before rapping his knuckles on the table. "If I text, will you reply?"

"I will."

Another curt nod. Jake wasn't giving anything away. "I'll be in touch." He didn't say when, and I didn't ask. I'd probably lost that right when I'd left him hanging for so long.

As he got up to walk away, I caught Sage's wide eyes. "Jake?"

He turned back. "Yeah?"

"Go easy on her, okay? I know she scared the hell out of you—"

"Don't worry about Sage. We've got her taken care of."

With those sharp, parting words, he collected his daughter, arm circling her narrow shoulders, and led her out of the building...and what felt like my life.

Before I trudged back upstairs, I grabbed the rest of my donut. This wasn't one of those times chocolate cured everything, but the taste of it brought me back to my mother holding me and telling me everything was going to be all right. I needed a little bit of that right now.

Chapter Forty-four

Jake

Jeremy was sitting on my porch when I pulled into my driveway after dropping Sage off at her mom's.

I hadn't spoken to him since I'd walked out of our building two weeks ago. Seeing him brought on an onslaught of mixed emotions, dread being the biggest.

I was a big fucking hypocrite. I'd managed to be angry at Clara for avoiding having a conversation when I'd been doing the exact same thing with my brother. He'd texted, called, showed up at my place, and I'd turned my back. First, because I'd been so damn mad at him, then it had come down to not wanting to vocalize the decision I'd made the moment he'd asked me to pick him and MZ over Clara.

I walked up the porch steps warily. Jeremy stood, his movements creaky, like he'd been there a while. He probably had. I'd called him when Sage had gone missing on the off chance she'd gone to see him or Anne.

"Sage is at Carly's?" he asked.

"Yep." I unlocked the door, leaving it open for Jeremy to follow me in. I was just about wrung out from that hour between Sage's school notifying us she was absent and the call from Clara, but it was time to face this.

"She's okay?"

"She is. Grounded but no worse for wear."

He chuffed. "I bet you and Carly can't say the same."

"No, we can't."

I didn't stop walking when I reached the kitchen, only paused to grab a beer then headed out to the deck. If this was going to happen, it'd be over an icy drink with my favorite view as the background.

Jeremy took the seat beside me, his own beer in hand. For a while, we were just two brothers, sipping from our bottles, watching the sun go down.

Jer spoke first, but not about what I'd expected. "Sage went to Clara."

"Kid loves her. I made a decision that has kept them apart."

Clara hadn't helped, but I wasn't mad at her anymore. Now that I'd seen her in the flesh, the tears in her eyes, the way she'd gripped the table with all her might... Her fear had been palpable, but she'd still asked me to go easy on Sage because she cared about my girl.

I'd dropped my anger, replacing it with a determination to bring us all back together where we belonged.

"Right." Jer's head dropped. "A decision I asked you to make."

"Mmm." I took a long pull from my bottle. "You shouldn't have asked, and I shouldn't have gone along with it. You knew I would, though, because I've always supported you."

"Like I always support you."

"Maybe." I put my empty bottle down and rested my head on my chair's cushion, watching the sky explode in oranges and pinks. "You crossed my line, Jer. I think you did it because you were sure I'd stay, no matter what. And you might've been right. Before Clara, that is."

He exhaled slowly. "I know she means a lot to you. In retrospect, there was no need to keep the story from her. At the time, I was grasping at straws, trying to save the deal if I could."

"I know that. You're not telling me anything new. Retrospect or not, you shouldn't have asked."

"This is a subject we'll have to agree to disagree on."

I turned my head, glancing at him. Jeremy wasn't a bad man, but he'd learned to be cold from the people who should have given him warmth. He could turn his emotions off when they got in the way. He adored his wife, but if I'd asked, he would have kept the same secret from her. No matter how long I'd tried to give him what he'd grown up without, he wasn't going to change. My loyalty and sacrifice were appreciated, sure, but they weren't sacred. Jeremy might not ever outright betray me, but he'd trod over me if he had to.

Hell, he already had.

"I'm not coming back to MZ," I stated.

He jerked like I'd surprised him. It shouldn't have, though. I'd told him what would happen if he kept secrets, and I was a man of my word.

"This is not the time to walk away. Without the Rossi deal, we'll have no choice but to close more stores. You're the only one I trust to handle—"

"It's done, Jer. The minute you learned about Dallas Fox and chose to call Roman and the others before telling me what was going on, I was gone. The only way you and I are going to be able to get good again is if I have nothing to do with MZ. You can't be my brother and boss. It's not going to work. You're no good at it, and if I don't walk, I'm afraid I'll bow under your pressure and fuck up again."

"Come on, Jake. There won't be another Rossi deal. You know that. There's no chance for you to have a conflict of interest with Clara again."

"That may be true, but I don't like who I am working at MZ. It's not me, Jer. I don't need or want it."

He scoffed. "You don't want the salary that bought you this house?"

"I don't. If I need to, I'll move somewhere smaller. Hell, I'll take a page out of your book and sell my shares to Roman."

"You're not selling your shares," he gritted out.

I shrugged. "I lived a long time without our grandfather's money. It was a good, comfortable life. I'm going to get back under the hood—do what I do best. If that means I need to give up my shares, they're yours."

His gaze bore into the side of my head, but now that I'd told him my intentions, a weight had been lifted off my chest, and I could take my first deep, clear breath since before he'd asked me to work at MZ with him.

"You're serious."

I smiled at the horizon. "Deadly."

"When I need you most, you're walking away?"

I drummed my fingers on my stomach, calm as I'd been in a while. "Not walking away from you, Jer—walking away from a job I don't want and get no joy from. If I stay, you and I are gonna end up hating each other."

"We've been fine the last few years."

I raised a brow. "You've been keeping secrets. I imagine there's a lot more I don't know about, and that's okay. I don't want to know. MZ is your legacy—it's never been mine."

He shot up from his seat and crossed to the railing. Gripping it tight, he tipped his head back to the sky and hollered his frustration.

"*Fuck!*" he cried. "*God-fucking-dammit.*"

I got up and stood beside him, placing my arm around his shoulders. No matter how old we got, he was still the kid who had come to me on empty and allowed me to fill him up. I was honored I'd been the one to do it, and I wasn't relinquishing that role. Brothers didn't do that, even when they disagreed.

"I'm sticking, Jer. You hear me?" I turned to him and took his shoulders in my hands, giving him a jostle. "This doesn't mean I'm not sticking. We're gonna get back to the good we've always been—when the favors you asked of me were fixing your car or helping you plan a surprise for your wife—things I'll jump at the chance to do. Always."

He nodded. If he was more than frustrated, he didn't show it. Jeremy's emotions were buried deep, only ever surfacing for brief, fleeting glances.

"I hear you." He bowed his head like it was too heavy to hold up any longer. "And I'm sorry I asked you for too much. You're right to get out now. Chances are, I would have continued asking."

Neither of us had to fill in the unspoken words, that he'd needed to test how far I would've gone for him. Inside his tightly controlled exterior was an insecure kid who had a hard time believing anything good could be his. Even his brother.

"Come here," I gruffed, pulling him against me.

He was slow to reciprocate my embrace. For a while, he stood stiff, but I'd done this dance with him. I kept on hugging, and little by little, his tension eased.

"I'm sorry," he repeated.

"I know." I slapped his back and took a step back. "We'll get through it."

He dug the heel of his hand into his forehead and grimaced. "Are there rules now? Can I talk to you about MZ? Or is that forbidden?"

I almost laughed. "Nothing's off-limits except you asking me to come back. I told you, we're no longer coworkers, but I'm here. Always."

Jeremy stayed a while after that. We switched to soda and went from watching the sunset to counting stars. I asked for his advice on getting Clara back. He was shit at it, but it was good to laugh at his suggestion of copying his move by sitting on her doorstep until she wanted to talk.

Once he was gone, I walked through my empty house, the silence beating down on me. I started to go upstairs to turn in early then stopped and asked myself what the hell I was doing. Why was I wasting more time not being with Clara?

I picked up my phone, but I didn't call or text. If I gave her the opportunity to say no, she might take it.

To hell with that.

The time for waiting on her had passed.

CHAPTER FORTY-FIVE

Clara

My phone was silent. I'd taken Jake's texts for granted, to be sure, but I guess, after today, I thought I'd hear from him.

He'd said he'd be in touch, just not when. When Nellie had been awake, I had been distracted enough not to constantly check for a message, but she'd been asleep for a couple hours, and I'd done nothing *but* check since.

I swiped to our messages, reading his last few, practically begging me to text back. My stomach clenched, guilt and frustration at war inside me. Why had I waited so long to face this?

This was stupid. I'd told Jake I'd reply, but why would he believe that? The least I could do was reach out first. It was more than my turn.

Me: *Hey…just checking in. When you're ready to talk, I'm here. I hope Sage is okay and not in too much trouble.*

I sent the message then instantly regretted it. It wasn't my business how he punished Sage. He'd made it clear he and Carly had it handled.

Me: *Whatever you and Carly decide will be right. Sorry if I implied something else.*

I threw my phone across the couch and groaned at the ceiling. How had I become this person?

Fucking Miller.

I groaned again. As much as I wished I could put the blame for everything on my ex, he was locked up far away. This mess was mine. Jake had a hand in it, no question, but I'd been the one to keep digging my hole deeper and deeper, and now I didn't know how to get out.

I picked up my phone and sent another text. This message wasn't as polite and formal. It might've been somewhat desperate, but Jake had bared himself to me, so maybe it was my turn.

Me: *I want you to know I love you very much, and I want to try to work through this with you. My heart broke when you kept things from me, but it's ten times worse without you. I miss you, Jake. I want our beautiful life back, and I want you to find a way for that to happen. Please find a way.*

Out of fight, I fell back against the cushions. I'd either hear from him or not, but I wouldn't give up. I'd try again tomorrow, the day after that, and—

Vroom, vroom.

What the hell?

An engine revved, and it sounded like it was right outside my house. Another rev. There was no mistaking the sound of a motor-cycle. A Rossi, I was certain of it.

My heart leapt into my throat, and I vaulted off the couch, running for the front door. Yanking it open, I stepped out onto my porch.

There he was.

Jake Hayes, leaning against his motorcycle in my driveway. His arms were folded over his chest, long legs stretched out with his ankles crossed. He looked cool as a cucumber while I was trembling.

"I texted you," I called out.

He patted the pocket on his chest where he kept his phone. "Haven't checked. I was riding."

"Okay."

He pointed to the ground in front of him. "Come over here."

Like always, drawn to this man, my feet carried me to him before I'd made the conscious thought to step off my porch. An arm's length from him, Jake raked his eyes over me, landing on my feet.

"Where're your shoes?"

I peered at my bare feet and wiggled my pedicured toes. "I didn't take the time to put them on."

His head cocked. "You heard the motor and came running?"

"I knew it was you."

"That's some urgency," he murmured. Then he slipped his phone from his pocket, the glow illuminating his inscrutable face. He took his time studying the screen before raising his eyes to me. "I want our beautiful life back too."

"How do we do that? What do we change so we don't end up right back here?"

"There won't be a next time."

"You can't know that."

"I do," he said simply. "I haven't been back to MZ since that day, but before I came here, I talked to Jer and made it official. I'm done. As of right now, I'm unemployed. Don't know if that's a selling point, but it is what it is."

It was too dark for me to get a read on him, so I stepped closer. At least, that was the excuse I'd used. Once his scent hit me—leather and wind—I couldn't deny I'd just wanted to be near him. His warmth filled the inches between us, and my toes touched the ends of his boots.

"I never would have asked you to quit," I said softly.

"But I needed to. I've been unhappy there since the day I started. And I couldn't come to you with promises unless I made the changes to make them irrefutable. When I tell you I'll never put business before you, you can take that as fact. I hope you'll give me the time to prove my word trustworthy. That's all I'm asking for, Clara. I need that time."

My guts were twisted in knots, and a "yes" caught in my throat. There were things to say before I could throw myself into his arms like I so desperately wanted.

"I used to measure my life in *before Miller* and *after Miller*. I could look back and see the distinct delineation of who I was and who I became. The truth is, I had to rebuild myself from scratch and decide who I wanted to be because I had formed myself around him. I chose the woman standing in front of you. And you love her."

"I love the hell out of her," he agreed gruffly.

I smiled. It felt damn good to hear that out loud, and I really didn't want to cry another tear. "I love you back." I put my hand on his crossed arms, his muscles rippling beneath my touch. "I can't divide my life that way anymore. Now, it's everything that came before you and—"

"Don't say after me." His arms came loose to grip my waist. "There's no after me. We're gonna ride this out in the middle until we get to the end."

"I would really like that. I don't want there to be an after either."

He looked at me with fierceness and all the promises in the world. "There won't be."

Heart hammering, I reached for his face, the bristles of his beard tickling my palms. "We can only have honesty."

"I agree. I've got nothing to hide, and I won't be putting myself in a situation where I'll need to keep anything from you." He hooked a finger into the waistband of my pajama pants. "I'll help you work through your fear, but you have to be standing beside me. No more hiding from it."

I shook my head. "I won't hide—so long as you're with me."

"I'm with you, Clara. I can't be without you."

I smiled again and slid my hands along his jaw to circle his neck. "I don't *want* to be without you, baby."

Eyes slamming closed, he released a shuddering breath and yanked me against him, burying his nose in my hair.

"Make sure you mean that. I'm an unemployed mechanic, mama, not exactly the guy in the suit you fell for."

"Oh, please. I fell for my motorcycle man long before I saw you in a suit." I kissed the center of his chest then rested my head there. "And I don't know if you noticed, but I make my own money, so..."

He huffed a laugh, squeezing me tighter. "That's my girl." Balling my shirt in his fist, his lips grazed my temple. "That's my fuckin' girl."

I tipped my head back, and he took the opportunity to press his lips to mine, sweeping me up in the pure, easy beauty of being loved by Jake Hayes.

I still had my fears, but my love for this man and our beautiful life was strong enough to beat them back. One day, even defeat them entirely. As he held me tight yet was oh so careful not to step on my bare toes, I knew that to be true.

We'd ride this thing down the middle, leather and wind all the way to the end.

Epilogue

Jake

Three Years Later

"Daddyyy!"

"Dad!"

"Daaaaaa!"

I grinned down at Clara, and she smiled back at me.

"Thwarted," she whispered.

"Little cockblockers," I murmured against her upturned lips. Louder, I called out, "Hold your horses, I'm coming!"

Clara snickered. "Good thing they're cute."

"Damn right."

I rolled off my wife and threw on a T-shirt. "Sleep a little more. I'll see what the ruckus is about."

My beautiful Clara stretched languidly in our bed, her eyes already fluttering closed. A lot had changed over the last three years, but she was still a night owl who loved her sleep-ins. I tried to give her that as often as I could. Our kids, on the other hand, didn't always cooperate.

All three were waiting in the hall. Nellie's hands were on her hips, but her sass was hard to take seriously when her hair was a tangled cloud of brown on top of her head.

"Hi, Daddy," she greeted. "Nico went into my room. Can you tell him not to do that, please?"

Nearly seven, Nellie had long since stopped saying "peas," which had just about killed Clara. Our girl was growing up faster than either of us was ready for, but she was full of the kind of vim and vigor that made a dad proud as hell. I didn't have to worry about her being pushed around at school or in the world. She handled her business and sometimes tried to handle other kids' too, which they didn't always appreciate.

"He was saying good morning." Sage bounced her brother on her hip, and he melted into her. Clara and I had been worried about the vast age difference between them and whether they'd bond as siblings, but they were two peas in a pod.

Nellie stomped her little foot. "He was trying to steal my capybara stuffie."

Sage ruffled her sister's messy hair. "Don't worry, Nell-Belle. I wouldn't have let him."

Nico waved at me, the dimples in his round cheeks popping. "Hi, Da!"

"Morning, buddy." I plucked him out of Sage's arms, kissing the top of her head as I did. We only had a couple years before she was off to college, so I made sure to get my affection in when I could. "Let's get out of the hall so Mommy can sleep. All right?"

Our noses led us to the kitchen, where Marina was cooking breakfast like she did every morning. When Clara and I had gotten engaged six months after that night in her driveway, we'd planned where we'd live together, and whether Marina would come too had never been a question.

That meant buying a new house near my old one and adding an apartment over the garage. Sage could still walk back and forth between the new house and her mom's, and I still had the view I'd loved most about my old place.

Here, we had room to spread out. A big garage for our bikes and the kids' toys. And most importantly, there'd been room to grow.

Clara had once said she'd thought she was too old to have more children, but we'd both wanted to share that experience together. The moment we'd said, "I do," we'd started trying. A few months later, she'd taken five pregnancy tests before finally believing it was happening.

I'd gotten to take care of her through her pregnancy and delivery the way she deserved. As long as I lived, I'd remember the feeling of holding her hand as we both saw our son for the first time. That squalling, angry pink thing of beauty who was part of us both.

Being a team with a newborn had been brand new, but we'd rocked that phase, just like every phase since. We were good together and balanced each other out.

Clara joined us in the family room a while later. Sage was on the couch reading, Nellie was dancing along to her favorite pop star's music video, and Nico was using my stomach as his own personal trampoline.

A typical Saturday in this house.

I couldn't think of anything better.

"Mommy, look!" Nellie twirled and kicked, then did some complicated hand motions. "Did you see that? I did it just like Sabrina."

Clara's eyes flared. "I saw, Nell-Belle. Your practice is paying off, don't you think?"

"Yep." Nellie beamed and spun back to the TV. "I'm going to do it again. Watch me all the way through, please."

"You got it, honey."

Clara perched on the couch by Sage, patting her knee while giving Nellie the attention she demanded. Nico instantly got tired of me and abandoned me for his mother. He pulled himself up onto the couch and climbed into her lap. She situated him there, her arms around his little round body, never taking her eyes off Nellie.

I sat on the floor, looking at my family, my wife at the center. Life was good.

Great.

Fuckin' grand.

It wasn't perfect, though. I'd opened my own garage a few months after leaving MZ, which had meant a lot of time and work. Almost three years in, my business was doing well. I was proud of what I'd made, and more importantly, I didn't have to drag myself to work every day. But I was busy as hell, as was Clara, and time was at a premium.

We made the most of what we had. Lazy mornings like this were my favorite thing. All of us in one room, together, enjoying each other's company. This was why I got up every day. These people, my whole world.

Later, when Nico was napping and the girls were keeping each other busy, I cornered Clara in the kitchen, pressing my front to her plush ass. Humming, she leaned her head against my shoulder and tipped her face so I could kiss her.

I took her offering, sipping from her lips. "I love you."

"I love you too, baby."

I closed my eyes and groaned. Her saying that would never not affect me.

She tried to step away from me, but I wasn't ready to let go. I growled and held on tighter, making her laugh.

"You're distracting me."

I nibbled on her neck. "That's the point, mama."

"I'm trying to use nap time to get things ready for later."

I licked a line from her shoulder to her ear and nipped her lobe. "That's what I love about you. Always so organized." I slipped a hand beneath her shirt to touch her silky-soft abdomen. "But truly, fuck 'em. They can fend for themselves."

She snorted and shoved my hand out of her shirt. I let her turn around to face me, pleased to see her smiling.

"You know, you're the one who thought inviting your brother and mine over for dinner was a good idea," she reminded me.

"Yeah." I thought about it for a second and decided I stood by my original statement. "Fuck 'em. We'll cancel."

"We won't. The kids are looking forward to cousin time—and so are you."

We weren't the only ones who'd expanded our family. Saoirse and Luca's twins—Aiden and Guilia—were a month younger than Nico, and Jeremy and Anne had had their first, Oliver, last year. When we all got together, it was the kind of chaos that fed my soul.

"Yeah, fine." I kissed her temple. "If I don't get to fuck you, let me help you out."

"Are those two things equal?" she teased.

"I'm never going to complain about the time I spend with you."

Sighing, she leaned into me, her tits pressing against my chest. "That is one of the sweetest things you've ever said to me, and you're definitely going to get to fuck me later." She touched her lips to mine.

"Not why I said it," I told her.

"I know, which is exactly why I love you."

I loved her for a thousand reasons. Too many to name. And each day that passed, I continued to add another and another to the list.

At the very top was her bravery. It was the reason we were here.

She'd gotten on her bike and ridden it to a little dive bar all on her own. There, she took what she wanted and, despite everything, kept coming back.

She'd said yes to me when the odds of us working out were stacked high.

When it might have been easier to be alone, she'd grabbed on to *us* with both hands and held on with all her might.

We'd had smooth roads and rough. At times, we'd had to carve our own path and fight our way through. But no matter, we had each other, which meant our ride was always, *always* gonna be beautiful.

Preorder Shira and Roman's book, By The Letter: https://myboo k.to/ByTheLetter

Luca and Saoirse

Read Luca and Saoirse's love story in Sincerely, Your Inconvenient Wife:

https://mybook.to/SYIW

Blurb:

I have this thing about saying 'yes'. I do it frequently, and with abandon.

Skydiving on a whim? Yes.

A last minute getaway to Ireland? Yes!

Agreeing to a **marriage of convenience** with sexy and arrogant Luca Rossi for two years? Um...yes?

It should have been a simple arrangement. Luca needs a wife to clean up his image as the new CEO of Rossi Motors, and I need my mother to stop trying to fix me up on terrible dates. In two years, we'll part amicably, no attachments or hard feelings.

Anything that happens between us will be outside the confines of our arrangement.

And by anything, I mean falling into Luca's bed. Which I also do frequently and with abandon.

But nothing is ever as simple as it seems. It isn't long before I fall for my **motorcycle-riding, dirty-talking, sexy-as-sin husband.**

I know I should be careful. This is just temporary, after all, and Luca and I want completely different futures.

The thing is, when I'm with Luca, all I want to do is say, 'yes', no matter how reckless that would be.

(Saoirse and Luca's story has a guaranteed HEA. No OW drama or cheating!)

STAY IN TOUCH

Join the Sublime Readers to hang out with me and be the first to find out bookish news:
https://www.facebook.com/groups/2086152844974595

Author's Note

Since Clara first appeared on page in Sincerely, Your Inconvenient Wife, I knew I had to write her happy ending, especially after putting her through *fucking Miller*. I had to give her the best hero I could come up with, and Jake popped into my mind. Someone unexpected, who Clara would never pick out on her own. Someone completely different from her ex, who would take care of her and her girl. I'm pretty proud of where she and Nellie ended up!

If this is your first time reading my books, well, hello! Welcome to my little world, where most of my books have either a big or small connection. This series is a spinoff of The Harder They Fall, so be sure to check those books out and meet Clara, Shira, and Bea at their inception.

If you've been around for a while, hey! Thanks for continuing to read my books and letting me widen this fictional world I've created.

As always, I'd like to thank my peeps: Monica, Rose, Jen, and Kate. I couldn't put out books without you. I also have to thank my right-hand gal, Amber. My professional life was a mess before you stepped in and whipped me into shape!

Whether this was your first book of mine or your fortieth, thank you for reading! I appreciate you more than I could ever say.

About Julia

Julia Wolf is a bestselling contemporary romance author. She writes bad boys with big hearts and strong, independent heroines. Julia enjoys reading romance just as much as she loves writing it. Whether reading or writing, she likes the emotions to run high and the heat to be scorching.

Julia lives in Maryland with her three crazy, beautiful kids and her patient husband who she's slowly converting to a romance reader, one book at a time.

Visit my website:
juliawolfwrites.com